ANDERS ROSLUND

Anders Roslund is an award-winning journalist and one of the most successful and critically acclaimed Scandinavian crime writers of our time. His books have been read by millions and he is the recipient of the CWA International Dagger and the Glass Key award, among many others. His work is published in thirty-six languages and regularly tops international bestseller lists.

T0332994

ALSO BY ANDERS ROSLUND

The Ewert Grens and Piet Hoffmann Series

Three Hours
Three Minutes
Three Seconds

The Ewert Grens Series

Two Soldiers
Cell 8
Cox 21
Pen 33
Knock Knock

ANDERS ROSLUND

Sweet Dreams

Translated from the Swedish
by Elizabeth Clark Wessel

VINTAGE

1 3 5 7 9 10 8 6 4 2

Vintage is part of the Penguin Random House group of companies
whose addresses can be found at global.penguinrandomhouse.com

First published in Vintage in 2023
First published in Great Britain by Harvill Secker in 2022
First published in 2020 with the title *Sovsågott* by
Albert Bonniers Förlag, Sweden

Copyright © Anders Roslund 2020
Published by agreement with Salomonsson Agency

English translation copyright © Elizabeth Clark Wessel 2022

Anders Roslund has asserted their right to be identified as the
author of this Work in accordance with the Copyright,
Designs and Patents Act 1988

penguin.co.uk/vintage

A CIP catalogue record for this book is
available from the British Library

ISBN 9781529113068

Printed and bound in Great Britain by Clays Ltd, Elcograf S.p.A.

The authorised representative in the EEA is Penguin Random House Ireland,
Morrison Chambers, 32 Nassau Street, Dublin D02 YH68

Penguin Random House is committed to a sustainable future
for our business, our readers and our planet. This book is made
from Forest Stewardship Council® certified paper.

This story contains content that some readers may find troubling. You'll find links to resources in the back of this book.

PART
1

It's always cold in the cemetery.

DIZZY.

So dizzy.

He tried to stay still. As usual.

A deep breath.

He closed his eyes, waited.

Until it passed. Until the world ceased spinning, and he was able to reach out for the flower he liked so much. Life everlasting. That's what it was called. A tall plant that arrived, proud and smiling, at the end of every summer. Ewert Grens momentarily forgot the pain in his hip as he gathered up its fallen leaves and moistened its buds, which bloom in clusters, with a watering can. He ran his hand slowly over the white cross – as close as he could get to her. His fingertips followed the ridge that formed her name on the simple brass plate. The only person he had ever held tight and who had held him tight.

I miss you.

He'd refused to come here for a long time. The eastern side of the Northern Cemetery. He used to park his car by the open gate and trudge down the winding gravel paths where his footsteps ruined the straight lines of the rakes. Surrounded by memorial groves and gravestones that rose up from the ground to stare at him. But as soon as he'd gotten close he'd given in to the pressure on his chest, his legs lost their will, and he would turn back to his car and the city and the police station – back to the corduroy sofa in his office, which was the entirety of his comfort, collected in a few worn cushions. Until one morning he finally understood. What he feared most had already happened. And once you realise that, you have to keep moving forward or fear might catch up and push you down again.

I miss you, though less and less.

Ewert Grens had hung the empty watering can on its hook in the garden-tool area and was just about to put the rake back when dizziness returned. A fierce wave through his body – an uncontrollable force that hit him more and more often with increasing intensity – and he only avoided falling over by leaning against the wooden fence, and if Anni were still here she would have dragged him to the hospital.

He did as before, stayed completely still, waiting for the wave, troubling and wild, to ebb. When it did not, he sat down on the park bench, which over time had come to be his own, staring at the patch of lawn some bureaucrat had named Block 19B, number 603. It had taken him several years to move two kilometres from his home on the bustling and heavily trafficked street of Svea Road to the well-kept and expansive spaces along Solna Church Road, to dare look at where she lay here among so many others, just one of the thirty thousand graves – a small distance from each other so as not to disturb, but close enough so as never to be alone.

He let the August wind play across his cheeks, which since then had become rougher, and his hair, which seemed thinner with every visit. And he could feel it. The calm. Even inside him. Enough to push away the dizziness for a while.

Right then, right there, the ground beneath him started to heave.

The whole world started to shake.

Grens looked around quickly. It wasn't the world. It was the park bench. All the times he'd been here, and he'd never shared it. Now a woman had sat down just half a metre away.

On *his* bench.

Right beside him and without a word, even ignoring him.

He glanced warily at her. She was around his age, if he had to guess, short dark hair, the kind of eyes that would not look away from a threat or even from shame. She reminded him a little of Mariana Hermansson. One of the few people he'd ever trusted, whom he'd hired himself, and promoted above others with much more experience. One of his closest colleagues for many years, and thus one of his closest friends, who

6

suddenly at the end of an investigation told him she'd applied for another job because she could no longer stand him. He didn't blame her, he couldn't stand himself often enough. He hadn't seen her since, which was probably why he often seemed to catch glimpses of her in other people.

It took several minutes. Then the stranger spoke.

'Are you grieving for someone?'

Still with her eyes staring straight ahead.

'I mean, that's what we do around here, right?'

He didn't answer.

'I'm sorry – perhaps you'd rather be left alone? It's just that I've never seen anyone else sitting on my bench.'

Now he answered.

'On *your* bench?'

She smiled.

'Not mine. Not in that way. Just that I'm usually . . . well, alone. You don't see many people in this part of the cemetery.'

They sat a while longer, without words.

She stared straight ahead, he stared straight ahead.

Everything else remained still.

'My wife.'

Grens nodded towards a white cross a few metres away.

'Her name was Anni. And when I think about . . .'

'Yes?'

'You're rather like her actually.'

'Excuse me?'

'I just mean . . . It's her I'm sitting here for. She's the one I mourn.'

The woman next to him also nodded, not as if she pitied him, it was pointless in a place where everyone was visiting death, more as if she understood what he was saying and found it reasonable.

'How long? Since your wife died, that is.'

'That depends.'

'Really?'

'She . . . There was a workplace accident. Thirty-five years ago. A car drove over her head, and it was my fault. She never spoke again, didn't really function. But to me, she functioned. There were many who considered her already dead. And then, when she died in a scientific sense – well, that was almost exactly ten years ago.'

'And for you?'

'A couple of years later. Now I know she's dead. That she no longer exists. To other people. But for me, she exists – in our way.'

Every morning and afternoon and evening he'd spent here, with Anni. And not once had anyone approached him at her grave. He assumed he must seem like he wasn't interested, nobody had ever thought about interrupting his time on the park bench.

But now, it felt neither bad nor wrong.

Just unfamiliar.

'And . . . you?'

'Excuse me?'

'Who are you mourning? Who are *you* here for?'

He had never been very good at small talk. And starting in a cemetery made it feel even more awkward than usual. But she didn't seem to care, maybe didn't even notice.

'It's . . . there. Next to the big birch. You see? Also a simple white cross. Just like your wife's.'

She pointed, away somewhere.

'Or you may not see it – there are quite a few rows in between. But this is the best seat. I usually visit the grave first, and then sit down on the bench – you can still feel it from here.'

Ewert Grens said nothing, it was clear she wanted to continue.

'Although that wasn't what you asked. You wondered who I was visiting.'

'Yes. But you don't need –'

'The answer is that I don't really know.'

'Excuse me?'

'No one is buried there.'

She looked at him.

'No one is inside the coffin.'

A HAND.

Soft and hard at the same time.

And the ones who are holding me say if I don't want to, I mean if I'd rather stay here by myself, then I don't have to.

Go with them.

EWERT GRENS FROZE. A sharp gust of wind cut through his body and then settled somewhere in the region of his chest.

'What . . .'

He'd learned that early – it was always cold in the cemetery.

'. . . do you mean?'

'Just what I said. The coffin is empty. That's probably why I come here so often.'

For the first time, Grens turned towards the woman on the park bench, waiting for her to continue, and met eyes that never looked away. She really did have that kind of gaze: it didn't apologise, but remained empathetic.

'Because no one was laid inside it.'

He didn't know her, had never met her before. Still, he understood her seriousness. She wasn't playing with him, wasn't crazy, had no ulterior motive. She said things just as they were.

'Come with me.'

The world shook again as she stood up and the rickety park bench rebalanced. She walked down the raked gravel path and stopped at a grave five rows away, marked with a white wooden cross exactly like the one he'd put up for Anni. He was here so often – how could he have missed it? The unknown woman stood there waiting for him to join her, so she could begin to tell him a story that should never be told, because it never should have happened.

'I lost her.'

And then he saw it. In the middle of the wooden cross.

The metal plaque with just three words.

MY LITTLE GIRL

'She was four years old. Almost to the day.'

The detective stepped closer, as if to see if there was anything else there.

No.

It was as if the words formed two first names and one last. My Little Girl. Two more letters than comprised Ewert Grens.

'A dirty, ugly car park on Södermalm. That's where she disappeared. Wearing her new dress and with her long hair in a beautiful plait.'

There were more flowers on this grave than on the one he cared for. More varieties, more colours. A beautiful, soft bed of blue and red and yellow. He surprised himself by recognising nemesia, starry eyes and petunias, not because he was much interested in plants, he wasn't, but because these were plants he'd learned over the years to avoid at Anni's grave because they required frequent watering.

The woman next to him evidently came here often.

'The police investigated, of course. Intensely in the beginning – I was interrogated several times. But weeks turned to months and their search turned more and more sporadic. After a year, they didn't know any more than they did on the first day. No one talked about her, ever asked about her. It was almost as if she'd never existed, as if she were nobody. So I chose not to put her name on her grave, I'm the only one who misses her now, her name belongs only to me. So my little girl. It's enough.'

'You said . . . a parking garage?'

'Yes?'

'My wife, we were expecting a child when . . . it was also in a –'

She interrupted him.

'I had left the door open, was just a short distance to a parking meter.'

She stared at the cross, still caught in her own nightmare.

'So I didn't see the other vehicle. Until it was too late.'

Grens waited. While she gathered her strength.

'According to the surveillance cameras, it took exactly seven seconds for my reality to change forever. My daughter was sitting in her car seat, the driver of the other car stopped right next to her door, opened *his* door, climbed out, grabbed her, got back into his car, and drove away.'

This unknown woman, who was so easy to talk and listen to, then did something he often did at Anni's grave, she squatted down and cleared away the fallen leaves and the occasional weed. And she probably did so for the same reason – not so someone else would think it looked nice, but just to be able to do something even though it was already too late.

'It was a very strange funeral.'

She pushed her hands through the sea of flowers that separated her from the one she mourned.

'It was me. A policeman. A social worker. And a priest – people she'd never met, who meant nothing to her in life and therefore could mean nothing in death. That small hole in the ground that a caretaker dug! That tiny white coffin with a red rose on it. Empty inside and so light as a feather to carry! They rang the church bells for her and the cantor chose a lullaby. "Sandman." It was a beautiful day, sunshine, and with the brittle music of the church organ behind us, it somehow seemed even more absurd to watch a coffin meant for a body who had barely begun to live be lowered into the ground, never to come up again.'

She fell silent.

But soon began to sing with her face turned towards the flower bed.

'*Sweet dreams. Goodnight to you.*'

'What's that?'

'That's what we sang. The last verse of the lullaby. Which felt so . . . yes, different from when I sang it for my daughter at home.'

Now she turned round.

'Maybe because when she was asleep in her bed I knew it would come to an end. She'd wake up. Not like this – the eternity of death.'

She looked at him, pointed at the grass they stood on.

'Her coffin is here, under our feet. Isn't it a strange thought?'

Yes. It *was* a strange thought. One he had thought so many times. That his beloved Anni was a few rows away, but could neither see nor hear him. He wished he could relive the days he'd been shattered by grief – he should have gone to his wife's funeral.

'I usually think of her as Alva, now that I took her name away. Alva is so sweet, almost like an elf's name, and they only exist if you believe in them.'

She held out her hand, small-boned, verging on skinny, but with an unexpected strength. It was as if she were holding on to him, pulling him inside.

'Almost three years have passed since she disappeared. And almost six months since I had her declared dead. Once a week I come here so she doesn't have to be alone, which I think she is, despite all the others who are lying here. Usually on Thursdays, like today – it's easier to slip away from work for a bit. Now I have to go – maybe I'll see you here among the graves again. If not, I'd appreciate it if you stopped by here when you came. Not for long, not like an obligation, just so she might feel like someone is close.'

He watched her back retreat down the gravel path that wound behind well-tended bushes and the larger gravestones from an earlier time – and realised he didn't even know what her name was. Nameless, just like her little girl.

He should go too, his day was waiting for him in a detective superintendent's office at the City Police Station with at least a dozen ongoing investigations on his desk, but he wasn't quite done with Anni. So he sat down on the park bench again, alone now, without any of the shaking.

Sometimes when he sat here he'd start thinking about children. How Anni probably never knew that the child she was carrying was the daughter they'd longed for. With heart and lungs and eyes that could open and close. And whose life ended when Anni's life ended in one way. Or, maybe he was the one who never talked about it? Well. He tried. To tell her. Especially in the beginning at the nursing home when he couldn't hold her tight enough, but it seemed as if she didn't really understand.

My Little Girl.

So goddamn unfair.

From time to time, when all his hours were taken up by violent criminals shooting at each other, he was overcome by the feeling that he just didn't give a damn. Of course he did his job, investigating as best he could because that's how he worked – nothing was ever done half-heartedly in the world of Ewert Grens, every stone would be turned over because that was the only way he knew how to live with himself – but he no longer really cared about the kind of victims who made a clear choice. A child, on the other hand, one who was injured, even killed, had no choice. A child was robbed of so many more days of life. And therefore it hurt so much more.

He forgot about the time.

Just letting in sunshine that warmed every place but this one, let a biting wind hunt him down in this enormous cemetery.

Almost an hour had passed by the time he stood up and broke off a couple of stalks from Anni's flower bed. He'd leave them beside another wooden cross, while he asked questions of a little girl who wasn't there.

Who are you?

Why did you disappear?

And where are you now?

I DON'T WANT that. Don't want to be left on my own. If Mum and Dad are gone already.

It feels nice to have a hand to hold that is both soft and hard at the same time.

A hand that knows where we're going. Where Mum and Dad already went.

Where they're waiting for me.

AFTER ANNI WAS injured, after the baby girl growing inside her died, and she herself had stepped into another closed room, locked into her own world inside a nursing home, her husband had been sent to a police psychologist. In order to deal with the fact that he was the one who had run over her. That their life together no longer existed. That his greatest fear had already happened. Thirty-five years later, he still remembered meeting that therapist who was trying to get closer to a man who had lost everything. How young police officer Ewert Grens failed his first task as a patient completely – imagining a safe place in his mind to go to when treatment got too demanding or his emotions too intense. Even then, it was clear that his whole life had been torn apart. He could not find a safe place. Even in his mind! Not at home, where his bed had become a black hole to fall into, not with friends or colleagues, not in that huge police station he liked so much. No place gave him peace. Until one day he bought the sofa he was now lying on in his office. Brown, corduroy. Neither remarkable nor particularly expensive, but comfortable, and big enough for him to stretch his long body out on. By now it was far too soft and the corduroy stripes were almost erased. Wear from three decades of lying there, occasionally during working hours and quite often at night instead of heading home to sleep.

But this afternoon he found no real peace there, no matter how long he listened to his ancient cassette player, to the voices and songs of the sixties, which he played endlessly and with which he was so familiar. His legs, his arms, his whole being buzzed with anxiety as he was cast in and out of short, confused dreams.

He sat up on the edge of the sofa.

Then lay back down again.

Tossed out an arm and grabbed a cup of black coffee and gulped it down.

Stared at the ceiling for a moment and followed the tangle of cracks that usually led him to calm.

He'd tried to flip through the preliminary investigations stacked in thick piles on his desk, full of people affected by violence. It was pointless. The crime scene descriptions stayed blurry no matter how close he leaned in.

And he knew why.

The similarities.

His mind was still on an unknown girl who – just like his and Anni's – had taken her leave in a dirty parking garage and who was now just a memory in a deserted cemetery. And whom he'd promised to visit so she'd feel a little less alone. Even though he didn't know what she looked like, what her voice had sounded like, or whether her eyes smiled at those she met.

There was only one way to meet her.

The archive.

There, in one of those brown cardboard boxes, were the only traces that could confirm she once existed.

He hurried out into the corridor and past the offices of his colleagues, who were all hard at work on open cases just as he himself should be, and stepped into the lift to go down to the basement of the police station. The archive had no windows and not much ventilation, but he always enjoyed punching a code into the keypad and opening the heavy steel door. Down here was a separate society of sorts, where another kind of order reigned, and perhaps even another kind of justice if a closed case contained evidence that might lead to prosecution and sentencing.

He walked through the aisles of the archive, further and further beneath the police station, all the way to the City Police's archive computer, which was pushed into a corner, and logged in to start searching. The nameless girl was in here somewhere, among tens of thousands upon tens of thousands of living and dead.

He remembered how the woman looked as they stood next to each other in the cemetery, how she whispered *it was a very strange funeral*. He entered 'LOST' and 'GIRL' in the search field, pressed enter and waited in front of the screen.

Nine hundred and seven hits.

He tried to recall what she'd said, and after a while added to the search with 'SÖDERMALM'.

One hundred and fifty-two hits left.

He clearly remembered her shaking with grief and anger as she told him about the ugly and deserted concrete.

'PARKING GARAGE.'

Twenty-two hits left.

And then, how had she described her? Wearing a dress? And the girl's hair in a beautiful plait?

'DRESS.'

Five hits left.

'PLAIT.'

One hit left.

He got up quickly and now headed in the opposite direction towards the tall metal cabinets with seven units – rows of identical storage boxes in rough cardboard, thick stacks of folders organised in a colour-coordinated system he'd never quite figured out, bundles of paper tied together with coarse string, wide-backed binders, overflowing plastic pockets and occasionally the kind of seized goods that were too awkwardly shaped to box up. Case after case and there – at the very point that might be at the heart of the whole archive – it stood. Aisle 17, section F, shelf 6. He climbed up on the rolling ladder and was just able to reach. A file box that was easy to lift down despite a stiff leg and a sense of balance that was long past its prime. He sat down at one of the reading tables and unfolded the box flaps like two cardboard wings. There wasn't much inside. A police report that noted the course of events. The report from the technical department, which failed to secure any DNA or fibres from a perpetrator. Dead-end interrogations with people who'd been in the area for various reasons.

The woman at the grave had been right.

No answers here despite decent investigative work, not a single clue.

A small child had been taken, and no one saw or heard a thing.

IT'S A VERY nice car. And very long. And brand new. And I have the whole back seat to myself, that never happens because Jacob and Mathilda and William always take up all the space. I can even lie down and stretch out as far as I can without touching the doors. When I sit up and look out the rear window, I can see the big store getting smaller and smaller and smaller until I can't see it at all. I ask why Mum and Dad couldn't stay, why they had to go, why they didn't have time to tell me themselves, and the man driving the nice car says they know where I'm going, and they'll find me, and we're on our way there.

I can't wait.

Until we get there.

Can't wait to see Mum and Dad.

EWERT GRENS HAD just stepped out of the lift and was striding towards his own office when he changed his mind and stopped abruptly. But not at the coffee machine like usual. Instead, he opened the office door of a detective he rarely spoke to, one he'd never really got to know despite being colleagues – as sometimes happens when detectives are immersed in various cases that lead them in different directions.

'Do you have a minute?'

Elisa Cuesta. That was her name, a colleague in her forties who looked up from a desk surrounded by still packed cardboard boxes. An office with bare walls, no personal belongings anywhere – a person who'd never really dared to move into what would always feel like a temporary hotel room.

As far from a worn corduroy sofa as you could get.

'Can I come in?'

'Sure. But there's no need to, Grens. Come back. I was the one who –'

'Back?'

'I just mean, we never talk to each other otherwise, and now a whole month later – it's too late, I took a chance then.'

'*A whole month later*? *Chance*? Now I'm not following you at all.'

She looked at him. Just held up both hands. Dismissively.

'Sorry, I thought you were here on . . . a different errand. Let's start over, Grens. Sit down on that cardboard box over there, it's sturdy, people always do. Now what is it you wanted?'

Ewert Grens zigzagged between the boxes and sank down onto one of them, hesitantly stretching out his stiff leg as best he could, trying to ignore the swaying feeling, while searching his colleague's gaze.

'I want to ask you some questions about an investigation that I assume you, as head of missing persons, discontinued a couple of years ago.'

Cuesta's expression was usually as neutral as her office. She always looked the same. It wasn't a memorable face, and if they had met out and about in town Grens wouldn't have recognised her an hour later. But now it was suffused with personality, the anger of a person who felt challenged.

'Is that so?'

'I'm not here to criticise you.'

'You and I never talk, Grens, we don't give a damn about each other. It doesn't matter, I don't long for your company – but then you come in here for the very first time wanting to talk about a case that *didn't* go to court? So if you're not here looking to find fault, what do you want?'

Grens shifted his position and the half-full moving box almost overturned.

He stood up; that felt safer.

'I want to find a little girl whose empty coffin lies under a white wooden cross.'

'Really?'

'And I want to know everything. See every single frame from every relevant surveillance camera from the morning of the twenty-third of August 2016. I want to comb visits to hospitals, social services, pre-schools. I want to relive the conversations you had, the doors you knocked on. All the way up to the moment you reached a dead end and deprioritised the case.'

'I don't know what you're talking about.'

'The investigation into the girl who was ripped out of a car and taken away.'

'Still not sure which case you're referring to.'

'The four-year-old girl who was in the passenger seat while –'

'Grens, look around. The boxes. Every single one contains *active* cases. My own and others. And I hate it as much as you do. But as for this *long-ago discontinued case*, you'll have to go elsewhere – I don't recognise it, and I don't need more to do.'

Ewert Grens didn't sigh. Just turned round.

'Thanks so much for the help.'

And started to leave.

'Why, Grens?'

'Why, what?'

'Why *this* investigation? Now? Where did it come from? Why are you rooting around in something so old when we're drowning in new cases?'

Ewert Grens shrugged. Maybe he should tell her about his wife, whose grave he couldn't bear to visit for years. Or about the child who had lain inside her, whom they lost and who now lay in an anonymous memorial grove he still couldn't visit. Or about a strange woman who did the opposite – visited the empty coffin of a little girl to make her feel a little less alone.

But he didn't.

'I'm not really sure.'

'Excuse me?'

'I met someone in the cemetery today and ... well ... someone who ...'

'Grens?'

'Yes?'

'How's it going?'

'How ... What do you mean?'

'You're pale. Look ragged, confused. Almost as if, well, if you'll excuse me, but I noticed it when you arrived, almost disorientated. Are you feeling OK? You don't look well.'

She leaned forward, expecting an answer.

'I ... just got a little dizzy. When I was in the cemetery.'

'Dizzy?'

He started to zigzag back through a room full of boxes, away from a person who was just as afraid of getting tied down as he was of breaking free.

'I had an ... unpleasant experience, which is connected to a previous unpleasant experience. That's all.'

He approached the door, and she watched him go, trying to make out what he was mumbling.

'The child in the cemetery, it hit me hard . . . the little kids always do, especially the little girls, I don't know why and . . .'

The detective superintendent almost staggered out into the corridor, and she could no longer hear him. She got up, followed him. He had reached the coffee machine – and this time he would stop for two cups – when her voice reached him.

'Grens – you never looked into the other one, did you?'

Elisa Cuesta had called out from the doorway of her office.

'The other one?'

'The other investigation. The other little girl who was four years old. Also a complete mystery.'

His colleague who lacked a memorable face became ever more diffuse from a few doors away.

'The girl who disappeared the same day – the one who was never found. Neither dead nor alive.'

MUM AND DAD say I should never go anywhere with strangers – but this can't be dangerous. Not if they know my name.

And we'll soon be there.

And I can wear my jacket.

The one that looks like a zebra. The one I never want to take off, not even inside when adults say I have to. It's probably my favourite. That and the butterfly in my hair. Which is blue and flies when no one is watching. The people driving the car, the people who know where I live, don't nag me to take it off, not like my mum, they understand.

We're probably getting close now.

To home.

THEY WATCHED HIM the whole time.

They didn't even blink.

Stared, stared.

The girl in the photograph to the left of Ewert Grens's desk had ceased to exist, according to the rest of the world, in a parking garage. She wore the same dress in the picture as she had when she disappeared. At the time of the photo, she was just over four years old, one hundred and eight centimetres tall and weighed nineteen kilos, her hair in a long, beautiful plait.

The girl in the photo on the right was jammed into a cherry-red child-sized armchair in front of one of those unpleasantly fake backgrounds studio photographers use, the ones that make the whole world seem imaginary. Her hair was shorter and lighter, she was about the same height, but a couple of kilos heavier, age four years and seven months.

They became the main subject of their respective police investigations on the same day.

The girl from the cemetery was no longer alone.

Ewert Grens moved the two photographs closer to the centre of his desk, closer to each other. They were connected. He didn't know how, they themselves may not know, but he didn't believe in coincidences, never had.

Every year more than seven thousand Swedes were reported missing.

Almost all were found within a couple of days.

But about thirty never returned, neither alive nor dead – they remained riddles, vanishing without a trace.

The girl on his left, now called Alva, and the girl on his right, Linnea, were two of those.

He got up, pacing anxiously back and forth across his office as he had done so many times before. Between the bookshelf and the corduroy sofa. From the window overlooking the courtyard of the police station to the closed door facing the corridor. Until he collided with himself and sat down again in front of two girls who just kept staring at him.

Maybe they were wondering who he was.

Why he was sitting there, why he thought he had the right to move them around.

He'd tracked down the folder from the long-abandoned investigation of Linnea Disa Scott this afternoon in an overcrowded cupboard in a dusty room in the police station in Skärholmen – and it reminded him of the cardboard box he'd lifted down from a shelf in the City Police archives in the basement just hours before. Equally solid work, equally fruitless. But while Alva had only a mother missing her, Linnea had many relatives who had desperately participated in the investigation, tried to answer every new question, be helpful at every new track. He flipped through the report to the Missing Persons Register, the issuance of the nationwide alert, the copies of her description that went out to patrol cars and bus drivers, the interrogations, the witness statements, the forensic reports. He'd return to all that, later. Right now, just two pieces in the puzzle of an investigation of the disappearance of a girl named Linnea were interesting to him: the surveillance footage showing the moment when she disappeared – and a document signed by her parents that might just change everything.

THE CAR STOPS.

I sit up, even though it was fun stretching out all by myself across the whole back seat.

We're there now.

I fix my zebra jacket and my blue butterfly clip. I want to look nice when I get home. Those who have soft and hard hands, who were driving the brand-new car, now unlock the doors, open one, and I jump out.

This is not our house.

This isn't our home.

An airport. I know that much. We met Grandma and Grandpa once at the entrance with the glass doors, when they visited us over Christmas. I can even hear the huge planes landing and taking off again.

I look around. Nobody I know is here.

So I ask the ones who know my name.

'Where are my mum and dad?'

EWERT GRENS STARTED with the surveillance footage.

Plugged the flash drive into his computer and opened the file.

The first girl, Alva, was torn from her car early one morning with almost no one nearby. But the circumstances of this little girl, Linnea, her sudden disappearance, which he was now watching, were quite different from the silence of a dim parking garage. The time stamp at the bottom of the footage showed eleven hours later that day, early evening, and the camera was located on the ceiling of a crowded supermarket, filled with both laughter and stress. Hundreds of people getting in each other's way. Overfull trolleys and high pyramids of TVs and bags of crisps and a speaker system calling out this week's specials.

Grens waited.

After a while, he leaned closer to the screen.

And saw her for the first time.

A little girl walking out without a care from between the shelves and into the frame. Linnea. It's clear even though he only knows her from a soulless photograph. A zebra-print jacket, with a hair clip that looked like a large butterfly placed sweetly in her fringe. Sometimes she stops – looks at her reflection in a shiny toaster, turns a box with candles upside down and shakes it a little, pokes a soft pack of napkins. She looks happy – going shopping with her mother and father is an adventure. One minute and twelve seconds later she is passing by and is on her way out of sight when a hand extends towards her. An adult hand, which belongs to someone just outside the frame. As if he or she knows exactly where the camera's angled. They seem to be talking to each other, the girl and the unseen adult. Until she's convinced, the outstretched hand takes hers, and they walk away.

Ewert Grens was shaken against his will, like the sharp wind in the cemetery. He'd just relived the last moments of a person's life.

At least the last moments as far as those who loved her know.

He let the film roll on and soon a woman and a man in their thirties run into the picture, out of the picture. Then back, and out again, and back.

Worried.

Soon angry, upset.

Then frantic, crushed.

That's where the detective superintendent stopped the film. While the shoppers at the supermarket continued to pack their goods into already full shopping trolleys, the woman and the man – probably the mother and father – stood in their midst, holding each other tightly.

He wondered if they already knew they would never see her again.

A PASSPORT. That's what it's called. And it's really, really, really for real.

With a pretty picture of me. No one else I know who is just four years old has their own passport. Not even Jacob. And Mathilda and William are way too little. But I'm not.

In the picture, I almost look like I'm six years old. That's what we're pretending. I'm trying to guess what the game is. No. Can't. But it's fun to pretend. That's why I have a new name, too.

I haven't really learned to read yet, but those who know my name, my real name, say that it says Lynn, and that my birthday is in the summer, even though it's actually in the winter. And that's what we should pretend until we finally get to Mum and Dad, who came up with all this and who will be waiting for us when we arrive.

HE TOOK THE flash drive out of the computer, the pictures of a family that had ceased. A single document remained to be examined in his thick file. The one that could change everything.

Form SKV 7695
Application for Declaration of Death —
missing person

Small, square boxes. The missing person's personal data, name of applicant, next of kin. A dull, colourless paper like any other, smelling of authority.

The difference was that this ended a life.

The parents, who held each other so tightly on the surveillance footage, who hoped to see their daughter again soon, now, a few years later, hoped for her death. Because that was better than nothing. This is how they justified their reasons on the back of the form, the box that was a little bigger than the others, where they wrote tightly, tightly with a blue ballpoint pen.

An appeal.

To the members of the Special Committee for Declaration of Death.

To – just like with the girl named Alva who was already buried – make an exception from the five-year rule and expedite the announcement of Linnea Disa Scott's death.

Ewert Grens had sometimes thought that of all the duties of a detective the most terrible was delivering death. He'd knocked on so many doors and told so many people that a son, a daughter, a husband, a wife existed no longer. He'd taken a life from them – for until the moment he was standing in front of them, telling them about their dearest one, the one who meant everything to them, that person had been alive in their minds. But these officials were even worse off. They had to decide on the very moment of a death. And had – in this case – truly done so.

> Based on a) the circumstances of the
> disappearance, b) the unsuccessful search
> and c) the time that had passed, the board
> finds a high probability that the person has
> died.

A former government councillor, a professor of medical ethics, a writer, a dean, and a lawyer had, according to the boxes filled in at the bottom, come to the conclusion that the girl in the footage – reflected in the toaster, poking at the goods on shop shelves – no longer existed.

> With regard to the suffering of the
> relatives, the case period has been reduced
> to three years.

Grens read the board's ruling again.

Three years.

He remembered the woman in the cemetery again.

Almost three years have passed since she disappeared.

She was talking about another child, but the same day.

He stood up. Sat down.

It might be very soon.

He knew how it worked. In order for someone to die in this bureaucratic way, the notice had to be published in good time in a national paper and only then, if nothing arrived to contradict it, was the person declared dead.

He logged in to the computer, googled to the right website and searched among the announcements.

A total of twenty-two people were waiting there right now for their deaths.

He scrolled past people who were last seen in Thailand, in Katrineholm, in Syria, in Malmö. Only two children. A seven-year-old boy, last seen in Norrköping, and a girl, last seen in southern Stockholm.

> Linnea Disa Scott, 131101-2449, has been declared dead.
> She is registered in Stockholm. Linnea Disa Scott was last
> seen at a supermarket in Skärholmen in August 2016.
> Linnea Disa Scott is, in accordance with Section 7 of the
> Declaration of Death Act (2005: 130), called to register with
> the Swedish Tax Agency no later than 23 August 2019.

The twenty-third of August.

My God.

Just to be sure Ewert Grens checked the calendar beside him on his desk.

It wasn't just soon – it was earlier than soon.

Tomorrow.

It was tomorrow.

She really was going to die then. And another four-year-old girl would have a strange funeral; a coffin with no one inside would be joined by another.

THE VERY FIRST person who sees my new picture has a blue airport jacket and blue airport trousers and very, very big hair and when she laughs she sounds just like Mum. But she's not Mum. She looks at me and opens my passport and looks at me again, and it's like I'm in two places – at the same time! She likes my zebra jacket and asks if I've ever flown in a plane before. I haven't. But neither has Jacob. She says that it's almost like being on a train, but you have to swallow and hold your nose and exhale air at the beginning and at the end. When she hands me back my passport, I put it into a secret pocket, and she winks at me and tells me to have a good trip.

THE WARM AUGUST evening hid a soft darkness that made it easy to breathe. Ewert Grens walked through the suburb of nice houses, past lawns that were deep green despite a dry summer. The ticking sound of rotating sprinklers cut through the silence, like living guardians of their gardens.

His destination stood at the very end of a row of square plots and met him with every window blazing with light. The detective opened a gate that squeaked wearily and then wound his way down stone slabs dotted with an obstacle course – a football, two bicycles with training wheels, a Frisbee, and an overturned skateboard lurking here and there. He knocked on the round window of the front door and rang the doorbell at the same time.

'I'll get it!'

Several voices, in chorus. Several pairs of feet racing to reach the door handle first.

A boy of about seven or eight soon stood in front of him with two pyjama-clad younger siblings right behind.

'Hello, is your mum or dad at home?'

'Who are you?'

'My name is Ewert and I –'

'My name is Jacob. And this is Mathilda and William.'

'Hi, Jacob. Hi, Mathilda. Hi, William. Is your mum or dad home?'

'Both of them are.'

Then they were gone. Feet racing again, now into the hall and towards what seemed to be a living room and, if he heard right, they also continued through that and out onto a back porch. A few minutes later, a woman and a man approached from the opposite direction. The mother and father from the supermarket surveillance footage. It was only three years ago – but they'd aged ten.

'You were looking for us?'

'Ewert Grens. Detective superintendent at the City Police. Do you have a minute to talk?'

They chose the kitchen. That was often the case during home visits – Grens had drunk countless cups of coffee, chewed on countless sticky cinnamon buns while threatened or suspected or victimised people sought to feel secure. This kitchen looked like so many others – a round table with a tablecloth and various chairs for children and adults, a refrigerator humming its refrigerator breaths, a meowing grey-striped cat drinking water from a half-full glass bowl and an antique sideboard with a burning candle.

They didn't know why the detective superintendent had knocked on their door uninvited, or why he was there, but they didn't have to ask for whose sake he was here – in recent years this family of five had been focused on the sixth. The man and woman who'd aged so quickly now looked at each other, as if deciding which of them would talk about her this time.

'Jacob, who opened the door, was Linnea's twin brother. My wife and I have been through hell – still, he's the one who's surely suffered the most.'

The father's eyes were tired, deep wrinkles chasing each other towards his temples and the whites of his eyes shifting to red. It had been a long time since this man had slept through a night.

'His younger siblings, on the other hand, don't remember her at all. Mathilda was two and William only six months when she disappeared. To them, she's just the girl in the photographs. The girl who makes everyone a little sad when they talk about her.'

The mother's eyes were more sombre than tired, she might sleep better than her husband, but she didn't laugh much.

'Look.'

Grens pulled a folded piece of paper from his inner pocket. A copy of the document he'd found in the file of their daughter's missing person's case.

'You've applied to have her declared dead.'

It wasn't an accusation. He hoped it didn't sound like one either.

'I'd like you to reconsider.'

He moved his coffee cup and the plate of buns and put the application between them on the table. As if it proved something – like a sharp-edged weapon with fresh fingerprints on it. Which, in a way, it was.

'Excuse me?'

'Yes, I . . .'

'I heard what you said. Both my husband and I did. But what we don't understand is what that has to do with you. Our beloved little girl disappeared without a trace three years ago. And you, Superintendent Grens – if that's even your name – haven't participated in that search for a single day. But now, with only a few hours to go, you sit down at our kitchen table, and ask . . . *that*?'

She wasn't aggressive, even though she very well could have been. Not frustrated, desperate, resigned, even though those would have been reasonable as well. She sounded matter-of-fact. Because she was presenting facts that should have made an unknown police officer apologise, stand up and leave.

'Yes. That's exactly what I'm asking.'

Instead, she was the one who stood up. She did exactly what he did when presented with a reality he couldn't make his way through – she paced back and forth across the room. In her case, between the dishwasher and the fridge, between the kitchen window and the antique sideboard. Where she stopped and looked at him.

'And you want us to do this because . . . ?'

'If she's declared dead, neither I nor any of my colleagues can request resources for the investigation. Can't seek cooperation from other departments inside or outside the police station if it's needed. It's . . . over.'

'Yes. Yes! That's what we want!'

The mother had raised her voice.

'We *want* this to be over.'

And just a few seconds later, their son Jacob almost ran into the kitchen.

'Mum, what is it? . . . Are you OK?'

Seven and a half years old. With the intonation and vocabulary of an adult. A sense of responsibility far beyond his years.

'Everything's fine, sweetheart.'

'You were screaming.'

'I wasn't screaming. I was just a little upset.'

'Because of Linnea?'

He knew, of course. Could have been standing in the hall listening. But probably didn't need to – he'd lived long enough to know the subject of every conversation his parents had at the kitchen table with a police officer.

'Yes. Because of Linnea.'

He walked over to his mother, arms outstretched, gave her a hug.

Comforting her.

'Can you leave us now, Jacob? So Mum and I can talk to the police officer? We'll be done soon.'

The father laid his hands on his eldest child's shoulders, carefully steering him out of the kitchen, and closed the door.

Which opened again.

'Mum? Dad?'

'Yes?'

'I'm watching TV. In me and Linnea's room.'

The father nodded, patted the boy's cheek. And closed the door a second time.

'They still share a room in his world.'

He cleared his throat. It was his turn to speak for the family.

'You all already explained to us that the investigation was being downgraded. That was why you stopped coming around here asking questions, stopped calling us to check details you'd already checked.'

His coffee cup, like his wife's, remained untouched. Now he dipped his cinnamon bun into it, slowly chewed on the softened bit, and gathered his courage to continue.

'We waited. And waited. You never came back. So we tried to solve it ourselves. Put everything we owned, all of our time into it. Hired private investigators. Advertised in newspapers. Put up posters and signed agreements with the post office – there isn't a household in Stockholm that hasn't had information about Linnea's disappearance put into its mailbox.'

He turned to Grens, looked at him, for a long time.

'But then one day you realise you can't take it any more. Your whole life revolves around something you can't change. You give up.'

And those tired eyes truly struggled.

'You've had your time. Three years. Tomorrow she is going to be declared dead, we won't change our minds. We're going to say goodbye to her with our family and relatives and a few close friends, as far from investigations and the authorities as possible. In fact, you, Superintendent, will be the only one outside of our inner circle who knows.'

The father put his hand on Grens's shoulder, much as he had put it on the boy's just now. To steer him out of the room.

'Come with me. We're going to go see Jacob.'

He waited until the detective picked up speed at the door, turned right and headed up the stairs to the first floor. The room was the third in a short hall, after a bathroom and what appeared to be the parents' bedroom.

'Hello, Jacob. I thought we'd just show the police officer your room. Is that OK?'

'Sure, Dad.'

The boy had invited them in without turning round – the TV show, some cartoon with blaring music, required all the concentration this seven-year-old had within him.

'In that case, Grens, take a look around.'

The father gestured across the doorway.

'Then I think you'll understand.'

Yes.

He understood.

The room didn't just belong to *one* person. Two lived here. Divided into identical halves, like mirror images. Each with the same bed pushed against opposite walls, each with the same desk, each with the same aquarium with shimmering golden-yellow and pink fish, and each with its own teddy bear wearing a red-spotted scarf at the foot of each bed.

And each had its own sign hung on its own bulletin board.

JACOB LIVES HERE. LINNEA LIVES HERE.

'He still refuses to talk about her as missing. "Is Linnea coming?" he'll say when we're packing the car. "Where will Linnea sit?" when he helps us set the table.'

Three years had passed. And nothing had changed.

'I think Jacob needs some closure. In order to make sense of this. To agree that she no longer exists. Become whole again, if that's even possible as a twin. We definitely need this, me and Maria. In order to be able to say goodbye. For real. To grieve, for real.'

Ewert Grens knew all about that. Daring to say goodbye, daring to grieve. Daring to stop fearing what has already happened.

Yet he was here to ask them not to do so.

Not yet.

'We have tried.'

The father whispered, his tired eyes now desperate, careful so that his words wouldn't pierce a cartoon world.

'Tried to change air. We even moved in order to . . . But it's impossible. The new room had to be furnished exactly like the old one. *Their* old one. He . . . can't. But if she was buried. If we say goodbye. We hope that it may be possible to think of her in a different way, which would make it possible for him to make some progress.'

Grens had seen this before with grieving parents. Untouched children's bedrooms like tiny museums dedicated to someone who was no longer alive. As if moving something, unpacking, making room for something new, would implicate them in the erasure. But this was different. It wasn't the parents who wanted to stay in the past. It was a seven-year-old twin brother.

'My experience when it comes to twins and police investigations is that sometimes . . . they just know. Feel each other's anxiety. If one of the siblings is in danger. If they are alive or dead.'

Ewert Grens looked at the boy in a bedroom, which was actually two bedrooms.

'The connection between twins is unfathomable. Ties we don't understand.'

The father of four, who now had only three children in his house, nodded slowly.

'You're right, I'm sure of it. That's what we've seen and experienced between Jacob and Linnea. But, Superintendent – a person is not just a twin. You are also yourself. Right? And Jacob needs to become that, needs to be given *the right* to become that. Himself. To live for his own sake, and not become swallowed by someone else's death.'

'All I'm asking is for you to postpone your application for a declaration of death. Give *me* time to investigate. A month? A week? Let *me* try. I think you're wrong, and it's Jacob who's right – it's too early to give up.'

The father didn't answer, didn't even glance round as he left the room and headed down the stairs, to the kitchen and his wife. That was where he was sitting with a new bun in his hand, dipping it into coffee, as Grens returned.

'And now *I* want *you* to explain something to me, Superintendent.'

'Yes?'

'Why . . .'

Still almost no emotion in his voice. Matter-of-fact. Calm. Even though he was temporarily on the attack.

'. . . is this suddenly so important?'

'Because there could be a connection to another case, which no one has examined before. And – tomorrow it's too late.'

'OK. I'll rephrase it: why is this suddenly so important *to you*?'

Ewert Grens stared blankly ahead.

He'd come here to ask the questions, not to answer them.

He didn't – just like when Elisa Cuesta asked about his sudden interest in the other little girl – have any clear explanation for what drove him. He was just doing what he always did: being affected and reacting. Rushed ahead, confident his mind would eventually catch up with him.

'I think it's time for you to leave, Superintendent.'

Now it was the mother who took over again. These parents knew each other so well, had done this so many times, knew when the other was exhausted and needed relief.

'You said what you came here to say. And we have explained our reasoning. So I will ask you to leave us alone.'

'How would the formal declaration of death help a seven-year-old to understand?'

'Did you hear what I said?'

Then she burst. The matter-of-fact voice long gone.

'We can't take it any more! For three years we've gone through everything, thought through everything, seen and heard and felt *everything* a stranger could have done to our beloved daughter!'

At each new sentence, the mother had taken a step towards the man she was screaming at. Now she took the very last, her face close to his.

'Linnea has died in my arms every day!'

Ewert Grens exited a few minutes later into an August evening that was as warm and quiet as when he arrived. Like stepping into a soft embrace. As if what happened inside couldn't touch life as it went on out here. And after winding his way through the toys, reaching the street and turning round, he stared into three pairs of eyes. In a window upstairs stood a little boy who was convinced his twin sister was still alive, and in the kitchen window downstairs stood a mother and a father who had decided their daughter was dead.

I SLEPT FOR sure. First I looked out at the clouds we were inside of, but not. Then I fell asleep. And when I woke up everything was blue. The sky. I'm in the sky! Hello? I'm going to tell Jacob. When I see him. Maybe he's also waiting for me to arrive, maybe that's why I couldn't see him when we left the big store.

I probably miss him a little.

Just a little.

AN EMPTY COFFIN.

All these years living with death – his days spent investigating it for the Stockholm police – and he'd never been to a funeral for someone who wasn't there.

He understood what the mother and father meant.

Might even be able to sense what they were feeling.

Linnea has died in my arms every day.

But despite that, he was pulling open Erik Wilson's door, heading straight in and speaking without waiting for his boss to hang up the phone.

'I want more time.'

Wilson waved, annoyed, shushing Grens with a finger to his mouth.

Ewert Grens didn't seem to understand the gesture.

'A week? Two weeks? Even more?'

Now his boss hung up. Halfway into a sentence. And didn't look especially happy about it.

'My door was closed. I was in the middle of a call. I chose to stay later than usual so I could wrap up a few tasks that require quiet and delicacy. So, Ewert, why do you think you can just storm in here, under –'

'Three weeks? Four weeks? Maybe more?'

'– those conditions, and in any way make me want to listen to what you have to say? Reconsider my decision?'

'Because I'm sure that the case was never fully investigated. She's out there somewhere. Alive or dead.'

'Sit down.'

'I want to find her. Bring her back. Home to her family or her coffin.'

'Ewert, sit down.'

Erik Wilson waited. Without speaking, or heading elsewhere, or doing anything other than observing the detective superintendent while he spat and hissed in front of him. Until Grens finally grabbed one of the visitor chairs and sank down.

'You don't seem to be doing very well, Ewert.'

'No more nagging. I'm old, not dying.'

'Elisa. She was the one who informed me. She was worried.'

Ewert Grens sighed loudly.

'So she's the new Hermansson now? Always worried about my health? Carrying on relentlessly.'

'Elisa cares. Sees. Thinks.'

Grens threw his arms wide.

'Sure. Maybe I was a little . . . dizzy. Earlier. But it's better now.'

'Better? Ewert – you seem even more tired, even more worn down than usual. But then you've never looked particularly spry. You're pale. Not exactly the picture of health. I've noticed it for a while now, so it was a good thing Elisa gave me a push. Because I'm not just your boss, I have personnel responsibilities. *Responsibility – for you.* You've worked your arse off in this station for over forty years, but your days are still longer than almost anyone else's. By a margin. You've seen all that people are capable of doing to each other. And I think, it wouldn't be so strange if you were finally approaching some kind of PTSD. A stress response to trauma. Maybe not from a single event, but from . . . well, everything.'

Then Ewert Grens shifted. Sat down again. *On* Erik Wilson's desk.

'Come on, Wilson.'

'I've taken care of tough, strong, experienced officers who pretended the warning signals weren't there. Just something other people were inventing. It usually ends pretty badly when they refuse to see it until it's too late.'

The slightly too heavy detective stayed sitting where he was. Even though the desk swayed hazardously.

'Yes. I *have* seen everything. But I've learned to shut it out.'

'It doesn't work like that.'

'It works just fine. Always has.'

'Until you *can't* shut it out any longer. Until it catches up with you. Because you can run fast – *but it will always catch up*. Sooner or later you have to deal with all those ghosts. Even you, Ewert.'

And when Grens, as he did now, leaned towards his boss, the gentle creaking of the thin desk turned to a metallic whine.

'So how long can I keep going, would you say? Five weeks? Six? Maybe even seven?'

Erik Wilson was tall, wide. Maybe that's why he never raised his voice, he didn't need to, his authority had always been self-evident.

But now he did.

'You're not going anywhere! Because, as I told you this afternoon, you don't have that assignment. Never had. When you leave here, you'll focus on the investigations already on *your* desk. The official ones! This one, Ewert, a seven-year-old about to be pronounced dead tomorrow, you'll just have to give up!'

It wasn't far from Wilson's large imposing office to Grens's much smaller and more lived-in one.

But he never made it there.

He turned when he reached the copier and left the police station and the corridor whose walls had ears. He was about to make a few phone calls he didn't want anyone to overhear – to people he would never otherwise talk to.

Ewert Grens, who had always maintained that the police should hold their press conferences as far from him as possible and say as little as they could.

Ewert Grens, whose contact with journalists was always no more than a yellow Post-it note with a phone number on it scrawled by one of the poor receptionists and left in the hall, which he would then toss with a satisfying arc into a bin.

Now he would call them. He needed them.

And he'd keep the conversation short, just like everyone who left an anonymous tip-off. Information that was private and therefore could only be shared with a few select newsrooms, and which was part of a story that began three years earlier, and had been written about a great deal back then – the story of a little girl who disappeared without a trace.

Now they would have their follow-up.

A funeral.

For the girl who never found her way home.

NOW WE'RE ALMOST there. The voice in the speaker just said so. (Which I think has to be one of the people who works in here and walks around asking if everything is OK and if I want something to eat or drink. Which I do, every time.) We're on our way down, and inside the clouds again, *inside*, or maybe *through*, I don't know, but that giant blue sky is still high up there somewhere, I know it for sure.

I guess I miss Jacob more now.

Yes.

But just a little more.

HE'D TRIED TO sleep at home but the black hole in his bed just kept expanding. He might have nodded off for a moment, or at least it felt that way, because surely he'd been dreaming? Dreaming of the woman on the bench whom he now knew from the discontinued investigation was named Jenny and who looked just like Anni, spoke like Anni, carried their unborn child as Anni carried her. Until he woke up, in a cold sweat. It felt so real. As if she were alive. But she wasn't, was she? He then wandered through the huge apartment, which he shared with no one, through rooms that were foreign to him and wondered why he was here. He walked out onto the balcony as the big city below played out its night, but couldn't find the peace he usually did out there. As dawn arrived, the first light touching the rooftops, he made his way from his home through the empty streets back to the police station. There, on his sagging corduroy sofa, he finally fell asleep properly. Heavily. And when the first steps from his early-bird colleagues echoed in the hall, he felt marvellously well rested despite the short nap. Breakfast, as was so often the case, was at his desk, purchased from the vending machines outside the kitchenette, two black coffees and a plastic-wrapped ham and cheese sandwich, while he gathered his courage to make a call that was quite different from last night's.

'Hello . . . ?'

'Hi . . . we don't know each other. But we met once.'

'And – who are you?'

'We sat on the same park bench a couple of days ago. In front of two white crosses.'

Silence. Barely even the sound of breathing. And when her voice returned, it was quieter, more careful and alert.

'The same park bench?'

'Yes.'

'It's . . . you?'

'Yes.'

'And you want – what? And how do you know my name? How did you reach me?'

'From the police investigation. About the girl from the parking garage.'

'It was never brought to court.'

'I know that.'

'And never became public. Something about the secrecy of the preliminary investigation, in case it might be picked up again.'

'I . . .'

He didn't get further than that. Unsure how to proceed. It almost felt good when she took the words from his mouth.

'So you're . . . a cop?'

'A detective superintendent.'

'You never said anything about that.'

'I was at the cemetery as a private person. Just like you.'

She fell silent again. For so long that he started to think she might have hung up.

'Hello, are you –'

'I'm here. And I'm wondering what you want.'

Now it was Grens who fell silent. He was normally so good at this – tracking down witnesses in an investigation, making them talk. But this was not normal. Because this was no investigation.

'I'd like to see you again. At the cemetery.'

She laughed, dropping her vigilance for a moment.

'You make it sound romantic.'

'Strictly professional. I promise.'

'Police work? At a cemetery?'

'If you only knew how much of a detective's work in Stockholm consists of death. I want to meet you and show you some pictures. And there – it will feel less formal. No paperwork that needs filling in, no obligatory documentation of what we say to each other.'

She breathed carefully again. Maybe she hesitated. He probably would have done the same if their roles were reversed – a stranger suggesting he meet them among the headstones.

'When?'

Her voice.

Less suspicious.

'Now. If you can.'

'I can stop by on my way to work. In one hour. Is that OK, Superintendent?'

Exactly one hour later he was sitting on the park bench in front of grave 603 in Block 19B. He'd watered the plants, removed the withered leaves, and cleared the weeds. He and Anni were done with each other, this time he was here for the sake of other people. One much younger, whose empty coffin was just a few rows away, and another just as young who in the same symbolic way would be buried in just a few hours.

Ten minutes later he was still sitting there, alone. She was late. So he stood up, started pacing between the rows of crosses and stones. Stopped from time to time, reading date of birth and date of death and figuring out the age they died – it upset him how unfair life was, some had so long, others so incredibly short.

He thought of his father. A man he only met a couple of times, but whose grave he was now also responsible for. A beautiful stone: smooth, black granite and gold letters that a stonemason chiselled in with force.

Parents who were in two other cemeteries in another part of town. A woman lying right in front of him. A daughter lying in the memorial grove some distance away.

Who are you when every layer of human contact has been peeled away?

How can you find a context when nothing seems to fit together?

He didn't know, yet. But recently he'd tried to reconcile himself to things not going as planned, tried to find new strength, to stand up. Not so he could be the same as he once was, live the same life – but to come back again different than he was before, since sometimes different is the only way.

'I'm sorry I'm late.'

She was taller than he remembered. Her short dark hair clipped back, but those eyes still had the same intensity, a gaze that never wavered.

'Thank you for coming. Shall we sit down?'

He pointed to the not entirely stable park bench, and they sat down at the same place as last time. As if it were already their habit.

'You mentioned pictures. That you thought I should look at.'

No small talk. He should be grateful, since he didn't like it.

Still, he felt a slight, unexpected disappointment.

'You were her mother. Alva – was that what you wanted to call her?'

'Alva.'

'I'm not going to ask about her father. Or about other relatives. About why you were alone. But that's why you're the only one who can answer my questions. You were her whole world. You know exactly what she was like. You more than anyone else.'

The envelope that had been in the inside pocket of his jacket was now wrinkled, and he smoothed it out as best he could against the wooden slats of the bench before handing her its contents.

A stack of photographs.

'The same day you lost her in the parking garage, another four-year-old girl was reported missing – she also never came back.'

The first was a photograph in a studio. An uncomfortable smile, stiff posture.

'Who is she?'

'Linnea. She disappeared just a few hours later, just a few miles away. First I want to know – have you ever seen her before?'

'Maybe.'

'Maybe?'

'Not really. But in a missing person's photo. I think I got a letter in the post. With exactly this photo. I remember it because . . . I . . .'

Her parents' desperate search for answers. It really had reached the greater public.

'But never in real life?'

'No.'

The next photo was a copy of what stood in a gold frame in the bedroom Linnea still shared with her twin brother. A child laughing with happiness, peering into the camera with eyes full of a zest for life. Grens had chosen it – and the following photographs – because she was surrounded by other children.

'And if you look at this picture?'

'Yes?'

'Not at her. At the other children.'

She instinctively counted how many were there. Nine little kids. Running around and looking happy, just as Linnea did.

'What do you want me to look for?'

'If any of them could be your little girl.'

She looked quickly at the photograph. Then the next, where Linnea was also in the company of several children, and the next, and the next. Until she'd gone through the whole stack.

'No.'

'You're sure?'

'I'm sure. Alva isn't there. In any of them.'

She handed the pictures back to him, and he put them back into the envelope and into his inside pocket. Then he sat there, silently vacillating. An elderly couple offered him temporary reprieve when they came walking by, greeting them as people do in a place where everyone is united by loss. Grens greeted them back, and they listened as the couple's crackling steps disappeared down a gravel path. But with the renewed silence came renewed reluctance, and now it was the woman by his side who saved him.

'I have no idea what your name is.'

She smiled, gently.

'You never mentioned it the first time we met or on the phone, and you haven't offered it here either.'

'Ewert.'

He cleared his throat.

'Ewert Grens.'

'Hello, Ewert. My name – as you probably already know – is Jenny. And I do wonder what it is that you *really* want.'

'Really?'

'You can't expect me to believe you brought me here to look at some meaningless photos.'

'They were not meaningless.'

'No? Come on.'

She threw her arms up.

She was still smiling, but her meaning was clear.

No more bullshit.

'OK. Maybe I wanted something more than that. In addition to the possibility that we might be lucky and find Alva in one of those pictures.'

'Yes?'

She held her arms wide again. Waiting for an answer.

'I think your little girl and the girl in the pictures might be connected.'

'Connected?'

'They're the same age. Disappeared within hours of each other. Their investigations were never linked. One is completed, the grave you visit, while the other has been deprioritised to such an extent that both the police and her family have given up. Tunnel vision. As often happens when cases land in different precincts and have to be solved with the same resources as hundreds of others.'

She lowered her arms and leaned back against the park bench. The whole rickety construction trembled at this small movement.

'And why are you talking to me about it?'

'I'm not sure. But I think it's because you were the one who started all this. It could also be that *if* both cases are to continue being investigated, it has to be done unofficially. I can't talk to either my colleagues or my bosses. But mostly it's because I swore never to go to a funeral again, and this afternoon the girl in the pictures you looked at will be buried, become a new empty grave – and I can't bear to go there alone.'

WE BOUNCE.

Hop. Hop.

That's what happens when an aeroplane lands. That's what the ones who know my name told me. It's not something to be afraid of, and I'm not.

Not much.

THE MAN IN front of him did not look his best.

His blazer wouldn't button across his stomach, his trousers had mysteriously shortened even though he hadn't grown, his shoes needed shining, and his tie wouldn't knot no matter how hard he tried.

Ewert Grens backed further and further away from his hall mirror. As if that would help.

The black suit he was never going to wear again had been hanging in his attic storage space. The white tie he was never going to wear again had been stuffed in between some towels and pillowcases in one of his bedroom wardrobes. The only sensible thing would have been to drive to the police station at Kronoberg and ask Sven Sundkvist, his oldest colleague and now best friend, for help. It would have been just as sensible to ask Erik Wilson, whom he'd come to respect over the years, to tie his tie. But he couldn't show either of them his funeral outfit. Wilson had already made it clear that this investigation was over. And Sven would remind him of how things often went awry when Grens engaged in unsanctioned investigations – how he ended up making emotional decisions that led to the events around him spiralling out of his control.

So he pulled off his tie, which immediately scrunched into a wrinkled state again, then he straightened his thinning hair, which fell in the wrong direction, sighed and left his reflection – it would have to stay here while the rest of him locked the front door and headed down the stairs to the street.

As he made his way to his car, he wasn't sure he knew what he was doing. Why didn't he just drive to a doctor instead, check if his dizziness was a symptom of a blockage or haemorrhage or some other unpleasant thing? Why was he putting time and energy into something he didn't really need to care about, which didn't affect him and wasn't his responsibility? Maybe this time he really should turn round, head back.

They met as agreed at the bottom of the Northern Chapel's long stone steps in almost imperceptible rain, drops dissolving before reaching the ground. As she stood there, dressed in black, protective paper wrapped around the red roses in her hands, she reminded him – just as she had the first time – of Anni. Something about the way she held herself, or maybe her expression. She hugged him, and he instinctively backed away, unused to being touched, but realised people heading into a funeral could hardly just shake hands, and it meant no more than what it was – a sharing of warmth in the face of this accursed cold.

They were early, only a couple of press photographers were waiting nearby, and Grens had to suppress the impulse to go over and thank them for coming. And when they entered the beautiful church – which seemed to lean against its symmetrical wings and vault towards the sky with a soft arched dome – all the seats were still vacant. They chose a wide aisle to the right after the entrance and sat down at the back, beside a small display that partly obscured their view, so there was little risk anyone would notice them.

Soon the rows of benches at the front were full.

A quiet murmur made its way along the walls of the church.

In the middle of a heavy stone slab, surrounded by lit candles, stood the empty coffin.

'Thank you.' He leaned in close and whispered. 'For coming with me.'

Jenny looked round, as if to make sure they weren't the only ones talking.

'I'm still not really sure why I'm here.'

'Because I'm not good at funerals.'

'Or why *you* are here.'

'Because it's the last chance to see something the other investigators didn't. Maybe understand something they didn't.'

An organ – difficult to see but somewhere in the vicinity – interrupted any attempt at conversation with an opening hymn as solemn and serious as this irrevocable ceremony.

The worst was the walk around the coffin.

When all the visitors, one at a time, went forward to say their goodbye to a little girl whose parents and the authorities had decided no longer existed.

No one could ever be more exposed than at that moment.

Face turned to the congregation. Pain and grief with no refuge.

When Grens saw Jacob, Linnea's twin brother, standing there, fighting against those around him who were trying to tear down his final defence, his belief that despite everything she was still alive, that nothing had changed, it was unbearable. It had been a long time since he'd wanted to hold anyone that tightly.

It was easier to breathe when they went outside. The drizzle still hung in the air as the sun broke through the clouds. They kept their distance as the mourners moved towards a newly dug hole and dropped their flowers onto the coffin. Yellow, red, white roses, and perhaps some of the older women were holding blue irises. After a while it was hard to make out what was happening because everyone stood packed so tightly together, but he could hear someone say *God, who holds the children dear* and someone else sing a psalm Grens had never heard before, and then in a gap, which appeared between a couple of mourners, he saw Jacob hesitantly making his way towards the open grave then seemed to change his mind and hurry back. The detective lingered beside Jenny near a grove of straggly birches until the whole group had dispersed, and two church caretakers prepared to fill the small hole with soil. Then they walked forward and both dropped a red rose onto the coffin lid.

'I thought I saw you inside the church!'

Grens had been staring down at the empty coffin.

That was probably why he hadn't noticed the girl's father.

'And now you're standing here – at her grave!'

His voice was broken, just like a man who has said goodbye to his daughter. While the eyes boring into the detective were those of a man who hadn't slept in three years.

'So what exactly about *leave us alone* did you find so hard to understand?'

The father had broken away from his family and the irrational anger getting ever closer to Grens was as unexpected as it was strange.

'It was you! Wasn't it? You called the photographers!'

Grens simply couldn't understand it – and he rarely had a problem understanding aggression. People who shouted at him were often entitled to do so, because he could be pigheaded. But not this time.

'No one outside our family circle knew about this! No one – except you!'

'I don't understand.'

'What is it you don't understand!'

'Your family was the one who contacted the newspapers, asked them to write about you. Now they're following up on their articles. Tying up loose ends. Just like you. Why does that upset you so much?'

'You were supposed to leave us alone! We begged you! This long process has to come to an end. For the sake of our whole family. And most of all for the sake of our beloved little Jacob.'

'No.'

'No . . . ?'

'I still don't understand. Why you're so mad. How could it be so wrong to care? Why does it upset you? I'm here as a police representative. For your daughter's sake. Because –'

'We're leaving now.'

Jenny took Grens's arm as she interrupted his stumbling attempt to explain himself.

'Our intention was never to disturb you. You and I are leaving here, *immediately*.'

Now she pulled him by the arm. Away from a father with tired, angry, despairing eyes, away from the grave and the small white coffin covered with flowers. They walked silently across the lawn that had turned slippery in the rain, past the chapel and the caretakers' tool sheds all the way to Solna Church Road. Only there, just as they were about to exit through one of the large gates, did she stop.

'Is it true?'

Her voice was quiet, sharp.

'What that father said? That he and his family asked you not to disturb them? Not to go near them?'

Grens didn't answer her. Which was answer enough.

'You asked me to come along because your boss and your colleagues wanted nothing more to do with this investigation, and I said yes – for the sake of the grieving family. For Alva's sake. I was glad there was a police officer willing to set aside his own time for others. And now – now I learn that it was the family, the victim's relatives, who didn't want to keep going! That they, on the contrary, *begged* you to let it be!'

The detective remained silent. Never had his funeral suit felt so tight.

'The next time you see me sitting on that park bench, you better not come near me. Stay away until I'm gone. And also, never call me again. It's been a long time since I've felt this ashamed.'

Her steps were as long as they were forceful, she even walked like Anni, a regular clattering rhythm that slowed as she turned onto a side street where he assumed she'd parked her car.

He lingered long after she'd disappeared. With no direction, not knowing where he was headed. The rain fell harder, but he didn't notice. And when he did, he didn't care.

He waited until he was sure that all the visitors had left the cemetery. Then he turned back. To the grave. He stood there a long time, watching the two caretakers shovel earth into a hole with an empty coffin inside. The symbol of the death of a little girl.

'Hello.'

Grens spun round, towards somebody who was good at sneaking.

'I forgot this.'

Jacob. And there, in the grass not far away, lay what he'd intended to put into the grave but then dropped. The teddy bear. With a red polka-dot scarf. One of two that had sat at the foot of the twins' beds now held safely in his arms.

'You're a policeman, right?'

'Yes. Yes, I'm a police officer. That's why I was at your house.'

'And you're going to find her?'

Those eyes. Jacob stared straight at the older detective superintendent who wasn't quite as convinced.

'Yes.'

He had to answer.

'I will . . .'

In the only way he could answer.

'. . . find her.'

Without adding that last word.

'Alive.'

'That's good. Because they say she's sleeping. That that's what you do. But I know we'll see each other again. I can feel Linnea. In my stomach. I know she's out there.'

The little boy was still just as convinced of the only truth he could accept. He wrapped the teddy bear in his jacket to protect it from the drizzle when someone shouted his name.

'Jacob!'

His mother. She hurried towards him, determined strides across the lawn.

'You come here now! We have to . . . today, Jacob . . . we have to be together!'

Grens watched them disappear hand in hand, into the distance, then he continued alone across the lawns and down the path towards the white cross where another girl's coffin had been buried. It was raining even harder, almost pouring now, and he settled on the bench near Anni's resting place – it felt good to just sit without seeing much in front of him. Rarely had he been so soaked. His white tie shrivelled, tightened, and he loosened it, threw it in the bin next to the bench.

Just then his phone rang.

He saw who it was and didn't answer. But it kept ringing. Until he gave in.

'What the fuck, Ewert!'

Erik Wilson. His boss.

'You were supposed to leave them alone! This is not your assignment! So why am I sitting here in front of my computer looking at pictures from a funeral on the *Daily News* home page? And there you are – clearly visible near the edge!'

In the same mood as before.

'The family called us – a conversation that landed in my lap – wondering who you were, why you went to their home, why you were asking questions. *In an investigation that is not yours.* And I had to sit there listening like a fool with no good answers! I get what you were trying to achieve by calling the newspapers. Attention! Thought you would force me to change my mind! A last-ditch effort, I guess. I made it very fucking clear to you that this case is closed. And I also said you seemed worn out. Should take time off. Now we're back to that again. But this is no longer a suggestion. It's an order. Ewert – no matter where you are right now, you are not coming back. Here. You're going home. And staying there.'

'Home?'

'From now on you're on holiday. Free. Call it whatever the hell you want. Getting paid for doing nothing. In the meantime, I want you to go to a doctor – both for your body and mind.'

'And what exactly am I supposed to do at home?'

'Rest. Go for long walks. Take care of yourself.'

'I don't rest. I work. That's how I stay healthy, and if I don't –'

'That's your problem, Ewert. You can't stay here if you're this worn down, this close to burning out, and maybe never coming back from it. It's not good for you. And it's definitely not good for us.'

'I'm not exhausted, I'm just affected by a case that . . . also an experience I had here at the cemetery . . .'

'An experience? What kind of experience?'

Ewert Grens didn't continue. So Erik Wilson did.

'Look, Ewert. Listen to me now. Apart from a couple of times when you've been suspended for misconduct, you have never left the police station. You don't take your holidays, even though I remind you to, and they no longer let us save them. Now you will take them. You still have all the days you accrued this year, just like last year – you can't have more than that, otherwise you'd be able to stay home until retirement. It's a total of twelve weeks. You are going to be gone for that long. When you come back, you will have no holiday left, but you won't need any either because you will have done *exactly* as I asked you to – gone to doctors who can deal with both your body and mind.'

Ewert Grens stared up into the rain.

And then lay down.

On his back. On the bench.

His face turned to the sky, water streaming down his forehead and eyelids and cheeks.

Maybe he fell asleep. If not, he was in that shapeless world between sleep and wakefulness where thoughts are both everything and nothing. *You're a policeman, right, and you're going to find her?* It went from a dream of a boy who was slipping into his sister's grave to a dream of two women who looked like each other burying their common child. He floated, he drowned, he ran as fast as he could but only got further away, and he couldn't save the boy who was falling onto the coffin. *I can feel Linnea. In my stomach. I know she's out there.*

He lay there until he finally grabbed hold of it.

The direction.

He knew where to go. Or at least where he would start, a place to begin.

He stood up with difficulty, sat on the water-soaked bench for a while, squishing his feet inside his shoes, then started to walk. Towards the eastern part of the cemetery. Towards the memorial grove. Where he'd never been. After thirty years, he was finally ready to visit the daughter they'd never had, who had lain here alone because, unlike Jenny, he'd decided she was someone who didn't exist and never had. And if today he dared to make it all the way there, maybe even talked to his unborn child a little as he did with Anni, then afterwards he'd go home where he'd sleep during the days and spend his nights at the police station, searching for a connection between two empty graves. Because little girls deserve to have someone who cares about them. Because he'd been wrong this whole time – people exist for as long as other people believe they do. Because a police officer can file some paperwork in the archive, but cases have an irritating habit of going on anyway, they don't seem to mind that nobody cares. Because sooner or later something always happens to change everything, to bring the past back to life – someone remembers, someone regrets, someone decides to talk.

And gets in touch one day.

WE'RE STANDING IN a very long snake. All of us. The whole plane. Winding slowly down the aisle between empty seats. I'm the only one who doesn't have a bag, I don't need one, I'm headed straight home to finally find out what game we're playing, why Mum and Dad tricked me in the big supermarket – before the nice car and the plane in the clouds – and most of all why they went there ahead of me, without me. When the giant snake has wound to the very front, it keeps winding down a flight of stairs and onto the asphalt and towards an airport bus and a new airport terminal where everyone is surely waiting to give me a hug and say *oh how I have missed you, my little girl* and *look how good you are at flying* even though I haven't even been gone a whole day.

I wonder what it will feel like.

Wonder if Jacob is there, too.

I think he is.

PART
2

PART

2

They were about to knock on the door of the darkest darkness.

HIS OFFICE WASN'T big enough. Ewert Grens had paced back and forth between the window and the door, the sofa and the bookshelf, and kept colliding with himself even harder and more often than before. So he started down the deserted corridor of the investigative division and his limping steps echoed loudly here, the slam of his heel bouncing ahead and behind him as he passed by the closed doors of his colleagues.

Two forty-five.

Alone, just like every other night.

Around ten o'clock, a couple of hours before midnight, it was usually safe to sneak in the back way and go up the stairs without being seen. He avoided the lift – if he met someone there he'd have no escape route. Turning his days around had been as easy as remaining unseen in the darkness. He now knew the sound of the coffee machine's periodic hum, like the cough of an autumn cold, and then its return to sleep, and the low hiss of the copier, a new friend he'd never before perceived during the day.

He pulled out his phone and dialled Mariana Hermansson's number. Fourth time tonight.

No answer.

Mariana, who he'd started to talk to after Anni ceased to exist, who always asked him the right questions and kept his thoughts from flying away. Mariana, who – like Jenny, who he didn't know but wanted to meet beyond just his dreams – kept her promise of never seeing him again. And he missed her just as much as he'd expected.

Eleven weeks ago he'd left the cemetery in a rain-soaked suit, after an empty coffin was lowered into the ground, covered in red roses and blue irises, and he hadn't been able to shake off those two little girls. They were beside him day after day, chattering and disturbing him. They refused to leave him alone. All these years as a police officer, and he hadn't even learned the most basic rule of the profession: *perpetrators and their victims are your work, not your life.*

He continued walking through the dry, dusty air of a quiet police station. Eight laps back and forth and two stops at the vending machine. An almond tart in an aluminium tin and a cheese sandwich with red peppers. In the meantime, dawn was preparing to paint the darkness on the other side of the windows a brighter shade.

'Grens?'

He was startled. The voice had come from somewhere behind him.

'That has to be you.'

Ewert Grens turned round.

At the far end of the corridor stood a slightly crouched figure, a tall and skinny shadow. Oh, shit.

He'd been discovered.

Then the shadow began to approach him, its long, thin legs taking long, thin steps that were much quieter than Grens's own and made no echo at all.

'Werner?'

'Yep.'

Grens had known the stooped detective Gunnar Werner for as long as he could remember. They'd started their service the same winter, and now they were both in their last years as officers with no plan for what to do when their time here was over.

'I knew I'd find you in the division's hallway in the wee hours of a Friday night. Though you're not supposed to be here at all.'

'And how did you *know* that?'

'You kidding me? Ewert Grens outside the station for any length of time? Everyone knows, my friend. They know you sneak in here after dark when you think nobody's watching. I bet even your boss knows, but doesn't want to go to the trouble of doing anything about it as long as you stay away during the day.'

They fell silent, walking side by side. Until they reached the lift a third time.

'I'm starting to get why you do this, Ewert. You won't find a solitude like this in very many places.'

Werner had worked for decades in wiretapping. That's how Grens still thought of him – headphones on, surrounded by cords and monitors. But after the major reorganisation, he'd moved from the wiretapping division to the National Operations Department and traded sound for image. Now he was one of the detectives fighting criminals online.

'But I wonder if that's really a good thing, in the long run. You have to take care of yourself now and then. Shouldn't burn the candle at both ends. As you often do, Ewert.'

'I have to keep going until I can find a way out of this investigation I entered way too late to have any reasonable chance of cracking it. But now . . . I can't let go. I've tried, but I just can't.'

'That's why I'm here.'

Werner stopped abruptly. Grens did, too. Between the kitchenette and the cloakroom.

'Yes?'

'You came by my office a couple of months ago, Ewert, and you wouldn't give up until I promised to tell you if we ever came across a couple of very specific keywords.'

'I talked to you. And to every sensible detective in Sweden, in the whole Nordic region. And to representatives of almost every one of the hundred and ninety member states in Interpol. And to –'

'*Zebra-striped jacket. Blue butterfly.*'

'Yes?'

'Keywords. Which you gave me no explanation for.'

'And I'll continue to keep that to myself for a while longer.'

'Why?'

'Because there are those who don't want me on this case.'

They looked at each other with the kind of trust that only a whole career spent at the same job can create.

'Then I won't ask again. But I want to give you this.'

The image Werner had printed out on copy paper wasn't very sharp nor was its object centred – but it was still the most vivid image Ewert Grens had ever seen.

That's why he took a quick, involuntary step back.

'What the hell is that?'

'We were contacted just over an hour ago by a Swedish aid organisation whose mission is to prevent . . .'

Now Werner held out the picture again.

'. . . the sale of children online. Sexual exploitation of children on the Internet.'

So Grens was forced to look.

'Someone sent this picture anonymously to their tip-off line.'

And he did exactly what he'd learned to do in order to deal with the dead. First, concentrate on everything around the body. The details beyond the person. Slowly build the image from the outside in, become accustomed bit by bit. He therefore saw a dull room, brightly lit, brown wallpaper ripped and adorned with just a simple mirror, blinds that had been pulled down and entangled with each other.

Gradually he allowed his gaze, his consciousness, to approach the heart of the photograph.

It did not help this time.

Never with this kind of picture.

The girl smiling at him, at the photographer, was around nine, ten years old. Grens had never seen her before. She was stark naked. A dog leash around her neck. The man standing obliquely behind her, holding the other end of the leash, whose face couldn't be seen because the picture ended at his chest, held in his other hand a scrawled sign: '*This is the first image in a series of nine.*'

Grens couldn't bear to think of how it might continue.

'Why did you come down here to push this fucking shit in my face? Why do you think I –'

'Your keywords.'

Grens had turned his head away. So Werner had to step behind him and snake an arm around until he was pointing to the middle of the picture.

'There.'

In the girl's hair.

'The clip. Holding her fringe to the side.'

After a while, Grens gave up. Followed his colleague's slightly crooked finger. And saw it.

'A blue butterfly, Ewert. One of your key phrases.'

A blue butterfly.

It truly was there.

After all this damn time. After waiting and waiting. A hit.

A blue butterfly that looked exactly like the one Linnea was wearing in her hair the day she was taken from the supermarket. A butterfly made by the girl's own mother, given to her daughter as a gift when she turned four, completely unique in the world. Admittedly, an eternity in the life of such a young person had gone by, three years since the last photographs included in the investigation were taken, but the girl in the picture was *not* Linnea – he was sure of it.

'I'm leaving this with you now. Won't log it. Because I assume you're doing what you need to do, Ewert, investigating as far as you can go.'

Ewert Grens accepted the sheet of paper with some hesitation.

'Are you sure?'

'When I sit down at my computer in my office with my beautiful view of Kronoberg Park, and continue my search for those types of pictures, I find more than I have time to write down. *More than I have time to write down, Ewert.* I come across a hundred Swedes a week easily who own or share these pictures over various channels, and there's no way I can process them all.'

The skinny man, who had always, even when young, seemed too sweet to be a cop, quite unlike Grens himself, and was too much of a good person to spend his days dealing with the dirtiest crime imaginable, looked sincerely exhausted.

'And that, Ewert, is if I search. By myself. If we add in outside tips – my God . . . a few years ago we received ten thousand. Last year it doubled to twenty thousand. Just *two per cent* turn into preliminary investigations – one in fifty of the tip-offs. A case we solved just two days ago, one where we're talking documented sexual abuse – images of rape and torture – remained untouched for two years while the abuse continued. Even though we had names, cities and phone numbers! Because if the suspect doesn't work with children or have one of his own, then, according to our guidelines, it will end up in priority group two. My whole job these days, Ewert, is to prioritise. So if you take one of them, I not only *know* that something is happening, I know *you* will be investigating it and doing a damn sight better than anyone else.'

Werner laid a cautious hand on Grens's shoulder.

'Besides, if we're lucky, a colleague I like very much might finally stop sneaking in and out – *during his involuntary holiday* – pacing down these corridors all night long.'

THE DOOR TO the corridor was carefully closed. The sixties music filled the void around him, and the corduroy sofa was just as soft as when it allowed an ageing body to find rest.

The time was approaching four.

Now dawn was truly not far away. He'd almost made it through one more night. He'd never been particularly good at counting, and the mathematics of this escaped him completely – that the shorter his time on this earth became, the longer his nights were.

He'd put the sheet of paper with its horrendous picture upside down on his simple coffee table.

A photograph traded between people who didn't have to leave their homes to commit the most heinous of crimes. Someone had sent it to an aid organisation, who in turn contacted the police. Someone wanted to tell them something.

Victim? Perpetrator? Witness?

Someone who was scared and seeking refuge? Someone who was proud and wanted confirmation? Someone who'd been wronged and was seeking revenge?

Ewert Grens still knew nothing.

But he didn't have to be good at maths to figure out when anonymous actions were more than just tips. There was a bigger story behind that picture.

He reached towards the table, turned over the sheet of paper.

This time he would not allow his gaze to reach the centre of the photograph, not meet the unknown girl with the blue butterfly – instead he'd concentrate on the perpetrator. The faceless perpetrator.

Grens pulled the paper closer, straightened his reading glasses.

A man in his younger middle age. That much was clear, even without a face. His build, posture, arm musculature. His skin was pale, body hair normal. The shirt was blue. A thin ring on his left little finger and a wristwatch with a red dial and silver-metalled strap. The dog leash in his right hand gleamed in the cold light.

Someone sent that particular image because it contains a larger story.

'Werner? Are you awake?'

Grens had called Gunnar Werner's phone hoping the skinny inspector was still in the complex of buildings that constituted the epicentre of Swedish police operations.

'Night shift this week.'

'The photo you gave me.'

'Yes?'

'Can you send it digitally?'

'Then we have to register it. And we want to avoid that for a while, right?'

Of course. That's why he came in person.

Paper doesn't leave as many tracks.

'Can you enlarge it?'

'Yes. But the original is not spectacular.'

'I'm coming up to you now.'

'I don't think that's a good idea, Ewert. In case this errand leads to any questions. Stay on that corduroy sofa of yours and listen to some more music – and in twenty minutes head to your pigeonhole. OK?'

Twenty minutes later, Grens walked down the dark corridor towards a mailbox he never emptied. On top of the pile of unopened letters and unread newspapers lay a manila envelope with no addressee or sender. He walked back, closed the door, and ripped it open with his index finger.

Twelve sheets of equal size.

Werner had divided the rectangular photograph into twelve equal parts and enlarged each one twelve times.

Grens sank to his knees and started to puzzle them together on the floor.

He had to dive into the giant picture, read every detail, see what it was someone wanted him to see.

Bit by bit, he shifted his focus from the headless man's body. Above the naked girl. Above the spartan room. But in the high magnification, the sharpness also disappeared so that it was sometimes difficult to perceive where one object began and another ended.

Top to bottom. Left to right.

With his knees in pain and his hips complaining, he crept again and again over the sheets of paper without finding what he was looking for.

Nothing.

He gave up, got to his feet.

Then everything changed.

Oh my God.

His last glance had landed *behind* the girl and the man, on a small round mirror, the only thing hanging on the wall. That's where he should look! Inside that! He'd assumed that the small grey dots on the mirror were just dust or picture noise.

Ewert Grens was in a hurry. That feeling in his chest again. In one of the bookshelf compartments he had a decent old magnifying glass, with a handle and everything. He picked up the sheet of paper, made room for it on the desk, and angled the table lamp down.

It just might be.

Those slightly lighter shapes in the mirror might be letters on the man's back, on the upper part of the dark shirt.

He moved the magnifying glass up, down, close, far away. Nothing became clearer – enlarging it only made the details harder to make out.

Grens hurried out into the corridor, passed by three closed doors and opened the fourth. Went into Sven Sundkvist's office and over to the desk drawer where he kept a small bottle of something that back in the days of typewriters was used constantly, something absolutely no one ever needed now. An almost full container of white Tipp-Ex correction fluid.

And it was odd.

When he sat down again to examine the sheet of paper with the perpetrator's back unintentionally reflected in a mirror, neither his knees nor his hips ached any more. It was always like that when he was getting closer to a person who believed they had the right to use force on someone else, believed that person's life had less value than their own. The adrenaline that rushed through him when an investigation grabbed hold, lifted him up, the intoxication that was like nothing else and came from deep, deep inside.

So.

Since the resolution was too low – and only got worse by enlarging it more – he would instead work with the image contrast.

It was worth a chance. He'd sometimes made it work in investigations in the past. If the contrast was insufficient it *could* help to dab whiteout on grey areas – the ones he assumed were dust and visual noise on the mirror's glass, but which just might be letters. Simply make them clearer.

Ewert Grens had never had much in the way of fine motor skills and felt clumsy, awkward, as he brushed white on all the grey parts as carefully as he could. He then took a step back, trying to make the now lighter dots come together in a pattern that would form letters.

No.

Nothing.

He dabbed again, in more places and with a steadier hand, white ending up in the right places.

Took another step backwards.

Yes. Maybe.

Letters, space, letters.

Ewert Grens took a deep breath, from his diaphragm, like he'd been taught.

Until he was completely sure of the first letter.

He focused on more bright dots that were fusing together.

Then the next one formed.

The third letter, however, wouldn't appear.

Refused to coalesce.

No matter how much he brushed and concentrated, the parts floated too far from each other.

. . . .
. . . .

It went better with the fourth.

The fifth.

And the seventh.

ᗡ
I
. . .
. . .
K

That *could be* it.

If he guessed, filled in the two missing letters.

The first clue to a blue butterfly that had flown to a new little girl.

N-O-R-D-I-S-K *(mirrored)*

He let the next word appear just as slowly – brushed, stepped back, brushed again – and after a while he'd managed to interpret four of the first six letters.

When everything was cut to pieces. Abrupt. By the frame of the mirror.

The rest, the end, was missing.

M-Ø-B-:::-:::-F *(mirrored)*

Ewert Grens started the computer, opened the search field and entered what he had – 'Nordisk Møb.'

And didn't even have time to take a sip of the cold dregs of coffee at the bottom of his mug.

After he scrolled past the paid ads at the top that got in the way of his actual search, only one reasonable hit remained. Two words with another fourteen letters: 'Nordisk Møbelfremstilling'. He clicked on the link and was taken to a website with Danish text and a logo that was identical to the one on the man's shirt – a company with a street address in Rødberg, a small town he had never heard of. A quick check of the map, and he ended up a couple of miles south of Nykøbing Falster on the island of Falster, about as far south-east in Denmark as you could get.

He stood up, not wanting or needing to look at the abuse any longer. Only a single paper was relevant now. The one with the mirrored text.

It was also the part of the picture that gave him doubts.

Could it truly be possible? Or was someone just messing with him?

Would a paedophile so advanced that he sold his perversions online to like-minded people – no other possible way to interpret a sign promising eight more pictures in the same series – be so careless that he'd allow himself to be photographed in a shirt with a company logo? Would a detective superintendent in Stockholm a couple of decades into the 2000s be able to unmask a representative of the darkest side of digital technology using the kind of tools his colleagues had in the nineteenth century, a magnifying glass, and another tool, Tipp-Ex, that was already old-fashioned by the end of the twentieth century? Or was he just seeing, spurred along a line of thought by a single hair clip, what he so desperately *wanted* to see?

Ewert Grens squatted down and collected the sheets of paper, turned them over.

Didn't want to meet them again, be pulled back into them.

But maybe also to avoid formulating new questions that could lead to the final one, something he wasn't even sure he wanted the answer to: did the tipper have a goal, had the image ended up with him because it contained a larger story, and if so, was this unknown girl connected to another little girl who also wore a blue butterfly and whose sham burial he'd attended just a few months ago?

SATURDAY MORNING. Half past five. A time when most people allowed to do so chose to sleep. That had never meant much in the world of Ewert Grens. His co-workers had learned to live with the fact that he might call them up in the middle of the night, the very moment he needed to talk, which often seemed to arrive at exactly those times when others least wanted to talk, and it was probably also when he realised he was lacking a context.

So he called again. Fifth time in just a couple of minutes. And she still didn't answer. Just like she hadn't for a whole year. But he wouldn't give up tonight. And it was as if she somehow knew it. Because after he called again, and again, and again, she finally answered.

'Ewert? What the hell –'

'Good morning, Mariana.'

'– don't you understand about the words *I. Don't. Want. To. Talk. To. You. Ever. Again.*'

'I understand. But I've always thought that was a bad idea.'

'I'm hanging up now. Don't force me to change my phone number.'

'Don't hang up. It's *not* you I want to talk to.'

She fell silent. And even though she hadn't exactly been whispering, he could hear deep breathing in the background, someone sleeping heavily beside her – his boss Erik Wilson.

'So who do you want to talk to? Erik? You see each other at work every day.'

'Ideally, I'd rather not talk to him about this at all.'

She fell silent again. He understood her hesitation. After a year of calling her regularly to try to start a new conversation, repair a friendship broken because it was his fault that she'd left the division, and now she finally answered, and he claimed he really wanted to talk to someone else. It did sound a bit suspicious.

'Oh, really? And what exactly does that mean? Who exactly do you want to talk to if you call here *in the middle of the night* and don't want to talk to me or Erik?'

'You know I want to talk to you. More than anyone. But right now, Mariana, just this *morning*, I want you to help me get a hold of that young guy you brought in last year, the one who could do things no one else could – open up and stare straight into a closed digital world.'

'Billy?'

'Maybe. Late twenties. Skinny. Pale. A little pimply. Has an attitude.'

'Billy.'

She fell silent for a third time. What had initially been irritation, and then hesitation, had become caution.

She lowered her voice.

'What are you up to, Ewert?'

'An investigation.'

'And you need help from someone who *doesn't* work at the station? Just like you *don't* want me to talk to your boss about it?'

'An investigation that isn't . . . completely official. Yet.'

And for a very, very brief moment, he felt that closeness again.

She liked this.

His habit of occasionally skirting around the system.

'OK. I know where he is. How to get a hold of him. I'll contact him and then send you his address – because I'm guessing you'd prefer he didn't come and meet you at the station?'

Then the moment was over. The closeness gone.

'And, Ewert?'

'Yes?'

'You do understand that this doesn't work any more, don't you? People who make calls at this time of night aren't well. They're trying to work themselves to death. They're escaping – and you and I both know from what.'

Her voice was sharp, cold again.

'Ewert – I sincerely wish you luck with whatever you're up to right now. *But never call me again.* And by the way – I've just made up my mind. I'm changing my phone number today. Take care of yourself.'

She hung up.

And the electronic silence was, as always, worse than any other kind.

Ewert Grens couldn't stand to wait in his office. It felt empty – a solitude that hadn't been chosen and therefore felt loud and intrusive. He walked to a cafe on Hantverkar Street that opened early. And after three hot cinnamon buns and two cups of coffee as black as it was strong, he received a text with an address and door code. From Mariana's usual phone number, for now.

He didn't take the metro often, but unofficial investigations required unofficial means of transportation, not registered with the police, and when he exited at the Skanstull station, it occurred to him how rarely he visited Södermalm like this. How lovely walking around Stockholm could be. Because as he crossed Göt Street and ambled down the wide avenue of Katarina Ban Street towards Ny Square and found himself enveloped by all the lively street life there, he was flooded with a temporary calm. Maybe this neighbourhood wasn't quite as hip as its residents thought, or quite so unique, but it had a soul and a warmth that the centre of the city, where he'd lived most of his life, lacked.

Five flights of stairs or a lift that looked older than him, which would be so cramped when its metal gate closed it would be hard to take a breath. He chose the stairs, floor by floor, and by the time he knocked on the right door, his problem was rather the opposite: too many breaths and too fierce.

'Good morning, Detective.'

Ripped jeans and a washed-out sweatshirt. And surprisingly alert.

'Good morning, Billy. Already up?'

'Haven't gone to bed yet, Superintendent. Got stuck at the computer.'

'You don't have to call me "Superintendent". My visit here is in a private capacity as you probably understand. Can I come in?'

A small apartment. But not what he'd expected. No piles of empty Coke or energy drink cans. No pizza boxes or Indian takeaway cartons. It was tidy, smelled clean, and the furniture looked expensive. But it was still a life that revolved around a virtual world, that much was obvious. The table by the living-room window was clearly the centre of the home, packed with advanced computer equipment.

'What should I call you then?'

'Ewert.'

'That feels weird.'

'I've been called that for as long as I can remember, and I myself have always thought it was a little weird, would definitely have chosen otherwise. But your name is your name.'

'I mean it feels weird to be on first-name terms with you – you aren't really the type.'

They sat down, the young IT genius in front of the screen and the older detective superintendent on a stool to his right.

'Before we start, I need to warn you.'

Grens lowered his voice without being aware of it.

'We will be working with images that are as terrible as anything humanity can create.'

The detective laid the sheet of paper on the table in front of them. And noticed the young man made the same move he had the first time – backing away as if hoping what he saw wasn't real.

'Here, on the other side, the person who gave me the picture has scribbled down a row of letters and numbers that don't make any sense to me, but which may mean something to you?'

Grens turned the paper over, replaced the image of a sexual assault with Werner's spindly handwriting, and now Billy's movement was the opposite: he relaxed, leaned closer.

'An address from the unindexed Internet.'

'Oh, really?'

'The darknet, Superintendent. I'm sorry – I have to call you that. Otherwise it feels unnatural.'

'Dark . . . net? That tells me absolutely nothing.'

'Seriously?'

'Seriously.'

'But how could you even be a detective superintendent and . . . it's been around for a long time.'

'There's the problem. I've also been around for a long time.'

Billy smiled. Friendly.

'Encrypted networks beneath the regular web. Part of the Internet that's completely outside official search engines. Websites with hidden IP addresses. So you can't just stumble across them by googling around a bit. And if you did happen to stumble there, you won't even be able to view it without the right browser.'

'That's exactly why I'm here.'

'That's exactly why you're here.'

When Ewert Grens sat down in front of a computer, he always smashed on the keys, tormented them, like so many trained on heavy, sluggish typewriters. Billy did not have that problem. His fingers danced across the keyboard, they liked each other, belonged together.

'In order to open the darknet you need special software. An anonymity service. I have a couple to choose from. Do you see there, Superintendent?'

Grens looked at the screen. Or the screens – there were a total of four.

Using Werner's seemingly random letter-and-number doodle, it didn't take long to fill them with the same kind of horrific pictures. For the first time he was met by it in its original form.

'Listen, Superintendent, I have to ask you something.'

'Yes?'

'Why are we sitting here and not in the police station?'

'Because this is the only way to get results in this investigation.'

'You understand that it would be a big deal if someone were to look into what I'm downloading. What addresses I'm visiting.'

'If there's any risk of either of us landing in prison, I'll make sure it's me.'

'Can I have that in writing? That you take responsibility?'

'If you want to stop, we can do that. No pressure, no questions asked. I'll leave now, and I won't hold it against you. Or you can help me move ahead – get closer to the faceless man.'

They both looked at the man holding a leash that circled the neck of a naked little girl with one hand, while with the other he held a hand-written sign telling them this was the first in a series of nine.

'So there are at least eight more?'

'So I understand.'

'And he's offering them to other people?'

'So I've also come to understand.'

'A paedophile ring, Superintendent?'

'That's what I'm trying to find out.'

Then neither of them could stand to look at the naked little girl any more. Grens stood up and peered out the window over Söder's varied rooftops, while Billy headed over to his minimalist kitchenette and turned on the coffee maker.

'Do you want a cup, Superintendent?'

'Only if we're going to keep going.'

'We are.'

The young voice suddenly sounded older.

'Because I want you to get that fucker. And others like him.'

He placed two giant porcelain cups between the keyboard and the screens, half a litre of coffee each, and then held up the back of the sheet of paper.

'This doodle – your words, Superintendent – is the picture's unique name. Almost everyone, other than a computer nerd like me, catalogues in the absolute simplest way when they add new objects. So if I just change a number in the image's name, like this, look now . . .'

He did. Changed a 1 to a 2.

'. . . I'm pretty sure we'll come to the next and . . .'

He fell silent.

Neither of them could speak for a moment.

On the screen at the top right, the next image had been conjured up.

'You can see there, Superintendent, where I'm now pointing, that the previous picture was posted by someone on the fourteenth of July. And this one the day after, the fifteenth. He's created his own serial story. So if I change the number again, and again . . .'

One at a time, the images filled the screens.

An adult man abusing a ten-year-old girl from start to finish in nine steps. Just as advertised.

'That's all, Superintendent. For this delivery.'

'Can you save them?'

'Already done.'

The giant cups of coffee had been drunk.

Ewert Grens had been given a flash drive, which he slid into the inner pocket of his jacket.

'You know, Superintendent, when I was little, they had to copy VHS tapes one by one and then go to the post office and send them in taped-up envelopes with a name and address and stamps, and it took a couple of days for the other fucker to receive it and . . . I mean, I'm not even twenty-eight yet, it wasn't that long ago. Now? With that memory stick, you can upload images faster than you can say "My name is Ewert Grens" and send it to file-sharing sites and cloud services all over the world. I love the Internet – but they really didn't know what the fuck they were unleashing when they invented it.'

The young man held out his hand.

'You owe me one, Superintendent. You can trust me to cash it in.'

Billy remained in front of the screens while his guest headed towards the front door.

'Can you imagine how much more evil shit like this is out there, Superintendent? Hidden on the darknet.'

Grens shook his head.

'No. I can't.'

'Not many can. And maybe it's just as well. It's easier to live like that.'

Ewert Grens went down the five flights and stepped out onto the beautiful avenue of Katarina Ban Street again, where he stood completely still for a moment and just breathed.

In, out. In, out.

A different reality than the virtual one he'd just visited.

And here he knew the rules of the game.

He knew that this was serious. Knew it was now he should go to his boss and hand over the flash drive and the analysis of the shirt that probably read 'Nordisk Møbelfremstilling', which was a company in a town called Rødberg just a couple of miles south of Nykøbing Falster.

But that's not what he did.

Instead, he walked to Göt Street, waved down a taxi and asked the driver to take him to Arlanda Airport as fast as she could.

He'd been pushed away from this case by both his boss and parents who had declared their child dead, and he didn't intend to let go of it again. He and a little boy agreed on that much – teddy bears with red-spotted scarves should not be left alone beside an empty coffin.

IT WAS RAINING when Ewert Grens sat down at the window seat of the East Side Grill. Those few passing by outside looked wet and cold, his chicken burger costing eighty-nine Danish kroner had no scent, and when he looked more closely at the business premises in the building opposite, he realised they were all vacant and available for rent. Rødberg's only restaurant on Rødberg's only main street had given up, just like the rest of this small town.

It took just over an hour to leave Arlanda and Stockholm, an hour in the air to Kastrup and Copenhagen, and another hour and a half on a bumpy train to Nykøbing Falster. He liked the neighbouring country that separated Sweden from the continent, understood most of the Danish language and was always happy to visit – but not this time. Not this errand. This journey had begun at two graves for two four-year-old girls.

According to the map on his phone, the Nordisk Møbelfremstilling company was less than a kilometre away, and he was able to borrow a forgotten umbrella from the restaurant owner, who was more likeable than the food. The sense of abandonment turned into desolation as he walked. He passed an elderly lady with an elderly dog and a hunched-over teenager cycling through the downpour, otherwise no one. He'd lived his whole life in a large city surrounded by its sounds and movement, and he realised he wasn't made for this – without life pressing in on you, there seemed to be no life at all.

He saw the white brick building with its now familiar logo in the distance after the last bend in the main street. A small factory building connected to an office area, and he headed towards the latter. The young woman at the front desk smiled and greeted him and asked how she could be of help.

'First, could you confirm that this item of clothing comes from here?'

Ewert Grens handed over what was left of the white paper sheet after he'd cut out the young girl and the sign in the man's hand.

'I'm sorry – but what do you mean?'

'The shirt. The one that says "Nordisk Møbel" on it. I want to know if it's one of yours.'

The receptionist had reflexively taken what he'd handed to her, now she glanced down at the paper and then up at Grens.

'Who are you? What's this about?'

He searched for the police badge hidden in the fabric of his jacket, then laid it on the wooden counter.

'My name is Ewert Grens, detective superintendent at the City Police in Stockholm.'

She opened the black leather case, compared the photograph to the man standing in front of her, ran a finger over the coat of arms with its golden crown.

'A detective superintendent?'

'Yes.'

'From Sweden?'

'Yes.'

'And you want to ask about our uniforms?'

'I want to know if that *is* your uniform.'

She looked at Grens, at the badge, at the paper, and at Grens again.

'We have two different shirts, one for summer and a long-sleeved one for winter. And yes – that's our winter shirt.'

Grens exhaled in relief and hoped she didn't notice.

His intuition had been correct. The journey was justified.

This was exactly the place to start searching.

'How many employees do you have?'

'I'm not sure if I'm allowed to answer that. Not even if you were *Danish* police.'

He heard clearly what she really meant.

Without pretending otherwise.

He really didn't want to involve any of his local colleagues yet.

'Well, in that case who exactly am I speaking to?'

She turned back towards a glass-walled conference room. Four people with stacks of paper and binders, engaged in what seemed to be a fairly hostile discussion.

'Looks like they're pretty busy. Despite the weekend.'

'We have more orders than we have time for.'

'Then maybe it would be easier for everyone if you help me? How many?'

Another glance back to check that nothing has changed – an interruption would hardly be appreciated.

'Twenty-two.'

'How many men?'

'One, two . . . five . . . eight . . . fourteen.'

'How many between twenty-five and forty?'

'What?'

'How many of the male employees are older than twenty-five but younger than forty?'

'No clue. Haven't worked here long enough to know.'

'I assume you have a personnel list. Maybe we can take a look at it?'

For a third time, the young woman turned back towards her superiors – now hostility in the meeting seemed to have broken out completely.

Collective anger behind her. A demanding police officer in front of her.

She didn't look particularly happy about any of it.

'Wait.'

She pressed on the keys as lightly as Billy in Stockholm just a few hours earlier. An extension of the body for a whole generation.

'Four of them. Twenty-six, twenty-nine, thirty and thirty-eight.'

Grens leaned over the desk and looked at the screen upside down.

'Excuse me? What are you up to?'

'I see that you have pictures of them.'

'Stop that!'

'I'd like to take a look at them.'

She no longer turned back for confirmation. Didn't even sigh. Just pushed the computer screen closer to Grens while she pointed.

'Him, him, him and . . . him. Those four are between twenty-five and forty. Satisfied?'

The detective superintendent smiled, nodded, and examined each one closely.

But soon stopped smiling. None of them were right.

Too thin, too fat, narrow shoulders, too short forearms.

'And that's . . . everyone?'

'Like I said. Are we done?'

He leaned heavily against the desk.

He'd been so sure.

'No.'

'No?'

'We're not done. Let's move on to *former* employees. Let's say . . . well, people who have worked here in the last five years – basically as long as a shirt lasts?'

She let him peek over her shoulder while she scrolled through the sizeable group who'd ended their employment at a company with very high turnover. They'd gone through fourteen different files, read their personal info and studied photographs, when Grens flinched.

That upper body.

'One moment.'

He held up the paper with the cut-out image next to the computer – the man on the screen was even photographed in the same shirt.

Shoulders, torso – identical.

Skin, arms – identical.

His way of standing – identical.

'This one?'

Even the ring. Little finger on the left hand.

'Yes?'

'Who is that?'

'That was before my time.'

'Can you view the file?'

After she opened the former employee's file with a few keystrokes, the portrait of him enlarged. Grens felt as if he were staring into someone who was staring straight into him.

Dark brown hair.

Winter pallor.

Slightly overweight, but muscular.

Pockmarked cheeks and a three-day beard and lips that remained full even though he unconsciously tightened them in front of the photographer.

'Carl Hansen.'

The receptionist had opened the next window on the personnel file.

'Salesman, employed here for . . . well, what would that be, eight months? Quit a year ago.'

They looked at each other again – Ewert Grens and the man who until now had stood faceless on a sheet of paper next to a naked child.

'Address?'

'When he worked here . . . Lærdal, it says. About twenty kilometres from here.'

'If you look him up in a regular search engine – does he still live there?'

She gave him a look as if to say *and why the hell would I do that*, but soon she opened a search window, as if realising that the quickest way to get rid of this Swedish police officer was to give him the information he was asking for.

'Yes. He does.'

'Can you write down the address on the back of this paper?'

Grens turned over the picture of part of the man who was probably named Carl Hansen and placed it next to the keyboard.

She wrote. A pencil that scratched loudly.

'Do you want to know who else lives there?'

'Can you see that?'

'Usually you can.'

She pointed to the screen, underlining the text with a fingertip.

'Two more at the same address with the same last name. A woman who is thirty-four years old named Dorte, and a child, a girl who is nine years old, named Katrine.'

'Good. Thank you.'

She seemed relieved, sensing that they were done. But he continued.

'And you understand that what we just talked about, this case, is not something you should spread around? Not outside this building or even to your colleagues?'

She looked at him, not exactly friendly, her back to the meeting in the glass cage.

'Listen – I promise – if they ask me I'll tell them exactly what happened. A nasty old Swedish man came here asking about something that has nothing to do with us. And I asked him to go away before I called the *Danish* police.'

When Ewert Grens stepped back into the pouring rain, he forgot to open his umbrella. Just like on the bench at the cemetery. But he didn't lie down on his back this time, didn't let drops stream freely down his face, even if that would have felt good. He didn't have time. He didn't know how and why, but a feeling of urgency was growing inside with each step between puddles of water on the main street. It wasn't just chance that sent that abominable picture his way. Someone knew any good investigator would end up here.

Time meant something.

That was probably why he started running.

THE TOWN OF Lærdal wasn't much bigger than Rødberg, and Grens's meeting with two policemen who travelled there from the capital of Nykøbing Falster – an older officer very close to retirement and a much younger one who had just finished his education – ended just as the Swedish detective had hoped. The nine photographs that Billy had found and transferred to the flash drive, together with the identification Grens had made at the furniture factory, were justification enough for a search warrant of the home.

A few hours later, they knew the family had been together for five years and during that time they'd lived in several different towns – every time a school or anyone else started asking questions or commenting on how Katrine didn't seem to be feeling very well, they packed up in a hurry and moved. They also knew that the family avoided socialising, that the girl was always dropped off and picked up at school by her parents and that the father – or stepfather as one of the neighbours corrected – worked as a salesman at a new company and was described as domineering. Just now, they'd received confirmation they were all at home.

The apartment sat above a small bakery on Lærdal's centre square in an older two-storey building with a grey and slightly shabby facade. In order to access the apartment, which according to drawings from the city planning office contained three rooms, a visitor would turn off from the main street, make their way to the courtyard, and take the stairs.

The older Nykøbing police officer went up first, Grens just a step behind.

After waiting for exactly five minutes as they'd agreed with the younger colleague, they looked at each other and nodded silently. They were about to knock on the door of the darkest darkness.

THE DOOR REMAINED closed.

For lack of a functioning doorbell, they knocked again, harder.

'Open up. It's the police.'

Ewert Grens counted to five. Ten. Fifteen.

But just as his patience ran out, just as he was about to do much more than knock on that simple wooden door, he was met by the metallic click of a lock being turned.

He recognised her immediately. The girl from the picture someone sent anonymously to an aid organisation. She was clothed. Hair up in a ponytail. She was even smaller than he'd imagined. But it *was* her.

'Who are you?'

Two old men wearing no uniform. The question was understandable from a nine-year-old's point of view.

'Police. And you – your name is Katrine?'

'I'm not supposed to say.'

'We're here because we want to talk to your mum and dad. And we know they're home.'

'Dad is doing something at his computer first.'

Just then a woman started screaming hysterically inside the apartment. Soon there were male voices and the sharp crack of a floor lamp knocking over.

'Mum, what's going –'

'Stay here.'

While the Nykøbing police officer prevented the desperate girl from running towards the fear and anger in her parents' voices, Grens rushed down the narrow hall. And as the Swedish superintendent stumbled among the armchairs and sofas in the living room, he was grateful he'd listened when his younger colleague suggested they split up, that one take the fire escape as soon as the other two knocked on the front door. The young policeman had broken in through the balcony door and, with gun raised, stopped the apartment's occupant from opening his computer and erasing what was on the hard drive.

Because they'd been right.

Grens felt just as sure now as when he saw the girl, as he exchanged glances with her stepfather.

The man he was looking at was also the man in the photograph who stood next to a naked child offering all nine pictures in a series, an entire rape, to people just like him.

WHEN EWERT GRENS sank down at the kitchen table above a bakery in a Danish town he'd never heard of before today, it was with a feeling of having accomplished nothing – even though he'd made it so much further than should have been possible. In less than twenty-four hours, he'd gone from alarm to arrest. From Werner handing him a photo at four o'clock in the morning to being alone at ten o'clock that same night after the forensic technicians had finished their work in a different country where the crime in that picture had been committed. And he knew exactly where that feeling came from.

A blue butterfly.

That was why he was here; it was in another little girl's footsteps he was travelling.

A trail that had now gone cold.

He looked around the kitchen where the family had eaten dinner just a couple of hours ago. Their last meal. Because while the mother and stepfather were being arrested and transported in handcuffs to Copenhagen for interrogation, two female social workers had taken the nine-year-old girl into their custody and were headed to one of the municipality's institutions.

Grens ambled slowly around the apartment.

To the hall where the suitcases had stood. Two large and a small one intended for the daughter. Packed. According to an email, which was printed out and lay in the same envelope as three train tickets, they would have travelled to Brussels the next morning for a private filming commissioned by a man who, according to the Belgian police, was previously convicted of both child rape and the sale of large volumes of child pornography. The commission would include full intercourse, the first time outside the family, which the daughter was now ready for according to the email exchange.

By sending that picture, someone had managed to prevent this trip.

Time really *had* mattered.

He continued on into the parents' bedroom. In the wardrobe hung several more shirts with that same company logo. In a cupboard was a tripod with camera equipment and in an antique chest of drawers they'd found dildos, ropes, sex toys. Empty boxes stamped in the western and central United States, Switzerland, Belgium, Germany, England had been shoved under the bed. It was while the older Nykøbing police officer was pulling these out that he said quietly *I don't know how it all connects, or where it leads, but this is way bigger than we thought.*

From the parents' bedroom, Ewert Grens continued on into the daughter's room. It looked much like any nine-year-old girl's room. He sat down on her bright yellow desk chair and scanned the walls covered with posters of pop stars whose names he didn't know and whose music he wouldn't recognise. Toys and puzzles and games were stuffed in a wooden box with no lid; on a bookshelf dolls stood in a row watching him.

She'd lived in this room. This was what normal felt like for her.

Just as normal as the abuse, the performances that were photographed or recorded at the request of others. Grens had encountered this in all kinds of investigations into relationships characterised by power imbalance and violence, regardless of whether the victim was a woman, a man, a son, a daughter. Manipulate. Normalise. Until the abnormal is your normal, your daily life.

A car drove down the narrow street outside, one of the few in the last half-hour. The town of Lærdal went to bed early.

He stood up from the child-sized chair, not very comfortable, and headed into the third room. The living room was where the computer had been, which his young colleague had saved by climbing up the fire escape.

A computer that was now being moved to a locked room at the local police station.

That was what he'd come here for.

And now they were waiting for a special investigator from Copenhagen to deal with it.

Every finger needed to land right.

No one would be allowed to touch anything until it was secured. No one would attempt logging in and risk destroying the evidence that would make a trial possible.

Only after that hard drive had been cloned, once there was a copy, would they visit a world none of them knew.

THEY HAD A very short time to gather sufficient evidence for an arrest. If not, the mother and stepfather would be released. And by the time a detective superintendent and a computer expert from the National Investigation Centre arrived from the Danish capital even less time remained.

That's probably why Ewert Grens didn't expect them to spend some of that precious time questioning his presence.

'And who are you?'

The woman, whom he guessed was in her forties, had sat down to start work on cloning the hard drive, and Grens was on the chair just behind her. As she turned round and stared at him as if seeing more through than at, he wished he'd prepared better.

'Ewert Grens. Detective superintendent at the City Police in Stockholm.'

'If we're going to cooperate across national borders, I'll need confirmation of your assignment.'

'I was the one who brought in the tip-off to begin with.'

'Written confirmation. From your boss, for example.'

'You'll get it tomorrow.'

'Then I'll have to ask you to leave the room.'

Ewert Grens had never had a problem with conflict. He sought it out, needed it, thrived on it. But this was the wrong moment. Now all he wanted was to avoid attention.

'Can we talk? In private?'

She looked at him, seemed to be considering her options. Then a quick glance at her Copenhagen colleague and the two Nykøbing police officers in the large investigation room to see if they were out of earshot.

'Sure. But make it quick.'

The small kitchenette was nearby, and Grens closed the door behind them.

'I *have* no assignment. Because neither my boss nor the family whose daughter is missing want to give it to me, and the mother of another girl, who actually started all this, no longer wishes to talk to me. If I'm being perfectly honest, they forced me out and put me on paid leave.'

He pulled out the simple plastic chair.

'But I just know, with forty-two years of experience as a police officer, that I'm in the right place. If it turns out, despite my gut, that this is a dead end, I'll leave you in peace and go to Helsingør to get some of that great ham you can only buy there and head home. If, on the other hand, there is a lead, I promise to get you all the papers you need once no one can deny them to me any more. Listen to what I have to say, and then decide if you can let me fly under the radar for a few days.'

She didn't say anything. But nodded briefly. Ten minutes later when he was finished telling her about a grave that was now two small graves, about coffins with nobody inside, she nodded again.

'Until Monday morning.'

'Thank you.'

'My name is Birte, by the way.'

He met her outstretched hand.

'Ewert.'

'Well then – welcome, Ewert. To the most fucked up of worlds.'

'The darknet. Encrypted networks that lie beneath the normal web.'

She looked at him in surprise.

'You know about that?'

'Encrypted networks beneath the regular web. Part of the Internet that's completely outside of official search engines. Websites with hidden IP addresses. You can't just stumble across them by googling around.'

'As a woman in this line of work I know all about being judged pre-emptively – but I'll admit my first impression was wrong this time, prejudiced. You really do *know* this stuff.'

'At least since this morning.'

He smiled. Just like her.

She sat down in front of the computer, while he returned to the chair behind her.

'They did a good job, our friends from Nykøbing Falster. It's not everyone who . . . it's always who's *first on site* that's most important, making sure the computer is secured so we can access the content in a way that the defence lawyers won't disqualify.'

She turned round, like before. In order to question his presence, like before.

But for another reason.

'Passwords and key codes – this may take a while. Most are encrypted automatically and this is highly encrypted. I'm damn good at what I do, but I'm still asking – are you sure you want to sit there and watch me go through all of this?'

'Yep.'

'It's nearly midnight. Borrow a room, I'll wake you once I'm in.'

'This is why I came. I'll stay right here. And it's been a long time since I slept through the night. Thirty years, approximately.'

The night in Lærdal was darker than in Stockholm.

Staring out the window of the small police station felt a little like drowning, or at least that's how he imagined sinking to the bottom of the sea.

But he liked sitting here watching the Danish computer expert perform her single-minded search, it soothed him. Not the reasons for her search, which remained twisted, but her professionalism. There was something comforting about people knowing how to do things he couldn't. Felt good relying on someone. Being dependent. He alternated between staring in concentration over her shoulder at the resistance of a locked computer, and listening to the recordings of the initial interrogations with the family that had just been made available as files on his phone.

The first interrogation – which was more in the form of a conversation – was short because of the late hour, but Birte's Copenhagen colleague wanted to prepare the girl mentally for the recorded interview that had to be held as early as tomorrow so as not to lose fresh impressions. According to the detective inspector, memory had a way of distorting reality, diminishing or enlarging it on the basis of a change in the emotional state. Grens adjusted his headphones so as not to disturb the ongoing computer work an arm's length away, but the nine-year-old girl didn't say much. Either she was in shock and scared, or just didn't like to talk. A couple of times she returned to whispering that it was a 'secret'. Her parents said so. But the little she said was enough. He understood what they were dealing with when she confirmed that each time included being naked and touching each other, that both her stepfather and mother held the camera, and that the ropes rubbed too hard against her skin one time when she was tied to a chair.

'Everything OK?'

Birte looked at him worriedly.

'Is it, Grens? OK?'

'Sure. Just listening to some of what I hope you find evidence to support.'

'Because you made a sound.'

'What?'

'As if you were in pain.'

'I didn't say anything.'

'You're sitting a metre behind me. The sound hit the back of my neck – you were in pain.'

Ewert Grens took off his headphones. He hadn't been aware that he'd been so affected. That he was living what a nine-year-old girl had lived.

He nodded at the computer screen.

'How's it going for you?'

'I'm closing in.'

While Birte searched for a way into the encrypted hard drive, Grens pushed forward into the first interrogation with the stepfather, which was also now available on his phone – the two Danish investigators had divided the work and seemed equally effective. While the computer expert mapped the digital world, the detective was responsible for the conversations. According to the voice that formally read the time and place on the recording, this took place in a visiting room at Vestre Prison in Copenhagen, and it reminded Grens of other interrogations with paedophiles he'd conducted or listened to over the years. But that's not what the stepfather was – a paedophile. Not in his own mind. And in order to prove it, in response to the introductory questions, he described real paedophiles in detail. They were slime. Total sickos. Not normal guys, like him.

> Interrogator (IR): You're exploiting a minor. Abusing her.
> Carl Hansen (CH): I'd never do that.
> (IR): You sell pictures. And you yourself participate in them.
> (CH): Do you see my face anywhere? If I did shit like that, I wouldn't leave a trace.
> (IR): You perform very violent sexual acts. With a child. Your own stepdaughter.
> (CH): Not me. But if you just knew how sick these fuckers are. I got one question. From one of these guys in Portugal. He wanted . . . he wanted a film with a girl lying on a mattress and . . . ah, I'm not saying another goddamn word. But I didn't do it, of course.

'Grens?'

Birte waved him forward eagerly, not even taking the time to turn round.

'I think . . . I got in.'

You could feel it in that small room. How everything changed. An alertness present only at night. Their senses sharpened. Scents becoming more intense, the light brighter, the keyboard's clicking louder.

'I've opened the hard drive – two folders with pictures.'

She pointed to square symbols on the screen.

Bad girl 1 (16 pics) Bad girl 2 (27 pics)

'There's a large encrypted file that contains significantly more – and it will take time to open that one. So far we only have these two. For some reason he decided not to encrypt them.'

'Bad girl? Seriously?'

'Seriously, Grens.'

As Birte clicked on the folders, allowing them to fill half of the screen, it became obvious how one or both parents had manipulated what followed as if it were a fun game.

As each picture got rougher.

In the folder 'Bad girl 1', the girl in the first picture pretended to be happy with her nice gifts – new clothes. In the next picture, the game developed into walking out onto a balcony and leaning out, the perspective angled from below, so that the viewer caught a peek under her skirt. On to the next where she was undressed. Then the next where she lay down with her stepfather.

The abuse escalated step by step until sixteen images had played out.

Step by step, the expression on the girl's face also changed.

What at first might be interpreted as delight at play-acting, being in a film, soon turned to humiliation.

'There are twelve more pictures in that series. And they get rougher. Much, much rougher.'

Birte watched the detective from Sweden who just a few hours earlier had involuntarily shown how he empathised with this vulnerable girl's experience.

'But this is probably enough for you, Grens. You might not need to watch to the end.'

Ewert Grens met her gaze gratefully.

'No. Your investigators will have to do that. I get the idea.'

'Not "your investigators". Me, Grens. That's my job. I'll sit here all night until every document is open. We have enough to keep both detained. Possession is a crime. The distribution these images advertise is a crime. But we also have to prove that the stepfather and mother were the ones who committed these violent acts. So far we've only seen parts of bodies, but not the parents' faces. Somewhere on here there has to be a picture that shows more. I'm going to find it. And when I've made sure the perpetrators are properly locked up and can't upset the investigation – then you and I can focus on the people committing the greater crime.'

She tapped her fingers on the monitor.

As if they were inside it.

'The people he delivers this to.'

Which in a way they were.

'A billion-dollar industry.'

WHEN BIRTE WOKE Grens at quarter past seven, he'd been sleeping hunched over in the chair behind her, close enough to feel his regular breathing, and the quiet darkness outside the police station had just started turning to a whispering November grey. As she gently shook his shoulder, she considered again how much to show him of what she'd found. What was absolutely necessary to see for a man who clearly lacked the ability to allow those criminal acts to remain just work, without any personal feelings involved.

'I've gone through every image and film. And the stepfather has unknowingly simplified things for us – each one is timestamped. We know exactly when each crime was committed. And based on those times, it will be much easier to build a case for the prosecution.'

She pointed to four folders that formed a line at the bottom of the screen.

'A series of eleven photos shows a male forcing Katrine to perform oral sex. The next fourteen photos show the same man abusing her by alternately pouring hot and cold water over her thin body. A short film displays a woman violating with her hands. In this folder, explicit close-ups of a male who –'

Rage.

Sudden, unexpected rage as Birte's eyes narrowed and seemed to change colour and her voice dropped.

'She doesn't cry even in the worst pictures. Sexual intercourse – and a nine-year-old girl doesn't even cry.'

Because it was as if she finally heard what she herself was saying. Felt it.

'But she will when she gets older. Cry. When she understands.'

She looked at him then.

For a long time.

'I'm sorry.'

'You don't need to be sorry. This hell . . .'

'I've investigated all kinds of violence in every part of the country. When I was first starting out this used to happen, before I learned to keep a distance between my own life and others'. Maybe it's you, Grens? I mean, I usually make sure to work alone, and when I saw your face, heard your reaction . . . The reality. That's probably what it was.'

Her voice was steadier now, her rage dissolving into sorrow.

'These people . . . No. I can't call them that. They're not people. Not to me. These *monsters* groom, train, influence. Every chat I find, Grens, between these paedophiles in closed rings, that's what they talk about. *Have you tried this or that? No, I haven't got there yet. OK – but when, do you think? I'd guess a month, then she'll be ready.* The constant psychological calculation, persuasion and revision, deliberately pushing sexual boundaries just a little bit at a time.'

Ewert Grens wasn't particularly good at physical contact. Always worried that it would be taken in the wrong way, too much or too little or too long or too fast or . . . but right now he wished he knew if it would be appropriate to put a hand on her shoulder or if her forearm would be better. Or maybe even a gentle hug. She seemed to need it.

'Just like during the stepfather's first interrogation. When he tries to explain how normal he is. That, Grens, is the other big topic in these chat logs. Give me confirmation. I'm not alone in my twisted world. If others are doing it too, then I can't really be a freak.'

Then he did.

A hug.

And she didn't pull back or try to free herself – she seemed comfortable with some human contact. Even though he'd just realised what drove her. Why she forced herself to explore and chart such gruesome worlds, such lost *monsters*. And when they looked at each other without saying a word, it was clear she knew that he knew that the unpunished abuse of a little girl long ago meant many years later that others who abused children would be punished, would be put behind locked bars and high walls.

'We'll soon have enough for the parents' trials – but now, Grens, we're going to take down the others.'

The Danish computer expert clicked on a folder isolated in the left corner of the screen, opened it.

'I wasn't going to show you more pictures. But in the ones I've collected here, the girl is fully dressed.'

Fifteen different photographs. Each one with Katrine in the centre – holding a sign. Each with a name and a greeting. *Hi, Paul. Thanks, Mike. Vielen Dank, Dieter.* Written in her handwriting with felt-tip pens of various colours.

'She has to communicate with the other men in the ring. They're supposed to feel connected. In other pictures, like this – do you see, Grens? – she's supposed to hold up a gift she's thanking them for. The dress someone wants to see her in. A camera for a new set of photos, and there, a dog leash, a dildo, the presents for specific images. She's even thanking them for that.'

Birte's rage was no longer uncontained, didn't reveal any of the feelings she'd decided to let go of years earlier.

Control it – don't be controlled by it.

'But we will track them down, find them. One by one.'

A face that was calm.

'We'll secure evidence they can never wriggle out of, no matter how anonymous "Paul" and "Mike" and "Dieter" think they are.'

And a voice that was full of power.

'We'll blow up the whole paedophile ring.'

LATE AFTERNOON IN a small Danish town. A little autumn humidity, a little autumn wind, a lot of silence. Ewert Grens wandered through deserted streets – the rain had stopped, but that didn't seem to matter, people were still staying inside, at home.

His steps were surprisingly light and his thoughts strangely clear despite only a couple of hours of sleep. Sharp. Strong. Far from dizziness and confusion. He'd told Wilson he needed work to stay healthy. But he also recognised something else. Hope. That's what he was walking around with. Sent to him by two little girls he'd never met but was trying to find his way to.

When he turned off the main street and into the courtyard of an old, shabby building with a small bakery downstairs and an apartment above, it was with that sense of hope. Every time Birte managed to restore chat logs or find more pictures, Grens had gone here for a new search and returned with more evidence. This time he was looking for two dolls and a dress with glittering gold sequins.

It felt as if the three-room apartment became more abandoned with every visit.

The people who used to sleep here, eat here were never coming back.

He found the sequinned dress immediately. It was hanging among the girl's other dresses in one of the hallway closets and hadn't drawn any attention to itself until it was mentioned in a chat between the stepfather – who they now knew went by Lassie in that kind of conversation – and a suspected member of the paedophile ring who went by the handle *Lollipop* and had an IP address in Switzerland. Suddenly the value of the glittering garment rose dramatically. If it truly existed, and if it had been sent *from* the customer who wanted it to be worn during the abuse *to* the perpetrator who was arranging the image, then they'd have another connection that could become evidence. Evidence that Grens, wearing a pair of thin plastic gloves, was now lifting from the closet and dropping into a sealed plastic bag.

He knew exactly where the dolls were.

When he'd sat down on the bright yellow desk chair in the girl's room, he'd imagined them all watching him.

But he had no idea that one of them was just about to give him the strength to make it through every long night of this investigation.

The two dolls, who according to toy shop ads were named Aimee and Victoria, were mentioned in a chat by another of the ring's members who ordered a video with 'your daughter playing naked with naked dolls'. And become truly interesting after they appeared in a set of deleted photographs that Birte had managed to recreate. Because of those pictures, Grens again entered the girl's only free place – the abuse, also intercourse in various forms, had, based on what he'd seen, always taken place elsewhere in the apartment.

He held up the photo next to thirty-seven faces and motionless eyes that were lined up on the bookshelf. They all looked the same. At least to a Swedish detective on the wrong side of sixty who'd never stepped foot in a toy shop.

After comparing features in two rounds, he was pretty sure he had found Victoria who had long chestnut-brown hair, and that the doll on the far right with blonde hair and rosy cheeks was the one the manufacturer called Aimee. And it was as he was about to drop them both next to the sequinned dress in the evidence bag, that he saw what would keep him going.

At the ear of a plastic face. Under the curls.

The blue butterfly.

Ewert Grens carefully loosened the thin piece of metal. He had never been closer to the two girls who had disappeared from Stockholm. He held it in the palm of his hand, wrapped his fingers around it, opened them again, could see that it was indeed identical to the hair clip that held the unruly hair of a four-year-old in place in a supermarket and which had been made in a single copy. He hadn't imagined it, didn't just see what he wanted to see. Nor was it a coincidence because he didn't believe in coincidences. A blue butterfly had been worn by Swedish Linnea the day she disappeared, a blue butterfly had been worn by Danish Katrine in a picture posted online that brought him here, a blue butterfly was now sitting on a doll that a customer sent for use as a prop for sexual assault.

The detective superintendent had never been particularly agile, his lameness had increased over the years inside Kronoberg's corridors, but now he floated back to Birte and the cramped computer room in Lærdal's police station, he passed an empty center with the evidence bag in his hand without worrying about the humidity penetrating through his skin to his bones – at this time of year it was seldom truly cold in Denmark, but still you're freezing.

'Did it go well, Grens?'

She was still sitting in front of the big screen. With that calm determination he liked so much, so different from her short outbursts of anger.

'Everything's been bagged. Both the dress and the dolls.'

He told her everything. Except the bit about a blue butterfly, he'd keep that to himself for a little longer.

'And how's it going for you – here?'

'I think it's time to show you more. Sit down.'

He did as she asked, sank down onto the uncomfortable chair behind her right shoulder. And even though they were about to dive deeper into the most broken of broken worlds, her calm felt contagious, so he almost relaxed, something he rarely did.

'I've restored the data from a couple of hundred chats and found a total of ten members who order, exploit and abuse children in a closed ring.'

She clicked on one of them and a long list of posts rolled down.

'Inside these different programs, there are some configuration files that –'

'In Swedish, Birte. Or at least Danish. I don't have a clue what you're talking about.'

'. . . So, I go into the settings in the program they used to transfer files from one computer to the next, and therefore we'll be able – *follow along now, Grens* – to prove that Carl Hansen, who calls himself Lassie, is in contact with this man – *look here, Grens* – who calls himself Wasp and has an IP address somewhere in the USA. And with this man who calls himself Lenny, also from the USA, and with someone called Gregorius who's in Belgium, and a Swiss man and . . .'

She pointed at the screen. At the absurd dialogues between men.

03-11-2019 01:10:57 Message from 133438297: *OK. Sounds nice. How about a little spanking?*

'That was just sent the day before yesterday. From a member I'm becoming increasingly confident is their leader. There's always someone with the highest status in a ring, who decides the conditions, manipulates the others to go past the next limit.'

03-11-2019 01:11:09 Message from 238437691: *Sure. That too.*

03-11-2019 01:11:38 Message from 133438297: *I want sound. Hear her yell. When you beat. And abuse.*

'Grens, we've stumbled on a gold mine. I'm compiling profiles for each handle, and they're growing gradually. They've been chatting for several months now. They have IP numbers and personal information that can be puzzled together into their real names, where they live, what their children's names are. I've made a small sketch here . . .'

Redcat, ? O	O Master, Schweiz
Meyer, Tyskland O	O Uncle J, Belgien
Wasp/Geronimo, USA O	O Gregorius, Belgien
Lenny, USA O	O Lollipop, Schweiz
Onyx, USA O	O Lassie (Carl Hansen)

'. . . and everyone knows each other in this ring. Quite well. A closed circuit. A true paedophile ring. Trading images, fantasies, what they've done to their own children and what they think others should do to theirs.'

Then she pointed at the screen, drew a circle around the name at the bottom right, leaving a temporary trace of moisture that soon evaporated.

'But even a closed paedophile ring is no stronger than its weakest link. Lassie, alias Carl Hansen. The FTP program I showed you, where the images are transferred, it led to the files he deleted – and they are recoverable! All his transmissions were logged there. Timestamped. Connected to the IP addresses. What he sent. And because we can only link an IP address to the right person if we have the exact time . . . Do you follow me? Soon I'll contact, informally and without explaining the context, colleagues I trust in the countries concerned, people who occasionally and just as informally need my help. They in turn can contact the network providers and find out which individuals connect to certain IP addresses at certain times, and then, Grens, then we've got them! Their identities! By God we've got 'em!'

She looked so happy. He liked that.

'But it wasn't Hansen who tipped off the aid organisation. I'm sure of it. His language in these chats, his reaction when you knocked on his door and seized his computer – it's his ignorance that has us sitting here. So someone else must have chosen to break the code of silence. Leaked the picture, aware he could be identified via the reflection of the logo on the back of his shirt. Someone was pissed off enough to risk everyone's anonymity.'

'One of the others in the closed circle?'

'Not necessarily.'

Birte clicked on the sketch.

Redcat, ? O	O Master, Schweiz
Meyer, Tyskland O	O Uncle J, Belgien
Wasp/Geronimo, USA O	O Gregorius, Belgien
Lenny, USA O	O Lollipop, Schweiz
Onyx, USA O	O Lassie (Carl Hansen)

Easy, GB

Julia, USA

John Wayne, GB

Ingrid, USA

Sherlock, GB

Queen Mary, USA

Marie Antoinette, NL

Ramses, Belgium

Ruud, NL

Mariette, USA

Friend, Italy

'Hansen doesn't just participate in the closed ring. He also has eleven external contacts that he trades pictures with on the side. A small circle of people who communicate directly with him. They don't know each other, only Hansen, just send pictures to and from Hansen – paedophiles who exploit children, but not part of the closed ring. It could very well have been one of them who burnt him.'

'And we also have profiles on them?'

'Soon. Working on it. Like I said – his computer is a gold mine.'

She smiled. Her serious face brightening for a moment during a workday that didn't allow for many smiles. Hope. What he'd been walking around with since this morning – that was surely what they shared.

'So how long do you think you'll need . . .'

Grens nodded at the screen.

'. . . before we move on to the next step?'

'Difficult to say.'

'Hours? Days? Weeks?'

'Yes.'

'Yes?'

'For the eleven who aren't in the ring, just trading rough pictures and videos with Hansen, and for eight of the ten who are part of the closed circle and order child abuse from each other, I'd say at most a couple of days. By then I'll be able to piece together enough for us to put out an alert and to go to our international colleagues.'

'But?'

'But when it comes to the last two, I don't know at all. Everyone connects via Tor. The Onion Router. And it's basically impossible to find the IP address at the other end of a conversation. Or rather: they all *almost always* connect via Tor. Because I've found moments for each – except for two – where they are careless. Upload files using standard FTP. This is not entirely uncommon, they become impatient, craving their new images, and communication over Tor can sometimes be painfully slow if you're eager.'

'In Swedish, Birte. Or at least Danish.'

'A system where the IP address bounces between a lot of different servers so that it becomes impossible to find the origin.'

'Then we'll wait on those two until later. And take the rest.'

'That's exactly what we won't do.'

She was no longer smiling. And her calm – he saw she was struggling with it.

'In a worst-case scenario, I can live with not getting one of them. For example, this guy, who calls himself Redcat and who I placed at the top left of the sketch. You see, Grens? The one who has a question mark next to his name because I'm not even sure where he's from. If we don't succeed in identifying and seizing that monster, I can live with it. *But I can't stand it if we don't get that fucker!* At the bottom left of the ring. Onyx. The leader. He's the worst of them all, he controls them. If you'd . . . Grens, when I read what he writes to his friends, who he calls his friends, they're all just looking for more pictures, but when he . . . he . . .'

Ewert Grens had misinterpreted her – it wasn't the calm she struggled with, it was rage.

'I'll wait. You don't need to rush it.'

'When he writes how his own daughter will soon turn thirteen and be too old for sex, that he'll . . . adopt a new child then, Grens . . . he's utterly depraved! And I've seen it before – if we grab the rest but not the leader, and if we don't do it at the same time, he'll just replace them with new friends. Do you understand? He'll start a new ring. New children will be raped.'

EWERT GRENS LENGTHENED his stride, pushing into it. It had been a long time since he'd walked with someone by his side without any goal besides movement. That was probably why it felt so good. Just a break to gather their strength and no talking. With Birte next to him, they made a wide circle around the small town of Lærdal. It was unclear whether the wetness on his head was heat from within or a light fog from without. He even dared to treat her to a hot dog and lemonade when they passed the sole open kiosk, and only after they'd finished chewing and wiped the mustard off their chins did they break their silence as if in unspoken agreement.

'I'm thinking of the last thing we read.'

'Me too.'

A chat between Danish Lassie and American Lenny about some particularly rough pictures that Carl Hansen had got from one of his external contacts, Friend from Italy. As Lenny begins to understand what they depict, he tries to trade for them, too. In return, he offers films of a total of forty minors, whom he's molested in his medical practice.

'And those Italian pictures, Grens, I saw in another chat when you were filling the evidence bag, Hansen was actually going to receive them in person. It appears that they'd planned to meet for a whole day, spend time with each other's daughters and violate them. Like a hobby. Two dads just hanging out. A meeting which was cancelled and the pictures were sent in the traditional way. However, the Americans, Lenny and Onyx and the man who sometimes calls himself Geronimo, have met on at least four occasions in California. If you read their conversations, they traded children with each other, exploited them and filmed it. These kinds of meetings have also taken place between the German and the

Brit, and the Swiss men. When people talk about crushing paedophile rings with several thousand members, about websites that anyone can access, then we're talking about a billion – no, a *multi*-billion dollar industry. People buying child pornography with their credit cards. But these aren't paedophile rings – in a paedophile ring, nothing is shared openly without knowing each other. Like this, meeting in real life to violate children.'

It was getting dark, and they were walking down artificially lit streets. As they passed the bakery with the family's apartment on the second floor, they both stopped and stared up at the lowered blinds.

'No matter what we do, Grens, it will never be right.'

She scanned the row of lifeless windows.

'We rap on a door where a father and a mother and a child live. And when, as police officers, we do what we're supposed to do, remove the child from physical and mental abuse and throw her mother and father in jail, we are destroying a family. We take the child from the only thing she knows, *the only people* she knows, the people who've raised her, from what is normal to her and therefore her security, no matter how destructive and abnormal it might be. So in the short term – she's going to feel distraught, no matter what.'

They looked at each other. But really only a glance.

'Grens – I have to find a way to get to him. *Stop him.* The leader. And I have to do it even though the bastard connects through a system where the IP address bounces back and forth and is impossible to track. Despite the fact that he seems to live somewhere on the West Coast of the US, and I'm just in a little Danish backwater. *He will never build a ring again.*'

They left the bakery and those lowered blinds. Still just as deserted. An elderly man was parking his whining car nearby and in the distance beautiful music leaked from an open door, but that was it.

'I *may* have a way.'

They slowed now, as if they weren't quite ready to go back to the police station yet.

'A way, Grens?'

'Like you said – a way to get to him.'

So they stopped at the same time, again.

Between two street lights, probably hard for anyone to see them.

In the distance, they could make out the other Copenhagen investigator and the two Nykøbing police officers in the large, well-lit windows.

'You keep doing what you're doing, Birte, mapping their identities in Hansen's computer, until we can contact the authorities around the world in a coordinated action – strike at the same time, everywhere. Nobody should get any warning, any chance to escape or destroy evidence. In the meantime, I'm heading back to Stockholm, and I'll contact the person we need. An infiltrator. An expert on accessing secret organisations. With his help, we can get close to this nameless leader – and I know exactly how.'

PART
3

That kind of fake laughter
seldom sounds good.

JUST AFTER MIDNIGHT. It felt like a homecoming now. The silence more silent, the desolation more desolate. The solitude more solitary.

Ewert Grens would have preferred to stay in a small Danish police station, sitting behind a computer expert named Birte, but instead he'd drunk lukewarm coffee in Kastrup then listened to Top 40 radio in a taxi from Arlanda. Once he reached his apartment on Svea Road, he didn't even take off his coat. The apartment was a sinkhole that pulled him straight into vast emptiness. Another taxi, this time to Kungsholmen and an office at Kronoberg and a corduroy sofa that he was just going to sit down on for a little bit, just to rest his feet.

And that was where he woke up now. Still had his coat and shoes on, and a gentle sun was caressing his face through the window. A quarter past seven. After all these incoherent nights, finally he'd slept coherently.

He snuck into the lift and took an icy shower at the police station's swimming pool, managed to steal down to his car in the underground garage, just in time too, since the sun was starting its slow climb up the sky. There wasn't much traffic even though it was a Monday morning, and within a few minutes he'd passed by the Globe Arena and was turning onto the residential streets of the Enskede neighbourhood, which criss-crossed each other as if laid out in a game of spillikins. The Hoffmann family had finally moved back here after rebuilding a house that had been blown up. He'd missed them more than he realised – their voices, which had filled the rooms of his apartment for months. After they'd lost their home, he'd surprised himself by inviting them to move in with him. He, who'd had exactly three guests in his kitchen since Anni left permanently for a nursing home over thirty years ago, and none who had slept over. He'd never imagined it would feel so satisfying to have new breath so near. The energy. The unpredictability. The mess. Wills colliding. Irritation. Relieved laughter. Checkered pancakes. The occasional Rasmus-hug. Humanity, basically.

He rolled slowly by red picket fences and mailboxes with lids left slightly ajar after a newspaper was picked up. The one he stopped in front of was different from the others – labelled with a child's large scraggly handwriting, by a very young Hugo who'd just learned to spell both family names.

KOSLOW HOFFMANN

The mailbox had been the only thing left intact after the night of the bombing. The house and the garden, all of it was blown away. Footage from a distant war on television, that's what it looked like, a civilian target hit by mistake. But it happened in a perfect Swedish suburb, and it had been a warning from the arms mafia to former infiltrator Piet Hoffmann, the toughest threat there was, made towards family members. That time they'd helped each other, Hoffmann and Grens, infiltrated for each other in what was supposed to be their very last collaboration.

Until now.

The detective sat in his car for a moment, listening to the morning radio without hearing it. He hadn't been here since they'd moved back into the house. With each new invitation his excuses – which were never very good to begin with – got worse. It was as if he'd become aware of the difference. How it sounded when voices fell silent. And how it was easier to ignore it if he didn't go there, since there was no way to bring them to his home again.

They saw him through the kitchen window as soon as he opened the gate. Rasmus's steps pounded down the hall, and he opened the front door before Grens could even press the doorbell.

'Ewert!'

His small arms couldn't really reach up and around the large guest so his hug was somewhat mediocre, but still it remained the most sincere and sweet human contact Grens had experienced in the latter half of his life.

'Hi, Rasmus, look –'

'Come in.'

'– how big you –'

'We're eating breakfast – you can join us, Ewert!'

'– got.'

Rasmus pulled him by the arm, and Grens just had time to kick off his shoes before they headed into the kitchen.

'Morning, everyone.'

They sat just as they had around his kitchen table. Piet and Hugo on one long side, Zofia and Rasmus on the other, and Luiza in her high chair on the short side. Grens had always sat opposite her, in the only vacant spot, and that was where he headed now.

'Coffee, Ewert?'

Rasmus had fetched an almost full coffee pot that was trembling alarmingly in his hand. He poured and managed to hit his mark for the most part.

'And no milk. Like Dad drinks it. Right, Ewert?'

'Right, Rasmus.'

It took so little. A warm hug, a sincere smile, coffee served by someone who was glad to see him. Ewert Grens felt such happiness, such ease for a moment.

'Why are you here?'

Hugo carried a heavier heart than his little brother. Worried more. Rasmus had followed his mother and father back and forth between countries and continents and safe houses without a care, Hugo had a harder time adapting to life on the run as the son of Piet Hoffmann, infiltrator of criminal organisations. It took longer for him to build a sense of security and earn his trust. Believe in people. Therefore, he always asked the uncomfortable questions and always sniffed out the danger hidden in other people's agendas.

'Ewert, I'm happy you're here, you know that, right? But you haven't visited us in a very long time, and here you are in the middle of breakfast on a school day.'

Hugo was not someone you lied to. Not if you wanted to stay close friends. And Ewert Grens did want that.

'Feels good to be sitting here. Eating a sandwich, looking at your little sister, who's learned so much. I should have come sooner and more often – and I will change that. That should be reason enough. But you're right, Hugo. I have another reason, too. Something I have to talk to your dad about after you leave.'

Quick glances exchanged by Hugo and Zofia. The kind that could turn to anger. Or maybe it was fear – the same emotion in two expressions.

'About what?'

Fear. That became clear when Hugo spoke.

'What are you going to talk about?'

'Sorry, Hugo. But what I have to say is for your dad's ears only.'

'I knew it! Something dangerous. And it's going to reach us here, even in our *new* house. Always, always when it comes to Dad.'

'It won't reach you. Not this time. It has nothing to do with you or Rasmus or Luiza or your mum. I promise.'

'Mmm. You and Dad always say that. But it ends up the same way.'

So far Piet hadn't said a word. Just watched the meeting between two boys who'd lived without a normal social life for so long, with only each other, and an old detective superintendent who'd chosen solitude as his companion. It was sweet how they'd got close to each other over the last few years. But now Piet put his hand on Hugo's shoulder and turned his gaze to his elder son, and then to their unexpected guest.

'Hugo – my big guy – it *is* true. It's not coming here again. Because Uncle Ewert and I are never going to work together again. *He's* promised *me*.'

Hoffmann now stared only at the detective. They had. Promised each other. Piet Hoffmann had promised to abandon his old life and never commit a crime again, and Ewert Grens had promised that the police would never demand their most skilled infiltrator risk his life by exposing organised crime.

He stared until the detective chose to look down.

Yes. Now he knew. That was the reason for Grens's visit.

Breaking that promise.

'Hugo, Rasmus – time to hurry up. Finish those sandwiches, drink up your juice. You have to leave for school in . . .'

The ticking clock hung on the wall above the worktop.

'. . . four minutes. And you still have teeth to brush, and Rasmus, you need to pack up your homework.'

As Grens realised in the middle of all this chaos – which was clearly a well-rehearsed part of family life here – that Zofia was also searching for her coat and bag to leave, he too hurried into the narrow hall.

'Zofia – you're heading out at the same time?'

'To the same school. But while Hugo and Rasmus spend their breaks out in the schoolyard, I stay warm in the staff room.'

'French, if I remember correctly.'

'And Spanish. And Polish, when needed.'

'I would have liked you to hear what I have to say to Piet. Because I promised you a "last time" too. But it will, of course, be in Swedish, my best language.'

He smiled. She did not.

'I'm sorry. Our first classes begin at the same time. And frankly, Ewert, I don't really feel like listening. You said it yourself. You promised "the last time". I'd assumed you meant it. But feel free to finish your coffee.'

If Hugo's eyes had been full of fear, Zofia's held the anger. And she had every right to it. Because she *was* right. His reason for knocking on their door was what made his visit unwelcome.

In the kitchen, Luiza was still sitting in her chair, and Piet in his. Grens also sank down at the same place as before.

'Are you in a hurry, Piet?'

'I've got about half an hour. Luiza is heading to preschool, then I'm installing some security doors and surveillance cameras for a customer in Solna.'

Grens waited while Hoffmann wiped yogurt and orange juice off Luiza's cheeks and helped her down from her high chair. Such mundane tasks and Grens realised he'd never performed either of them.

'I guess you know why I'm here.'

'Zofia knew. Hugo knew.'

'I wouldn't come here if this wasn't a matter of life and death. A person you could save.'

'You heard what Zofia said. And I have no real desire to listen either.'

'Still, I want you to.'

'No, Ewert. I want you to listen to *me*. After we clear this table.'

An everyday task Grens was more accustomed to. During those six months the house was being rebuilt, he'd cleared his table after breakfasts that gave his large kitchen in his large apartment some meaning and substance. While Hoffmann put food back into the fridge and pantry, Grens loaded the dishwasher and chased crumbs off the tabletop and floor.

'So. Let's start upstairs. Come with me.'

Just as a few months ago Linnea's father tried to explain by showing him Jacob's room. Now Hoffmann was waiting for him, climbing up wooden stairs that smelled as new as everything else in this house, which had been rebuilt as an exact copy of the blasted original.

'Rasmus's room is here on the left, like before, but furnished differently. Hugo's room is in the middle, and it's identical to the original – he was insistent on that.'

Grens didn't really remember what it looked like before. Probably didn't find it very relevant. But if Piet said so . . .

Piet Hoffmann looked a little proud as he continued on to the next room.

'And this is all new. Luiza has her own room now. A big girl.'

Ewert Grens glanced into a normal kid's bedroom. With normal kid things. But he didn't say a word, since Piet was so obviously proud.

'And now down. To my office.'

They followed each other down the wooden stairs to Hoffmann's workroom in the basement, just like in the old house, with the desk and wardrobe placed exactly as before.

'Identical to the old room, don't you think, Ewert?'

'Because it *is* identical.'

'With one big exception.'

Hoffmann opened the spacious wardrobe, stepped into it and motioned to Grens to come in among the shelves loaded with the family's sweaters and shoes and hangers with suits and dresses and a section intended for winter clothes.

'You see?'

'See what, Piet?'

'There's nothing past this. No more hidden levers that open secret doors. No entrance to infiltrator Piet Hoffmann's innermost room.'

The wardrobe in the previous house had very cleverly hidden another room where this wall seemed to end. With storage cabinets full of weapons and bulletproof vests and safes filled with piles of cash and passports with false names. A hideout.

'The rooms I showed you above – that's the entirety of my life now. Hugo, Rasmus, Luiza, Zofia. That's why there are no hidden rooms down here either. I don't keep secrets any more. All I do is sell security cameras and alarms and bulletproof doors to companies and spend the occasional weekend as a bodyguard. I'll never risk any of this again.'

Ewert Grens had once given the command to shoot to kill Piet Hoffmann. That was before they knew each other. Another time, he forced Hoffmann to infiltrate by threatening to publish evidence of a huge cache of smuggled drugs that would have seen him locked away again, for a long time. By then they knew each other, but not well. But now, after they'd lived together for six months, after Grens finally experienced what it was like to be part of a family, it was no longer possible to force his cooperation via guns or blackmail. Even manipulation was out of the question, a way of getting results that Hoffmann had honed during his years as an infiltrator. So instead they stood in a basement wardrobe and did their best to outstare each other. Until Ewert Grens finally gave up trying to be smooth.

'You say no. But –'

'Don't ask me again.'

'– you don't even know what the hell –'

'Stop nagging! Stop pushing!'

'– I want to ask you about!'

'Goddammit, Grens – what exactly didn't you understand in what I just said?'

Long ago the doctors and counsellors at various juvenile detention facilities who evaluated Piet Hoffmann, repeat offender, had diagnosed the cause of his actions as low impulse control. Over the years, first as a criminal and then as a prisoner, that characteristic of his personality had gradually been replaced by extreme impulse control. He'd already made up his mind. Never again would the rage inside take control. Never again would his environment determine who he was. A perfect tool, it had turned out, for someone who wanted to earn the trust of his enemies. The ability to use his rage only when the moment arrived to expose and destroy an organisation – and also to protect himself.

Ewert Grens was well aware of all that. That was also why he recognised it now. Hoffmann was close to snapping.

But it didn't matter.

His own rage made it impossible for him to let go.

'This is about children.'

'Never again, Grens.'

'No older than Rasmus. Several who are even younger.'

'Not for the Swedish police, not for any foreign police.'

'This isn't for a police force – it's for me.'

'And not even for you. So for fuck's sake stop it! Stop pushing me, Grens!'

Piet Hoffmann stood trembling in front of him now. This was his breaking point. They both knew it. How hard Hoffmann sometimes had to fight against the desire to go back. Not for the money, but for the adrenaline, the kick, what he was. How difficult it was sometimes to resist offers from the criminal world or from various police forces of *just one more time*. How he'd promised Zofia and the children and been given one last chance to be part of his own family, and that if he broke that promise there would be only loneliness as vast as Grens's own.

'Piet – I helped you. I was there when you needed me.'

'And I helped you people! So many times! It never ended well – at least not for me. Right? We both know how it works, Superintendent, they just squeeze and squeeze until there's nothing left.'

Ewert Grens had an envelope of pictures and printouts of chats folded in his inside pocket; now he almost threw it down.

'*This is what you don't want to stop!*'

'Go.'

'You owe me this.'

'I don't owe you or anyone outside this house a goddamn thing!'

Grens pulled out the contents of the envelope, held up pictures and chat logs, waving them in front of Hoffmann's face.

'Just a small selection. Not even the worst. *These are the children you don't want to save!*'

'Go! Get the hell out!'

Hoffmann took a step forward.

'Go now, Grens! Don't ever pressure me again! Go for both our sakes!'

He was standing in a wardrobe that no longer contained a secret life. Pushed up against the wall like a fucking rat. Nowhere to go, eyes staring into eyes.

'I'm not leaving until you look at this filth, Piet. Until you know what you're saying no to. Until you –'

There was nothing else left.

Other than the urge to protect himself by fighting his way free.

A fist hit a face, a nose, and part of a right cheek, and Detective Superintendent Grens collapsed.

He lay there on the floor, motionless.

SURELY THIS WAS the best moment of his day. The entire house, the whole neighbourhood, had settled into stillness in the dark. Luiza was asleep, Rasmus and Hugo were each in their own bed, about to tumble into the peace of night. He'd missed their first years – criminality and imprisonment and the life of an infiltrator had consumed more of his life than his family did. But he hadn't been living back then. Not really. On the run. That's what he was. Maybe that's why he was usually so grateful to be able to sit here, with his children, no longer on his way anywhere else. Just stillness. Even deep, deep inside.

But not tonight.

Worry. Imbalance. Anger blowing up in small series of explosions in his chest, and no idea how to stop it.

It was just like before, and he hated it.

'Dad?'

In Rasmus's room, that's where he was sitting.

'Yes?'

'What did Uncle Ewert want?'

And it was his younger son's head he stroked.

'He . . . just wanted to say hi.'

'At breakfast?'

'Yes . . . it's been a long time. He probably –'

'Excuse me?'

Hugo's voice. Coming from the room next door.

'Come on, Dad – after this long?'

'Yeah, you know . . .'

'"Just say hi"? Seriously, Dad. Who do you think we are?'

They fell asleep. Finally. And Piet Hoffmann headed down the stairs to what was usually the continuation of the best time of the day, a glass of wine with Zofia at the kitchen table, a final hour together with no other demands.

This was unlike a normal night as well.

Zofia put the glasses out, poured, and was on her usual chair.

But she wasn't her usual self. Because he wasn't his usual self.

'Piet?'

'Yes?'

'I'm going to say exactly what Rasmus and Hugo said. What was this morning's visit about?'

He looked at her – the only person he could never hide from.

'This.'

The envelope that Grens had pushed into his face.

Now Piet Hoffmann held it above the pine table, turned it upside down, and let its contents fall onto the tabletop.

Her first look was hasty.

'What . . .'

The next disgusted.

'. . . is that?'

'Just a small selection. Not even the worst. That's what he said – Ewert. The pictures you can see for yourself . . . and the text, I glanced at it – chats within a paedophile ring.'

She stared at the pile. Stared without seeing. Blankly.

'He wove these in my face, even though I promised to never do another job. He should have left me the fuck alone. In peace! And here he comes with those fucking pictures! Just like when he showed up in West Africa and forced me to infiltrate the trafficking operation. Both he and I know that's not going to work any more! I've lived an honest life since then! He doesn't have shit on me!'

He stood up, struggling to speak quietly, so as not to wake the kids.

'Is that all, Piet?'

'Isn't that enough?'

'No. Maybe before – but not any more. Not enough to make you look like that. Act like that.'

The only person he could never hide from.

'It didn't end so well, the visit, we didn't part as friends.'

Zofia's gaze was pulled towards the picture on the top. She flipped through the pile. Her face – Piet saw it so clearly – changed. Grief. Memories. Twice while she was looking, reading, he had to apologise, go back upstairs, make sure the children truly were asleep. Because he was worried about them – it had taken a long time, but he'd finally learned to think about other people. But also he needed some distance from her reaction. He knew where it came from. Zofia, on the other hand, sat there, trying to make sense of what Hoffmann had spent the day not even daring to get close to.

Then she did what he wished he could.

She wept.

'What are you thinking about?'

She didn't answer. So he let her cry it out.

'Honey? Zofia?'

'You know what I'm thinking.'

'Do you want . . . ?'

'No.'

They had tried to so many times. *He* had tried. To be a part of her past. To understand what had happened. A very long time ago.

'Maybe I should never have . . . shown you.'

'I was the one who asked.'

'I don't understand, Zofia. After fifteen years together? After three children? After death threats and torpedoes into our homes and a house bombed and . . . you still can't talk about it? To me? About you?'

'I'm sorry. I can't, Piet. Can't put it into words. Even to myself.'

He gathered up the pile of pictures of naked children and paedophile chats and slid them into the envelope, trying to be rid of it all. He'd done everything he could to gain her trust over the years, there was nothing else to do. He'd been given her love, he knew that, that was obvious and unconditional and wonderful, but never access to what had happened to her as a child, which never seemed to lose its potency for her.

'So, Piet, what did you say?'

She stared at him through the silence.

'Say?'

'To Ewert?'

And he met her eyes. They were done, for now.

'What we agreed. What I promised you. Never again.'

EWERT GRENS WAS stretched out on the corduroy sofa, a cup of black coffee balanced on his chest, listening to the late-night silence of the police station.

The detective superintendent had left the spillikins streets of Enskede just as morning rush hour was ending. He'd turned onto Nynäs Road and driven back towards the inner city and to a large hospital on Kungsholmen. High-velocity violence. That's what the radiologist said. Fractured nasal bone. A face that several hours later looked swollen and bruised.

He'd understood what Hoffmann was demanding from him, perhaps even begging.

But he hadn't let it go. And that resulted in blows.

The kind that leave no chance of a future path together.

He forced his neck up from the armrest, doing his best to ignore the pain, and took a drink of his coffee, then put the half-full cup back on his chest. When he'd snuck into the police station earlier, he'd stopped four times at four doors, almost knocked even though he knew no one was there. First at Elisa Cuesta's door – would have been nice to sit on those unpacked boxes and discuss Alva, who wasn't in her coffin, maybe learn a little more. Then at Mariana Hermansson's door, where he'd gone so many times to spill all his thoughts while she listened and received them back better than before – until he allowed himself to remember it was someone else's office now. The third time he stopped was outside Erik Wilson's door, wanting to talk more about Linnea, the girl who was also not in her coffin and who'd got him suspended from work. Though he was well aware that that was impossible too, the existence of two children could only be assured as long as he conducted a non-sanctioned investigation alone and in secret. The fourth stop was outside Sven Sundkvist's office, where he'd normally go for help with the question of how, without Hoffmann's participation, to proceed most wisely – but even if Sven *had* been inside, *had* been able to advise him, Grens had no desire to withhold parts of the truth from his closest colleague so better to say nothing at all.

Finally he'd gone into his own office, to try to find the answer in his corduroy sofa instead. Until he gave up and called the police station in Lærdal, Denmark, for an update from Birte.

It took a long time for her to answer. He wondered if it was deliberate.

'Hi – Grens here. From my office in Stockholm.'

'Ewert? Is that . . . you?'

'Yes, I –'

'I'm having a hard time hearing you, something's up with the line. Can you call again?'

The line? More like a nose that wasn't really intact any more.

It took a while for her to answer the next time as well. He again wondered if it was intentional.

'Sorry – it cut out. I just found out more about two of the guys exchanging images directly with Hansen who aren't part of the closed ring. I think I pinned down their identities.'

She wasn't avoiding him. For some reason, that made him happy.

'The one with the handle *Friend* is actually Anthony T. Ferrara, who's serving a long sentence for raping his daughter repeatedly. How he managed to access the Internet from inside an Italian prison is incomprehensible to me. Handle *Sherlock* is actually John Davids who served two prison sentences in the north of England for child abuse. It's clear locking them up has not cured them.'

Grens heard her tapping away on the keyboard, the impatient click of someone who wanted to make progress.

'I'm approaching two more – will have them very, very soon. Both inside the ring. The German, *Meyer*. And *Lenny*, the paediatrician from the United States, who I now know has ten children of his own.'

Ten. Ewert Grens couldn't even stand to think about it. Yet that was what he did.

'Their pictures?'

'Nothing you need to see either.'

'Still that terrible?'

'Yes.'

She was writing like before, or at least tapping at it.

'Birte – how can you bear it?'

'I sleep like you do, not much.'

'I mean: how can you handle more pictures?'

'I've been doing this for so long. I think it's like . . . looking at corpses, death. Terrible. Still, there are people who autopsy bodies every day. I guess . . . after a while you don't think about it, don't store it in the same way as someone who's new to it.'

'Like me?'

'Like you, Ewert – at least with this. And the infiltrator?'

He hesitated a moment. So she had time to continue.

'The expert at getting into this kind of organisation? When does he start? Or she?'

For a moment, the tapping stopped. She really wanted to know.

'He.'

'And?'

'I'm . . . working on it. We'll be there soon.'

Ewert Grens stayed there on the corduroy sofa. Without finding any peace.

Faceless men with long prison sentences for rape or with ten children they abused stared down at him, wouldn't even leave him be when he closed his eyes.

Half an hour later, it was his mobile phone ringing, and when he saw the number on the display, he turned it over. So it rang again. And again. First on the landline and then the mobile. The sixth time he counted the rings, four five six seven eight nine, his whole body tense until they finally fell silent.

He really wanted to talk to her. But how could he?

He'd had just one task. While Birte was shut up in a little police station in the Danish countryside working round the clock to identify members of the paedophile ring they'd drawn out from a disturbed shadow world, he'd gone to the Swedish capital to make sure the infiltrator he'd promised would be sitting next to him on an aeroplane headed back south.

Instead, there'd been high-velocity violence. Fractured nasal bone.

Now she called again. Seven eight nine ten eleven rings, the most so far.

Ewert Grens had, of course, met other criminal infiltrators who worked for the police authority. But no one as skilled as Hoffmann, a man he'd learned to trust, even come to know. So for an assignment that was already unofficial, which under no circumstances could be discovered or go off the rails, there really was no one else. And since he no longer existed, there was absolutely no point in answering Birte.

'Grens?'

A voice in the hallway outside his closed door.

'Ewert Grens? Are you there?'

A male voice he didn't recognise, which sounded quite young.

'Who's asking?'

'Officer on watch.'

Grens waited. Someone new. It sounded like he was still there.

'Yes?'

'Sorry to have to disturb you, Superintendent, but a colleague, a very nice one, called from a town near Nykøbing Falster, and convinced me in Danish I nearly understood to come up here to you. She said she tried to reach you by every other method. Email, landline, mobile phone. She also said you knew who she was and had her number.'

Grens hoped that his sigh was inaudible. He couldn't avoid her any more. It was apparently still the case that problems don't just disappear when he pretended they didn't exist. He pressed her number and she answered, unlike him, after the first ring.

'I've been trying to reach you, Grens.'

'I . . . Well. You did now.'

'Because I found our opening! The one we need your infiltrator for!'

He should laugh. Rejoice. He heard the seriousness, the joy, she really had found a way out that was now a way in.

'Oh, really?'

But that kind of fake laughter seldom sounds good.

'I also identified the first two inside the ring – both Meyer and Lenny. Meyer's real name is Hans Peder Stein, and he was convicted twenty years ago for a series of child rapes in a small town north of Munich. Conditionally released and outwardly well behaved – German state police were hoping he really had changed. Lenny is the father of ten children and the doctor who bragged about documenting the rapes of forty children in his practice. We now know that his name is James L. Johnson and he lives in a city called Visalia, somewhere between Los Angeles and San Francisco.'

She was amazing. He wanted to say it, shout it. A single day had passed since they'd parted ways, and she had four names. He didn't say anything.

'But that was not why I chased you down. I found something else. In one of the chats, it appears that Meyer and Lenny are preparing to meet, in person, again. And not just them – listen now – Onyx, the leader, is supposed to be there too! One of two that I have nothing on, at all! The one I won't allow to get away! Meyer, Lenny and Onyx will – if I interpret their lightly coded conversation correctly – each bring their own child and trade them. Everyone will be allowed to play with everyone. Meeting place probably California, in a little less than four days. This is our chance! If we can map out everyone else, if we can coordinate with all police authorities, if we . . .'

My God. She wasn't amazing. She was so much more than that.

'When you talked about the infiltrator, Ewert. Just before you left.

You said he was the tool we could use to get close to the leader – *and that you knew exactly how*.'

He never should have answered the voice that came through his door. And certainly never called her back.

'Hello? Ewert? Answer me.'

'Carl Hansen.'

'Yes?'

'Lassie.'

'Yes.'

She waited for him to go on.

'Carl Hansen is the key that opened the paedophile ring to us and to his contacts with access only through him. But – he is also the key to the next step, even though he's locked up in Vestre Prison in Copenhagen. Because no one knows what he looks like. They all know each other through handles and photographs that reveal only an arm or a leg or the upper body – but never a face. Only those who've met in person have seen each other. And there's not a single reference in all the material you've gone through to Lassie meeting any of the others in real life. He and the mother and the girl were on their way to their first meeting abroad, the one with the Belgians, when we knocked on the door.'

Shallow, regular breathing. She was full of expectation.

'Yes? Grens?'

'The infiltrator I was talking about. He would take Hansen's identity. Become Lassie.'

Her silence changed.

'As Lassie, he would then approach the leader.'

Deeper breaths.

'Suggest he participate in the next face-to-face meeting.'

As if she were thinking, appreciating his suggestion.

'Their names, addresses, appearances. We would get everything, Birte.'

'And the infiltrator, he . . . ?'

'Yes. Highly capable. In every way. Even at an international level.'

'So the meeting I just found out about? Our chance? With your . . .'

She was happy, he could hear it.

'. . . infiltrator, Ewert – it really *is* our chance!'

A slight scratch through the phone. The pressing of keys again. Eager to continue.

'From now on, I'll send all communication I find that I think might be of interest so that your companion can prepare himself. What time do you get here?'

Ewert Grens awake, again.

But at least this time he knew why he couldn't sleep.

What time do you arrive?

He'd gladly have remained beside her, but at this moment he was grateful to be six hundred and fifty kilometres away in another country with no chance of meeting her eyes. His frustration increased with each new email of Birte's findings. Each new absurd communication between the members of the paedophile ring that came from her search for their identities.

05-10-2019 03:11:36 Message from 433228295: *A candle.*

05-10-2019 03:13:02 Message from 135311671: *Yes?*

05-10-2019 03:13:24 Message from 433228295: *You light both ends and pour the wax over her naked body.*

05-10-2019 03:14:07 Message from 135311671: *Perfect! I think I need one more week before she is ready. LOL.*

Ewert Grens did what he always did when what was inside became too much to handle.

That sick asshole in his fucking locked room!

He slammed the coffee table first.

That's the only place they reign as kings!

He stood up and hit the wall just as hard.

Driving each other further, further! Patting each other on the back!

Now bleeding from his knuckles, he struck again with his other fist.

And they write to each other like some kind of diary about how good they are at destroying their own children!

'Hello?'

A new voice from the corridor.

'Ewert? Are you OK?'

The door opened. One of the cleaners, they often said hello and chatted a bit when Grens stayed late on the sofa while the wastebasket was emptied and the floor vacuumed.

'Yes . . . it's fine.'

'You screamed. And you seem to have hit yourself, your face – that doesn't look good at all.'

'No.'

'Yes. You screamed loudly. And you *have* hurt yourself.'

A candle. You light it at both ends and pour the candle over her naked body.

Grens soon closed the door. Alone again, he contemplated what he'd done – just like at the Lærdal police station while listening to the recordings of the first interrogations – screamed aloud without being aware of it.

Was he losing his mind?

What was it about these children that affected him so much more deeply than any other form of human violence he'd encountered during his forty years on the force?

In order not to fall, losing his footing as the floor disappeared, he sank down onto the sofa and tried to breathe into his diaphragm as he'd learned.

He simply did not understand it.

But now there was blood on the knuckles of both hands.

If he read a little more of what she sent, surely it would pass. He would have to get used to it at some point.

The next email was a review of the correspondence to and from one of the untraceable addresses. The leader who called himself Onyx and lived somewhere in the United States. A synthesis that didn't offer much more than a confirmation of the power structure. How it was Onyx who guided the other members of the paedophile ring and set the rules – for example telling them to use encryption to avoid detection.

While Grens kept reading and doing his best to suppress his outbursts – there were enough people as it was wondering why he was screaming – another email arrived from Birte. In a few introductory sentences she described how she would continue to work intensively until Grens arrived with his infiltrator, and here she was sending a selection of newly found chats that offered smaller pieces to the larger identity puzzle.

Until Grens arrived with his infiltrator.

There it was again. Insomnia.

He went out to the coffee machine for his two cups of black coffee. Might as well if he was going to be awake anyway. And started reading the attached file, a total of twenty pages of new text from a twisted world.

It was at page 11 that the blow struck his chest.

The kind that spread simultaneously up and down, to the gut which felt and the brain which became conscious.

In a message from handle *Spirit* – which Birte noted was likely the same individual who called himself Lenny – there was a sentence containing the two words Ewert Grens dreamed of every time he managed to fall asleep these days.

14-08-2019 02:23:33 Message from 763923245: *A white dress, silver shoes, and a blue butterfly for her hair.*

And a blue butterfly for her hair.

He read the passage, the sentence, over and over again.

The message from Spirit/Lenny to Onyx was about an order to Lassie. About which garments and jewellery he'd sent, and what he wanted to see on the girl in the next photo series.

The blue butterfly. Finally.

The hair clip Linnea had worn, that sat above the left ear of the doll in Danish Katrine's bedroom, which stood in the picture that started all this – a completely unique blue butterfly that now lay in the lower drawer of the desk in his office. The decoration sent to be used as props. Now he knew by whom. And from where. Ring member Lenny, who according to Birte was named James L. Johnson and came from a place somewhere between Los Angeles and San Francisco.

Now. *Now*.

There was only one choice.

Even if his face still ached from the kind of violence that excluded any future together.

He got up from the sofa, grabbed his coat and hurried towards the car that was parked on Kungsholms Street, drove the short distance to a small apartment on the fifth floor in a neighbourhood called Södermalm, which he'd visited just a couple of days ago.

'Superintendent?'

Billy. Obviously newly awake. In the same torn jeans and washed-out T-shirt.

'Do you sleep in those clothes too?'

'It happens – but what the hell happened to you, Superintendent?'

The young man stared at the much older one.

'Your face, it's banged up, taped up, and black and –'

'I need your help.'

'You need a doctor.'

'I've already seen one.'

'Sure. Suit yourself. But it's easier if you come in.'

'And it will be even easier if you come with me.'

Billy didn't seem surprised. He probably solved as many problems via other people's networks as his own. He was only surprised as they drove for a while, and Grens revealed that this wasn't about computers at all.

'Really? I don't know about much else. Why do you think I work from home and only leave to go to 7-Eleven to buy some dinner? Why do you think I go to bed when others get up? Because I'm not very good with people. That's why you write your first computer program at nine, and while the other kids play football and get drunk, you hide behind advanced coding. Not because you're so damn smart. I was even part of a hacker network for a few weeks with other people who suck at people, but not even that was my thing.'

'I can . . . be a bit like that.'

'What is it then? If it's not about computers?'

'It's what you think you can't do.'

'Oh really?'

'Because I can't let even a whisper of this reach the police. And you're the only person in this country who knows what I'm up to.'

'Superintendent, what exactly are we talking about?'

'People.'

By the time they made their way down the street into Enskede and turned off the car engine in front of the Hoffmann family's mailbox, the whole world was shrouded in late-night darkness. As Billy sat there waiting for Grens to explain what he meant by *people*, he realised he'd probably been here before.

'We were here a couple of years ago, right?'

'Not this house exactly. But a similar one. At the same place.'

'Something to do with human trafficking. I think. And a computer with the tightest fucking encryption I've ever seen. I would have cracked it faster now.'

'You remember correctly. So maybe you also remember that there were children in that house?'

'No.'

'There were. Two. Now three. The oldest are boys, nine and eleven. And those are who you'll help me with.'

'How?'

'Babysitting.'

'Baby . . . sitting?'

'I *can't* risk anyone else finding out what I'm working on. And – I will owe you one more.'

Billy shrugged his thin shoulders.

'Which I do intend to cash in on as well. Big time, Superintendent. But sure, OK. I was just planning on chilling anyway. Might as well do it here.'

It was quarter to three and his second visit in less than a day.

So as Ewert Grens walked down the square stone slabs towards the front door, it felt as familiar as it did inevitable.

He started by knocking. When that didn't work, he switched to the bell. First a short ring, but with each new press his index finger pushed longer and harder on the round plastic button.

Finally the lights turned on in the hall, and the door cracked open.

Zofia. Eyes squinting sleepily.

'Did something happen? Are *you* in danger? Are *we* in danger?'

'No, but –'

'In that case – goodbye, Ewert.'

She closed the door. Almost. Because the tip of his shoe was stuck in the gap.

'You and Piet need to listen to me. One more time.'

'Damn it, Ewert, if you just –'

'Mum? What's happening? Why did you say damn it? Me and Hugo don't get to say that, and –'

Grens sensed a ruffled head behind her. Rasmus. Who then stuck that messy head into the doorway.

'Uncle Ewert, what are you doing here?'

'He's leaving. Now.'

Zofia turned to her younger son.

'Go back to bed, honey.'

'Why should he – *Oh, Ewert, what happened?!*'

'It's nothing, Rasmus.'

'But I can see you've been beaten up! Why should he go, Mum? He's hurt, and he just got here.'

'Because –'

'Because I'm disturbing you. In the middle of the night. Your mother is right about that. But if she and your dad just let me in for a little while, or rather let both of us in then . . .'

Grens moved, and Billy became visible behind him.

'. . . we'll be done, and everyone can go back to sleep.'

Now Piet had come down, too. And it was at that moment Zofia noticed the detective's badly bruised face and then looked at her husband

and realised what *it didn't end so well, the visit, we didn't part as friends* really meant, and she sighed and waved Grens in towards the kitchen.

It was a good thing he had Billy with him. Both Piet and Zofia kept their hostility in check, as so often happens when an outsider puts everyone on their best behaviour. It was probably thanks to Billy that they agreed to listen to him one last time. Billy, who didn't think he was any good at reading people, read each of them perfectly. He understood what Ewert Grens was after, that both parents were completely against it and that the way to reach them was through the children. When with a few, and for Grens completely incomprehensible, sentences about computer games, Billy got Rasmus to rush up to his bedroom and promise to go back to sleep afterwards, and in passing offered to babysit, he even got Piet and Zofia to accompany the stubborn detective.

On the way, they said nothing.

The four of them, Grens in the driver's seat and the two Hoffmanns and a sleeping Luiza in the back seat, were silent for the whole of the journey through Stockholm's darkness. Not even one question of where or why. Not until he, near Karolinska University Hospital, slowed down to exit the E4 for Solna Kyrk Road.

'What are you up to, Ewert?'

'Soon.'

A different kind of darkness lay over the enormous cemetery. When he turned into the entrance and asked them to get out, his passengers didn't look exactly comfortable. Zofia stood close to Piet, and maybe that's why she was whispering, but her voice wasn't very gentle.

'I repeat: what are you up to, Ewert?'

'I want to show you something. A grave.'

They were also silent over the next stage of the journey. Made on foot along the paths that cut oblong lines through green lawns, lit by sparsely placed lamps. The resting place they finally stopped in front of had been dug just a couple of months earlier.

'The girl, Linnea Disa Scott, was four years old when she disappeared in a supermarket and seven when she was pronounced dead in August. According to her parents, she had a zebra-striped jacket that she liked so much she even wore it at home, indoors, and a hair clip that looked like a big blue butterfly in her fringe. This one.'

From the outer pocket of his jacket Grens took the hair clip, which he had found on a doll in a Danish child's bedroom, held it out, then closed his hand around it – for a moment he'd been afraid it might leave its metal frame and fly away.

'I was here for the funeral, there were a lot of people, and it felt good to drop a red rose on the coffin lid. But in fact, that's why we're standing here now, no one was inside the coffin. Linnea didn't attend her own burial. She was quite simply not here. So it stands to reason, she must have been somewhere else.'

For a moment they listened.

For a moment he had their attention.

He had just started to tell them about a girl who took a strange hand in a crowd before being lost forever, and about the parents who could not bear to mourn her any more, when he was interrupted. By Zofia.

'Her?'

Face pale, voice thin.

'The girl from . . . the newspaper?'

The phone was in her coat pocket. Zofia took it out and typed something into the search engine with so little text that Grens couldn't read even though he did his best to peek, and soon held up an article from the largest-selling morning newspaper.

'This one, Ewert? A while ago?'

The detective fumbled with his reading glasses before he could follow the finger that pointed to a grave and a cluster of mourners. A photo he'd never seen – but had arranged – and whose publication Wilson used as a basis for his suspension.

'I read that article and . . . Ewert, is it *her*? Everything you left with us, the pictures and texts and . . . That was about you wanting Piet to infiltrate in order to find out about . . . *her*? Have you brought us here because she's there somewhere – among the children in those pictures?'

'That was what I hoped Piet would find out.'

'But what do *you* believe? Is she there?'

'I don't know. It could be. That's enough for me.'

'What I mean is: why did you give the pictures and texts to Piet – *now*? Why is it suddenly so urgent, *now*, that you pick us up in the middle of the night?'

'If I'm right, we have a deadline of three and a half days. That's how long we have to take advantage of a big opportunity.'

'And you need Piet for that?'

'His presence is crucial.'

Zofia was still pale.

But her voice sounded a little steadier when she looked at Grens and began to speak.

'I read the article and looked at the newspaper pictures – the grave, the mourners – because I recognised the story. *Knew* the girl.'

She grabbed her husband's hand, squeezed it.

'Linnea. That's her name. Was her name. Even though it doesn't appear in the newspaper. She was in the same children's groups as Rasmus. The same preschool. Never with Hugo, he's a little too old, but we knew her, the family. They lived in our area, back then.'

She turned to the newly dug grave.

'We all became . . . sort of a part of the disappearance. All of us who were around the family. Got involved, comforted them as best we could. Then they moved. Very suddenly. Cut off all contact. Didn't have the strength to live any more . . . well, in the past. They're somewhere north of the city, I think.'

Ewert Grens nodded slowly.

'North-west of the city. A nice house in a nice neighbourhood.'

'I especially remember the twin boy, Jacob, he took it very badly.'

'He still takes it very badly.'

She was deeply affected. Grens felt it.

'I brought you here, to this grave, so that you could understand. But I also want us to visit another grave, another four-year-old girl who disappeared the same day, who is also not in her coffin.'

He didn't know why he kept going, why he said what he said then. It had nothing to do with this. But he really wanted to hear Piet say yes.

'And after we've seen both graves, I want . . . well, I have a daughter here, too.'

'A daughter?'

Piet Hoffmann glanced down at his own sleeping baby girl before meeting Grens's gaze.

'Yes.'

'You've never said anything.'

'I'm saying it now.'

Now it was Piet who squeezed Zofia's hand.

'Do you want . . . this doesn't change my answer to you, Ewert, but do you want us to go there? Of course, we'll go with you to visit your daughter. Where is she?'

Grens looked down at the gravel path.

'I . . . don't really know. The memorial grove, I think.'

'Think?'

'I've never been there.'

He scraped his foot, the small stone fragments stuck to his rubber sole, and he had to pull them out with his fingers.

'It hasn't . . . I was on my way a few months ago, but couldn't quite make it there. I couldn't do it. But it took me a long time to visit Anni's grave as well.'

'You have . . . never been there?'

'No.'

'How . . . When?'

'Over thirty years ago.'

Ewert Grens stared at them. A long time.

'So – what do you say? Piet?'

'I say I'm not the right person for this.'

'You won't be exposed to danger. The worst that can happen is that you have to go home again and waste a couple of days and some of the police force's travel cash.'

'You're still not listening – I'm not the right person because I'm not the right kind of infiltrator.'

'Piet, I let go of my unborn daughter. I let go of Zana who was also my responsibility once.'

Hoffmann remembered. Grens remembered. Another little girl who faced violence, and whom they searched for together the last time they collaborated.

'I'm not letting go of any more little girls who need me.'

Piet never had the chance to answer. Because Zofia did instead.

'I think we're done here. We don't need to see the other grave. Or visit your daughter.'

'But –'

'Give us a minute, Ewert.'

They walked into the darkness of the cemetery, their contours soon too indistinct to follow. But if Grens had to guess, based on body language, it was *as if she said* of all the idiotic infiltrations you've done, Piet, this would be the only sensible one, and *as if he said* I promised you I'd stop, Zofia, because this never ends well, and *as if she said* the girls were only a few years older than our little sleeping Luiza when they disappeared. And when they came back and Zofia asked the detective how he knew for sure that the blue butterfly meant the girl in the empty coffin really was out there somewhere, then it was *Grens who said* he didn't know for sure, but he was certain that he had to keep going – for all the others in the envelope they'd received.

'In that case.'

Zofia looked first at Grens, then at her husband.

'One more time, Piet.'

'Zofia, I meant what I said before – I'm not the right infiltrator for this kind of criminal network. And I promised you. Because we both know how I get.'

'For Linnea's sake. And maybe for mine. For . . .'

They both looked down at Luiza, who turned over in her pushchair, mumbling something, even snoring a little.

'. . . if Linnea is part of those pictures Ewert showed us, if he thinks there's even the slightest chance she's still alive – well, in that case, please do it, Piet, please go.'

PART
4

Not hiding from someone.
Hiding in someone.

AS EWERT GRENS opened the heavy oak door of Lærdal's train station and took a deep, rain-soaked breath, he felt unexpectedly at home. Maybe it was because this town was so very small compared to Stockholm. Or maybe it was because Birte had sounded so happy when he called her from Arlanda to tell her he was on his way. Or maybe it was because he hadn't stepped off the train alone – but with Piet Hoffmann at his side, so he no longer felt ashamed, he was delivering on his promise.

They hadn't said much to each other afterwards, there in the cemetery.

He didn't need to tell him about how what should be a safe embrace – that of a child's parents – could turn into a chamber of horrors. Or about all the women and men who have to live with the memory of childhood abuse, but who are never truly free of the fear it might happen again, the images of a past that are online forever, passed from one paedophile to another, a crime with no end. And later, in the Hoffmann family's hallway, after Piet climbed up the wooden stairs to say goodbye to his children, Grens had followed. It felt good to stand by the door and watch as three children reacted differently to Piet's kiss on a cheek or adjustment of a pillow. Luiza, who had traded her pushchair for a cot, woke up briefly, turning from back to stomach just like before. Rasmus breathed as deeply as Grens remembered, so lost in sleep he didn't notice his father was near him. Hugo's anxiety, on the other hand, was palpable – he cried out, sweating, and plunged his hand into the dark towards nobody at all. For a moment, Piet glanced over at the doorway and the detective, and they both thought about what Zofia had said – that these children were the same age as the children whose pictures were in that envelope.

On the way to the airport, trapped next to each other in the front of the car with nowhere else to go, they didn't speak of the blow in the wardrobe or the face that was now swollen black and blue. And it didn't feel quite as terrible as Grens had feared to have spilled out his past, about a daughter he may one day visit.

They also didn't say much on the plane or on the train as Hoffmann read the chats between members of the ring, studied the pictures Birte had dug up, listened to the interrogations of the father and mother in custody now and to the interview of the girl at one of the municipality's institutions. It required no explanation because it could not be explained. A crime that did not resemble any other – violence directed inwards, not outwards. That's why this mission – *infiltrating the inner circle of a paedophile ring, revealing the leader's identity, securing evidence to lock everyone up* – was so different in its essentials from every one that Piet Hoffmann had done previously.

They'd barely made it through the front door of the small police station before Birte wrapped Grens in a big hug. Like an embrace between people who have known each other for a very long time. Or not seen each other in an age. A hug he didn't mind but that made him insecure – because neither of the two options applied here.

She met Piet Hoffmann with hand outstretched.

'Hello, I'm Birte. Welcome. I was starting to think you didn't exist.'

She glanced at Grens. She'd understood. Just another man who was full of shit. His relief to be standing here with Hoffmann increased.

'He exists. At last. And my own hours under the radar – without the approval of my bosses? Which unfortunately have come to an end?'

She smiled.

'We can probably consider extending them.'

She fetched an extra chair from the kitchenette and closed the door to the small room, which had temporarily become an unofficial liaison centre when the number of unofficial Swedes doubled.

'I paused my search when you said you were on your way – instead trying to hunt down another person who doesn't want to be found. I gathered most of what's public and much that Swedish police have tried to keep quiet. About you, Hoffmann.'

Piet Hoffmann looked both surprised and annoyed.

'I didn't know I was here to be evaluated.'

Birte turned round and changed the image on the computer's two screens.

Piet Hoffmann at different ages but in similar contexts.

The police authority's criminal registry, the National Courts Administration's archive of sentences imposed, the correctional agency's list of inmates.

'Ewert described you as a "good infiltrator". Or, more precisely, as "the best infiltrator". What he forgot to mention was that you did your infiltration as a criminal. Despite the fact that criminal infiltrators are banned in Sweden.'

'I'm no longer a criminal or an infiltrator.'

'I understand that. But from Grens's update it sounded like you were still pretty good at fighting.'

They both glanced at Grens's face. The swollen skin and splotchy colour.

'I have no problem at all, Hoffmann, with doing what Detective Superintendent Grens wants to do. Keep quiet. Forget to inform the US authorities that an outsider will be on their turf trying to solve crimes in their jurisdiction. I myself don't always trust foreign police; I've participated in investigations that were capsized because of corrupt police officers. In this case, we have a handler, Grens, who is already unsanctioned – but that's nothing to having an infiltrator over there as well. With no connection to the Swedish legal system, and only a very loose basis for investigating. Any inquiry from the US to the Swedish authorities would spell disaster – an unauthorised freelancer for the police, who, moreover, happens to be wanted in that particular country already.'

She nodded.

Yes.

She had found that out, too.

'So what I want to make sure we all agree on is that you, I and the National Research Centre have never had anything to do with each other. Just like I've had nothing to do with Grens.'

Piet Hoffmann glanced at Ewert Grens.

'The usual, then?'

'And especially . . .'

Birte clicked through more pictures – these were from a hostage drama in a high-security prison.

'. . . if everything goes to hell. If you end up needing the assistance of the Danish police. Then I'll have no idea who you are.'

Another glance at Grens. They had both been there for that. The hostage situation. On opposite sides. When the Swedish police abandoned their infiltrator, locked up and unmasked, behind bars.

The detective nodded.

'Yes. Like you said, Piet – the usual.'

'Well then . . .'

Hoffmann turned to the Danish computer expert, shook her hand again.

'. . . we're agreed. I'll infiltrate one last time. And if something goes wrong, we never met, and I'll expect no help.'

BEFORE PIET HOFFMANN could log in to the closed paedophile ring for the first time, hidden behind Lassie's identity, Birte and Grens had to make sure that the Hansen couple were locked in their cells with no way of contacting the outside world. Had to make sure no newspapers, radio, television or digital channels had leaked any information about the family. Ensuring that the arrest of the parents remained a secret and thus still unknown to that faceless community.

Externally Hoffmann was surrounded by order. But inside him, chaos reigned.

He'd always felt untouchable in his professional role. A manipulator who knew two lies made a better truth. Someone who lied so much, so skilfully, that he lost sight of where a lie ended and truth took over. A man who garnered trust and confidence, but easily tore it down again when a criminal organisation needed to be destroyed. Now, sitting in a small, shitty police station in rural Denmark, he realised that his unique skills and experiences were useless. He'd infiltrated the mafia in Sweden, drug cartels in Colombia, gangs of human traffickers in Libya, arms dealers in Albania – and now he knew nothing.

Not because he'd been gone a few years. Or because he now had something to lose, which always made this kind of life harder.

He simply did not understand these people.

These behaviours and thought patterns were so far removed from the culture of threats and violence that he grew up in, lived in, survived in.

That he was. That he became.

'What is it?'

Ewert Grens leaned forward when Birte left for the toilet.

'Nothing.'

'I can tell it's something.'

Piet Hoffmann was convinced he'd been keeping the chaos, the confusion inside. He was an expert at blending in among people who never truly knew him.

But Grens knew him.

Hoffmann shrugged.

'Playing a criminal – that's one thing.'

Whispering, without knowing why.

'When I do that I know how to think. Know how others think. Know what danger looks like. I can attack, retreat. But playing a . . . paedophile? No. I can't. It won't work. Zofia and you and sometimes even I have wondered what the hell my limits are, what will happen the day I cross over them. Now I know. This is where the limit is.'

Hoffmann nodded to the screen on the left.

'Right there.'

Towards the sketch of a paedophile ring with known aliases, in a couple of cases supplemented with real names.

'I can't act like . . . one of them. Can't sit here and come up with fake messages about what I'd like to do to a kid, how I want to harm her as much as possible. I'm sorry, Grens – it's not in me.'

'We have three days. Then you'll need to be in place.'

'Exactly. It's so little time . . .'

Hoffmann turned his back on the screen.

'. . . it's insane. Winning the trust of their leader. While mapping out the rest of the ring. While also prepping what I'll need to do the job.'

'Insanity – but it's what we have. And until then, Piet, while time is ticking forward, *more children are being abused*. And when time runs out, while the meeting we hope you can attend takes place, *more children will be abused*. And if you miss that meeting, *more children will be abused*. And –'

'Enough.'

'– while we wait for another chance, *more children will be abused*. And –'

'I said, enough!'

170

'What's enough?'

Neither of them had noticed that Birte had returned. But she noted the tension.

'More like *not* enough. Time. So I have a suggestion.'

Piet Hoffmann was almost whispering again. As if it were difficult to speak.

'I explained to the detective that I can't handle chatting with these sick motherfuckers about the best way to rape a child. I've done it all – tattooed corpses, watched my fingers being amputated by pruning shears, tortured caged people with electricity and barbed wire in the middle of the jungle – all so that cops could take down organised crime. But I won't do this. So instead of wasting all of our time and doing something I can't do well, I suggest we delegate. Use our time efficiently.'

Birte sat down. Nodded. The kind of nod that says *I'm listening*.

'Do you live alone?'

'What?'

'Birte – are you single?'

She examined him. Looked at Grens. Then answered.

'Yes.'

'And you live in Copenhagen?'

'Yes.'

'In that case, I'd like to borrow your apartment.'

She hesitated again. But not long. She dug out some keys from a bag sitting on the floor beside her desk.

'Sommerstedgade 24. Fourth floor. Ten minutes to Fisketorvet and about the same to Vesterbrogade.'

She started to hand him the keys – without letting go of them.

'I have a cat that the neighbour feeds. If you want to avoid any visitors, fill the bowls yourself. Tuna will be fine. And fresh water.'

The keys left her hand, and Hoffmann slid them into one of the long side pockets of his trousers.

'If I head there to figure out what I'll need for the actual infiltration. If Grens meanwhile becomes Lassie. And if you, Birte, continue to map their identities.'

He stood up and grabbed the jacket hanging over the back of the chair.

'Three tracks in parallel – it's the best use of our time. If we do it that way, then *maybe* we can catch up.'

He was already on his way.

'I need a day for prep. And if we assume this takes place somewhere in California, a day to travel – I just booked the last possible departure tomorrow, at 2 p.m.'

At the door, he turned round.

'That means we have exactly one day. Twenty-four hours – starting now.'

Tuesday 14:01 p.m.
(23 hours and 59 minutes remaining)

AFTER HOFFMANN EXITED the small police station a comfortable silence settled in, which surprised Ewert Grens. He, who usually found the empty spaces between people uncomfortable, was sitting there now, just a metre from Birte, as occupied with his computer screen as she was. He didn't worry about what he was going to say because he didn't need meaningless words to protect his shyness or mark the difference in their ages. The Danish computer expert helped him log in to the digital universe, where a closed paedophile ring existed, then instructed him how to navigate it, hiding behind the identity of Lassie – which was his task. Now it was up to Grens to communicate as credibly as possible about abuse and manipulation. Open the door wide enough for Hoffmann to slip inside.

Tuesday 2:10 p.m.
(23 hours and 50 minutes remaining)

It usually bothered her to have someone breathing down her neck while she was working against the clock. But with the Swedish detective in front of his own computer it felt different. Because he seemed to completely lack any social graces, didn't seem to grasp the most basic unwritten social rules, had no clue how to make small talk. Might not even be aware that small talk existed. So, he didn't distract her with any.

No unnecessary comments. No hand on the shoulder in an imitation of intimacy. A perfect room-mate, though possibly a not so perfect life partner.

Birte stretched, waving her hands back and forth in the air like she usually did to prevent mouse elbow.

Discovering the ten secret identities in the ring.

Discovering the additional eleven individual contacts directly linked to Hansen.

This was her mission for the next twenty-four hours.

She already had a handful: *Meyer*, a German named Hans Peder Stein; *Lenny*, an American named James L. Johnson; *Sherlock*, a Brit named John Davids; *Friend*, an Italian named Anthony T. Ferrara; and, of course, *Lassie*, alias for the Dane Carl Hansen. Deciphering the rest of the names wouldn't take as long – a lot of the research and cataloguing had already been done. So if Grens continued to sit there calmly, and if she could stay awake, then theoretically it might still be possible.

Tuesday 2:43 p.m.
(23 hours and 17 minutes remaining)

In one of the train's first-class carriages, Piet Hoffmann, after a slow first couple of miles, tore the back off the brochure in his chair pocket and started to write. Capital letters, easier on vibrating rails.

GANGSTER HUG
POTATO FLOUR
CITIZEN
BIRD GPS
USB CAMERA
SHORT-SLEEVED SHIRT
JAMMERS

He folded the piece of paper, opened it again, and added

TUNA

before stuffing it into the side pocket of his hunting jacket. The last might not make much difference in the success of the infiltrator's mission, but it was important to Birte, who reminded him of Grens – isolated and content to be so as long as their routines were maintained. He then glanced around to make sure no one else was sitting in this part of the train carriage and made three calls. The first was to a small studio on Södermalm in Stockholm, on the corner where sleepy Högalids Street met bustling Långholm Street, to a make-up artist who usually worked in film and who happened to be the best one he'd ever come across. The second was to a damp basement with small round windows on Istedgade, in the middle of Copenhagen, to a man who was one of the many special station hosts he'd established relationships with during his years in the criminal underworld. The third and final call was to the house and the people he missed as soon as he left them and who probably hadn't even noticed that he was gone – his home. His children, who were becoming more independent every day and soon enough they'd be seeking their own paths, their own relationships to call family.

When the train from Nykøbing Falster arrived at the capital's central station, he made sure to stop by a supermarket and fill a plastic bag with tins before heading to the address Birte had asked him not to write down. He was met by a white, blue-eyed cat, who expected first tuna and then to play with bouncing balls. He put his minimal luggage on what he thought was Birte's bed and his previous intuition was confirmed – an apartment as overflowing with solitude as Grens's place in Stockholm. The kind that was self-imposed. Without actually being chosen.

On his way to the first meeting – the basement room in central Copenhagen – he found himself humming in spite of the seriousness of his mission. He felt good here, always had, even when he was living his life destructively. People, houses, air – it was all a lot easier here than a few kilometres away on the other side of the strait. Iced water in a paper cup, a smørrebrød with liver pâté and onion rings in a napkin in his hand, as he walked down the cobblestones on Halmtorvet. When he arrived at the basement on Istedgade, he buzzed the intercom and waited for a *come in for fuck's sake, man*, then heard a click as the door unlocked. He was met by stairs and the stench of cigarettes. As if all the smoke that no longer lingered in Copenhagen's cafes was collected here instead. At the other end of the large storage room, Sonny could be seen faintly through the fog. The stationmaster for this city.

'Piet Koslow Hoffmann! It's been a hell of a long time!'

His arms outstretched for a bear hug of the kind all these small-time gangsters used, and Sonny now switched to Swedish, almost without an accent – if he hadn't decided to become the Nordic region's foremost fixer, he might have earned big money on his language skills.

The hug was hearty, adding the aroma of yesterday's wine to the smell of cigarette smoke.

'So you really got out?'

'Honest. For real.'

'And you still need my help?'

In Stockholm the name was Lorenz, and he kept his office in the boot of his car, in Bogotá it was Cesar who sat in a glass cage inside a Super-Deli, in Tunis it was Rob, who could always be found at Le Grand Café du Théâtre at tables shaded by yellow parasols. Here Sonny was the stationmaster – the fixer who took care of his own station, a place for goods to stop on their way to new owners.

'Making an exception. One last time.'

'Just like everybody else inside Vestre Prison, Piet – one last time.'

'I mean it.'

'Just like they do.'

Cigarillos. That's what he smoked. Sonny lit one more, had two in his mouth at the same time.

'You in a hurry?'

'Need it no later than tomorrow morning.'

'And a passport, Piet?'

'Yes. Just like usual.'

'If it had been like usual – using any name – you could have had it now.'

'Only one name works.'

'Appearance?'

'I'm sending a photo.'

'And weapons? The other things on your shopping list?'

'I need those waiting for me – in place. When I get there.'

'You don't make it easy on me.'

'That's what you get paid for.'

'That's what I get paid for.'

Another gangster hug and the stairs up to humid air that rolled in from the harbour and the Baltic Sea. A walk, a cold beer, some sleep and then on to Kastrup Airport to meet her on the first flight from Stockholm.

Tuesday 5:32 p.m.
(20 hours and 28 minutes remaining)

Every new keystroke, every new download of instant messages or images, was basically an immediate risk. Even an expert at covering your tracks always left some trace in a digital world. And the moment a ring member discovered any intrusion into their closed world, an alarm would go off and all evidence would be destroyed. Still she had no choice. They needed every identity to carry out coordinated raids with other law enforcement agencies.

That's why Birte rejoiced silently, not once but twice.

Because by compiling information about the three children who were called Lorna, Holly and Denise, aggravated rapes that were available for download at one hundred dollars a pop via a crudely constructed website, she was able to identify the handle *Queen Mary* as Jennifer Jackson, the children's mother, who lived in Grand Junction, Colorado, USA. And by cross-referencing information from a couple of their chats, within minutes she had identified the man with the handle *John Wayne* – who advertised the rape of his children in the same way and at the same price – as one David Paxton based in Brighton, England.

Tuesday 6:14 p.m.
(19 hours and 46 minutes remaining)

As soon as Ewert Grens logged on again as the paedophile Lassie, after a short break, it became clear that neither the members of the ring nor any other contact knew that Hansen had been locked up in a prison cell without any means of communication. Three detailed orders for videos with extreme abuse of Katrine were awaiting a response.

For Lassie's reply. That is, Grens's reply.

It was the worst assignment he'd had in his forty years as a police officer.

He'd investigated double murders, triple murders, opened a shipping container full of rotting bodies, reassembled corpses that had been torn apart by rats, had witnessed executions. But the repugnance he felt right now was beyond anything else. Because he *had to* do what Hoffmann refused to do – answer like a paedophile, appear to be a paedophile, while hoping to lay the grounds for a meeting in real life. Make contact with the man who called himself Meyer, or the one who called himself Lenny, or maybe even Onyx, the ringleader. If Grens, as Lassie, reached out to suggest a meeting he risked arousing their suspicion, because in their previous chats the other members had always taken the initiative, made the requests, while Lassie complied and delivered on the goods.

'And you find this kind of thing . . . all the time?'

He knew he shouldn't talk. Knew Birte preferred silence. But after answering a few of the members' requests to the best of his ability, he needed to speak a couple of words to a person who thought like he did.

'This is a little different. Not the degree of violence, but the fact that they have a system in place to trade children with each other in real life. And yes, I come across the kind who rape via the screen all the time.'

Grens didn't turn round. That would indicate a longer conversation and minimise the chances of getting an answer from her. So they sat there conversing with their backs to each other.

'My colleague who gave me that first picture, Werner, said he found more than he had time to even write down, easily a hundred Swedes a week.'

'And I easily find a hundred Danes a week.'

'So how will we ever catch up?'

'We won't. Catch up. Ever. Even if we put all of our resources on it from this day forward, we'd still never be able to investigate it all. But we can't give up, Grens. Can't allow ourselves to think . . . It's like drugs. They won't go away no matter how hard we work, but we keep going because we have to and we can't allow ourselves, I can't allow myself, to think it's meaningless.'

Tuesday 7:07 p.m.
(18 hours and 53 minutes remaining)

Birte was no longer listening, so Grens's final questions hung unanswered between them. But he didn't seem to mind – it had been enough to clear away some of the despair in order to make room for more.

She was close to discovering another identity with the help of her informal network of international colleagues.

And just like last time, this one would lead to *one* more and so on – so she had access to three more in less than an hour.

Handle *Lollipop* – who violated and allowed others to violate his daughters Chloé and Selina, who sent the glittering gold sequinned dress to Danish Katrine – was actually Jean-Michel and lived in Zurich, Switzerland. *Gregorius*, whose children were Sandra, Rahel and Frank, she identified as Matz Mechele who lived in a quiet suburb north of Antwerp, Belgium. And *Marie Antoinette*, with sons Jan and Tomas, soon turned out to be Stefan Willems from Zwolle in the eastern region of the Netherlands. In addition to bartering within their closed circle, these three were probably selling images on a larger scale via other platforms – all declared low incomes on their tax returns despite living very well indeed.

Birte now had the names and addresses of half of the members of the ring and five of the eleven in the chain who only communicated with Hansen.

It was still possible.

Tuesday 9:21 p.m.
(16 hours and 39 minutes remaining)

She was carrying a heavy leather bag in one hand, but she wound her way through Kastrup's arrival hall with light, almost springing steps. After his call, the best make-up artist he'd ever worked with had headed directly from her studio on Södermalm to Arlanda to take the next flight. She smiled that smile you could spend time with, leaned towards him, and he thanked her for rushing down to meet him.

'And this time, Piet?'

She'd sensed that it was an emergency – it always was – and had started to work on her assignment as soon as she was in the taxi to the airport.

'The little you could say on the phone – hair colour between regular and dark brown, eyes nut brown, stubble and a clearly hooked nose – helped me pack my bag. But more? Do you want to age like last time? Maybe get fatter? Bad skin? Cuts? Specific characteristics?'

'This time I don't decide. He does.'

Piet Hoffmann unfolded a copy of a photograph from the Danish passport register.

'Thirty-seven years old. Height: 185 centimetres. Weight 84 kilos.'

She studied the face in that frozen image.

'Who is he?'

She didn't expect an answer, was used to Piet not telling her anything, because as an infiltrator he simply could not. Never trust anyone. Always in danger, when exposure meant imminent death. But she still asked the question anyway – knowing the purpose of a mask, the context in which it would be used, was the foundation on which her work rested.

So when he answered, she flinched. As if something was wrong.

'A paedophile. Active. Extreme in his abuse.'

This time wasn't like the others. This time he wasn't infiltrating organised crime, which specialised in threats, violence and the death of adults. Instead, he would be searching through an unfamiliar world. And because he knew those who work with changing appearances prefer to know as much as possible about a person's interior so that outside and inside meld, he did something he'd never done before.

'Common Danish name – Carl Hansen. Regular small town – Lærdal.'

He whispered each new statement more quietly, so the taxi driver wouldn't hear.

'Stepfather. A member of a paedophile ring. Very recently locked up . . .'

They were passing over the water into the inner city via the Sjælland Bridge, and he pointed out through the car window.

'. . . five minutes away, in that direction.'

Still surprised at receiving an answer, she stared out the car window. Starting to understand. Hoffmann's transformation this time had a different purpose.

Not hiding from someone. Hiding in someone.

Tuesday 9:55 p.m.
(16 hours and 5 minutes remaining)

As the paedophile Lassie, Ewert Grens had received and answered two more vile chat messages when his phone buzzed silently in his pocket. Unknown number. He snuck out of the room to avoid disturbing Birte, who seemed even more preoccupied than before.

'Grens here.'

'Any contact yet?'

Piet Hoffmann was sitting in a car, that much was obvious. The ambient noise sounded like heavy traffic. A big city.

'I've received a total of five messages. Mostly Hansen's paedophile friends outside the ring. None of the three we're focused on. Those we need to make contact with for the mission to proceed.'

'We have to . . . *You* have to make contact, Detective Superintendent. Meyer, Lenny, Onyx. The clock is ticking!'

'I know. I *hear* the seconds. But I can't be too aggressive – I'd risk tipping them off. And ruin Birte's chance of tracking down all their identities.'

'We have a very narrow window.'

'And I *will* open it. By continuing to chat online, while waiting for an opportunity to arise. Swallow that impulse you have to act *now* so you can strike with full force when the time comes. Patience. The most important tool of the infiltrator. I learned from the best, right, Hoffmann?'

It was after that call, while Grens was brewing himself a fresh cup of coffee in the kitchenette that now felt as comfortable as his own kitchen back in Stockholm, that he heard a sharp ping wind its way through the small police station. The signal that meant an incoming message. He hurried to his computer, but hope soon turned to disappointment.

A message from *Ingrid*. Not one of the three who could make a difference.

Just another handle of Hansen's contacts outside the closed ring. Thus a person who Grens had neither the time nor the desire to answer. Still he had to. He couldn't risk raising any suspicions – so-called Ingrid and so-called Lassie had, according to the chats logs, always answered each other without delay.

So Grens opened the message of one paedophile to another – another request to trade pictures. In order to be able to bear it, he did as before, saw without seeing, followed the edges of the photographs, avoided the child's eyes. Until, at last, he happened not to. He was filled with astonishment.

It had to be . . . Surely?

Maybe.

Goddammit!

It could be *her*.

He enlarged the picture. The dress. The plait. The eyes – like a copy of those who belonged to a girl Jenny called Alva because it sounded so much like an elf's name. The one she called My Little Girl, who had disappeared from a deserted parking garage.

Ewert Grens leaned forward and took a slow, deep breath trying to banish the worst of the dizziness.

It didn't help.

If this was her.

When he read the accompanying text – the one he had to answer to prove they were old paedophile friends – it turned out that the sender, this so-called Ingrid, had 'dug up some old pictures just for fun' and as usual expected pictures in return.

Just like that she was real – *could* at least have been real.

The girl with a coffin in one of the two graves that had started him on his way here.

And Grens made a decision.

When this emergency was under control, when communication between the three key actors had been established, when Hoffmann was on his way to the people who traded their children – then the detective would contact Jenny again. No matter what she might think of him. And not just because he missed her and often dreamed about her. She had to see these pictures, had to decide if that little girl was the girl he was searching for.

Tuesday 10:19 p.m.
(15 hours and 41 minutes remaining)

She liked the white cat. And the white cat liked her. Before the make-up artist with the comforting smile even unpacked, she grabbed the loudly purring creature, carried it around the apartment cradled in her arms like a baby, stroking its belly and patting the top of its head. Hoffmann was pretty sure the cat was smiling, too.

Birte had an ornate, old-fashioned dresser in her bedroom with an oval mirror framed in dark wood resting above locked drawers – the make-up artist placed her tools there. The ones that would transform a father of three who could never physically hurt his children into someone who raped his daughter and documented it so that others could experience it as well. Among her tools, Hoffmann recognised pieces of most of his previous transformations. Plaster casts of his face that she'd taken. Gelatin and silicone and glue, the bottle of hair dye and the packs of contact lenses, the hairdresser's scissors, the comb, the electric razor, the bag of real hair and the wig needle, brushes and cotton swabs and a jar of something that looked like potato flour, but whose use he'd never really understood.

'The nose. We'll start there.'

At the right edge of the mirror, she taped up the face that would be his.

'You have a nice straight nose, Piet, but the one in the photo is dominated by a sharp bend in the middle. I'll model the clay until it's the same, a new nose that I'll put on top of your own.'

He remembered this, how she worked, from other masks for other missions. Remembered how she built up the edge of the clay and poured in plaster that would harden, broke off what needed to be removed and carved out the lump that would become his new facial feature, mixing in the silicone and pouring it into a mould and pressing it together. Bit by bit allowing him to meet another version of himself.

Tuesday 11:01 p.m.
(14 hours and 59 minutes remaining)

After a hectic but marvellous hour during which Birte finally identified the handle *Master* as Wolfgang Linden from Brienz, Switzerland, and *Uncle J* as Jacques Goor from Brussels, Belgium, and a couple of moments later found out that *Wasp/Geronimo* was none other than Claire Becker from Columbus, Ohio, and *Ramses's* real name was Thomas Van Vande from Florenville, Belgium, she made a decision. It was time. With eight out of ten members of the paedophile ring and six out of eleven of Hansen's other acquaintances tracked down, she would – very carefully – make contact with several police officers in the nations concerned. Hounded by time, they needed to prepare the coordinated arrests that would happen if Grens and Hoffmann managed to complete their tasks.

Tuesday 11:37 p.m.
(14 hours and 23 minutes remaining)

Ewert Grens barely heard the ping this time. Not because he was tired – though he was – but because he'd lost a little more hope with every new chat message sent to Lassie by one of the twisted individuals they *weren't* waiting for, and which he still had to muster the strength to reply to so that everything would seem normal.

Maybe that's why he didn't really react at first when, after a glass of cold water in the kitchenette and a few careful back stretches in front of the computer screen, he opened the message and read the sender.

From Onyx. The leader of the paedophile ring.

But slowly he understood.

The name that Birte had the most difficulty getting close to, which could only be discovered and neutralised in real life.

He's the worst of them all, their leader.

One of three participants in the meeting Hoffmann was trying to join.

If we grab the rest but not the leader, he'll just replace them with new friends.

The member of the ring who had enraged the self-controlled computer expert.

He'll start a new ring. New children will be raped!

The detective spun on his chair, turning with eagerness. Towards Birte. She needed to know. Besides, he needed her help to move forward. But she waved him away – did not have time, was herself at a turning point that meant success or failure.

He'd have to solve this on his own.

He needed to get closer to the faceless leader without arousing suspicion.

Wednesday 12:03 a.m.
(13 hours and 57 minutes remaining)

'His hair is darker. Not at all like yours. And that's good, Piet. Darkening hair is much easier and much faster than lightening it.'

She reached for the steel comb.

'But first we cut it. His hairstyle is almost a buzz cut. I'm guessing . . .

ten millimetres. Your jaw will look a little wider, but the one we're start-ing from is also quite strong, so the proportions will work.'

He usually closed his eyes while she worked her hands and scissors over his scalp, resting temporarily while someone else took all the responsibility, and he was relaxing his tense shoulders when she abruptly stopped working.

'Piet?'

'Yes?'

'What am I missing?'

'Missing?'

'You're always stressed. Like you're counting down the seconds. Or on the run. But today, I have never felt . . . this uneasiness.'

Then she did it again. Saw the man beneath the man.

'That's what you're radiating, Piet.'

'I wasn't aware of it. That I . . .'

'And it's very intense.'

'This . . . You're right. It's a twisted fucking world to live in, to adapt to. And I have to step into, act inside it, become an accepted member. Am I uneasy about it? More than I ever have been about anything before.'

She finished cutting, dyed his hair and eyelashes and eyebrows in the same brown shade, put in contact lenses. And took a plastic bag out of her suitcase.

'A few days' stubble. That's what he has in that picture – and that's all we have to go on.'

She opened the bag and emptied the contents onto the tray. Real hair, strands of black, brown, grey that she cut into tiny, tiny pieces, Hoffmann guessed two millimetres long.

'A mix – if you look at a man's stubble, study it carefully, everyone has a basic colour, but there are other colours present as well . . . Can you tilt your head back a little?'

She stroked his skin with the glue brush, his chin, cheeks, a bit down his neck, then clumped the hair she'd cut into a small ball, which she rolled from the bottom up until tiny hairs stuck.

'Feel it now, Piet.'

He rubbed a hand along the new surface. Just like his own three-day stubble, but in a darker shade.

'And it won't be visible? Say if I'm as close to someone as I am to you now – they still won't be able to see it? The glue?'

'If they do, I did a bad job. If you're worried it still looks shiny, I can use some of what you call my potato flour – the kind you put in your hair to make it fuller, do you remember those hairstyles? It's mostly used when we film under bright lights and then it *might* be visible, but this powder always takes care of that.'

Piet Hoffmann met the mirror image that was him and still not him. Comparing it to the photograph hanging beside. It should work.

'I need a picture with my new look. For the next step. Can you take it with your phone?'

'No.'

'No?'

'Not yet. We're not done.'

'It looks done.'

She pulled out another picture of Carl Hansen, held it towards him.

'If you lean really close. You'll see there's one detail left – the most obvious one of all.'

Wednesday 12:04 a.m.
(13 hours and 56 minutes remaining)

'Birte?'

'Grens, I don't have time.'

'If you don't take two minutes to listen to me now, go ahead and hunt all you want afterwards. It won't matter.'

'What are you talking about?'

'I'm talking about Onyx, the leader. He made contact with me – or with his friend Lassie who he thought he was writing to – a while ago and ordered new pictures of "slutty Katrine". More like demanded them. That was his tone. And I answered. Told him I'm on a business trip right now. In the US.'

'A business trip?'

'Well . . . since we want to meet him in person. Want to reel him in. Little by little. I thought since the stepfather works as a salesman, and I wrote "business trip", then it might seem natural if after the next time he contacts me I could write "since I'm in the US maybe we could meet up". And then I'll add that as soon as I get home, I promise to take care of his request. And Katrine will do exactly what he wants, while I take pictures.'

'But?'

'His response is taking a long time. I'm feeling uneasy. What if I . . . didn't do the right thing? Ruined our only chance? Wrote too much? Too little? Was too familiar? Too distant? Sitting here, waiting for an opening to ask to join them has taken over my whole mind. I want you to read it, Birte. Even though you don't have time. Decide if I need to send something again, adjust my tone, offer more, do whatever will get it past his radar.'

Wednesday I2:05 a.m.
(I3 hours and 55 minutes remaining)

'There. By the right eye. A scar, about a centimetre and a half long. Pretty faint, looks like he got it years ago.'

The make-up artist pointed to the photograph of Carl Hansen. Right between the right eyebrow and the temple.

'This is what I would look at first if I wanted to make sure image and reality were the same thing.'

Hoffmann saw it now. An elongated scar. The kind you pick up when you're young that sticks with you for the rest of your days. Hansen fell out of a tree or crashed his new bike or got hit by some opponent's hockey stick.

'It won't be a problem to copy it. All we need is this little jar and a tiny brush. The problem will be that it only lasts for a day. And then it needs to be redone.'

'I've got a long trip ahead of me. Once there I'll have to prepare a few things. And I'll need some sleep. So at least two days.'

'This is what we'll do: I'll give you the scar now, and you watch and learn exactly how to do it yourself. We take the picture, send it where it needs to go. You take a brush, sponge, some special glue and a small jar of scarring liquid. When you get there, buy make-up cleanser at any pharmacy and wash off what I'm putting there now. Then make your own scar.'

It was as simple as she'd said. At least when she did it. She put liquid on the brush, and as she gently applied it, it looked as if the skin contracted – appeared to be a real, inward-turned scar. On top, she dabbed the glue with a sponge and finally just normal powder. No one would think the disfigurement next to his eye wasn't a real one.

'OK – look straight into the camera.'

She took the first picture of a completely new face, and he in turn sent it on to a basement room on Istedgade. He'd soon be done with his portion of the preparations. And he hoped Grens and Birte had made it just as far.

Wednesday I2:06 a.m.
(I3 hours and 54 minutes remaining)

'The text looks good. The reply. You're better at this than you think, Grens.'

'And there's nothing I should change or –'

'Now all you need is patience. And whatever you do – *don't betray your uncertainty*. Do *not* send it again. Do *not* take it back. Let him read it, sit with it, ask his questions.'

Wednesday I2:07 a.m.
(I3 hours and 53 minutes remaining)

'By the way, Grens. Since you already interrupted me. We might as well talk.'

'Yes?'

'I've just finished making contact with the first round of law enforcement in the countries where we have secured identities. US, UK, Belgium, Italy, Netherlands, Switzerland, Germany.'

'So we risk destroying everything. If someone talks. Sends out a warning.'

'Yes. But *if* there's a coordinated operation to arrest everyone at the same time, then we have to start planning at some point. And we can't wait any longer.'

'If you say so.'

'Operation Sandman.'

'What?'

'That's what we're calling this operation from now on.'

'Like I said, Birte, if you say so.'

'Because our colleagues will expect an international collaboration to have a name. Because Sandman was written by Hans Christian Andersen, and this mission is led out of Denmark. And, if I'm being completely honest, because I was the one who named it, and I'm not very good at those things.'

'It's perfect.'

'I know there was Operation Sleipner, the first big operation in Sweden, not a real paedophile ring but customers who bought child pornography off websites using credit cards, as well as Operation Falcon, and those sound much better, but –'

'It's perfect, Birte. *Goodnight to you now.*'

She looked at him, surprised, listening to his off-tune singing.

'"Sandman" was the lullaby they sang at the funeral of one of the children I told you about when we first met.'

He sang again, loud and off-key.

'*Sweet dreams. Goodnight to you.*'

And for a moment, she could almost forget why they were sitting here, which is surely why she sang along.

Wednesday 06:24 a.m.
(7 hours and 36 minutes remaining)

'Come in for fuck's sake, man.'

This time, Piet Hoffmann was prepared for the fog of cigarette smoke that met him as he opened the door to the basement on Isted-gade, as well as the long gangster hug given to him by Copenhagen's most skilled fixer.

'Looking pretty handsome today. The buzz cut and the honking nose suit you.'

Sonny held his lit cigarettes, pointing into smoke that obscured but didn't hide what was there.

'A coffee? Maybe a drink? Or you still in a hurry?'

'Still in a hurry.'

'Next time.'

'Like I said: there's no next time. This is the last time.'

'And I said: that's what you always say.'

A fresh passport lay on one of the basement's many tables. Sonny picked it up, flipped through a little distractedly.

'New look. New name. New social security number. And I see you've gone and become a Danish citizen as well.'

As genuine as a fake passport could be. Signed and issued by the Danish authorities with the correct number and security markers. Piet Hoffmann looked at the picture of his own adjusted face. Carl Brian Hansen. He was now three years younger and had his birthday in January.

'And weapons? And the other stuff on that list that I could have done myself, but won't have time for?'

'When you land in San Francisco, take a taxi to a one-star hotel not far from the bridge to Oakland. Green Tortoise Hostel. The restaurant isn't great, but there's a pool table with not very cold Coca-Cola coolers and a few rickety shelves of old paperbacks. Grab a cue stick and hit the 4 and 5 balls back and forth until somebody shows up. Twenty centimetres shorter and forty kilos heavier than you and asks if you want to play a game of 9-ball. Stephen. California's Sonny. Not nearly as charming, of course, but almost as good.'

'Stephen?'

'Never say Steve. Or Stevie. Or you'll have to find somebody else to fix your stuff.'

'Your partner?'

'We usually trade services. I help Americans who need the kinds of things that can't be bought in the shops on Ströget, and Stephen helps out Scandinavians who aren't able to bring the tools of their trade onto a plane.'

Piet Hoffmann had a brown, bulky envelope in one of his jacket's inner pockets. Now he placed it on the empty surface the passport left behind.

'Just like you asked – only used dollar bills.'

'Where did it come from?'

'North Africa.'

'Guaranteed to be clean?'

'A human trafficker who is no longer with us. You don't need to know more than that. Unless you wanna tell me where the passport and my weapons come from?'

'You're right, my friend – I don't need to know more than that.'

Leaving the smoky basement room felt like taking a deep breath. But he was also hit by the realisation that seventeen of their twenty-four hours had expired. So when Piet Hoffmann stopped at one of the abandoned wicker chairs on Halmtorvet's winding cobblestones with the hot cup of coffee he'd refused when Sonny had offered, it was partly to cross out a few more items on his list – GANGSTER HUG, POTATO FLOUR, CITIZEN, BIRD GPS, USB CAMERA, SHORT-SLEEVED SHIRT, JAMMERS, TUNA – partly to make a phone call to the only one of the three of them far from finishing his task. And he sounded as impatient as he was.

'Yes, it's Gre—'

'How does it look? What's your status?'

'Please, go for a walk. Sleep. Anything that will make you leave me alone.'

'I need to know, Ewert. What is *our* status.'

'Not one damn bit better if you keep calling me all the time asking the same questions.'

'And what does that mean?'

'I've made contact. With the leader. Your target, Hoffmann. But no answer.'

'To your question about participating?'

'None at all.'

'Goddammit, we have to, *I* have to –'

'Don't you think I know that? If I heard the seconds ticking by before, I feel them now – heavy, nasty, stinging blows inside my gut.'

Wednesday 07:52 a.m.
(6 hours and 8 minutes remaining)

'Grens? You're talking too loud.'

'Sorry. Got a little excited.'

'So loud that I heard what you said.'

'I'll leave the room next time.'

'I mean – I understood the meaning of what you said. And I'm asking the same question as Hoffmann. But want a different answer. When, Grens, can you be ready?'

'I guess I have to –'

'Sit down.'

'I just promised to step out if I was getting wound up.'

'Listen – I'll only say this once. Hoffmann has done what he needs to. He's ready to go. I've done my job now – identified the last five in the chain. Handle *Easy* we now know comes from Wales, *Jan* from Holland, *Julia* and *Ingrid* and *Mariette* from three different states in the east or south of the US. All have been connected to verified addresses. The ones that remain are inside the ring itself, handle *Onyx* and handle *Redcat* with bouncing IP addresses; I need – as I warned you – more time to track them down. We hope Hoffmann will take care of Onyx in person, and we can simply cut the last one loose, when we can't wait any longer. Representatives of the relevant police authorities are on their way for a first meeting in Copenhagen, and I'm headed there in just a moment. To prepare for the coordinated arrests of these abusive parents who allow others to abuse *their own children*. So, Grens – now you have to figure out your fucking part, too!'

Wednesday 08:04 a.m.
(5 hours and 56 minutes remaining)

It was at this point that Ewert Grens usually slammed his hand onto a table or cupboard or swiped at a hanging lamp or at whatever happened to be in the way of his unbridled rage. Around the time he usually opened his office window and roared into an uncomprehending police station courtyard. But now he just sat in his chair with his back to Birte. Completely still, completely silent. Totally empty.

They were right.

He'd blazed ahead – first convincing the Danish police and then the Hoffmann family to follow the path that led from two little girls' graves. And now that they had – driven by various forces – come so far, so close, it was his fault alone that they'd go no further. Eighteen of twenty-four hours had passed since they split up and took on their respective investigative roles, giving Hoffmann a reasonable chance to be in place by the time the most violent members of the paedophile ring met in real life and traded children with each other.

13-11-2019 08:15:43 Message from 133438297: *Perfect. And I expect . . .*

But it was then – as the cop who never gave up was doing just that – the reply he was waiting for arrived.

What they were all waiting for.

Contact with the leader of the closed ring.

13-11-2019 08:15:51 Message from 133438297: *. . . violence. More this time. Much more.*

Ewert Grens didn't notice he had turned red and started to tremble.

But not out of anger. But from anxiety. Needing to do the right thing. Or rather, make no mistakes.

His hands shook so much that when they landed on the keyboard he couldn't press hard enough and had to try again in order to answer.

13-11-2019 08:19:51 Message from 238437691: *No problem. First thing when I'm back.*

13-11-2019 08:22:12 Message from 133438297: *Back?*

13-11-2019 08:24:40 Message from 238437691: *From that business trip I mentioned. Actually in US right now.*

Slowly closing in.

The faceless meeting the faceless.

With a reply that could either open a secret door a little wider – or close it forever.

He knew he'd never been very good at striking the right note in his dealings with other people, neither the sick nor the healthy. And after asking Birte about the last message he'd realised she was like him, lacking a social compass. A good, intelligent woman, easy to like, hard-working with a thirst for justice, but without finely tuned emotional antenna. Just like the other computer expert he'd cajoled into joining this investigation, young Billy in Stockholm.

Ewert Grens needed to reason this out, talk to someone with an intuitive insight that could open up the human psyche, someone who could guide him towards the right formulations – the key that would unlock this. But he didn't know many others. And the few who could have helped him, who had that ability to enter into other people, were impossible to ask. Both Sven, who had almost too much of just that kind sensitivity in him, and Erik Wilson, his boss who had a solid understanding of human behaviour, had to be kept in the dark so they wouldn't find out where he was and why.

Two male friends. That was all.

There had been a few more women. Anni, whom he continued to talk to even after she was at the nursing home, had always answered in her own way, but now lay silent in her grave. Laura, who helped him break out of his own prison and was soft even though the job she did was one of the most inhumane a person could do, cutting into corpses, but he could hardly call her now after two years of silence. Lena, Bengt's widow since he was blown up in a morgue during a trafficking investigation – Ewert met her fairly regularly, and she understood people, but that also felt wrong. This was her deceased husband's world, and it was Ewert Grens's job as her husband's best friend to protect her from it. Then there was Jenny from the cemetery, who he missed a little, and who didn't want to see him again. And finally Hermansson of course, the best of them all, who had finally answered her phone the other day, who had now changed her number to avoid him. She would have been perfect. Could have figured this out perfectly. Known exactly what to write and how.

Those were the only ones he had.

He was back where he started. Alone.

As the seconds ticked by while he struggled to find words sufficient to create an opening for an invite for himself – that is for Lassie, who was Hoffmann – to the meeting which would determine everything.

Wednesday II:44 a.m.
(2 hours and I6 minutes remaining)

He'd gone with her to Kastrup Airport, followed her into the departure hall, and when she turned on her way through the security checkpoint and waved, Piet Hoffmann waved back. To the make-up artist who – because Sonny was wrong – would never again transform him into someone else.

Almost twenty-two hours.

He was standing surrounded by travellers in constant motion as they repacked overweight suitcases or exchanged money into bright-coloured currencies they'd never seen before or stuffed liquids into sealed plastic bags or just looked at each other during their long farewells.

And not a word from Grens.

Wednesday II:44 a.m.
(2 hours and I6 minutes remaining)

Silence. The only answer he had received.

Ewert Grens stared at a computer screen, but it refused to meet his gaze. Updated the chat page again, again, again. Made sure the network was connected. Opened the tab for 'sent' to make sure that last message really had headed off like it should.

And still – that cursed silence.

Wednesday 2:00 p.m.

Deadline. Time had run out.

Still no answer.

Onyx, the leader they were hunting, who was everything according to Birte, was still absent. Maybe he'd guessed, become cautious, retreated into the anonymity of the network. Perhaps it was Grens himself whose wording had warned him.

It was over.

Their struggle to track an anonymous person had been in vain.

They wouldn't make it to the meeting.

He was no longer on the trail of the girl with the blue butterfly in her hair.

Wednesday 6:02 p.m.

It finally arrived – but four hours *after* the deadline. The next message.

13-11-2019 18:02:09 Message from 133438297: *OK*.

And Grens hesitated. Was it even worth replying? Risking the other arrests for a man that could never be reached? No matter how important Birte might think it is?

13-11-2019 18:02:15 Message from 133438297: *Have a pleasant journey*.

But when the second message arrived – *pleasant journey* – the only contact so far that didn't contain explicit orders for child sexual abuse, it was as if Grens's energy returned.

His courage. To at least try.

He pushed his note of prepared statements aside and answered as simply as he could.

13-11-2019 18:06:32 Message from 238437691: *Thinking: while I'm here, maybe meet?*

13-11-2019 18:07:04 Message from 133438297: *We are not supposed to.*

13-11-2019 18:07:52 Message from 238437691: *But maybe now – will take many years until my next US trip. Possible?*

Ewert Grens was no longer shaking. Because time had already closed the only door that led to the leader of the paedophile ring.

Thursday 2:09 a.m.

It took eight hours. Grens had walked several laps around the city. Eaten. Packed his bag and warned Birte of a final run-through the following morning in her office in Copenhagen, on his way home. Ate again. When the peculiar reply arrived, in the middle of the night.

14-11-2019 02:09:44 Message from 133438297: *What is your home like?*

What did that mean?

Some kind of password?

A test?

Or just as simple as it seemed?

Like Birte earlier, Ewert Grens didn't have much choice. He had to keep going until this was truly over. And he had to take risks. By writing the only thing he was sure of. That they wouldn't have shared these things with each other.

14-11-2019 02:12:15 Message from 238437691: *I don't know anything about YOUR home.*

For the first time, the next reply arrived immediately.

14-11-2019 02:12:32 Message from 133438297: *But I know all about yours. Describe it.*

Yes, it *was* a test.

Could the ringleader, whose confidence Grens still hoped to gain, know anything about how Hansen lived? Have information that could remain hidden until they – if ever – decided to meet, socialise?

14-11-2019 02:13:53 Message from 238437691: *I live in Denmark. A town called Lærdal.*

14-11-2019 02:14:05 Message from 133438297: *More.*

14-11-2019 02:14:46 Message from 238437691: *In the city centre. Above a small bakery.*

14-11-2019 02:15:04 Message from 133438297: *More.*

Grens exhaled, inhaled. He had to proceed very carefully. And so far he'd had just enough luck in order not to fall flat on his face. He'd actually been there. Inside Hansen's home. Several times, in fact, gathering batches of evidence based on Birte's instructions.

14-11-2019 02:15:58 Message from 238437691: *Grey facade. Entrance from courtyard. Three rooms.*

Was that enough?

A computer-savvy individual could find out that much if they knew Hansen's true identity. But the inside? Then they would have to have been inside. And that was impossible – according to Birte's summary, they had never met.

When the next reply failed to arrive – as if the faceless man at the other end was considering whether or not to go forward – Grens made a decision.

Ask the question. Now. The one that this was all about.

14-11-2019 02:22:33 Message from 238437691: *I did what you asked. Revealed myself. Am I welcome?*

The detective superintendent read those three short sentences over and over again.

While he waited.

And waited.

And waited.

For the computer's ding.

The reply.

14-11-2019 02:47:24 Message from 133438297: *OK. You can meet three of us. Santa Maria, California. Thursday. Noon. Preskier Park by the pond with the little fountain.*

Yes. Yes!

Detective Superintendent Ewert Grens was in.

That is to say, paedophile Carl Hansen was in.

That is, infiltrator Piet Hoffmann was in.

Thursday. Noon. Preskier Park by a pond with a small fountain.

Ewert Grens's effervescent joy bubbled up from deep, deep inside, probably from the same place where anxiety had just struck him hardest earlier. It was spontaneous and heartfelt and made every tense muscle relax. Until reality struck him. Check-in, the flight across the Atlantic and then coast to coast across the US, customs, then the pick-up that he suspected Hoffmann had arranged, from there another drive into a city called Santa Maria, maybe even some sleep. Those extra thirteen hours that it had taken Grens to solve his part of this mission were exactly what Hoffmann had needed to get there in time.

It was too late.

Thursday 2:54 a.m.

'Hoffmann? Grens here.'

'Detective?'

'I have good news and bad news.'

'The good first.'

'I . . . Where are you? There's a lot of noise.'

'Outside. Lots of people and noise.'

'So, I got us a way in. You're welcome inside. *You* are invited to their fucking meeting. You'll be able to meet three of them. Including the one we want – the leader.'

'And the bad news?'

'That I'm calling you half a day too late. And I realise what that means.'

Thursday 2:56 a.m.

'Grens? Can you hang on a second? I have to do something. Don't hang up.'

'What are you doing?'

'A security check. Going through a metal detector.'

'Already on the way home? Copenhagen or Stockholm?'

'San Francisco International Airport.'

'San . . . Francisco?'

'Just got off the plane. Nice and warm, not at all like Danish weather.'

'You're . . . Hoffmann – you're *there*?'

'I had the ticket. I was at Kastrup on another errand. And thought how shit it would be if you actually managed to get this done, and I was too far away to take advantage. I took a chance. On you, Grens.'

Thursday 3:02 a.m.

'Birte?'

'Yes?'

'Were you asleep? Still in Copenhagen?'

'I was home bribing my cat with some tuna and some ball throwing, now I'm walking back to the National Police Station. Have to keep preparing – I've invited law enforcement colleagues from seven nations, who need to think it's nice to come here even though the meeting will be cancelled immediately.'

'I have good news. And great news.'

'OK – and what does that mean?'

'I got in! We can go to their meeting.'

'But Hoff—'

'—mann is already there.'

'There?'

'In place. And with the time difference, if I'm counting correctly, it's now six on a Wednesday night in San Francisco. He'll make it! Birte, we got them . . . *goddammit, we got them!*'

Copenhagen, Thursday 3:48 a.m.
San Francisco, Wednesday 6:48 p.m.

As Piet Hoffmann took those last steps to the glass window and the staring customs officer, whose shirt was buttoned to the top and whose hair was perfectly parted, he became Carl Hansen. Now inside and outside needed to be one, no matter how wrong it felt, just as everything had to hold together tomorrow when he met them beside a pond with a fountain.

He pushed the fake passport through the square slot and smiled.

He'd always understood the conditions for an infiltrator – *only a criminal can play a criminal.*

He had accepted the most important rule in the life of an infiltrator – *always alone, only trust yourself.*

Even when it came to the very worst kind of crime.

PART
5

Only the eyes of the vast sea reached here.

THE CAR THAT rolled past the United Airlines terminal smelled strongly of plastic and leather. Newness. Normally, he would have pre-booked through some rent-a-wreck company and driven out of San Francisco International Airport in the kind of regular-looking car that wouldn't attract much attention. Usually, he would have leased it as Piet Hoffmann, Piet Koslow, Peter Haraldsson, Verner Larsson or any one of the other names he had a valid passport and suitable background history for. But this was no usual situation, there was no time to build any story besides that of a Danish paedophile on a temporary business trip to the US, and that was why he signed with Carl Hansen's pointed handwriting and paid for a huge, shiny vehicle that was anything but discreet, with advertising for an international rental car company emblazoned across the rear window.

Sixteen miles north. In big-city traffic.

He'd visited this part of the United States only once before, but according to his map if he stuck to the edge of San Francisco Bay he'd soon be in sight of the bridge to Oakland. And as West Coast jingles played over the radio, the sun beat down warmly and he rolled down his window, it hit him again. The cleavage. The shame. The awareness inside every cell of what the organisation he was here to infiltrate actually did. At the same time there was another awareness, which was why he felt so alive in a way that made his other life seem like a dry husk.

Presence filled him. Emptiness was banished by adrenaline.

This was what he'd been missing the whole time. What he fought against every single day. Tried his best to seek out in that other world. The strength to resist criminals or cops who came offering just one more time. The strength to be happy with Zofia, his children, his normal life.

The one-star Green Tortoise Hostel was balanced a bit precariously in that San Francisco way along a steeply sloping hill somewhere between the financial district and Fisherman's Wharf. Hanging, unconcerned, down over the next street. And Sonny was right. The shabby restaurant, the pool table, the Coca-Cola coolers and the rickety shelves of old paperbacks stood just where he said they would. He followed the instructions, picked up a pool cue and chalked the tip haphazardly then started hitting ball numbers 4 and 5 back and forth in an unfocused way. It didn't take long. Before confident steps approached from inside the restaurant. A new pool cue, also chalked, and someone who gestured in a way that might mean 'How about a game, you and me?'

Piet Hoffmann smiled as politely as he could.

'I'm sorry. I'm waiting for another player.'

'No.'

'Yes, you'll need to move, I'll –'

'– bond a little with a new friend named Stephen.'

Hoffmann looked at the other player.

A woman.

Short and round – that much fitted.

'Stephen?'

'Stephen. Never Steve. Or Stevie. Otherwise you'll have to find some other idiot to help you. Do you have a car?'

'Yes.'

'There's a Ford pickup parked just outside the entrance. Red. I'm leaving in five. Follow me.'

Then she was gone. The pool cue rolled slowly across the table, balanced precariously just like the whole building, hanging off the far edge. He grabbed a lukewarm can out of the soft-drinks machine and hurried down steps, covered in a thick carpet that hadn't seen a vacuum in a long time.

She drove fast.

He had to push both himself and the rental car to keep up as she swerved without warning onto Bay Bridge and over churning waters towards Oakland, then eastwards at high speed on major roads that became smaller roads that became narrow streets in a city called Walnut Creek. Then she finally parked. In an area where residential homes gave way to fenced-in factories. Next to a factory's high chain-link fence topped with rolls of barbed wire stood a simple – though not what you would call well kept – house with a lawn that looked like a bath towel.

She didn't even turn round, just headed straight inside, leaving the front door open behind her, sure that he'd follow.

'Here. Down in the basement.'

A short spiral staircase and a narrow corridor, which led to the house's garage.

'Welcome.'

Inside the oil-smelling garage, framed photos hung on the filthy walls. Stephen in uniform. And other photos with a man in similar clothes.

'Two tours in Iraq, both of us. That handsome man with the moustache is my husband Jerry. He's the one taking care of the kids upstairs.'

She pointed to the roof of the garage. The unmistakable sound of children messing around.

'That was the end of it. Have to believe in a system to make it, right? But we made contacts. And we took those with us.'

A garage that was never home to vehicles. The smell of oil had nothing to do with car engines. It was gun oil. The entire area was crowded with locked boxes of various sizes. She opened one of the smaller ones.

'"Carl Hansen", you said?'

'Yes.'

'If that's true then my husband runs faster than I do. But this is yours, right?'

At the top lay a piece of paper. And she ticked it off as she handed him the contents.

'Radom, Polish pistol, with fourteen bullets in the magazine, leather shoulder holster. Hunting knife with wooden handle, double-edged, leather shoulder holster.

He grabbed what had always been his standard equipment, could already feel those two holsters resting against his shoulders.

'And here's a miscellaneous bag from your shopping list.'

She dug into the wooden box, which was painted in military green.

'Five untraceable burner phones. Look like they usually do. Take these? And here, the jammers with timers, strong signal that's guaranteed to find the frequency you need turned off – blacks out everything. Then, this, the world's tiniest GPS tracker with a couple of weeks' battery life in it – twenty-four by fourteen millimetres and nine measly grams. And finally, when it comes to micro-cameras with built-in microphones, this is probably the one I like the best – it has a motion detector and records as soon as someone waves in front of the lens.'

He lifted the jammer, which was similar to ones he'd used before. But the GPS didn't take up any more space than a SIM card, and the microcamera was an exact copy of a regular flash drive.

'It also works as a normal flash drive. In case anybody gets curious. So the pictures you asked for are already loaded on it. Never would have believed you were the type – you don't look it.'

Never again let the rage inside take control.

Never allow your surroundings to determine who you are.

The first rules of the infiltrator. But this time there were none.

This time he really couldn't follow them.

He couldn't stand there and be judged as . . . *that.*

'*And I'm not the type.* That's why I need all this! Do you understand that?!'

She looked at him. Nodded after a while, slowly.

'I deliver the shit my customers ask for so long as they pay me – we need the money. But I feel a whole lot better now. I'll even throw in a few extra magazines with your purchase. Shoot every one of them. First the prick, then the forehead.'

Four full spare magazines for the Radom pistol. Piet Hoffmann placed them in his bag with the other stuff and handed over a stack of tightly rolled banknotes.

'What we agreed on.'

She didn't count it. There was an old-fashioned tin box on one of the shelves near the garage door; she lifted the lid, dropped the money inside.

'And Sonny?'

She actually wanted to know.

He wondered where they'd met, how these shadowy people from every part of the world found each other and started working together.

'Seems to be the same as always.'

'A good man. Still smoking?'

'Non-stop. Surrounded by a fog. Cigarillos mostly, I think.'

'I've told him he should stop. It'll kill you.'

When they got upstairs again Hoffmann took her hand, thanked her for the help, and caught a glimpse of her husband and children in what must be the kitchen. A metal prosthesis was attached to the once handsome and uniformed man's right knee; a landmine, probably a high explosive. A life changed completely from one moment to the next. Just like the life of a little girl who had been led away by a stranger's hand.

Sometimes it really was that clear. And the woman in front of him saw that he saw.

'Yep, what can I say? If the system doesn't work for you, you have to become the system. And as for you? Make sure you do what I said: shoot those fuckers, down then up.'

The house next to the belching factories and high barbed-wire fences shrank slowly as he wound his way out of the narrow streets that all looked alike. He left the residential area of Walnut Creek, but stayed on the Oakland side, searching for the mall former officer Stephen described as enormous, which should be located in San Leandro and offer everything he was missing.

It *was* enormous. A city within a city. And it *did* have everything.

He parked and walked inside among hundreds of other shoppers wearing the face of Carl Hansen, but still in Piet Hoffmann's clothes. When he exited seventy-five minutes later, long trousers had been exchanged for knee-length khaki shorts, hunter's jacket and white T-shirt were now a blue-checked short-sleeved shirt, black boots now sockless feet in brown sandals. He wore a watch with a red face that was a copy of the one in the abuse photos, a similar gold ring, glasses with frames in the same brown shade and of the same brand as in the wedding photo Grens had taken from the Danish family's home, and a rough silver necklace identical to the one in the picture from Hansen's driving licence.

At the far end of the parking lot a couple of virtually empty rows unfurled. He drove the car there, turned off the engine, and took out the handwritten list to cross off what had been left to do in his far too short prep time. ~~GANGSTER HUG~~, ~~POTATO FLOUR~~, ~~CITIZEN~~, ~~BIRD GPS~~, ~~USB CAMERA~~, ~~SHORT-SLEEVED SHIRT~~, ~~JAMMERS~~, ~~TUNA~~. He jumped over to the passenger seat and folded down the sun visor, which had a mirror on the back. He examined the curvature of the nose, which looked just as natural as the make-up artist had promised, ran a hand over the multicoloured hairs of his stubble, still as firmly glued to the skin as before – combined with the buzz cut and the custom eyebrows and nut-brown contact lenses, plus the clothes he'd just bought, he looked like the man he was supposed to be.

Almost.

Hansen's clearest characteristic had started to fade. The scar. By the right eye, between the eyebrows and the temple. The make-up artist had warned him that he'd need to redo it.

Piet Hoffmann grabbed the make-up cleanser from one of the plastic bags and started to gently wipe away the fifteen-millimetre-long skin incision. The brush, sponge, special glue and the small jar of scarring fluid he'd brought with him from Copenhagen – now it was up to him to make the final adjustments to appear just like the paedophile whose body he would work through over the next twenty-four hours.

HE TURNED THE steering wheel. Quickly, abruptly. The skid was loud and out of control. The rental car swiped against the steel railing of US Route 101 and then slid over three lanes on its way into a twenty-four-hour gas station. He stopped there. The engine was running, and he was a good distance from the gas pumps and people and car wash when he – just as he had a few hours earlier – flipped down the sun visor and stared into the mirror.

I am Carl Hansen.

I rape a little girl who is nine years old and then sell pictures of it.

I'm going to a park in Santa Maria to hang out with other people who also rape their children and enjoy talking about it, comparing tiny bodies, maybe sharing tips on how best to go about violating them.

Piet Hoffmann remained in the driver's seat, staring out over the asphalt of the gas station, trying to figure out what exactly he was doing here. Why speeding south through a dry, hot November California day, without even realising it, let alone planning it, he'd suddenly veered off the highway without even slowing down.

He stared at the mirror image, and it stared back.

That uncertainty again.

Or maybe disgust.

Even hatred.

He didn't have a fucking clue.

He felt out of his depth.

He was going to infiltrate for the first time without his emotions on his side.

This uncertainty was not related to his ability to overpower them. The violence perpetrated by this group had no connection to the violence he himself was an expert at. Once he had the leader's identity, he would strike – knew that he could keep three paedophiles under control with weapons and muscle power. That was not the source of his agony. It was in his disgust. In his doubts at how long he could play this role inside this body, when he only wanted to escape from it.

When, half an hour later, he pulled back out onto the highway, it was with no more clarity than he'd turned in there with. He increased his speed and halfway to his destination, at the point where the bridges and tunnels intersected with a town called Salinas, he left the monotonous asphalt for a much more beautiful route along the Pacific coast, until one of Santa Maria's many white churches appeared out of the darkness with its pointed roof, chiming three times. Time to check in at the hotel, make his final preparations and get some rest after a night spent on a plane and before tomorrow's meeting with those he'd come here to destroy.

PRESKIER PARK WAS a flat piece of grass that had been portioned out into a reasonably large square in a well-planned city. Skinny conifers leaned against each other as protection from a busy highway, park benches sat in their shadows, gravel paths led to small playgrounds. And somewhere in the middle, like a beating heart in a body forced to rest, a spraying fountain loomed over a well-sized pond.

Piet Hoffmann sat down on a rock, which seemed to have been placed there as intentionally as everything else.

Half an hour left. A couple of hundred metres to go.

He watched the children, watched them run and climb up and down a wooden tower connected by rope bridges and steep logs. He guessed seven or eight years old, girls and boys playing freely, all around the same age as the children he'd come here to save, who weren't at all free, who had been forced into another reality.

He had a mission.

And he wasn't sure he was ready for it.

Afraid he might take a wrong step.

Like the man with a shiny metal prosthesis from the knee down, tall and proud in his uniform in those framed photographs, now in charge of running his home while his wife hawked illegal weapons to strangers.

That man had also had an assignment. And took a wrong step.

Where is *my* landmine?

Who has hidden it?

When will I take a step and risk losing everything?

He got up from the rock that had looked hard, but was actually comfortable, walked slowly, gravel crunching beneath his sandals. Lunchtime. Work colleagues sharing a pizza away from the stress and routines. Groups of children on excursions with plastic cups and packed lunches sitting on colourful blankets. A young couple lying in the grass, holding hands. Togetherness. A very different kind than what he'd been invited here for, invited in through Grens's anonymous chats.

He approached the pond with the fountain, trying to make his arms hang as naturally as possible from his tense shoulders. Observed. Assessed. He could tell that much. Who? Where? He surveyed his surroundings like always, without seeing.

Until one of the men sitting in the grass, pouring steaming coffee out of a checked Thermos, rolled up his blanket and packed his hamper. A short, stocky man with a receding hairline. When he reached the broad stone edge of the pond, he sat down and leaned forward, dipping both his hands, rinsing them off. And at the same time glancing over – Piet Hoffmann didn't need to turn round to know what he was doing – in Carl Hansen's direction.

So that's what the leader looked like.

Forty-five years old.

White.

Looked like a petty bureaucrat.

A little younger than Hoffmann had expected – but it might fit.

'Hello.'

He'd finished rinsing his hands, stood up and almost crept over to Hoffmann, now stood right next to him while they both pretended to admire the beautiful park.

'I suppose it's me you're waiting for.'

But he didn't sound as Hoffmann had expected. A high, boyish voice, not at all like a man who was used to being in charge. This could be someone else here for a completely different meeting. With no connection at all to destroying children.

'I don't really know. That depends. Who are *you* waiting for?'

The man laughed. Again like a little boy. A gurgling, carefree sound.

'Good that you're careful. I am, too.'

Then it came again, that silly giggle, just a little too loud.

'If you turn around. Toward me. Look at me.'

Piet Hoffmann did as he was asked.

'Mmm.'

The leader was considerably shorter than Hoffmann. And because they were so close, it must have looked strange, one man's head bent low trying to look down and the other angling his whole head back to look up.

'Mmm.'

The humming.

'Mmm.'

Hoffmann wasn't sure if it was supposed to seem threatening, worrying or just thoughtful. Or – perhaps the shorter man wasn't even aware of it as he carefully examined Carl Hansen.

'Yep. Seems about right.'

'Excuse me?'

The man took a folded piece of paper from his shirt pocket and unfolded it.

'You.'

A photograph of Carl Hansen. The real Carl Hansen.

They really did know.

Not one of the portraits that Grens grabbed from the available government registers or personnel files from workplaces. Nor a photo of someone waiting passively in a studio or in a booth. This one seemed to have been taken from a distance and was more alive. As if the leader had taken it himself with decent magnification.

'And – yes.'

'Excuse me?'

'I saw you wondering. And the answer is yes. The leader of our little group took this picture himself. Without his target knowing it. This applies to all our members. Complete information on their identity. Family situation. Housing. And – our own pictures to compare. Even though we aren't supposed to. The group should be . . . anonymous. But the leader likes playing it safe. There are those who don't share our interests.'

The chuckling, childish laugh. A little longer this time.

217

'And you – yes, you look exactly like the picture.'

Piet Hoffmann stood there in a mask he himself had doubted.

First, doubting if it was even needed – a new face was always a calculated risk, bits could fall off and betray the next layer, betray him. Then, if it did hold, he'd wondered if interior could become exterior.

But it *had* been needed. And it had held, he had held, so far.

'So hello. Again. I'm Lenny.'

The chunky, thin-haired man compared the photograph to the man in front of him one last time before folding it up. Then he held out his hand.

Until Hoffmann took it.

'Lenny? I thought . . .'

'. . . that I was Onyx. That was the point. I only performed the test based on information gathered by Onyx. He's even more careful than the rest of us.'

Lenny.

Piet Hoffmann looked at him, trying to remember Birte's summary.

You have ten children of your own.

You brag about having filmed forty rapes of other children in your medical practice.

A large bird with a long, thin neck landed gently on the pond's surface. Another one. And another. Hoffmann had no idea what they were called, but they looked so proud as they glided forward. As if the world were a simple, peaceful place.

'The time has come . . .'

The man raised his arm to look at his watch.

'. . . twenty past twelve. In two hours and forty-one minutes. Exactly three. At this address.'

He was still holding the photo, now he turned it over. In pencil, on the back, stood seven lines of detailed directions.

'It's very beautiful there. And very isolated. By the way . . .'

'Yes?'

Now the overweight man stepped close again, bending his head back, studying him. While humming, like before.

'The scar?'

'Yes?'

'The one by your eye?'

'The one I've had a long time.'

'How did you get it?'

Piet Hoffmann tried to stand completely still.

Was this a new test?

Did they know something they shouldn't?

Or – was it no longer whole? Had the scar make-up he'd done in the car started to fade?

'How . . . did I get it?'

'Mmm.'

'A really nasty fight. With a short, overweight man. He ended up in the hospital because he asked too many questions. And he wasn't nearly as good at fighting as me.'

The paedophile who called himself Lenny remained where he was, close.

Staring. Humming.

Hoffmann stared back.

Had he gone too far?

Had he just given himself away?

Had he . . . ?

Laughter. That crazy, fucking laugh. As Lenny broke the silence.

'That was really, really funny. I like you.'

Lenny handed over the paper with the picture of the real Carl Hansen on the front and seven handwritten lines on the back.

'Well – welcome then, just follow those simple directions, and all will go well. We'll . . .'

That laughter again.

How could a forty-five-year-old man sound like a ten-year-old boy?

'. . . have ourselves a very nice evening. Both adults and children.'

A VERY BEAUTIFUL, very exclusive house straight from some sweet American drama. That's what it reminded him of. In this ugliest of realities.

Piet Hoffmann drove the rental car slowly along a lonely, winding gravel road.

Gentle wind and the occasional bird call in the distance.

Otherwise deserted.

Several hundred metres after he passed the last house, the world seemed to open up. Sky. Sea. As if he were driving straight into infinity. It was impossible to go further west in this part of the world. There among the cliffs at the far end of the California coastline, just a few long steps from the dark, troubled waters below and beyond that on their far, far edge Japan and China.

The perfect place for someone who wanted to be left alone.

Wide-open spaces with nature as privacy and an eternally sound-proof environment.

The wide iron gate slid open as Hoffmann neared it, and he rolled into a natural landscape of wild grass with dark green bushes covered with small, bluish-red berries, while surveillance cameras captured their surroundings from every angle. He didn't even have time to turn the engine off before the short, fat man calling himself Lenny opened the entrance to this magnificent house and headed down the front steps.

'You found it.'

'I had very good directions.'

'Great. We aren't that used to having guests. *Adult* guests, that is.'

That accursed laugh. Shrill. Giggling. He leaned over in a deliber-ately exaggerated bow, sweeping an arm towards the front door.

'Welcome.'

Piet Hoffmann was to go first and the springing wood complained softly as his host followed just a step behind. A long, wide hall opened into a living room with high ceilings and outstanding panoramic windows that for the second time in just a few minutes made him want to step straight into eternity. Only the eyes of the vast sea reached here.

'Who lives here?'

'Nobody.'

'Nobody?'

Hoffmann looked around.

The interior matched the exterior – expensive, exclusive, tastefully furnished.

A dream house. With no occupants.

How the hell could they afford that?

A gold-coloured, antique metal drinks trolley held half-full bottles and fragile drinking glasses. The man called Lenny poured himself a smoky whiskey and turned to Hoffmann.

'What are you drinking?'

'Same as you.'

'Good. Still careful.'

The boyish giggle was shorter now, he had more to say.

'*Sanctuary.*'

'Excuse me?'

'You asked who lives here and no one lives here – because this is a sanctuary. For the group, people like us. The misunderstood.'

Sanctuary. The misunderstood.

In two words, their whole unreality became real.

'There's another room I want you to see.'

The other exit from the large living room led to the kitchen, also something from an American movie, a kitchen island in its centre and a view from the sink towards all that endless blue outside, sky and sea, and as they continued through it, past the small dining area for shared corn-flake breakfasts, they stepped into a room that breathed with something different. With anxiety. This is where they took the children. A large bed in the middle with fluffy pillows and stuffed animals piled together. The accessories were lined up on a shelf, waiting. Dog leash, sex toys, piles of clothes in tiny sizes. But something was missing. The only thing Piet Hoffmann understood. And was completely assured was here, just like outside. The extended eye. What he too liked to use to predict an opponent's movements must be hidden in this room to preserve these rapes. The camera that recorded the film that would later be shared with the other members of the ring.

It didn't really matter.

The jammer, now sitting in the trunk of his car waiting for the moment when it was time to strike, would knock out not only this camera, no matter where it was, but all other surveillance cameras. But starting it right now, turning this world into a black void on the monitors those cameras were connected to, would create unnecessary suspicion. This visit was supposed to be perceived as normal.

One last, quick glance through the room.

Behind that painting? Maybe there, in that slightly darkened corner? Or sewn onto that round pillow adorned with plastic beads of various colours?

'And . . . your daughter?'

Lenny signalled that they should leave the room.

'Yes?'

'Will she be joining us?'

'Excuse me?'

'Did she come with you? It must be exciting to be nine years old and cross the globe from a tiny, cold country in Europe and arrive here to the sunshine state.'

'I'm . . . pretty sure I wrote you about that. In my conversation with Onyx. Surely I did, right? She and her mother stayed at home. This is a business trip. But, of course, I'll take care of all your requests as soon as I get home.'

'That's fine, I just – ah, you know, one can always hope. Right? You should know that we all talked about that little story you sent us last time. That series of nine pictures, the one where she's lying there and then you . . .'

Piet Hoffmann came so very close to punching him.

Almost couldn't stand it.

Almost dropped his role.

'. . . well, I think it was almost as good as that last one when she comes home from school and you met her and . . . or the time she was changing clothes to go to the beach and instead . . . you always have a . . .'

Now.

I'm going to hit him now.

I can't take it any more.

'. . . yes, a playful journey. From image to image. Peeling away the earnestness one step at a time towards a more natural encounter.'

Piet Hoffmann did not strike him. But he was sure the other man must have noticed how it took all his willpower to hold back his rage. They passed through the hall, which had been converted into an office, and Lenny noticed that his guest was staring.

'Our business centre.'

'Oh yeah?'

'Onyx and I sell these encounters. Not the group's pictures, those are of course sacred, but other things. Which we record here. Or some things we arrange that don't quite meet the quality suitable for our members – but those credit cards out there pay our considerable wages.'

Lenny giggled proudly.

'Big money, Lassie. Big, big, big money.'

The industry. Birte had mentioned it. Where most were like Hansen, the face he now wore. The Danish father who sold his nine pictures in the same series to a select few, then fifteen other pictures in another series, using his own child for a couple of thousand dollars here, a couple of thousand euros there. But she said there were also really big profiteers, who ran businesses with huge turnovers based on the children they molested.

'Another whiskey?'

'Thanks, I'm fine.'

'Mmm. Smart. Pace yourself. For the little ones.'

He let out another of his irritating boy giggles, while Hoffmann lingered near the office equipment. How much could two men like Lenny and Onyx make? How much was *big, big, big money*? He'd infiltrated gangs of human traffickers, drug barons, arms dealers, and thought he knew everything there was to know about the money that drove crime, but he had no knowledge of paedophiles, naked children – they too were part of the multi-billion-dollar industry of organised crime. He'd thought of it as perverts trading pictures one-to-one. Because he was naive? Ignorant? Or just didn't want to know?

'Lassie?'

Lenny signalled that they should continue walking.

'Yes?'

'Why the handle?'

'What . . . do you mean?'

'Well, I'm just wondering. A little curious. Like – does it have something to do with the dog?'

Carl Hansen's handle in the paedophile ring.

His handle.

And Piet Hoffmann didn't have a fucking clue.

The few preparations he'd made were a joke in a world that was all about survival. Back when he worked, really worked, as an infiltrator, by far the most extensive and time-consuming task he'd had was to create a backstory that could hold up against any conceivable question from the criminal network he sought to uncover. Anything that would make those he was there to hurt and disrupt perceive him as their equal, that would slowly gain their trust.

'Lassie?'

'Yes?'

And only then, when he had that foundation of lies, was he protected.

Now?

He hadn't even had time to learn the answer to the simplest question – *what is your name?*

'You're right. It's the dog from TV.'

'I knew it!'

'Katrine. My daughter. She saw some old episodes somewhere. Talked all day about Lassie this and Lassie that and . . . I thought it seemed appropriate.'

Lenny snickered, accepting the answer, even liking it.

Hoffmann's fabrication would hold a while longer.

'And you?'

'Yes?'

They were back at the fantastic panoramic window with its fantastic view, stood in silence for a while, drowning in the sea below until his host started talking again. But there were no more questions. More his own thoughts.

'So . . . I've been thinking a lot about what we do.'

'Oh, really?'

'Or – *how* we do it. If we all do it the same way.'

Piet Hoffmann tried to avoid answering. Was this a new test? Or just regular, easy-going conversation between paedophiles?

'You, Lassie – children don't really feel for real, they *think* they feel. We just dull their imagination for them, help them reshape their minds. That's what we do. Make them understand that they're safe. That their anxiety is the wrong state.'

Wrong state.

Piet Hoffmann forced himself to keep his eyes on the sea, only there.

You're putting your own fucked-up wrong state onto a child.

The sea. He had to look at the sea.

Because you are the child. Because you . . .

'So how do you do it?'

The man who called himself Lenny looked at him, smiled, it was worse than the laugh.

'How? What . . .'

Hoffmann tried to smile back.

'. . . do you mean?'

'What are *your* methods? To make Katrine stop imagining? To make her feel right?'

'It . . . depends. I use well . . . a couple of different ones.'

'There is only one.'

'Oh, really?'

'Substances. Nothing makes children relax more. Feel the love instead of anxiety.'

Hoffmann's smile ended. He couldn't do it any more. At the same time, the other man's smile changed, but for the opposite reason, it grew, into grotesque laughter again.

'Because anxiety, Lassie, never leads to love. What we give them makes them feel a pulsating love bomb in their chests. Such power! You explode! These are substances you have to try for yourself. Then you'll understand. And your photos, I promise, will be even better.'

The short, fat man looked at him triumphantly. He had conveyed what he'd been thinking about for so long, analysing, trying to put into words. Perhaps his greatest discovery. His own path to happiness.

Substances. Love bombs.

Piet Hoffmann shook.

I'll fucking make you feel their anxiety, you sick bastard. I will . . .

And here he was at last. After all those years, all those smart choices. At his limit, which would mean dropping a role for the first time during a mission. Beating someone just for the sake of it. Without caring about the consequences.

He tensed his whole body, turned round, about to raise his arm.

Then a sound interrupted him.

A sharp squeak outside the window.

He listened.

A light thump. Steps up the front stairs. A door opening behind them.

'Hello there.'

The man who passed by the hat shelf into the long hall was carrying a helmet and wearing a very tight black cycling suit that ended at his knees. The zip pulled up to the neck, and the pocket on the upper arm was large enough for a credit card and phone. On his feet were shiny cycling shoes with thick straps instead of the usual strings, and the cleats beneath the sole slammed hard against the lacquered floor.

The handbrakes on a racing bike. That was the squeak he'd heard.

'Welcome. Are you our Danish guest?'

The paedophile leader didn't look at all as Hoffmann had expected.

The age was correct, around sixty. But that was it. This man was fit, on the verge of athletic. Hairstyle, features, attitude, all elegant in some way, he could pass as the smooth, successful CEO of some major company.

'If you're Onyx, then you *know* who I am. Because *you* wrote the questions I got in the park.'

A nice, polite laugh. Not at all like Lenny's bizarre giggles.

'You're right. In a way, I did ask you that already in the park via my representative. And because you answered correctly, here we are. Three secret friends together at last.'

'And if I understood it correctly . . . also a fourth, right?'

'Meyer will be joining us later. He's just taking care of a few of our other guests. The younger ones.'

The polite, pleasant laugh was somehow even creepier than the bizarre one.

'I'm going to take a shower. Need to look my best for dinner with our fine society. It was a little windier than usual today, and I had to climb quite a few hills to get here.'

He unbuckled the straps of his clattering shoes, put a bicycle key and thin gloves in a wicker chair, opened a white cupboard, and took out a bath towel of thick terry cloth.

'If you have to be on the move – might as well exercise. Do you cycle, Lassie? You look like you're in great shape. For me, it's cycling and a lot of qigong. Breath. Energy. That's all we need.'

The shower must be at the other end of the hall, because that was where the fit, elegant man was headed.

'And intermittent fasting, that's very good, too.'

Halfway across the threshold he stopped, looking at his friends from the ring.

'I've tried to make Lenny understand. Exercise, fasting, NMN, Recital – these things help us rejuvenate our cells. Exercise and eating right. It's that simple. If you want to prolong your life.'

Then he continued into the bathroom and closed the door behind him.

The nameless leader of the ring. The whole purpose and target of his infiltration.

The sound of running water soon rushed through the house's pipes. The octagonal window high up on the bathroom door fogged up and became blurry.

While Hoffmann was stuck with what the man out there had left behind.

Pure in his body. Pitch-black in his soul.

Rejuvenate? Live longer?

Obsessed with staying alive – with a life that was all about mutilating the psyches of children.

Ninety years? One hundred years?

How many more children did he intend to destroy?

'WE ALWAYS CONCLUDE with a small glass of vodka – alcohol that's very pure – along with a thin slice of lemon at the edge of the glass. No unnecessary additives.'

This was the weirdest night of Piet Hoffmann's life.

Two paedophiles eating food meant to rejuvenate their cells while conversing about naked children and how to manipulate them – all the while a third man sat on the opposite side of the table and emptied the last shards of his mind in order to continue *playing* a paedophile.

Algae and beetroot salad, chickpea puree with lemon-marinated carrots, mango chutney with lime and coriander, kale chips with cashew dip, and special water from a special source.

Pure in body – pitch-black in soul.

The one who called himself Lenny didn't say much, nor did the one called Lassie. The one who called himself Onyx did most of the talking. This elegant man spoke politely, expressed himself graphically in a pleasant voice as he expounded on how one day the world would understand, that it had existed in every civilisation, and the time would arrive when the love between adults and children would be accepted.

And meanwhile they – while waiting – had to hide.

Hide their love.

Meet in temporary sanctuaries overlooking the sea.

Piet Hoffmann still felt confident in his mask. It was holding. He resembled the Carl Hansen they saw in the photo. Conversations, movements, attitudes would also work as long as he contained his rage. His first priority – at the risk of being exposed, losing everything he was here for, losing the children they were speaking about – was the picture he'd promised Grens and Birte. A photo of an as yet unknown man so they could start searching through facial recognition programs for a match.

That's why Hoffmann apologised and stood up from his seat at the antique dining-room table, stretching his arms over his head, while swinging his back gently.

'Lots of sitting, the flight, the car, the customer visits, and then more sitting during this amazing dinner. Have to get my blood flowing.'

Onyx nodded, as if allowing it, or perhaps agreeing it was wise to take care of your body. Hoffmann leaned forward, back, forward, back until what he had in his shirt pocket suddenly fell down onto the thick, soft carpet. A couple of credit cards, a car key, a phone charger and a flash drive. He apologised again, knelt down and picked up each object, and when he grabbed the flash drive, which had slipped beneath the flower-pot of a green palm, he turned the short side towards Onyx and lightly pressed the opposite side with his thumb. Three times. Three photographs with a micro-camera.

Piet Hoffmann sat down again, his joints looser but also his chest – one crucial task completed – still in time to taste a bit of that pure vodka with a thin slice of lemon, the one that was supposed to finish their meal. A toast with the two men across from him.

But Onyx never raised his glass – instead he pointed to the shirt pocket where Hoffmann had just placed his small pile of belongings.

'Can I see that?'

Hesitantly, Piet Hoffmann pulled out one gold credit card, from Danske Bank with Carl Hansen's name on it, a farewell gift from Sonny in his smoky Copenhagen basement, provided free of charge with the new passport.

'No. Not that.'

'No? What then . . . ?'

'The flash drive.'

'Why?'

'Just thought I'd take a look at it. Or . . . is that a problem for you?'

Hoffmann felt like screaming.

Yes. It's a fucking problem. Because it's a micro-camera being used as part of a police investigation. Because the last three pictures are of you.

'Nope. No problem.'

He pushed the flash drive across the table towards the waiting hand.

'Lenny – can you grab your laptop?'

A laptop that had lain among the others in the hall office was now placed between empty plates and drinking glasses in front of the leader of the paedophile ring.

'As I said. Just a look.'

The tiny piece of plastic that could remember so much.

Now it became one with Lenny's computer.

'Well . . . I'll be damned.'

Onyx stared silently at the screen in front of him, moving the mouse back and forth, scrolling through the images, stopping sometimes, then continuing.

'Have you seen this, Lenny?'

Piet Hoffmann just stared at the back of the computer. Without knowing for sure what memories this contained.

'You really have . . . Lassie, this is really good stuff! Different from what you've done with your Katrine – not in a bad way, not that, it's just nice to see other children. Brand-new children. Danish, I would guess? Scandinavian?'

Now he could circle round the table without being perceived as too eager.

Stand behind the two paedophiles, to see what they saw.

Breathe again.

Because Stephen had done her job. Or maybe it had been her war-injured husband. Ninety-four images of naked, fair-haired children were stored on that flash drive. If anyone were to come across it. Want to check him out. Question this version of Carl Hansen. They'd drown in a flood of child pornography before reaching the hidden camera.

The last pictures taken.

'Yes, all the kids are from northern Europe. I usually . . . It can get a little lonely in the hotel sometimes.'

'And the memory stick, you carried it with you – in this condition?'

The polite voice had its own way of modulating not only tone but also volume as it changed perspective. High and quiet meant an underlying threat – *as I said, just a look* – deeper and louder meant impressed – *well, I'll be damned* – now it switched back again, to high and quiet and threatening.

'You brought it with you? Into the country?'

So here they were. At the lie, which was once an infiltrator's tool that he had mastered as well as violence.

'Yes.'

'Through US customs?'

The lie he no longer believed in. And if he didn't – how could he make some-one else believe it?

'Yes. Hard-encryption. If some stupid customs agent wanted to take a look . . . I promise you, it would not have worked.'

'Mmm. And yet this *isn't* encrypted even a little bit now. Is it?'

A lie could only be true when both the teller and the hearer believed in it. And in order to do that, they had to recognise each other.

'It was.'

'Was?'

'Until I decrypted it. At the hotel, my first night. Couldn't wait. You know how it is.'

Onyx studied the images on the screen for a long time.

Examining them.

Until he seemed to make up his mind.

He ejected the flash drive, handed it over. Without scrolling further. To the end.

'Good. Good. Then maybe it's my turn . . .'

He smiled.

While Piet Hoffmann, as discreetly as possible, exhaled again.

They'd just taken one step closer to each other.

'. . . though only if you want, of course. I'll show you one of *my* latest. Another kind.'

The leader double-clicked on one of the documents on the screen and, for those few seconds it took to open, seemed almost touchingly proud.

'Not sending these out to the society until tomorrow, but you can take a peek in advance. Just like Lenny did yesterday.'

Lenny stood up straighter, prouder.

Trusted. Chosen.

They rearranged where they stood so that Hoffmann could step forward and watch between the gap in their shoulders.

Then he saw it, realised what was depicted.

'I switched the bowl several times. Tried plastic in different sizes and colours. Both for dogs and cats. But when I found this, well – the picture was perfect. Made of metal, and a little smaller than the others. It's a better scale for the girl doing such a good job eating out of it.'

The child was older than the others who were usually depicted. Hoffmann's own Hugo was eleven and this girl a couple of years more. She lay naked on her stomach on a concrete floor, truly eating out of the metal cat bowl.

'The toilet?'

He couldn't do it. Couldn't stand still.

'That way?'

The voice, controlled.

'Or maybe one on the second floor?'

His breathing, controlled. His movements, controlled.

What was rushing uncontrollably up from his feet and burning inside his throat *must must must* be controlled.

'It's just past the shower. Third door on your right.'

Hoffmann thanked him and tried to keep his strides a normal length despite his legs itching to hurry.

Calm down. *Calm down.*

He managed until the door was locked, then sank down onto the toilet lid. And wished it was possible to cry. Uncontrollably. But he couldn't. Couldn't allow it. Red eyes from weeping couldn't be masked.

One of his burner phones – Stephen had done a good job there too, the very smallest available – was taped to the inside of one of his thighs, as far up into his groin as possible.

'Piet?'

Zofia answered at the first ring. As if she were sleeping with her phone in her hand, her fingertips resting against the answer button.

Her voice – he wanted to hold her, lie close to her, touch her warm skin.

'Piet, what –'

'I can't do this.'

'Where are you?'

'I give up. First time ever. I'm just empty – have nothing, Zo, there's nothing left.'

She let him speak.

About a girl who had turned thirteen, too old, but while she was waiting to be replaced by another child, they humiliated her instead, laid her down naked next to a metal cat bowl. About a man who called himself Onyx, who during their meal, between the healthy dishes, had explained that thanks to the income from online sales he had no need to work, but had still recently started a job at a school for autistic children because that was a good place for recruitment.

Talk until he really had emptied out everything.

And she, in turn, then gently began to speak, almost whispering, about how he *must must must* keep going, hang on to the version of himself that they were allowed to see. Just a little while longer. For the children in the pictures. For all the other children who would be harmed by the members of the ring. Because they were sick fuckers who would leave their mark upon every child every day of their lives.

He listened. Knew.

Knew she was talking about herself. About what she never let him see despite the fact that they had been so close for so long, despite the fact that he'd pleaded with her.

'I've . . . never really told you. How it was.'

But now she did. Trusted him. As he trusted her.

'When we met, Piet. I think you . . . or, I *know* you remember. My body. My sexuality. How I had no boundaries. That's what you said once. That you liked it. But still, it scared you. Sometimes . . . yes, all of it. And sometimes I just shut down, shut you out. Always on my terms. *My terms*. Damaged. That's what I was. What I still am. But I trust you now. My body trusts you. It understands without me having to understand how touch can be . . .'

She cried, never finishing the sentence.

The talk he had always wanted to have, he now lacked the strength to hear.

'Zo, I . . .'

He didn't cry with her. Resisted it. Despite not being able to stand it.

'I'll tell you more. All of it. When you get home. I know how these kids *don't* think. They don't think, because they don't dare. Understand. Feel. And if one day they're lucky – maybe they will also meet their own Piet. But until then . . . Piet – destroy it! Destroy that fucking ring! For my sake.'

Her breath. He could hear it.

'I had no one to save me. Save them. Do you hear me, Piet?'

He kissed the phone twice as they always did, always an even number, and hung up with her voice inside him.

He flushed the toilet. Let the tap run for a while. Rinsed off the traces of a man who was empty.

He then transferred the images from the hidden camera on the flash drive to his phone and sent them to Grens. Onyx now had a face. Now, through their various means, in reality and in the digital world, they could search for his name.

When Hoffmann returned to the dining-room table, the photograph of the girl on the concrete floor had been replaced by Carl Hansen's latest series of images, which at this moment meant it was *his* series of images, and it was hard to decide if it was Lenny or Onyx who'd sunk more deeply into them, looked the happiest.

'What room are you in?'

A question that didn't matter. Small talk. Between paedophiles.

That wasn't the case.

Piet Hoffmann perceived something else.

'When you share your daughter with the rest of us? Where do you take these nice photographs?'

The leader's questions sounded like an interrogation.

Even more control.

Piet Hoffmann hadn't even seen the whole series. The first photo of a nine-year-old girl that Grens showed him in the kitchen in Enskede had been enough, then. He was in a race against time at that point – in parallel with all his other preparations, getting an oversight of the network's pictures and chat messages. He managed to memorise only one example from each of the ring members' photo series to get a sense of the approximate content of their conversations, which, after a quick assessment, seemed most central. Now he desperately tried to remember what else the detective had told him. How Hansen arranged his photo sessions. The extent to which the girl's mother was involved.

'I'm usually in the pictures, so my wife takes them. Helps me. She doesn't mind.'

That's how it worked, right?

He was suddenly unsure.

The woman they arrested had also been involved, hadn't she?

'Your wife? That's great. And in which room?'

The images? What had it really looked like beyond the naked girl? Wallpaper? Furniture? Lamps? Rugs?

'Why does that matter?'

'The place is as important as the act.'

Piet Hoffmann grasped at the memory of the apartment his exterior supposedly lived in, but that he himself had never actually visited.

'In the living room. Almost always.'

'It doesn't look like the living room.'

He needed to sound as certain as he was uncertain.

'We're three people in a small apartment. Our living room maybe doesn't look like other people's living rooms. But that's how we chose to furnish it.'

'Really?'

'Really – what?'

'That wasn't how it was furnished when I was at your home, with you.'

A single look, out of balance. Piet Hoffmann hoped no one had had time to catch it.

'You say "at your home"? "With you"?'

'Yes.'

That didn't match the background information Birte and Grens had given him. According to their briefing, Carl Hansen and his family were preparing to go on their first trip, bags packed, to visit another paedophile, when the parents were arrested. According to Birte and Grens, the Dane had never met any of the others.

Or – had he?

Had Lassie and Onyx met but left no trace of it in the conversations Birte had managed to uncover?

'Fuck that!'

So Piet Hoffmann made up his mind. He'd do as he'd done before, when this was his job and his life. When being questioned meant not just death and danger and struggle, but also longing. Longing to be confronted – so that he could finally confront them after months, sometimes years, of answering their fucking questions smoothly, submissively, keeping quiet so he could dig deeper into the mafia structure he was infiltrating and destroy it.

'I've had enough, goddammit!'

He'd go on the attack. Cover uncertainty with certainty.

'You accepted me as a member and have repeatedly received – *enjoyed* – my pictures of Katrine without the interrogation! And when I get here, I have to go to a meeting in a park, and you test me and approve me. Goddammit, Onyx, enough of these little games!'

Aggressiveness usually worked in the world he knew. Here? Now? He had no idea.

He was as hollow as the silence that sucked all the air out of this beautiful room with its beautiful view.

'Your pictures . . .'

He'd been turned toward the leader now. It was the leader who would decide if Piet Hoffmann had gone too far. If the children he was here to save would be locked in a little tighter.

'. . . they are amazing. You're meticulous, my Danish friend. Beds are properly made. Tables are tastefully set. You care about aesthetics.'

'I repeat: you said "at your home".'

'Forget it.'

'You even said "with you".'

He took a risk. But he only had the information Birte and Grens had given him. And had to use it with all the conviction he didn't feel. Lean into it.

'What the hell did you mean by that?'

'You're right. I should let it be. I know just as well as you that the place is as important as the act.'

Piet Hoffmann relaxed, slightly. Aggressiveness had worked on this type of criminal, too.

Onyx smiled amicably. Until he didn't any more.

The skin on his perfectly aged face tightened, his lips narrowed to thin lines, his ice-blue eyes sharpened.

'You were the one who wrote that the place is as important as the act.'

Hoffmann didn't answer. The leader's way of breathing, his bridled anger, foreshadowed a continuation.

'Which I said to you, just now, more than once. But you didn't react. Even though it was *you*, Hansen, who wrote it first. When you asked us, *me*, to join. Become a member of our community. And we liked that. *I* liked it – you put into words something that I have always felt. It's why I allowed you in. You were the final piece. Then I closed the group.'

The tense lips. The ice-cold eyes.

Piet Hoffmann realised what the leader was really saying. He'd just given himself away. Betrayed himself before he could betray them.

'The place is just as important as the act. Yes, I wrote it.'

Hide the uncertainty.

'Because that's how *I* have always felt.'

With certainty.

'And I thought I was the only one who felt that way.'

Was this also a trap? Had Hansen never written that? Was the quote as fictional as the leader's visit to Hansen's Danish home?

'Until I got in touch with you and realized there were more like me.'

'And in that case, my Danish friend – also a little eager, right?'

The leader's voice and facial expressions remained the same. But it was impossible to tell. Had Piet Hoffmann imagined it? Was it a trap and if so had he just managed to escape? Or – was this another misstep for him?

'Eager?'

'I mean, *I* would have been. If it was me visiting you, in your special place in Denmark. At a meeting with a girl I had only seen in pictures.'

Only seen in pictures.

There it was. The admission. Onyx had never been to Denmark, never visited Hansen at his home. Piet Hoffmann had taken a risk and won.

He relaxed a little more.

Then a loud buzz interrupted. Someone was ringing the doorbell.

'Just as *you* will now be able to meet those you've only seen in pictures.'

The ringing again. A stubborn, hoarse pling-plong that bounced impatiently between the walls. Onyx nodded to Lenny, who opened the door.

Two little girls. Around Rasmus's age again. No, even younger. Seven, eight years old.

'Welcome.'

Lenny laughed his little-boy giggle. Bowed exaggeratedly. While the girls remained there, outside.

'You go in now. It's rude to make the adults wait.'

A man's voice. Behind the children. English with a heavy German accent.

The one who called himself Meyer. As unaware as Lenny that he'd

239

already been exposed, that Birte, according to Grens's summary, had identified him as Hans Peder Stein, conditionally released after a long prison sentence for repeated child rapes. And that Meyer – as soon as Hoffmann discovered Onyx's real name – would be arrested and detained at exactly the same time as a long list of other paedophiles in Operation Sandman.

'Our little exchange students. Julia and Lynn.'

The German gave them a small push, and they each held out a transparent hand. The slightly taller one, fair hair in a ponytail and eyes that had been a clear blue but now changed to red, looked at Piet Hoffmann without seeing. While the girl half a step away to her right kept her eyes on the floor while greeting them with a trembling hand. Or so Piet thought. Until he realized it was his own hand that was shaking, his own fingers that were damp with anxiety.

He now knew he was supposed to act eager. Now knew why the place was as important as the act. Now knew what the leader of the paedophile ring meant when he mentioned meeting those you'd only seen in pictures.

Now knew what they believed Hoffmann, wrapped inside Carl Hansen's exterior, had come here for.

'SKAOL?'

'Almost.'

'Skiiol?'

'Pretty close.'

They had filled up their vodka glasses. The kind that was pure even though it tasted more bitter than he'd expected. They were celebrating. That they were together. That the exchange students had arrived and were now waiting in the room with a large bed in the middle, framed by a shelf with special accessories.

'I love the sea. I love being here. And I love learning new words from our Danish guest.'

Elegant. Urbane. Almost friendly. Onyx had invited his new friend Lassie to speak a little Danish and seemed genuinely amused by it, for a moment beyond doubt. Piet Hoffmann spoke Swedish and Polish and a decent Spanish and English, but he still had no feeling for the language that was supposedly his mother tongue. He made it up. Swedish as a basis for some kind of pretend Danish. And not one of the three ring members – not even the man who called himself Meyer who spoke a language that was geographically close – noticed anything. They'd laughed, stood next to each other like old friends hanging out for the evening, toasting their fellowship and shared interest.

'Despite that, I must leave you. The sea will be here next time, too.'

At first Piet Hoffmann wasn't sure he'd interpreted his words correctly. But when the still nameless leader took his vodka glass to the kitchen, rinsed it out and put it in the dishwasher, it was clear from his actions Hoffmann had heard right.

He was leaving.

As anonymous as when he'd arrived.

Hoffmann tried to understand. It didn't make sense. Everything they'd said so far, everything they'd done, was all about spending the evening together. With the exchange students. But if the man he still only knew as Onyx left . . . if Hoffmann still hadn't managed to get close, to expose him without risking that the other members could be warned and flee . . . if he stayed here with just the two they already had names and addresses for . . . if the paedophile ring was blown, but its founder remained free to start a new ring with new paedophiles who raped children . . . if . . .

That could not be allowed to happen.

'You have no ashtrays.'

'Excuse me?'

'So I suppose you don't smoke inside?'

'None of us smoke at all. Not even Lenny, any more.'

Piet Hoffmann smiled, apologetically.

'I've really tried. To quit. But now, considering what's gonna happen this evening . . . I'll be right back. Just need a few drags.'

He pulled the pack of cigarettes out of his pocket that he'd bought then half-emptied before coming here. An occasional smoker. He didn't wait for an answer, that constant unspoken approval, didn't turn round either, just headed for the front door and down the stairs. He had a minute, maybe a bit more. First light the cigarette, eyes on him from the window, take a few deep drags. Then a carefree walk along the gravel path.

He'd planned to place it beneath a car. But Onyx had surprised him, cycled here. He'd also planned to wait to disrupt the surveillance cameras in order not to arouse unnecessary suspicion.

Now it was too late.

He had to improvise.

Take a chance. Risk discovery.

Hoffmann smoked the cigarette, strolling along slowly. Even though his whole body was in a rush. He left the gravel path for the wild grass, looked around as calmly as he could.

And there.

Leaning against the back of the house.

He made sure he was out of sight of the window, hoped no one had sat down temporarily in front of one of the surveillance camera monitors – and ran. Towards the side of the house. Towards a racing bike as exclusive as everything else here – electronic gears, carbon-fibre frame, the kind of bike that would cost you ten thousand dollars.

But no bell. That would have been the perfect hiding place.

The battery for the electric gears was second-best.

He turned the pack of cigarettes upside down, shaking it until a thin, oblong piece of plastic fell out. About the size of a SIM card. He held it between his thumb and forefinger and pushed it into the gap between the small, square battery and the frame, poking it in above the pedal and the chain.

The world's smallest GPS tracker. Stephen's suggestion.

Made for researching the behaviour of birds and small animals. Submitting locations and plotting them on Google Maps.

Sent directly to Piet Hoffmann's phone.

He ran back as well. Until he was in sight of the window. Then he walked slowly towards the front door of the house where, with gestures that were easy to follow, he stubbed the glowing cigarette against the heel of his sandal.

He'd made it – and knew exactly how to proceed. He'd have no problem overpowering Lenny and Meyer and leaving them tied up for the local police to pick up. Nor following the path the GPS would draw position by position on his phone, until the battery it was being sent from was at the bike owner's home. At that point Piet Hoffmann would park his car some distance away and contact Grens and Birte, who in turn would give their German, Swiss, Dutch, Belgian, British, Italian and American colleagues the go-ahead for a coordinated strike around the world.

Mission accomplished.

And so it would have gone.

If his thoughts hadn't started ricocheting around inside his head.

Ha. Ha. Ha. Ha.

Because as he opened the front door and stepped into the house and was about to start talking to the faces waiting for him at the dining table, it was as if sounds started searching, searching, searching for each other but never quite connecting, as if words and sentences were strangers who no longer belonged together.

Ten thousand slippery thoughts careened through his mind. While his arms and legs seemed to tangle with each other.

Hahahahahahaha.

Until he understood without understanding.

Drugged. That's what he was.

The pure vodka that had tasted more bitter than he'd expected.

Hahahahahahahahaha.

The boyish giggles.

The grotesque laughter flowing out of Lenny's gigantic mouth had turned into green bumblebees and yapping white hyenas and floating black seaweed that smelled like mud and tasted salty and felt sticky.

'Love bomb.'

Lenny sat in his place behind an empty plate and raised his vodka glass. He seemed like a very small child as he stared straight into Piet Hoffmann's wide eyes, into his soul.

'Substances, Lassie. A love bomb just exploded in your chest.'

IMPRISONED.

Inside himself.

Inside the darkness of his own mind, someone had locked a door that no longer existed.

He couldn't move, couldn't think, he was asleep but his eyes were open, unseeing.

He was a guard to his interior prison and could not escape.

BRIEF, BRIEF MOMENTS of presence.

As he perceives Lenny.

Perceives Meyer.

But not Onyx.

'Maybe we should give our Danish friend a little welcome gift.'

Tiny, tiny moments of transient clarity flying around.

And just as he was starting to see again, to understand again, to master his own body, transformed again into those crashing thoughts and tangled arms.

'Or maybe he's not really our friend after all, maybe he's . . . lying.'

The place is just as important as the act.

That was how they'd seen through him. How he'd failed. Fallen down.

Into drugging, into absence.

Piet Hoffmann tried – *really tried* – to break through his chemical captivity.

And it wasn't just his ability to think and move that was gone.

Onyx was, too.

The leader was no longer there.

Maybe that's why Lenny was speaking.

'Mmm. You are correct. Now it's just us left. You and me and Meyer. Because you ruined our night. Forced Onyx to leave us. You see, he's very careful not to be here when we record. And that's our plan now. We're going to record – you. So he went home, both to watch like he usually does and to find out who the fuck you are and what the fuck you're doing here. In our sanctuary.'

The hysterical boy giggle.

'Or, if you prefer – you can prove it to us now, voluntarily. Prove you're not lying. Prove you are truly one of us.'

Green bumblebees. Yapping hyenas. Stinking seaweed.

'Show us you are prepared to do *just about anything* with a child.'

Hoffmann stood up – *wanted, wanted, wanted to stand up* – but his legs remained still. His body lacked any will. Lenny and Meyer had grabbed him by the arms and were now dragging him across the floor towards the room with two waiting little girls.

'There you go.'

Piet Hoffmann flinched and tried to twist himself back and forth, but the weak, overweight men held him with ease.

Powerless. Apathetic. Resigned. Docile.

No strength to break free.

'Have a good time, everybody, grown-ups and kids.'

Hoffmann stared – *stared and screamed* – at the two girls.

They sat in front of him on the bed, drugged, just like him.

Love bomb in the chest.

Blurry and crystal clear. Silent and loud. Far away and right next to him.

'I can't . . .'

Even his voice had given up.

'. . . can't . . .'

Only a hoarse rattling of words came out.

'. . . when I'm . . .'

He searched desperately for the eye of the camera. The one recording. The film Onyx was going to watch after leaning his racing bike against his house, arriving at his home.

Might even be watching right now.

'. . . like this . . .'

'Oh, friend, don't worry.'

Hoffmann tried again and again to tear his arms away from Lenny and Meyer.

But nothing happened.

'We'll undress the girls first. Then you. They don't really have the same substances in them, and they know just what to do. We could see this as a . . . well, a punishment. Because you are not who you say, are you? You're somebody else. Somebody who tried to deceive us. The place and the act are important, right? We're filming. We're going to sell this. If only you knew how much they pay for new faces. And that's what we're going to do – show your face. The face beneath the face. A face brings in a lot of money, so much more than headless bodies. I'm guessing . . . in your case . . . with two little girls at the same time – at least a thousand bucks a pop. And we've got *lots of buyers* through our channels.'

Piet Hoffmann struggled, tore, screamed again. Without getting anywhere, without being heard.

'And the best part is that if anyone ends up going down for this, my friend – it will be you. We make a fortune – and you protect us! Our biggest prize in a long time, and it just knocked on the door! Hundreds of thousands of dollars that we can use to expand our thriving business. All thanks to you. More fake passports. More foreign exchange students. More recruiters to find beautiful children for us.'

He was getting nowhere.

He was stuck.

While those brief, brief moments of clarity were starting to return again.

So what I want to make sure we all agree on is that you, I and the National Research Centre have never had anything to do with each other.

Now came words and images from the meeting with Birte on what would happen in an emergency.

If everything goes to hell. If you end up needing the assistance of the Danish police. Then I'll have no idea who you are.

He had, of course, accepted it then.

That's how he'd always worked as an infiltrator – trust only yourself.

He hadn't known what the panic tearing him up inside now – as they tore him up outside – felt like back then.

Never knew what it felt like when a drug prevents you from striking, fighting back.

HIS LAST CRY was swallowed by a hoarse whisper, which made almost no sound at all.

Not sure where he was, or if he even existed.

Surreal reality?

In this case, two men were trying to push him down onto a bed.

Or real surreality?

In this case, two men were binding his arms.

Or unreal surreality?

In this case, two men were trying to take off his clothes.

Or real reality?

Because if this was happening – if someone was pushing him down and someone was binding his arms and someone was pulling off his clothes – it was happening right now, just like that.

And even though he lacked any strength, he hit.

Hit.

Piet Hoffmann had always done whatever a mission required to maintain his credibility, to continue dividing criminal organisations from within. Actions he would never be rid of, that haunted him, that woke him up at night while Zofia still slept heavily next to him, the kind of sleep that came from an inner calm, which once lost could never be recaptured.

Whatever it took – but not this.

Not.

This.

So he struck. And struck again.

He hit through the drug. Through his chemical limits.

Struck out with his hatred, his drive for self-preservation, his willpower.

What separated him from those who held down his arms.

But with the drug changing his mind, he had no sense of his own strength.

Whether his blows were hard or soft. *Too* hard or *too* soft.

So in one of his few conscious moments as he managed to tear himself free and his fist met Meyer's face, it did so with primordial force. All he had in him. Just to be sure. So as blood flowed from the German paedophile, Hoffmann was genuinely surprised by how hard he'd hit him, and by the fact that his blood ran bright red instead of pitch-black.

Once he started hitting, he couldn't stop.

Blow after blow connected with Meyer's head, neck. But the shrill, terrified screams were someone else's. Those belonged to Lenny, who had taken a shocked step back instead of helping his friend, and now tried to escape the face that would never be whole again.

'Why don't you laugh now, Lenny!'

The man was terrified of physical violence.

'Giggle louder, you fucker!'

The dog leash was still on the shelf next to the children's clothes and the sex toys, and as Hoffmann reached for it, he temporarily lost his balance, misjudged the distance, and fell against the sharp edge of the shelf, could feel the prosthetic nose being torn off.

'This – this is what you do to children!'

Lenny had reached the threshold of the room as Piet Hoffmann grabbed him by the arm, threw him against the door frame and interrupted his shrill howl by wrapping the leash around his neck.

'You wanna play? Let's play!'

Rage. Fury.

As, in the confusion of the drug, he pulled the dog leash harder, harder.

As Lenny's eyes turned red, were almost pushed out of their sockets.

As the noose shut off his airway, and there were only a few seconds remaining.

Until death.

That was when she screamed.

'*Sluta!*'

Stop. In Swedish.

'*Snälla!*'

Please.

Hoffmann stopped pulling. Came to a halt. Had *she* shouted at him in . . . his own language? Was the drug playing tricks on his brain? Were his own children standing there? Rasmus or Hugo or Luiza crying and screaming and . . .

'*Sluta! Sluta!*'

What kind of drug cocktail had they given him?

How long would it rule his mind?

'Are you . . . is that Swedish?'

'*Sluta!* Don't hit! Stop stop stop!'

While Lenny fell unconscious to the floor, Piet Hoffmann took cautious steps towards the little girl. She had fair hair up in a ponytail and eyes that looked at him without seeing. She was the one who had spoken, shouted.

'You speak Swedish?'

'A little.'

Her friend kept staring at the floor – just like when they arrived. Impossible to make contact with. So he concentrated on the girl who had made him let go of the stranglehold.

'What's your name?'

He asked her in Swedish, but she didn't answer. Just stood there, blankly.

'What's your name?'

In English, now. And she answered. A thin voice.

'Lynn.'

'And before that?'

She hesitated.

'I . . .'

'Yes?'

'Linnea. That was my name.'

THE LITTLE GIRL who was once called Linnea had shouted, *Stop! Please!* She'd done so in Swedish and saved the life of her tormentor. Now she stood as transparent as before beside an unconscious body which lay stretched out on its stomach. The victim had saved her perpetrator.

'Is he . . . ?'

'He'll live.'

He'll survive. Just like the girl whose life he'd stolen.

Linnea?

Was it . . . *her*?

The one the authorities, in agreement with her parents, had pronounced dead? Who Rasmus went to preschool with so many years ago? Who Zofia asked him to search for?

The girl he was here to find?

Piet Hoffmann wanted to sit down, take the girl he didn't recognise in his arms, hold her, ask her to tell him everything.

Not now.

As the fight against two paedophiles had now turned into a fight against time. He was unmasked. Not just here – the camera hidden somewhere in the room would soon convey what had happened to the ring's founder as well.

And that one could not be allowed to escape. To destroy the evidence. To warn the other members.

'Please. Stay in this room. Police are coming. They will help you.'

The girl pressed her lips together, silent.

No. She didn't want to stay. Didn't want to wait for the police. Not until he dragged Lenny's and Meyer's bodies to the kitchen and tied them to the railing that led out to the patio.

He stumbled then, again.

Dizzy.

Confused.

'What chemicals?'

Lenny had gradually started to regain consciousness, and Hoffmann kicked him.

'Hey, you fucker! What chemicals? How long – in my body?'

The overweight man still had a dog leash wrapped around his neck, which may be why he was coughing, gasping for air as he tried to answer. Words that drowned inside each other, inaudible.

Piet Hoffmann made sure that the two men's hands were fastened tight, with cable ties that would cut cruelly into their skin every time they tried to move, then looked over at the two girls one last time before hurrying to the rental car.

How skinny they were. How tiny.

How far from home.

PART

PART
6

As if he were staring into two mirrors facing each other.

HEAVY DROPS SLID down the glass.

On the *inside* of the window.

A room that had long since ceased to breathe – tension, hope, eagerness converted to body heat, painting the world outside blurry. Ewert Grens swiped his shirtsleeve across the condensation, drying the upper half of the window and catching a glimpse of morning rush hour in the Danish capital through a gap that would soon fog up again.

'Still no word?'

'Still no word.'

Birte looked at him. She had hoped for another answer.

'Grens – we can't wait much longer.'

'I know that.'

'We have to contact him! We need the ringleader's identity now!'

'Hoffmann makes contact – we never contact him. *Those* are the conditions.'

'You described him as the best in the business.'

'He is the best.'

'So why haven't we heard from him!'

Grens wanted to take her by the hand and pull her aside, tell her something, explain to her – anything to give her peace of mind. But he decided not to. He didn't want to undermine her authority as leader among this group of colleagues from all over the world. So he took a few steps back, away from the window, and kept his distance from the conference table on the top floor of the Danish National Police's substantial headquarters. From this vantage point, the unofficial participant could study the official ones. Birte – who had named the operation and managed to convince law enforcement agencies who had never cooperated before how important it was to do so now – had a detective inspector to her right, whom Grens had met on his first day in tiny Lærdal and who was responsible for all the Danish interrogations, and on her other side sat a young prosecutor from Copenhagen, who was building the case against the Hansen couple. Then there sat a long line of representatives from law enforcement agencies in Germany, Switzerland, Belgium, the Netherlands, the United Kingdom, Italy, and then a friendly man from Interpol, a not-so-friendly woman from DC, a prosecutor from San Diego, an agent from US Customs, and finally a young woman, who was standing up, and if Grens understood correctly was Birte's American counterpart at something called the Homeland Security Investigations Cyber Crimes Center.

They stood now in front of the large whiteboard, Birte and the Cyber Crimes woman, hanging up their chat message map in enlarged format, which, based on times and IP addresses, established how 'person A and person B are connected here' just like 'person B and person C there' – strengthening links that could convince a judge or jury that a child had been abused at a specific moment. More magnifications had been hung on the white stonewalls. More investigative results were exchanged during the day across national borders in the puzzle that formed the paedophile ring, and soon with a little luck this could be used as evidence. Just like the picture where one of the faceless abusers shows off a red dress he's mailing to Katrine could be connected to a name by a black-and-white bedpost looming in the background of the photograph – a detail police officers could search for during their upcoming arrests. Or like the picture where someone wrote 'Hi Katrine' on a cardboard sign to obscure their face, but revealed a green-painted wooden ceiling. Or how – it stabbed at the upper corner of Ewert Grens's chest, always at the same spot – in the pictures where a girl with sad eyes removes a hairpin in the shape of a blue butterfly from her own head and places it on a doll's, the same doll Grens later found on a shelf in the Danish apartment, could be used as proof if that particular girl was found during this operation.

'Ewert?'

It hadn't helped to take a step back, to do his best to disappear.

'Nothing yet?'

Birte still hoped for an answer.

'Nope.'

He shook his head gently.

'Nothing from our source.'

Ewert Grens saw her disappointment, understood her impatience.

He was left with a different feeling.

They had flown here from all over the world to wait for a breakthrough. But the Swedish detective superintendent carried inside him yesterday's long phone conversation with Piet Hoffmann, who had been on his way to a city called Santa Maria. He'd sounded like a man Grens didn't recognise, a version of the infiltrator he'd never met before. Hoffmann's bewilderment had been so enormous, his doubts so overwhelming. And for Grens, here in a room that was depending so much on Hoffmann's abilities, it all made him feel like a liar. He should, of course, talk to Birte, tell her the truth, but at the same time she needed total focus on the solution, not the problem, in order to manage this team.

While Birte prepared for the meeting and met and introduced each guest, Grens spent his time listening to all the interrogations conducted with Carl Hansen, Dorte Hansen, Katrine Hansen. The family they had destroyed because they had to.

That's when it had struck him. Hoffmann's voice.

Piet Hoffmann was *acting* the paedophile. Unlike other times Grens had heard him doing his infiltration work. Unlike the recording of Carl Hansen – while he repeatedly denied what he'd done – who really *sounded* like a paedophile in every way. And if an outsider were to compare those two, they'd perceive the dissonance, the contradictions, in the voice of someone who didn't really believe in himself.

The interrogations with the girl and the mother and stepfather had confirmed the impression of the preliminary conversations he had listened to that first night after the arrest. A daughter, who now and then let slip some horrific detail without really understanding it, raised as she was to assume that the life she lived was normal. A mother who constantly demanded to know where her daughter was, and how she was doing. And a stepfather who sneered – Grens of course couldn't see his expression, but after doing hundreds of similar interrogations he was fairly sure that was what his face looked like as he met every statement with a counter-question.

Interrogator (IR): We have the pictures. Of you and Katrine.

Carl Hansen (CH): Do you?

(IR): Yes and –

(CH): So you can see me

(IR): We see –

(CH): An arm, right? But can you see my face?

(IR): On the whole, we have –

(CH): On the whole, you don't have shit, do you?

But that wasn't what was disturbing him. The stepfather's lack of empathy. Grens had dealt with that his whole life, in all its variations. It was the mother's response that was giving him unexpected discomfort. Her obsession with knowing what her daughter was thinking. Possessing her. Like her husband, every statement was met with a question, but of a different kind. A mother who believed that she could regain herself, control herself, by controlling her daughter.

Ewert Grens sought out his own enlarged contribution, which lay in the middle of the conference table framed by coffee cups and half-drunk bottles of mineral water. The picture Hoffmann had sent from his phone, the last sign of life from the California coast. A furtive photo of the man who was assumed to be the leader of the paedophile ring. Perspective from below, as if the infiltrator was lying on the floor when he pressed the button on an advanced micro-camera. Objects not entirely in focus and lighting unsatisfactory, but despite that even enlarged several times, now measuring more than one metre in width and height, the face was clear. A man in late-middle age, not much younger than Grens himself, but in much better physical condition. No excess fat or even many wrinkles on his tanned skin, hair that was thick albeit in various shades of silver and grey, eyes with much more energy than this tired detective. A face that needed a name to be held accountable, a home address that could be linked to physical evidence. In order to be arrested, sentenced, locked away. Forever.

Grens had just taken the first step towards exiting the room, towards fresh air, when he paused at the door. His phone was ringing. And he wasn't the only one who had noticed it. The whole room had fallen silent. The meeting's participants, the representatives of law enforcement agencies that normally focused on their own separate problems, were all focused on one thing now. Hoping for one thing. That a ringing mobile phone, which was usually switched off during a meeting, might be the call that finally gave them the green light.

'Yes?'

The detective superintendent looked at the phone's display.

It fitted.

One of the numbers that existed for just a day and belonged to Hoffmann.

'Grens?'

'Speaking.'

Ewert Grens looked around. Everyone was listening to his side of the conversation. Birte, too.

'Yes?'

'Two of them can be picked up. Immediately. Send the local police to the address I texted you. Two – but not the one we really want.'

The sound of a car. Piet Hoffmann was in a vehicle, on his way somewhere.

'I'm following him. The leader. It's dark now, and I've lost sight for the moment, but –'

'How close?'

'I have a trail.'

'Good. Good. Well then . . .'

'But, Grens?'

'Yes?'

'I think I've been discovered.'

Ewert Grens now met only Birte's eyes. He needed to talk to her without the others listening. They'd been told that the green light was a final bit of data being decrypted, which would confirm the exact positions of suspected perpetrators – not a formerly wanted infiltrator travelling in the US under a fake passport on an unsanctioned mission on behalf of a Swedish detective superintendent and a Danish IT expert.

'Wait a minute.'

The detective nodded to Birte, who left her seat at the front of the group and followed him out into the corridor.

'I'll put you on speaker, Piet, and please speak quietly.' He whispered into the phone, holding it between them. 'I'm listening. Repeat the last thing you said.'

'It may be that I'm about to be exposed. Worst-case scenario – I already have been.'

Grens angled the phone slightly, so the sound from the limited speaker was better.

'I think we're getting close to his home – he's on a bike, and I'm driving through densely populated areas. As soon as he's parked his bike and sat down in his fine armchair to check this evening's tapes, he'll realise. Warn the others. And then – it will all fall apart.'

Another look exchanged between the detective and Birte.

'Piet, it's Birte.'

The Danish investigator leaned closer to the phone.

'I understand what you're saying. And you're right. I can't delay this any more – I'm activating Operation Sandman.'

Grens looked at her – really *looked* at her.

She'd just chosen the path she absolutely did not want to go down.

Ordering the raids to be made before establishing the identity of the leader. Risk losing him, just like the other one with a bouncing IP address. Live with the knowledge that the paedophile ring would soon re-emerge with new members.

And she made it knowing that *not* choosing this path would be even worse – it would mean alerting the paedophile ring, allowing them all time to escape.

'But before we hang up.'

She brought the phone closer, making sure Hoffmann heard every word.

'If you get hold of him.'

'Yes?'

Piet Hoffmann was driving slowly, at least that was how it sounded, according to the engine noise.

And now slowed even further.

'Birte? Did you say something – I can't hear you.'

'*If* you track him down at home – don't focus on him.'

'What the hell are you –'

'First the hard drive. Then the man. Always! The computer is the priority! Without it, without . . . *you must secure the hard drive*. If it were me . . . I'd look first for an NAS, a hard drive next to the computer, then pull out every power cable you can find. But, Hoffmann – be careful. If he sees you – he will destroy it! Erase it! Lock the door and throw away the key, all that evidence . . . *The hard drive, Hoffmann!*'

Ewert Grens had been on his way out of the room to get some air when the phone rang – now he made another attempt. Made his way along the hard, slippery stone floor, used his temporary access card to open two pairs of electronically sealed security doors and coaxed open the glass door to a narrow balcony which, judging by the amount of cigarette butts in musty metal cans must be where all the smokers in the Danish National Police hung out. After the first liberating breath, he sank down on a lonely wooden stool and ran his eyes over the roofs of central Copenhagen.

My God.

Didn't she hear? Didn't she understand? What I heard, understood?

Hoffmann has been drugged!

His voice. His intonation. That brief hesitation before every answer. His choice of words.

Grens was sure of it – Piet Hoffmann was under the influence of strong chemicals.

The detective superintendent stood up. Sat down. Stood up. His body as worried as his mind.

Maybe he should tell her?

Let Birte know that while she was declaring war on the whole world, their infiltrator in California was not only fighting the leader of the paedophile ring, he was also struggling against a drug that was weakening him?

No. Too soon.

She still needed to focus her energy on starting the operation. For now this was the detective superintendent's problem.

So *he* made the call, established contact.

Even though only the infiltrator was supposed to do that.

'It's me again.'

'Grens – I don't have time. Chasing flashing red dots on a map.'

'A simple question.'

'Hanging up now.'

'How do you feel?'

Piet Hoffmann didn't hang up. But didn't say anything either. The roar of the car engine lay like a protective membrane between them.

'I asked a question.'

'Mmm.'

'And you know I won't give up until you answer.'

The engine noise. There was something soothing about it.

'I've never felt this way. Ever.'

'How?'

'I . . . I can't get my thoughts together, Ewert. Or my body.'

'What do you have in you?'

'Don't know. Some shit mixed into alcohol. It's starting to pass. But slowly. I'm . . . not myself.'

'Stop.'

Ewert Grens hadn't planned what he was going to say.

The one thing he shouldn't say.

'Pull the car over and stop. Let him go, just like Birte said, but do it now and without that damn computer.'

Hoffmann had risked death in all of his previous missions – but this time he wouldn't even be able to defend himself if the danger became a real threat.

'Do you hear me, Piet?'

'Nope.'

'Stop this.'

'That fucker, if you had met –'

'Give it up now!'

'I'm not giving up. I'm not letting him go. Do you understand, Ewert?'

PIET HOFFMANN LET his phone drop onto the passenger seat as if ridding himself of Grens's voice. His own worry was now the detective superintendent's as well. A quick glance in the rear-view mirror. He looked different – and at first didn't realise why. The bridge of the nose. Carl Hansen's profile had been beaten down during the violent struggle. Also – the scar. Completely scraped off. And for a moment, he smiled the smile he lost right around US border control.

I'm leaving the paedophile behind.

With one hand on the steering wheel, he dragged the other over the mottled stubble until short straws of various colours stuck to his palm.

Dragged. Scraped. At what reminded him of shame.

While I search for myself.

A teenage boy was balancing his bicycle against a narrow roadside wall, a group of women were jogging towards him in the headlights, and two middle-aged men were arguing in a driveway using sweeping gestures. Hoffmann followed the red-flashing GPS trail along a residential street, which wound its way through an affluent American suburb with houses that looked just like every other affluent American suburb. Identical houses, identical lawns – it made him dizzy, as if he were staring into two mirrors facing each other.

Then the red dot stopped moving.

Turned into a fixed point just as he grabbed his phone from the passenger seat – that was where the trail ended on this map.

Piet Hoffmann estimated the distance. Four hundred and fifty metres separated him from a parked bicycle with an active transmitter jammed behind its battery.

He lingered in the car while another evening jogger passed by, making sure that the red dot stayed where it was. The man they were looking for, the man who had built a paedophile ring that violated young children, a man that an entire operation in both the US and Europe was waiting for in a police station in central Copenhagen, was barely a five-minute walk away.

Had so-called Onyx parked at his home?

Had he just started the film taken by the camera Hoffmann was convinced was hidden in the seaside house's assault room?

Or – did the leader of the ring already know what happened?

His shoulder holsters were hidden in the spare tyre in the trunk. Hoffmann adjusted one over each shoulder and waited for the familiar feeling of something tightening in his skin. It didn't come. He took out the pistol and the hunting knife that had long been his standard equipment, wrapped his hand around the grooves of the gun and felt the weight of a double-edged knife, but that didn't bring the familiar feeling back either.

Back to who I just was.

Because it's my own hand I don't recognise.

Just like when I was punching too hard through the chemical wall.

He grabbed pliers and the suction cup and the box of razor blades out of the glove compartment and let everything slide down into the side pockets of his trousers, down among the cable ties, then left the car, trying to walk at as normal a pace as possible.

Despite the fact that time was running out.

Despite the desperation in Birte's voice when she'd told him about the unique evidence that could make all the difference and yet could so easily be destroyed.

The phone in his hand. The red dot on the map. A little further down this street, turn at the next and about fifty metres ahead on the right. Past one, two, three, four, five, six houses of the same size on the same plots.

Movements you don't notice.

A face that has no features.

Become the neighbour who just lives around here somewhere.

Despite an interior that hid a ticking clock, he tried to convince himself to keep walking slowly, maintain an infiltrator's exterior that would be a part of the street scene, a man passing by who you won't remember later.

There.

The elegant, white picket fence. The perfectly groomed fruit trees that looked like security guards with their backs straight and long arms stretched along a path of circular stone slabs. The brick house was two storeys and ivy wound its way up beside the front door.

There.

Piet Hoffmann breathed in, breathed out, in, out.

He counted at least three surveillance cameras covering the front, probably supplemented by as many on the back. That usually meant alarms on the doors and windows.

In out, in out.

He covered the last bit of ground towards a cylindrical mailbox, the kind you opened with a key. Number 26. On the next row, below the property's address, a nameplate. Ten capital letters. RON J. TRAVIS. And there, past a couple of low bushes, he finally saw it – the bicycle, leaning against a garden shed.

He'd slowed down but kept walking down the street, only stopping when a couple of close-standing trees offered him cover.

In out, in out.

Whatever was buzzing in his head refused to let him go.

But he couldn't wait any longer, had to tear himself away from the drug that was trying so hard to hold him.

If he stretched out a little between the tree trunks, he could see the house, without being seen. His eyes wandered through a flowery garden, searching the brick walls, room by room, curtain by curtain.

A rectangular basement window.

That's where he would try to get in.

The jammer was in place next to the knife in his holster. He fished out the little bit of plastic and wedged it between two tree branches, making sure it stayed put. Stephen had promised long range, and as

Hoffmann aimed the jammer at the house that belonged to one Ron J. Travis – *is that your name?* – he hoped her professional knowledge was still reliable.

Because now he ran.

Towards the cylindrical mailbox and the classic fence, pushing the gate open and crouching down beside the far end of the house, next to the rubbish bin. The jammer, if it worked, would have found the same frequency as the surveillance cameras and started transmitting by now, turning every image to blackness. And by the time he scraped off the putty around the basement window with a razor blade and used pliers to pull out the small pins that held the glass in place and used the suction cup to loosen the entire window, the alarm would be completely shut off, all communication between the alarm system and alarm central broken.

A faint odour of mould seeped out.

Stuffiness.

He lay on his stomach in the soil of the flower bed with his head through the hole he'd forced open, pushed away with his feet and slid with outstretched arms down onto the basement floor.

Towards darkness.

Only the dim light from the street lamps reached here.

That's why they were so prominent. The eyes. The ones staring at him.

'RON J. TRAVIS.'

'Not now, Grens.'

'I just received this picture. Take a look at it.'

'In a bit.'

'A two-storey brick house with a white picket fence. If you concentrate on the surfaces right there, Birte, follow the edges of the image – surely it seems as if it was taken behind the cover of a couple of trees? And the photographer is close, I'd guess at most fifteen metres away.'

'*In a moment, OK?*'

'Hoffmann.'

'Hoffmann?'

'He sent the picture. Thirty seconds ago. Texted: "Ron J. Travis, 26 Bolford Street", followed by a question mark.'

Now the Swedish detective superintendent had her attention.

'"Travis"? And . . . a question mark?'

'Yes.'

Birte, standing beside the steamy conference room's huge TV screen, excused herself, asked her colleagues from the Cyber Crimes Center and US Customs to step aside a little to pass through, and pulled Ewert Grens aside.

'You mean . . . ?'

'Yes.'

'. . . that could be *the* house? *The* name?'

'I mean that Piet Hoffmann sent the picture in the middle of his chase. Which leaves only one interpretation.'

She had given up.

Had made the one decision she didn't want to make.

Lose the leader – so as not to lose them all.

'In that case . . .'

But now.

An opening.

An infiltrator near the target.

'. . . Grens, contact local police. Give them the location and –'

'No.'

'Grens – do as I say. *Order*. If you want to stay in this room.'

'If we head in there now, if the American police start running around outside the house in that picture and – you said it yourself, Birte – if the homeowner is warned, there's no way you will ever see the contents of his computer. If Hoffmann thought reinforcements would help, he'd have let us know. Instead, he sent a name. We should prepare what we can. But don't sound the alarm until we hear from him again.'

They looked at each other. For a long time. Finally, she nodded.

'You know Hoffmann.'

And Grens nodded.

'Take care of the world, Birte, while I compile what I can on the name Ron J. Travis.'

She returned to her place in front of the giant screen, which was divided into twenty equal squares so that visitors gathered in this room could follow the nineteen parallel raids. At the bottom of each frame, the member's handle and place of residence blinked in white. At the top left corner of the screen *Lollipop, Zurich*, then *Gregorius, Antwerp*, all the way to box number 18, *Queen Mary, Columbus*, and number 19, *Mariette, Portland*. The last box, number 20, was black. It had been reserved for Onyx, the leader.

'*In sixty seconds.*'

Birte held the wireless microphone, turning to her international colleagues.

'*In forty-five seconds.*'

She counted down while nineteen frames wobbled in constant motion, reality from a multitude of camera perspectives, mounted on the helmets of the police officers who stood at the front of each specially trained task force.

'*In thirty seconds.*'

And here, inside the ever more airless room, in another part of the world, the police chiefs who spoke a multitude of languages waited close beside each other.

'*In fifteen seconds.*'

Concentrating.

Impatiently.

Just as much in motion as the rocking images they were watching.

'*In five, four, three, two, one . . .*'

As if they too wanted to run to the TV screen, they too wanted to approach the house or apartment whose doors were being forced open, an opening for the rest of the police force to stream in with weapons raised.

'*. . . now.*'

But they remained where they were. Frozen. Silent.

While the movie screens that reminded Grens of fiction forever changed the lives of both victims and perpetrators.

While the audience's attention was switching back and forth between the images, whichever offered the most drama at the moment.

Just then the camera showed a police force assailing a large farmyard in the middle of the United States – the box marked number 8 that blinked *Grand Junction*. The female ring member *Queen Mary* according to their information was a nanny in a house where the family's children lived with the woman's own. At the very moment the doors and windows were opened, a boy lay in her bed, naked bodies close together, which didn't seem to bother the other children sleeping in the same room. According to the police chief's report, her carefully arranged photo series, along with those of the leader Onyx and the ones calling themselves Redcat and Master, contained the most serious abuse, the depictions with the most severe violence.

As the middle-aged woman was taken away in handcuffs, the audience on the other side of the world turned their attention to box number

11 and the blinking white *Zwolle*. There, in the eastern part of the Netherlands, *Marie Antoinette* was eating breakfast with his wife and two sons, when the only existence they knew exploded from both inside and out. Just like after the first crackdown on the Danish family, which started this whole operation, they were now separated, bewildered, the father locked away and the sons sent into institutions, where they were welcomed by social workers.

One box – in addition to the completely black one – differed from the others. Number 14, *Hartford* written at the bottom. A raid in a darkened apartment in a small town in Alabama, near the Florida border. When the police stormed the home, which according to the reconnaissance data belonged to *Ingrid*, one of the eleven paedophiles who communicated only with Carl Hansen, they were met with no reaction, no resistance. In a shaky film sequence, a large man appeared, in tight shorts, wearing a short-sleeved shirt that shone brightly with a stain. The apartment's owner, John Hector Pereira, who had been released just two months earlier for lack of evidence in the suspected abuse of four children, had put a rifle in his mouth and fired.

During the initial phases of the operation, Grens had kept his distance, studying the police officers' backs as much as the squares of moving film. Now, about the time the helmet camera started moving close to Pereira's blown-up head, one of those backs turned and sought the detective's eyes. Birte. And even though she didn't say a word, even though he didn't either, they both understood. She, silently, asked if Hoffmann had been in touch – and he, equally silently, replied that he had not. She asked about the risk of Hoffmann also being monitored – and he wondered that too and unfortunately suspected the risk was considerable. She asked what possibility Hoffmann would have to complete the mission if discovered – and he answered that knowing Hoffmann's previous work, the infiltrator's chances were good.

What he did not reveal to her, however, in their loud silence, not yet, was that Piet Hoffmann was under the influence of strong substances, and if he were exposed the battle would be lost.

In that case, everything was over.

THE FETID SMELL of mould was real.

As real as the hard, cold basement floor.

As the darkness.

But not the eyes. Surely?

Those large shining eyes that reflected in escaped light.

Which continued to stare.

At him.

Piet Hoffmann stood up. The eyes were still there. Had even multiplied.

The drug. I'm imagining it.

He took a step forward. Without getting any closer. Because the eyes simultaneously moved backwards.

But did they exist? For real?

One more step.

If so, I've been discovered. And need to . . .

Then he saw. Understood.

They exist. For real. But the eyes aren't following him.

They're scared.

They're hiding.

One more step, one more.

As the dim light from outside temporarily lit up the unknown figure and he saw a . . . child's face.

A girl.

He looked at her. Surely . . . was that her? The leader's daughter? Thirteen and too old? The girl who was to be replaced by a newer, younger, adopted sister?

Or – were there two of her? He counted eyes. Maybe ten? Counted again. Twelve? Six? Eight? Groggy. Confused. He looked down, looked up. Four? Looked down, looked up – four. Down, up – four. He decided. There were two pairs of eyes. Two children. Here, in the basement. In the darkness.

Here they are again, the ones who have to live with the consequences of this abuse.

He took one last step, a small one. Getting closer, without scaring them.

When a sound suddenly assailed him.

Hysterical.

Spinning round, round, round him in this unfamiliar space.

Metal. Clatter. A vibrating clunk.

Bouncing from wall to wall, drilling its way into his head, his brain.

I switched the bowl several times. Tried plastic in different sizes and colours. Both for dogs and cats. But when I found this, well – the picture was perfect. It's a better scale for the girl doing such a good job eating out of it.

The man who called himself Onyx, his pleasant voice explaining how the world would one day accept the love between adults and children. Just as when a child was hungry enough she accepted food served in a metal cat bowl.

That's what he'd tripped over.

The cat bowl.

Which now stopped rolling and came to rest on the basement floor in an increasingly violent, louder circling motion.

'Linda?'

Someone was moving up there, speaking sharply.

'Greg?'

The door to the upstairs of the house opened.

'Did one of you knock over the food bowl?'

The first steps on the stairs, halfway down.

'Answer me.'

The voice that Piet Hoffmann recognised. But this was a different tone, far from pleasant.

'Linda!'

'No.'

'Greg! Last chance.'

'It wasn't us.'

'Don't you ever lie to me.'

The basement door closed again.

Locked.

And it occurred to Hoffmann that with the drug in him, he lacked sufficient fine motor skills to coax it open.

It was no longer possible to avoid being discovered.

PIET HOFFMANN DIDN'T know what was going on upstairs. But he could guess. And he guessed right.

Because as soon as the elegant and well-spoken man who called himself Onyx closed and locked the basement door, he had known. Linda and Greg never lied to him. If they said they didn't kick the cat bowl, then someone else did.

Someone who didn't know where it was kept.

Who couldn't find his way in the dark.

So he slid the basement key into his pocket and ran to his study just a few doors away. To the computer and the screen that showed surveillance footage from twelve cameras, half on the property at the coast, which he'd cycled away from an hour earlier.

It was into that house that he looked first. And got no further than the first camera, which was sewn into one of the stuffed animal's eyes in the room with a bed as its only piece of furniture.

The picture was upside down.

Everything was filmed from the vantage point of the floor.

As if someone had thrown the soft toy to the side and left it there. They were always careful about that, it should always be in its place, especially the fabric head, which contained the camera and documented what would be relived.

The room, what was visible of it, looked destroyed or turned upside down. The shelf on the wall hung by a single screw. Large brown stains were on the bedspread and carpet and wallpaper. He zoomed in and felt more and more certain it was congealed blood.

He moved the cursor back in time. To around the point where

he – outside the house and beyond the lens – was climbing onto his bike and cycling away.

What he saw changed everything.

Lassie, drugged and compliant, pulled into the room and the waiting girls. Meyer and Lenny, each holding one of his arms tight. Their false friend had to be undressed.

So far, so good.

But – suddenly he tears himself free.

Punches.

A fist into Meyer's face. Punch. Punch.

Bloodstains all over the room.

No one screams. Not Meyer in pain, not Lassie in rage. It's Lenny who's making that noise. Until the dog leash silences him, too.

Neck red. Eyes red.

Lassie pulls the heavy body across the wooden floor. The leash tighter, tighter. But the screaming keeps on. It's someone else now. One of the girls, her language foreign.

Despair, that's what it sounds like.

An appeal.

They watch each other – the one who does the beating and the one who screams – as if they understand each other. And almost unconsciously, it seems, the man loosens his grip. Releases the choke cord.

That's as far as so-called Onyx allowed the film to roll.

He froze the image just as Lenny took his first breath and started to cough.

That was enough.

What he'd seen changed everything.

THE PAEDOPHILE LEADER lingered in his study, switching between images on the screen, now to the cameras on the house he sat in.

He started with the eye trained on the front.

The dirty white fence, the moss-green blackcurrant bushes, the bright red mailbox, the grey-worn pavement – it was all black.

He switched to the camera at the back.

Also a flood of electronic black.

Now the surveillance cameras covering the sides of the house.

Black, black images.

Not only had their sanctuary been encroached upon.

Someone had knocked out his entire surveillance system.

Someone who was here, now, in his home.

PIET HOFFMANN TURNED on his phone's bright torch and two bodies retreated, curled up, turned their shy faces away.

Accustomed to the dark. Unfamiliar with other people.

'Friend.'

Hoffmann whispered.

'Don't be afraid.'

He hurried past the two children on his way to the creaking wooden stairs, up to the basement door, grabbed the handle. Locked. Just as he'd suspected.

'Your cushions.'

He waited. Until they dared to look at him.

'Press them over your ears.'

He brought his hands to his own ears to show them.

'Like this.'

He'd glimpsed their simple sleeping places against the basement wall – thin mattresses with thin pillows that could at least protect their hearing.

He breathed in, out.

In. Out.

And fired.

THE MOMENT HE chose to shoot, that was the end. Too late to start over. The silence, the sneaking, the darkness – the conditions for getting close – no longer existed. Just alarm. Just hunt. Just seize.

He shot again.

Again.

Then the basement-door lock gave way.

If I'm only discovered now.

If the cat bowl didn't warn him.

If that fucker didn't know his house had an intruder.

I have enough time.

Piet Hoffmann pushed a broken door into a home he'd never visited, making his way along walls he'd never seen. He found himself in a hall. On one end was the front door with a shoe rack and coat stand next to it. On the other, the five rooms on the ground floor – and out of one, near the middle on the right side of the hall, streamed light.

His drug-influenced movements felt slow, clumsy.

But a single glance at that illuminated room was enough for Hoffmann to know exactly what could not be allowed to happen.

'You . . .'

There he sat, the leader.

Alias Onyx. Legal name Ron J. Travis.

'. . . stop!'

In front of the screen of a desktop computer connected to a . . . what was that?

An external hard drive? The NAS hard drive that Birte had spoken about?

The box next to the computer was black with two flashing lights.

Behind it sat another box, linked to four green and blue cylinders, the size of plastic soda bottles.

Piet Hoffmann had no idea what he was looking at – but realised Onyx had already known he was here when the basement door closed and locked.

He yelled again.

'Stop now!'

Piet Hoffmann, weapon raised, needed only two steps into the room to reach the desk and the man who looked so elegant and spoke so pleasantly and kept his children in a basement with a cat bowl. And who, with a gun aimed at his head, reluctantly turned round, staring at Hoffmann – at Carl Hansen's face, which had lost parts of its nose and a lot of its camouflage make-up.

At the same time the man pressed a button on top of the black box.

And a howling sound started.

'What just . . .'

The gun pushed harder into the man's smiling face.

'. . . happened?'

But no answer.

The mouth of the gun dug deeply into soft, tanned skin, the pressure increasing on the temple as blood started to flow freely. And the leader, after a stretch of silence, answered in his original tone; gone was the sharpness that ruled over two children, replaced by something calm, reasonable, convincing.

'I'm not stopping. No matter how you threaten me. No matter who you are, "Lassie". I mean, what are you going to do? Shoot me? How would that increase your chances of –'

Just then the black box jumped.

While the computer screen blacked out.

'– getting back all the content that's now being destroyed?'

Piet Hoffmann listened to the silence that arrived after the heavily encrypted content became unreadable. That was probably why he – with a confused level of violence that the drug continued to trick him into – grabbed the grinning paedophile leader and dragged him away, away from the lifeless screen and out of the room.

That was probably why he was so careless in his rage that he didn't notice Onyx grabbing hold of the door and pulling it shut.

And that was probably why he was now on the wrong side of a bulletproof barrier of thick metal, guarded by a code lock. While the evidence of abuse he came here to retrieve was being annihilated.

VIOLENCE. THREATS. FEAR of death.

Tools Piet Hoffmann had mastered over the years.

Whose proper usage always guided him.

He fired a total of five shots at the armoured door. Forced Onyx's upper jaw and lower jaw apart and pressed the pistol's barrel into his mouth. Rammed a fist into his face.

That fucker just laughed.

Hoffmann left him lying on the floor, bleeding. If Grens a couple of days earlier seemed to hear the seconds ticking by, now the Swedish infiltrator was sure he could hear inaccessible digital evidence being erased one bit at a time.

He also heard *sanctuary*.

Heard *misunderstood*.

He mostly heard *children don't really feel, they think they feel. We just dull their imagination for them, help them reshape their minds.*

He shot again at the reinforced steel door, in desperation. Screaming his rage. Kicked the man who laughed.

'The code! To the door!'

Unplug the power cables, that's what Birte said.

The ones he couldn't reach.

'Give me the fucking code!'

He sank to the floor next to that sneer, raining down blows that were probably too hard or too soft, the former since a couple of the leader's teeth fell out and he lost consciousness.

It was over.

This was as far as he'd get.

Piet Hoffmann was breathing heavily, looking around absently at the unfamiliar space.

Full of drugs, empty of hope.

When suddenly he ... Yes ... Well? ... glimpsed something at the end of the narrow hall that might be a solution.

He stood up and ran.

He'd been right.

The grey plastic door was the opening to an electrical cabinet.

He skipped the first rows of red and green buttons and glowing diodes, and the ones in the middle with small grey switches, but grabbed the large control at the bottom. The house's main switch. He pulled it down, heard a clicking sound as all the lights went out.

A DARKENED HOUSE. With hard drives that were no longer erasing. But also with unknown rooms and storage spaces and closets and stairs and corridors that meandered here and there.

Piet Hoffmann tried to orientate himself in the hall. It felt so much smaller without the lights on, as if what was left of reality had been compressed. The torch on his phone barely guided his way along the papered walls and over a thick carpet, back to the area outside the locked room. To the paedophile leader.

Who was no longer there.

Damn.

Damn.

The drug that stole his balance and strength had also taken his judgement.

Hoffmann had lowered his guard on a man who'd been beaten unconscious. Who'd allowed him to *believe* that. In a place the intruder didn't know, while the owner of the house was familiar with every nook and cranny.

He had done everything in his power to save the evidence on that hard drive – but lost the criminal the evidence could lock up.

Hoffmann spun round in the dark.

The man who called himself Onyx could be anywhere.

Behind him. In front of him.

Impossible to see in the dim light that leaked in.

Listening was easier. He perceived movements on his left side. Panting, wheezing, somewhere from the right.

Imagination.

The creaking and knocking and squeaking were just the sounds the house made, living material exposed to sun and wind.

Until they weren't any more.

A metallic click he knew all too well.

From out of the darkness.

Hands loading a semi-automatic shotgun.

HE STOOD THERE as a perfectly lit target.

That sharp beam of light in one more step, one more second would have meant his death.

Piet Hoffmann had learned early that panic was the worst emotion for an infiltrator, panic was counterproductive, panic was life-threatening, panic was your enemy's best friend.

But panic was exactly what he felt.

He turned off the phone's torch in a panic, sank into a squatting position in a panic, moved back in a panic. He was someone else. Scared. Dizzy. Wavering. Almost falling. The chemical mixture continued running through his blood, leaving him off balance, easily trapped. While Onyx was somewhere in the dark.

Intruder.

This is how it would be described and assessed afterwards.

Onyx could aim at his head, shoot him dead, and American law would be on his side. Furthermore, after establishing the identity of the deceased – one Piet Hoffmann, a foreign national who'd served time for a violent crime – the leader of the paedophile ring could not only continue to pursue his well-paid job of abusing children, he'd be praised by his neighbours for protecting the safety of their neighbourhood.

Hoffmann waited, motionless.

Did he see me? Does he know where I am?

While trying to take in every sound.

Very close.

Breath.

They were four, no more than five metres apart. Separated only by the darkness. Too far away to overpower him – and no opportunity to get closer.

A single careless move.

A single scratching sound.

It would happen that fast. How easily his life could end.

Slowly the blackness got lighter. His retinas, pupils, optic nerves adjusted, and Piet Hoffmann sensed a silhouette. A man's head. Arms, legs. And in his hands – a firearm.

Hoffmann wasn't the only one waiting quietly.

Onyx, too, stood frozen, hoping for something that would reveal the intruder's position.

Then a creaking.

Steps. The patter of feet.

But not the paedophile's, he was still immobile. Further away. Behind the silhouette with the rifle stood another silhouette.

The thirteen-year-old daughter.

She must have snuck up the basement stairs and out into the hall, while the two men were busy searching for each other. And Hoffmann suddenly realised – Onyx, who couldn't see her, would interpret those steps as Piet Hoffmann's.

And that was exactly what happened.

As the next step scraped against the floor, the leader of the paedophile ring spun round, weapon raised, and surely never heard as she gently asked 'Dad, why is it so da—' because the roar of the gun drowned out her voice.

AS THE SHOT was fired, trigger pulled back and magazine engaged, Piet Hoffmann braced his feet against the floor and pushed off with all the strength he could muster, despite his confusion and panic, and threw himself at the closest silhouette. The paedophile hadn't expected it, was turned in the wrong direction, and fell hard while the rifle was being twisted out of his grip and releasing hundreds of lead bullets. Hoffmann, the gun now in his hands, pounded the butt repeatedly into the leader's forehead and scalp before rushing over to the girl lying face down on the floor. The child – who was supposed to be replaced now that she'd outlived her usefulness – had saved his life and transformed her father's.

PIET HOFFMANN HELD her, stroking her hair and cheeks. She wept. She was struggling to hold back her tears, crying just a little more as she pressed her face to his chest, so used to no one hearing. Thirteen years old. And so alone.

Her father's shot hadn't hit her. All her injuries, both inside and out, had been received in another way. Hoffmann wanted to whisper to her that everything would be OK, but that would have been for his own sake, because that was too simple. This girl, who supposedly was on her way to being a woman, would never live fully, never achieve the kind of security or trust that came from childhood.

'GRENS?'

'Wait a second. I have to get out of here. This room and all these people and TVs and no ventilation and –'

'I got him.'

A thud. And another. The detective superintendent had come to an abrupt halt in the stuffy conference room on the top floor of the Danish National Police headquarters in Copenhagen, and it sounded like he'd dropped his phone.

'Sorry . . . you ended up on the floor. *You got him?*'

'Yes.'

'Neutralised?'

'Unconscious.'

'Piet . . . if you only knew! You've saved not just all the ones he abuses – the whole operation is depending on evidence from his computer, you should see this place, we're watching raid after raid on a big screen, and the members of the paedophile ring are being dragged out right and left by cops wearing so many different countries' uniforms and –'

'About the evidence. Something happened to the hard drive.'

The detective was still holding the phone in his hand.

But didn't answer.

'Grens? Are you listening? Something –'

'I'm getting Birte.'

When Ewert Grens walked fast, his limp became more obvious. Louder.

'Just a second.'

The heels of his shoes hit the stone surface unevenly. Even through the phone.

'You're on speaker. Now out in the hallway.'

The murmur in the background receded. The two Scandinavian police officers were alone.

'OK, first: the address I sent to your phone, Grens. *Now* you can send your American colleagues here, too. The fucker is lying in front of me in the hall, wrists and ankles in cable ties. However: the hard drive. Or whatever it is. I never got to it, I turned off the main power, but something happened before I could. He pressed a button, and the black box jumped.'

'A button?'

Birte whispered, leaning close to Grens's phone, even though none of their colleagues could hear them, or probably even understand.

'Yes, and –'

'Jumped?'

'He pressed a button and then –'

'Hoffmann, one moment. Grens?'

She lifted her eyes, looked at the detective.

'Yes?'

'That young guy in Stockholm who helped you get here?'

'Billy?'

'You would know better than me. Can you call him?'

'Now?'

'Immediately. A three-way call.'

Ewert Grens dialled a number stored in his phone and hoped his new acquaintance was awake.

He was.

Even though his voice sounded strained, as if he were lying down.

'Yes?'

'Billy – Grens here. Along with a Danish investigator. And soon with another colleague who's in California near a computer whose content we need access to.'

'This is starting to get expensive for you, Superintendent. Three favours to cash in.'

Birte grabbed the phone.

'Hi, Billy, I'm the Danish investigator. I know a lot about computers and how to find things inside them, but I'm not as up to date on their construction. When I heard Grens's description of you, I figured you might be. So I need you to listen.'

'Go on.'

Then she connected Piet Hoffmann to the conversation again – all three phones were now active.

'Describe again what you saw in that room.'

For a moment it sounded like he wasn't there any more.

Just electronic static.

'Your phone, Hoffmann? We can't hear you.'

'I'm calling from the house's landline – I knocked out everything else with jammers, even my own phone.'

The static subsided, and the infiltrator's voice became clearer.

'So I saw a desktop computer. Connected to a black box with flashing lights. And another box, a little smaller, connected to four green and blue cylinders, about the size of soda bottles. The button he pushed was on top of the black box, and when he pressed it it beeped, buzzed a little, and the whole thing jumped.'

Grens and Birte looked at each other, the crackling and hissing had increased again, but it seemed like everyone still understood.

'Billy?'

Grens brought the phone's microphone closer to his mouth.

'You heard?'

'Mmm. I heard an NAS, a power supply, four kings – sorry, capacitors – and a trigger. The button he pressed.'

'Yes?'

'This guy doesn't delete his disks in the usual way. I'd bet your colleague saw a degausser, and that the howl he heard were the capacitors charging up, building one hell of a magnetic field.'

'You're sure?'

'Let me put it to you like this, I have a . . . well, a friend, who was forced into some minor insurance fraud and didn't want to serve time for it, and say some Ewert Grens were to knock on their door to take a look, this seems like a variation on that friend's solution. I bet if your colleague took the lid off the NAS, he'd see a cable wound a bunch of times around a couple of hard drives, and then the capacitors work pretty much like batteries. You want a lot of voltage for a quick burst, and so you super-charge them with electricity. Because data is stored magnetically on a hard disk, every damn thing will be erased if you expose it to a very, very strong magnetic pulse. An electromagnet will kill the hard drive – and everything on it. That might make it jump, too.'

'*Fuuuuuuck!*'

Birte's scream was too loud, or too shrill, for the phone's electronics.

'. . . *Fuck!*'

And her voice was amplified by the walls of the hallway.

'Sorry, I just . . . *Goddammit!*'

Her voice, a little hoarse.

'It's too late, Grens. It's all over.'

'Over? Hoffmann turned the main power off and –'

'What your friend Billy is saying is that as soon as Onyx pressed the button and that box of hard drives jumped – that was the end. Having your computer clean such massive hard drives takes several hours. But this way, it was deleted in a fraction of a second.'

Grens loosened the phone from her tight grip, took it from her, spoke.

'So you, Birte, and you, Billy – you both think the hard drives have been erased?'

Billy's voice sounded firmer now, as if he'd stood up.

'Worse, Detective. They're as dead as hard disks can be.'

Birte had started walking towards her colleagues. Now she turned round.

'You get it, right, Grens? All the evidence is gone. We'll never be able to tie him to a single crime.'

THE PAEDOPHILE LEADER's face was cut, bloody, distended. One eye swollen shut. So he peered up with the other one as he came out of the next bout of unconsciousness, the one he hadn't faked. And Piet Hoffmann couldn't really believe it as he stood there in the darkened hall, guarding him, because it seemed like a faint smile was forming on those broken lips.

But the squeal of the capacitors as they charged had been all too real – they'd both heard it.

Heard as a supercharged machine on the other side of a locked security door destroyed movies and photographs of naked, tiny bodies, and electronic messages from one paedophile to another. Surgically removing the heart of the ring. Evidence that would have confirmed the members' abuse and connections.

'*You raped your daughter!*'

That was why Hoffmann, like Birte, started screaming.

'*Made her eat out of a cat bowl!*'

Screaming and kicking at the same time.

'*And you think you're gonna go free? Because of lack of evidence?*'

At the body who was smiling.

'*Because it's . . . too late?*'

GRENS AND BIRTE said nothing to each other as they walked back into the airless room and took their seats in front of the huge TV screen. There was nothing to say. During their brief absence, the numbers on the digital signs at the top of the wall, like queue numbers at a bank or a pharmacy, had risen from three to seven arrests in the United States – California, Florida, Texas, Idaho, New York, New Jersey, Michigan – and from four to five arrests in Europe – Denmark, Belgium, Germany, Switzerland, England. The number on the last sign, on the far right, represented the number of children rescued, and it too had risen – from seventeen to twenty-seven.

PIET HOFFMANN HAD stopped kicking and screaming. It wasn't enough, changed nothing.

The gun, on the other hand.

He pushed it against that broken smile, carving out new holes in the thin skin of the paedophile's face.

If no one else does it.

Punish.

He'd killed before. In order to survive. He'd never felt it.

You or me, and I care more about me than I do about you, so I choose me.

But this was different. Killing so that others could survive.

This he felt.

HE LINGERED IN the car with a view of the white picket fence and perfectly groomed fruit trees. The home where police cars were now arriving. He stayed until the children, the thirteen-year-old girl and her younger brother, were escorted by a female police officer into the light of the street lamps. Then he drove off. Back the way he came.

With thoughts that made sense. With nerve pathways and muscles that obeyed.

The chemicals had finally released his body.

The distance between the two places had seemed so great while he was desperately following the GPS signal from a tracking device hidden on a bicycle. Twenty-six kilometres. That was it. A short trip now that he knew where he was going.

This house was also surrounded by police cars.

Even more than the one he'd just left.

Ordinary patrol cars and slightly larger vehicles from the forensic department and over there, near the awesome view of the sea that was now only compact darkness, a couple of discreet vehicles that must belong to the social workers.

As soon as he reached the massive iron gate, Piet Hoffmann was stopped by raised uniformed arms. After a long discussion and an elaborate inspection of an ID issued to one Carl Hansen, he drove by the wild grass and stepped in through the front door heading towards the kitchen – the place where Hoffmann had left the paedophiles who called themselves Lenny and Meyer. Towards the detective who was the highest ranking officer and thus in charge. And after he had been introduced as the man who sounded the alarm, the detective nodded towards the railing of the terrace.

'That's where we found them. Bound. Beat up. One had a dog leash wrapped around his neck.'

'Sounds about right. As I remember it, that was where they were when I got here.'

'We were alerted by our colleagues in – Scandinavia.'

'I didn't know who to call.'

The American police officer read a few hasty lines from a notepad.

'Hansen? Carl Hansen?'

'That's right.'

'Danish citizen?'

'Yes.'

'And you just *happened* to pass by and waltz right in right then? Make your way to the kitchen?'

'I was walking. Out along the cliffs. I'm a tourist. The coast is unbelievable for those of us who didn't grow up here – it feels like you're all alone in the world. Then I heard the shouting. And ran over here.'

A forensic technician, who was shuffling around in plastic gloves with a zephyr brush dipped in sooty fingerprint powder, politely indicated that the officer and Hoffmann were standing in the way of their work. So the two of them moved over to the panoramic window, which looked out over an infinite dark sea, which the paedophile leader had proudly shown to his Danish guest not so many hours ago.

'Shouting? What kind of shouting?'

'As if someone were . . . well, in pain, I suppose.'

'They weren't just roughed up – I'd surely classify it as *aggravated* assault.'

The police officer looked at Hoffmann. Waiting him out. His voice contained not a hint of suspicion, more like idle curiosity.

'Might even classify it as attempted murder. That is, until the attacker managed to rein himself in. Or that's how I'd interpret it.'

'Maybe so.'

Now Hoffmann was the one waiting out the police officer.

'And perhaps – that might be something you, as an investigator of violence against children, are able to understand?'

Had the Swedish infiltrator read him wrong? Was the inscrutable expression on the police officer's face not curiosity at all, but rather the beginning of a proper interrogation?

'I mean, if I remember right – though, of course, it was pretty chaotic – there were children here. Girls, right? Being treated pretty badly. I imagine that the person who beat those men up probably thought those girls should be saved. Does that sound likely?'

Waited. Waited.

Waited for the nod that finally arrived, as if the officer might just agree.

'Possibly. But in that case, I wonder – as a police officer – at the degree of violence? Was it really necessary?'

'I imagine it was. Necessary. To make sure neither of them ever put the girls in danger again. Before someone – who just happened to be me – came by and called the police.'

Now it didn't take as long. The officer shrugged.

'Yep. That sounds reasonable.'

Could even have winked.

'That they deserved it. For the record – you never saw him? The man who did this?'

'No. I didn't see anyone else.'

'And if my co-workers dusting for fingerprints were to happen upon a few that belong to you?'

'Wouldn't be strange. Because I was inside the house when I called for help.'

'Just what I was thinking.'

Forensic technicians had started to circle alarmingly close and Hoffmann and the police officer moved further into the house along the taped line that indicated where the evidence had already been secured. Closer to the room with a single piece of furniture – the wide bed once watched by a huge stuffed animal below the shelf of the paedophiles' accessories. Toys and aids that were now scattered around on the floor in dried blood.

'The girls?'

303

'Yes?'

'Are they still here?'

Piet Hoffmann had almost not dared to ask, worried he wouldn't like the answer. Lenny and Meyer had been taken away and were on their way to their respective cells. But there had been vehicles from the social services at the back of the house.

'The girls are still here. Being tended to by professionals. Gradual progress – building trust so they can be taken away from here.'

'I'd like to see them.'

'Why?'

'We only met briefly when I was here last time. I'd like to leave knowing that they're OK.'

A guest house stood on the large plot. A couple of bedrooms, a nice little kitchen, and a living room with a TV and fireplace. From here the view was even better, nothing stood in the way, a few steps and he could jump down the cliffs towards the sea, infinity.

There they sat next to each other. On a sofa.

Two girls around the age of seven. Jittery. Small.

He approached them.

'*Hej.*'

He started in Swedish.

'How do you feel?'

Concentrating on the girl who had her hair tied up in a ponytail and who had screamed in the chaos *snälla sluta* in her high voice.

Linnea.

She didn't answer. But didn't look away either.

He sat with them while the social workers tried to build trust with the children. Every now and then silent glances were exchanged by him and Linnea, and he was sure that her empty eyes were reaching out to his from deep inside.

Later he discreetly took a picture of her with his phone, and as he made his way back outside to the cliffs that faced the great sea, he sent Grens the picture and a short accompanying text. *The girl with the blue butterfly.* He knew the detective superintendent would understand.

A PLEASANT BREEZE. And far, far below on the night-black sea, it was possible to make out a few scattered beams of light from passing boats. He had no idea how long he'd been standing there. It was peaceful, but he felt no peace.

Despite the fact that they'd blown up an international paedophile ring and arrested more than twenty extremely serious sex offenders.

Despite the fact that they'd rescued dozens of children who spoke a multitude of languages.

Even though he'd met Linnea and knew she was alive.

It was peaceful, but he felt no peace.

Because they'd never be able to build a case against the worst of them all. The man whose name was Ron J. Travis, so-called Onyx, who built the ring. That man was still alive – Hoffmann, in rage and frustration, had almost taken the shot, aimed his gun, and turned off the safety, but never fired – and, just as soon as his battered body healed, he would be released from prison and start recruiting new members to abuse more children.

Piet Hoffmann picked up a stone, which fitted his right hand perfectly and threw it straight into the blackness. You could hear it bouncing from rock to rock, but not whether it fell into the water.

One more thing to do before he got into his car and left this place forever. He was going to call Zofia. He had no idea what time it was at home, maybe morning, maybe a school day, but he needed to hear her voice.

Maybe he would also tell her what had happened.

That Linnea was alive. But that the perpetrator who'd injured her would soon be free.

That it was over now. A good ending, but also not good. As it sometimes goes.

Three hours later.

THE GIRL WITH the blue butterfly.

It really was her.

Ewert Grens had tried to question those sad eyes, find fault with her straight nose and thin lips, ignore the fact that her cheeks had exactly the same roundness and her dimples sat in exactly the same places. But even the way she stood was the same, her right leg straight and her left slightly angled, her arms hanging loosely in Hoffmann's recent picture, just like in photographs of her when she was four years old. This *was* the seven-year-old version of Linnea from Stockholm, the girl buried in an empty coffin.

He stretched, yawned, and for the first time in a very long time came close to something like calm. It felt good to sit some distance from the argumentative police chiefs and the chattering TV screens, all by himself on the narrow balcony with a view of Copenhagen's rooftops and an autumn wind cooling a face that had healed like it should, but sometimes still hurt more than he wanted to admit. In that stillness, allowing himself to accept that one of the two missing girls had now been found. He put his phone in his jacket pocket. And took out a picture he hadn't yet dared to fall into, never truly examined.

A photo, dark and gloomy but with decent sharpness, of another little girl. A dress and a plait and eyes that might just be the ones Jenny saw for the last time in a parking garage. The picture that Grens had clicked open a few days ago when he was emailing as Lassie in order to get the members of the paedophile ring to meet Carl Hansen aka Piet Hoffmann in real life. He remembered how he'd trembled and how that terrible dizziness had got worse – just as it was right now when he tried to think about it.

Alva? Could it really be her?

He had made a decision back then. Once the emergency phase was over, and Hoffmann was on his way, he'd contact Jenny. Even if she'd insisted she never wanted to speak to him again. She alone could decide if this was what he hoped – a trail worth following.

Now he couldn't delay any longer.

The emergency phase *was* over. And Hoffmann wasn't even on his way, he was on his way back.

Ewert Grens decided to call her. This Jenny who – like Anni long ago – had disappeared from his life in a cemetery.

He searched through his phone's contact list. Then among the outgoing and incoming calls. He couldn't find a number to match hers anywhere. Hadn't he saved it? Had he unconsciously deleted it from his call list? To protect himself? Not sure if he would be able to resist calling her late some night in a dream and end up making matters even worse?

He'd often wondered where she'd gone. Sometimes when he thought about her when he was awake, it almost felt like she'd been erased. He couldn't remember her features. Nothing about what she looked like. As a cop, he was usually good at that. But the more he thought about her, the more indistinct she became.

If the number was no longer in his phone, it surely had to be in his office at the Kronoberg police station in Stockholm. But calling Sven or Wilson and asking them to go in there and search for it wasn't really something he should do – neither of them was supposed to know where he was, and more importantly what he was doing.

But he did so anyway.

Eager.

Now that he'd finally mustered the courage to contact her despite the risk of being rejected.

He first called the officer on duty, who didn't have the time, what with a shooting in Råby and a suspected explosive device in the city. Then Elisa Cuesta and a couple of new subs in the investigations department, whose names he barely knew – all of them had their phones switched off and messages that said they were in a meeting, probably the same one. So then it would have to be Sven. No answer there. Though he called and called and let it ring a total of twenty-two times. Only Erik Wilson, his immediate superior, remained. His last choice. He'd hoped to avoid any bureaucratic scheduling questions for a while longer.

'Hello, this is –'

'Ewert? Is that you?'

'Yes, and I'd like to ask you to –'

'Good to hear from you – how's it going?'

'Fine, I –'

'Last week of your holiday – what are you wasting it on?'

'I'm doing what you told me to, of course – resting. Travelling a bit.'

'Travelling?'

'In Copenhagen right now, you know, red sausages, the occasional Carlsberg beer, and they have that lovely amusement park.'

'Sausage. Amusement park. I'm proud of you, Ewert!'

Detective Superintendent Grens took a deep breath. Returning to his errand, contacting Jenny – while that little spot to the right of his heart still held some courage.

'There was one thing. Which I need help with.'

'Oh, really?'

'An acquaintance. A phone number I can't find. Written down in my office.'

On the desk. That's where he asked Wilson to start looking.

And you could hear the rustling and scraping as his boss flipped through piles of criminal investigations at various stages.

'Nope. No handwritten note with a phone number.'

'You're sure?'

'I turned over every single piece of paper in every single folder – and I won't do it again. Completely sure.'

'The desk drawers.'

'*On* the desk is one thing. But rummaging around in your drawers doesn't feel quite right.'

'I need the number. And like I said, I'm pretty far away. Among those carousels.'

'Ewert, you're . . . well, a very private person. More private than anyone I know. And I really don't want to snoop through your private world . . .'

'Wilson?'

'Yes?'

'Rummage. Snoop.'

The three overflowing drawers on the left side of the desk squeaked loudly as they were pulled out. This was followed by thumps of varying pitch as the contents rolled onto the floor. Then that squeaking again, as they were pushed in.

'Nope. No phone number here either. And yes – I'm sure.'

'On the bookshelves? Or in that small gap between the table and sofa? Maybe on top of the safe? In the plastic pockets hanging on the inside of the cupboard door?

Erik Wilson laid the phone on the desk with the microphone facing down, so it wasn't really possible to follow his journey through a very lived-in office. Until he returned.

'Nope. Nope. Nope. And nope. It's not on shelves or in gaps or in plastic pockets.'

Grens didn't answer.

'Did you hear what I said, Ewert?'

'I heard.'

'Why is it so important? And what does it have to do with your holiday?'

'I'll tell you. When the time's right.'

No saved number in his phone and no notes lost in his office at the City Police, the place where he spent most of his time. Wilson searched as badly as he did. He'd have to keep looking when he got back to Stockholm, try to muster up the courage again.

The detective stood up, leaned against the railing of the balcony. Far below lay the Danish National Police's stone courtyard. It was much like when he stood at his own balcony and stared down at the asphalt of Svea Road. Feeling for a moment like anything was possible. Standing there, enjoying the view and the fresh air, you could even try flying, floating for a while – living. Or, even easier and therefore thrilling: you could push away with your legs, jump, fall towards eternity. He did neither. He sank down on the stool behind the tin can of cigarette butts and opened the files on his phone with interrogations of the Danish stepfather, the mother, and her nine-year-old daughter Katrine. To continue listening. The stepfather's denial and lack of empathy sounded the same no matter how the interrogator formulated the questions, and the daughter's hesitant responses about what she'd been exposed to were equally evasive. But he wasn't interested in either of them. It was the mother – her obsession with the girl, controlling her, asking constantly where she was and what she was doing, after spending years devoted to destroying her – that interested Grens. Why didn't she deny it – like the father? That would have been easier to understand, a way of protecting herself, tolerating her own actions.

He listened to her interrogation, listened again. Became familiar with the voice of a person he didn't know at all. Her intonations. Pauses. Hesitations. Convictions. Fear and aggression, retreat and attack.

Until he was freezing.

But not because of the Danish autumn winds. This cold came from deep inside. Like always when something felt wrong, and he didn't know what or why. And it gnawed at him and wouldn't stop gnawing until he turned what he couldn't see inside out.

He told Birte he was taking a walk, stretching his legs, had to get the blood pumping in his far from fit body. And he did walk. From the Danish National Police towards Vestre Prison. Just over half an hour through Copenhagen until he arrived at an arch-like entrance that resembled the gates of a castle in a fairy tale where the people are allowed to enter and bow and curtsy. Denmark's largest prison. Explaining who he was to the guard, who became the manager, who became the middle manager, who became the senior manager, didn't take long, but convincing them he should be allowed to visit the detainee Dorte Hansen took much longer. He supposed that was a good thing – if it was difficult to get into a prison unannounced, it was probably even harder to get out. In the end, the solution was the police officer from

Nykøbing Falster who was at his side when they knocked on Hansen's door, the one who wrote the original police report. After a long telephone conversation and Grens's stubborn, sometimes clumsy pressure, he agreed to assure the Danish Prison and Correctional Service that the Swedish detective was assisting the investigation with an emergency interrogation, and the locked doors that led to the exercise yard and through the prison's gloomy corridors were finally opened. To a visitor's cell identical to every other he'd ever been in, a plastic-covered mattress, a basic table surrounded by basic chairs, and a dirty window behind thick bars.

How broken she looked.

Led in by two guards, handcuffed, she shuffled along with hurried steps, her hair matted, her face pale, and her timid eyes on the stone floor.

Grens assured the two prison guards he was fine there on his own – the interrogation would go faster and yield more if he were allowed to spend time with the suspect alone while the uniforms waited outside the metal door. He fetched two cups of coffee from the machine at the entrance to the visitor's cell and when she took one of them feebly, she said nothing, drank until it was empty. Then he gave her his, still steaming, and waited until she emptied that one halfway.

'I've listened to your interrogations. But I don't understand them.'

Grens stood up from the table, made his way round the cell, stopped at the barred window overlooking the prison wall.

'Well, that's not quite true. I didn't understand. Before. When I first listened. I couldn't make sense of why you answered the way you did. But *now* I think I can.'

He looked at her.

'Because your feelings are true. That's why you ask the interrogator the same questions over and over again. What is your daughter doing. Where is your daughter. How does your daughter look. Because you . . . are protecting her?'

She said something.

So quietly that he didn't catch it.

'Dorte – I didn't hear you. Try again. Did I guess right? You haven't been asking about her over and over again in order to control her?'

'No.'

Still a whisper. But enough to reach him.

'You're not trying to dominate her?'

'No.'

'You want to protect her?'

'Yes.'

That last *yes* wasn't much louder, but by the time it reached Grens it was a roar that made the gnawing inside him cease. He'd suspected as much, guessed right.

'There's a theory among my international colleagues who are currently here in Copenhagen because of you and Carl Hansen. They believe a ring member leaked that picture of your husband and started this whole investigation as some form of revenge. For some reason, this closed circle cracked and one participant opened a forbidden door. Perhaps they felt singled out or despised in some way, perhaps they felt excluded when pictures were sent out, it could be anything that makes an easily offended person lose their temper. I never bought that theory. It doesn't make sense. Both you and I know that, right?'

She didn't look away. But didn't say anything either. He had to continue formulating his thesis on his own.

'Because you sent the picture, Dorte. Leaked it. And it ended up with me.'

There was a rattling outside the cell door, and one of the guards peeked inside.

'Everything OK?'

'Everything's fine. Could you please close the door again?'

That large bundle of keys scraped against the handle as the lock was turned, and it occurred to Grens that he'd never understand how a person could live with the sound of metal hammering against metal hundreds of times a day.

'Dorte?'

'Yes?'

'Now I want you to tell me if it was you. Because it's important. Both for me and for you. But most of all, it's important for Katrine who you claim to be trying to protect.'

Her lips moved. Inaudible. So quiet, so quiet.

'Yes.'

'Yes, what – Dorte?'

'It was me. I sent the picture to the Swedish aid organisation – they had a tip-off line you could contact anonymously. I have a hard time with people like you. Cops. Especially if they're Danish.'

A first image sent to an aid organisation and not directly to the police. Only Werner and Birte knew that. She was telling the truth.

'The picture of your husband? And of Katrine?'

'Yes.'

'Why?'

'It was . . .'

She was shaking. He should comfort her.

'. . . I mean . . .'

Hold her.

'. . . he'd decided, she would, we'd packed our bags and were going to . . .'

Tell her she did the right thing.

'. . . she was ready, that's what he said, ready to go all the way with others, and I . . . I . . .'

But Ewert Grens did nothing. Just waited her out. Like all experienced interrogators.

'. . . I couldn't let that happen! Just couldn't! It was always me who took the pictures, and I knew his back was visible in the mirror in that one, I even asked him to move a little so that . . . he was very, very careful and always checked the images so nothing could expose him, but I finally found the one I needed on the computer and sent it away and then . . . *Arrest me*, so you can save her, *please arrest me and arrest him*.'

For a moment he was sure she would collapse.

'Dorte, if that's true – then explain to me why you didn't just run away?'

But the fragile body didn't fall, it stayed upright.

'Why didn't you just open the door and walk out with Katrine by the hand?'

She was silent.

'Instead, you took even more pictures.'

And stayed silent.

'Did he beat you?'

She shook her head.

'Did he threaten you?'

Shaken again.

'Then I need more of an explanation if I'm to understand you.'

She cried, but quietly.

She kept herself upright with one hand clutching at the table.

And started to talk.

About a cry for help – at some point the only escape that was left. About boundaries that were incrementally pushed until the abnormal became normal. About his control over Katrine, and how through that control, he controlled her mother. About participating in the abuse because the mother answered yes to a question that she was never really asked.

Ewert Grens listened until it was his turn to speak. Explain.

About how pictures of part of an arm or a hand were enough for a trial, but not a conviction or a long sentence. About how not even a shirt with a company logo in a mirror is enough evidence unless the person on the other side of the camera testifies to who it is. About how if she didn't identify her denying husband, testify against him, this perpetrator would soon be released just like one of his paedophile friends in California. And her daughter would never be safe.

They stared at each other for a long time.

The girl's mother cried as she made up her mind.

Restrained, muted tears. As if in relief.

'Yes.'

'Yes?'

'Yes.'

She then hurried to the metal door and knocked, shouting she was done. As if not wanting the time to change her mind. The guards unlocked with their scraping and rattling keys, and she turned round.

'I'll testify. Tell them everything. Even if it means I never see Katrine again. At least I'll know she'll escape what's in those pictures.'

Seven hours later.

A CLOCK COUNTING down. Until time no longer mattered.

Piet Hoffmann had checked out of the small hotel in Santa Maria, a city that was filled with beautiful white churches. If you were to climb up onto one of their pointed roofs, you'd have a magnificent view of the Pacific Ocean and the world beyond. Before his trip back, he stopped in front of one of them and thought about just that. He didn't feel like driving on. Hollow. Like always, after a mission's seconds, minutes, hours, days finished ticking down. But it wasn't only that. He just didn't *want* to leave. Like always, he missed Zofia and the children in that piercing way that reminded him of pounding, red passion – but he wasn't ready.

Unfinished.

That's what this felt like.

He climbed out of the car and walked down streets he never had time to become familiar with, glanced inside sleeping windows. The lives of others. How many men like Onyx and how many broken teenage daughters were hidden behind the seemingly carefree walls of these houses? How many films of the violation of naked children were being sent through the air around him to anonymous computers? Never-ending acts of cruelty would only decrease in number for a short time – for the weeks it took the leader of a broken paedophile ring to be released for lack of evidence and start all over again.

This really was the best time to explore an unknown place.

Dawn.

Just like a few hours ago beside the night-black sea, the waking light was peaceful – but gave no peace.

He walked slowly with his arms outstretched like barriers trying to capture answers that didn't exist. He wandered by shop windows and closed restaurants. He even lay down in the middle of the street and stared up at the cloudless sky trying to feel *something* besides frustration and anger. But couldn't take in that bright blue, or the birds flitting here and there, all he saw was a grinning, bleeding face while hard drives on the other side of a locked security door had already been destroyed.

He was lying there when his phone rang.

'Hel— hmmm – hello?'

'What are you doing?'

'Lying down.'

'It's morning there, right?'

'Earlier than that.'

'You lying down – at the airport hotel?'

'What do you want, Grens?'

'Don't fly home. Yet.'

Piet Hoffmann sat up, still in the middle of a deserted city street.

'I'm not at an airport hotel. Never got that far. Still in Santa Maria. Twenty miles from those godforsaken houses.'

'Go back there.'

'To which one?'

'Onyx's home.'

'Grens – they're guaranteed to return there today. Forensic technicians.'

'Take care of it.'

'Because?'

'Go to where the computer was. We'll talk again when you're in place – don't have much time.'

'That computer is in a well-guarded police station now.'

It crackled, sounded like the line was breaking up, and Hoffmann was about to hang up and call back when the detective's voice returned.

'It's not that one I'm interested in.'

'Oh, really?'

'I need you to get over there and check about a copy that might still exist. And if it does, this one he *couldn't* delete.'

YELLOW POLICE TAPE fluttered in a gentle breeze, and wheel tracks cut deep grooves through the well-kept lawn. But no people. Not the house's owner nor the investigating police officers.

Piet Hoffmann walked closer.

Maybe he should have stayed in the car, made sure the property was truly deserted – but he had to get in and out before the neighbours woke up. So he did a repeat of yesterday. Opened the gate in the white fence. Ran towards the brick wall. Took cover next to the garbage bin. The basement window he'd made into an entrance had been nailed down by yesterday's police force, so he went on to the next one, took the razor blade, the pliers, the suction cup from his backpack and loosened that glass pane instead. On his stomach in the flower bed and then the same musty smell as he landed on the basement floor. But no staring eyes.

The stairs creaked like before, and the door to the ground floor was ajar, the lock out of order. The morning lit the way through the hall where he'd come so close to death in the evening darkness. The security door to the study was open again, and just as he'd expected, only dust remained in squares on the desk where the computer and all its home-made boxes had stood.

'Grens – I'm here. I'm in.'

During his last call, the detective had been walking the city streets of Copenhagen. Now it sounded like he was inside, probably back with the Danish National Police headquarters.

'Good. The computer and its accessories?'

'Gone. Just like the American police.'

'Exactly what I was hoping for.'

Hoffmann searched along the floor and walls of the room, then pulled out the desk drawers. Traces of additional belongings that were missing. Police technicians had taken more than just the computer with them for further examination.

'Piet – do you remember the young man who was with me when I showed up uninvited not so long ago?'

'You barged in uninvited more than once.'

'He stayed behind as a babysitter while I showed you and Zofia the Northern Cemetery?'

'I remember him.'

'Babysitting is not his primary occupation.'

'I understood as much.'

'He freelances for us now and then when all of our other computer experts have failed. Yesterday he was the one listening to your description of Onyx's devices.'

'And?'

'He called back. Turns out he might have a solution. There *might* be one more copy – which Onyx wouldn't have had the time or means to erase.'

Piet Hoffmann sank into the chair the paedophile leader had sat in while he distributed those pictures. His heart. It was pounding. So . . . there was still a chance?

Rotting away in a locked cell.

Dying a little more every day.

Much better punishment than me shooting him in frustration and finishing it all.

'I'm connecting him now. Three-way call, like yesterday.'

It took a moment. The detective fiddled with the buttons and swore and fiddled a little more. But finally managed to add a new voice.

'Superintendent? What's up?'

Hoffmann listened to the young voice, which was cheeky without much effort. There weren't many who could address Grens like that and get away with it.

'Electronics and gadgets, not my best subjects. That's why you're here, Billy. Piet – can you hear us?'

'I'm here.'

'Good. And you, Billy?'

'Still on the phone.'

The cheeky voice was back.

'And to my way of thinking, Superintendent, since these fucked-up pictures are their most valuable possessions then they absolutely could *not* be allowed to just disappear, so, of course, a backup has to exist. I mean, what if one day he accidentally presses the wrong button? A fumble and bit of a mistake just like a fellow such as Grens? Or what if the house starts down? Or if there's a burglary? Or if –'

He stopped. Drank something. Smacked his lips.

'I saw the shit they're up to. How they handle it, technically. Not what you'd call super hackers – even though that degausser thing was pretty fucking cool. So if they want a copy that doesn't leave any unnecessary physical traces such as flash drives or extra disks, then I'd bet it's on the cloud. The man you call the leader could very well have everything – the entire contents of those hard drives – encrypted in a file that he uploaded to the cloud.'

'Wait.'

Piet Hoffmann whispered.

'I thought I heard something.'

He allowed his arm to hang, the phone still in his hand. The dull thump of car doors slamming shut, that's what he'd heard. Not so far away. He waited. Straining his ears for sound. Which didn't repeat.

'The neighbours. They're starting to wake up. Go on.'

'The cloud. Someone like him could hide a copy of his shit there. And if that's the case, it couldn't be deleted the same way.'

New sounds. Voices from the same direction as he'd heard the car doors.

'Just tell me what to do. I might not be alone here for much longer.'

'His router.'

'OK?'

'We'll be able to find his backup through his router. The connection between the computer and the Internet. There are logs in there that could lead us to it – an IP address for a cloud service. You take the router with you out of the house and send it to me by UPS or FedEx or whatever, a day or at most two if you're not stingy, Superintendent. And since you're cops, you contact the network provider and get access to the backup. Then I start processing it, testing, and testing with a bunch of passwords – until I succeed. Get in.'

More car doors. But closer now.

Just like the voices.

Hoffmann hurried to the window that faced the gate and narrow alley and peeked out.

Police officers. They had returned.

'The router? Where? Thirty seconds. Then I have to get out of here.'

'I'd have put it on the same floor as the computer.'

'Yes?'

'Not in the same room. But . . .'

Something sharp.

That's how it sounded.

One time. Two times. Three times.

The barrier tape on the front door. It was being pulled away.

'. . . max three, four metres into the house. Maybe –'

'I know where it might be.'

The electrical cabinet. Where, in confusion and panic, he'd turned off all power to try to interrupt the computer's aggressive attempt to wipe itself out. There had been something on a shelf next to it – with glowing green diodes.

Hoffmann rushed through the hall.

Yes.

Surely?

There it stood.

He gathered up the cords and grabbed the lightweight plastic box. But couldn't lift it. It was stuck. Onyx had fastened the router to the shelf with two screws.

There may be a copy. Evidence, Piet. We still have a chance.

Hoffmann pulled hard, pulled again, prised it back and forth. It sat there. You needed different tools to get it loose. Or so much force that he'd risk revealing himself.

So the sound he heard now was coming from right outside.

Detectives and technicians scraping with keys.

Turning the lock.

Pushing down the door handle.

Piet Hoffmann let go of the router and ran. Down towards the basement. Just as the first rays of light streamed in from the entrance outlining the shadow of an arm, the basement door slid closed behind him, and he crept down the creaking stairs, towards the removed window.

Heavy steps over the ceiling of the basement.

They were inside the house.

He grabbed the window frame and lifted himself out of the missing window. And managed to push half of his upper body through the open hole – until his movements were interrupted.

He froze.

A uniformed police officer was standing by the fence. Not far from that stood another. They were searching for tracks, even outside.

He had no escape route now.

PUSHED AGAINST THE wall like a fucking rat.

Nowhere to go.

Just like in another basement. His own. Where he'd struck, and Grens had fallen flat. Now there were more pieces in play. In a house he'd broken into and whose owner he'd beaten badly, in a country where he was working under an assumed name for a foreign police force that wouldn't even admit he existed.

Piet Hoffmann put the window back in place as best he could; only if you got really close would you see that it was loose, lacking most of its putty and the pins, which held the pane of glass in place.

Some of the daylight made its way in, leading him helpfully.

The children's mattresses and pillows remained on the floor and the rest of the basement seemed to be drowning in debris, old furniture and removal boxes and clothes stacked along the walls. The feet above his head continued to slam down on the ceiling, investigators moving from room to room.

Until one of them didn't any more.

Until the basement door opened and the steps were met by creaking stairs.

'Say that again.'

In English. With a slight Spanish accent.

'I can't hear you.'

Steps that paused on the stairs waiting for someone up there to say something, again. Just enough time to throw himself down, crawl into that pile of furniture, press his body beneath an antique wooden cabinet.

'I just need ten minutes. I want to take a last look. OK?'

Someone called back *OK* up above and the heavy steps continued downward. Hoffmann lay on his back and every silent breath pushed his chest into the underside of the cabinet. The man not only walked heavily, he *was* heavy – slow footsteps made it clear the policeman was getting closer.

Overpowering, neutralising, in the worst case harming a single investigator was as easy as it was impossible. Because the one would be followed by another and another. And this was their territory, they knew it, he'd have to escape surroundings he'd never visited before.

Piet Hoffmann turned his head gently, pressing his cheek against the cold surface.

The metal of the cat bowl gleamed in the feeble light.

In front of it loomed two black shoes – a single step away.

HE COUNTED THE seconds. Ready to attack. He thought of Zofia and their life together, which had always been determined by his choices. This had been her choice. He stared at a pair of shoes and listened to a man rummaging through drawers and emptying boxes and opening cupboards. He pressed his body more tightly against the floor and held his breath as the investigator took the very last step, and now he was beside him.

THE AMERICAN COP wandered around in the dark basement for eleven minutes and twenty-eight seconds. Along with his colleagues, he moved around above the basement ceiling for a total of eighty-four minutes and eighteen seconds. After the police cars' doors slammed shut and the vehicles drove off down that quiet residential area, another fourteen minutes and thirty-seven seconds ticked down. And that was what Hoffmann did. Counted time. Breathing quietly. Pressing his back against the floor. On two occasions he was sure it was over for him, unconsciously tightening his grip on the knife in his hand. The first time a flashlight passed by the cabinet, its rays bouncing below it, even touching parts of his body. The next time the investigator squatted down with his black-trousered knees just a few centimetres from Hoffmann's staring eyes to photograph the contents of a cardboard box.

Piet Hoffmann remained beneath the cabinet with his breath blowing against the antique wooden bottom of the furniture.

For a long time.

Even though he heard the front door's double locks turning, the tape carefully put up again.

He stayed there while the day lived on, until darkness fell and evening's silence arrived.

Until he was sure he could go back upstairs and unscrew the flashing device undisturbed, put it into his backpack and find his way out through a window in the living room.

Four days later.

STRETCHED OUT ON the kitchen sofa Ewert Grens had a perfect view of the apartment's only clock. Bright, flashing figures at the upper corner of the stove, sandwiched between the oven door and the hot plates. 1:34. That meant he'd been inside the home of someone he barely knew and had absolutely nothing in common with for over forty-eight hours. Two whole days without once opening the front door and walking out onto the autumn-damp, slippery pavements of Stockholm.

'Are you sleeping, Superintendent?'

Billy's voice was still sharp, focused.

'Yo? Superintendent?'

'Yes. I'm sleeping.'

'Carry on. I need a little more time.'

Grens had arrived in Sweden at about the same time as the package from California. Spent the last days of his holiday on the top floor of an apartment building on Katarina Ban Street. Mainly at the coffee maker, which he was now on his way to again.

'More coffee? Since I'm making some anyway?'

'Seems like you're definitely not sleeping, Superintendent.'

'The big cups, then. Like last time.'

This life continued to surprise him. Arriving with new ideas and peculiar inventions. Like *Detective Superintendent* Ewert Grens, locked up for decades inside his own prison of safe routines, now climbing out of his corduroy sofa, leaving his office to go abroad on a trail that was little more than a blue butterfly. Like *the widower* Ewert Grens, who had chosen solitude for so long, who never felt comfortable in the company of new people, hunkering down in a cramped kitchen instead of fleeing for his home. Like how *sixty-five-year-old* Ewert Grens, who was far from youthful in his thoughts and actions, and who didn't really want to be questioned, now finding himself relaxed and comfortable around a twenty-seven-year-old who loved to ask questions. All of it was as incomprehensible as the various computer programs and files now being methodically explored.

'Here. No milk or sugar. Same as me.'

'Thank you, Superintendent.'

He placed the giant cup next to the keyboard in the apartment's only room, while Billy's dancing fingers continually entered new algorithms. Trying password after password for encrypted material that – via the router Hoffmann had taken with him and the network provider that Birte eventually wrestled into submission – had been found in exactly the place he guessed. A copy hidden in a cloud service.

'Again, I want to make sure you realise what we'll be facing. When you finally manage to get by those passwords.'

'You don't need to protect me, Superintendent. I know. Though I really have tried to forget those pictures from last time.'

'This will be worse.'

'I haven't changed my mind. We *will* get that bastard.'

Just as when Grens lingered behind Birte in Denmark, he did his best not to worry and pace around and unknowingly drive those in his vicinity crazy. So he abandoned the giant coffee cup and the computer screen and Billy's dancing fingers and returned to the kitchenette and the sofa, which had proved almost as comfortable as the one in his office. He had his own mystery to solve. Searching for Jenny, who he wanted to meet again. For several reasons. For one, to clarify a saved image – found during the most hectic stage of the investigation, when by chance he'd clicked into the river of orders that flowed between the members of the paedophile ring – which now lay in front of him on the kitchen table. And maybe, if he were lucky, Jenny would identify and confirm who it was.

But first he had to find her.

On his way from his own apartment to Billy's, Ewert Grens had stopped by the Kronoberg police station and turned his entire office upside down. Every drawer in his desk and every tightly packed binder on his bookshelf and every plastic tray overflowing with papers lined up along the walls. The result was the same as Wilson's search – no note with her number. He'd considered, in parallel with the hunt for Onyx's password, asking Billy for help with this as well, search for her digital tracks, but decided against that idea. Jenny and the story of her daughter were not the focus of the international investigation at the moment, they were part of his own journey. And moving forward also meant travelling alone.

'Superintendent?'

'Yes?'

'Are you still sleeping over there?'

'Yes.'

'Good. Because it's time.'

'Time?'

'I just figured it out. We're inside the paedophile leader's encrypted material.'

It took a while, sitting side by side in front of those big screens, to really take in the breadth of what they'd found behind the secret door.

Because the man who called himself Onyx had hidden not only his own pictures, not just the ones he'd sent and received – he had copies of every single photo that had ever been exchanged inside their closed ring. His files, according to the table of contents, hid a total of eight hundred thousand examples of child pornography. Once they sorted the lists of passwords for bank accounts and email addresses, once they catalogued orders and invoices and payments from every corner of the world, they had a turnover that was the equal of a small publicly traded company. All the commercial activities Onyx and Lenny conducted – selling pictures and films – were now available on the screen in front of them. And without even counting particularly carefully, the detective estimated revenues of tens of millions of dollars.

'This . . . Billy . . . I have no idea how to thank you.'

'I do. I'll get back to you about it.'

'I live in fear of that day.'

Grens smiled.

'Now we know it exists. That *everything* exists. But it's still not enough.'

'Not enough? I know you're a bit jet-lagged, Superintendent, after that long one-hour flight from Denmark, but – surely you have eyes? It can't be any clearer!'

'It's not enough – legally.'

Billy stood up. Upset. His thin arms became sweeping wings in front of the computer screen.

'What the hell are you saying? Did we do all this for nothing? Is that fucking monster gonna go free because . . . because you sit there talking about –'

'What I'm saying is that justice and the law are not always the same thing. That if we want justice, we'll have to deceive the law a little.'

Billy was still waving his arms.

'And what does that mean exactly?'

'We have to find a solution, make sure what we have here won't be ruled out as evidence in a future trial. You and I – two unauthorised persons outside of official channels – *might* be suspected of having tampered with the encrypted file. Right now, it would be easy for any moderately adequate defence lawyer to argue this is all incorrectly handled evidence.'

He looked at the young man. The pride that had just been so palpable, the smile, was no longer there. But Grens could see no qualms on that face. More like concentration, purpose. That's what Billy was showing. This was someone who preferred staying up all night solving puzzles so as to avoid going outside during the day, who would rather find his way through digital labyrinths than figure out how to socialise with his fellow human beings.

'In that case, Superintendent, we'll just do like the paedophiles did. Hoist them on their own petard.'

'Expand?'

'We send this as a tip-off to the American police from an anonymous source. A message that bounces and bounces until they can have no idea where it came from. Never guess it was sent by an old cop, whose face has gone from black and blue and swollen to yellow-brown and basically normal, and a computer geek, who has terrible taste in clothes and too much time on his hands. All the information will arrive as an anonymous tip-off, a strong encrypted file that their computer experts will have to crack, just like I did. We'll let them work for it a little bit.'

Ewert Grens had slowly started to exhale.

It could work.

'And are there any?'

'Any what, Superintendent?'

'Who are as good. As you.'

Billy looked away, suddenly shy. He understood it was a sincere question. But also Grens's way of giving praise. Praise from someone who surely was unused to giving any.

'I know it sounds unlikely, doesn't it, Superintendent?'

He turned back, shyness gone.

'But they do have a few who are as good as me. And it's kinda fun – seeing the fucking leader destroyed by his own methods.'

Then they fell silent. Sat next to each other and studied the screen and the contents of an encrypted file that would prove everything. Possession of eight hundred thousand files of child pornography. Revenues of tens of millions of dollars. More than enough to send every single member of the ring – with the exception of the still unidentified Redcat – away for as long as their home nations allowed.

'You're not as bad as you think, Billy.'

'What?'

'At hanging out with other people.'

'Neither are you, Superintendent.'

They had arrived. They had succeeded.

Evidence to sentence every one of them. Even the creator and leader of the ring.

That was probably why, for a moment, they glanced at each other and smiled.

Nine days later.

THE INTERNATIONAL TERMINAL breathed longing. A mumbling throng of anticipation. Everyone crowded together, nudging and poking, but with no anger or irritation – each collision was followed by another look at the electronic doors sliding open silently as the next passenger exited with heavy suitcases and tired eyes. Ewert Grens had been watching people meet for almost half an hour. Hug, cry, laugh. Airports were so full of contradictions – at their best when the ones who were moving stopped.

Then they arrived.

Behind an elderly couple struggling furiously with awkward luggage and a cluster of businessmen carrying identical briefcases. Piet Hoffmann and Linnea. Hoffmann carried a small bag and his other hand rested lightly on the girl's slender shoulder, leading her gently towards the exit and the waiting horde.

Grens waved at them as best he could, then pulled back, searching for a calmer place. And as they approached, he squatted a little to be able to look into a pair of eyes so much older than the seven years they'd lived.

'Hello. My name is Ewert, and I'm a police officer, Piet's friend, and I'm here to help you.'

She looked at him, listening, with no reaction. Blank. Shut down.

'Yes, and as a policeman I'll –'

'You have to speak English. For her to understand. She only remembers a few Swedish words.'

Hoffmann looked at the detective, then turned back to the girl and spoke to her in English.

'Right, Linnea? English?'

She nodded. After a long hesitation. Very carefully.

And Grens saw so much more:

With her Swedish as good as gone.

Maybe *that* was what she'd shut down. Her past.

In order to survive.

'OK. English. Linnea, I'm a police officer and I . . .'

It took longer to explain to Linnea using his rusty English. And was quite a bit harder. Especially about her parents. How they didn't know yet, weren't aware of her arrival – because Grens didn't want to give them a hope that might be snatched away if it all went wrong after all, if their daughter wasn't on that plane, didn't step out into a new world that was also her old one.

The detective took them on a detour via an airport kiosk to buy them all an ice cream – the girl looked at Hoffmann as she received it, awaiting his nod of approval – then they all picked out sweets and fizzy drinks. On the drive back to Stockholm, Grens took the opportunity to glance in the rear-view mirror when he thought the girl wouldn't notice, fully occupied with unwrapping rustling paper from the kind of caramels that stuck to your teeth. She was still empty. Face neutral, no joy, no anger. Pale skin, dark circles beneath her eyes, a mouth with narrow and dry lips. Her hair was shorter than three years ago in that film from a super-market surveillance camera; he wondered who had cut it for her or if that was something she'd taught herself. A couple of times he tried to talk to her, just nonsense about nothing, but received no answer. And he understood. Or, he understood why. How a small child, whose beautiful joy of life had been obvious as she examined her reflection in a toaster or over-turned boxes of candles and pressed her index finger into soft packs of napkins, a girl with thoughts and hopes and language, would have had to lose all of it in order to survive. But with shy glances she continued from the back seat of the car to check in with Hoffmann. The trust she had in the stranger who'd helped her escape hell on earth was touching – the infiltrator, in a very short time, had managed to reach a heart that sick people had spent years doing their very best to destroy.

At the Central Station she broke down. It was there that Hoffmann repeated one last time what he'd tried to convey to her several times on their long flight – that when they landed in Sweden a friend named Ewert, whom he trusted totally, would be waiting for them, and when they got to a city called Stockholm, Piet Hoffmann would have to leave her, and she'd drive on, home to her family. Linnea threw herself around Hoffmann's neck, pressing herself close, hugging him and weeping until no tears were left, and they had to prise her off, one tiny finger at a time.

Grens understood completely. He too didn't trust anyone because he'd learned life was simpler that way – and if that was so, where would this little girl find any trust after all she'd been through? How terrible it must feel to be left in the hands of an elderly man she'd never met before?

But they had no choice.

The Swedish superintendent's unofficial colleague could not be made official in connection with a living girl who had been declared dead. Ewert Grens already had enough questions to answer to his boss and didn't need to add the question of why – even though it was illegal – he had used a private citizen as an infiltrator. And Piet Hoffmann, at all costs, wanted to prevent both criminals and the police from becoming aware that he'd been persuaded into one more assignment, thus risking any new offers.

Alone in the car with the fragile little girl he was assailed by unease. Intrusive, ruthless. Pain concentrating in the detective's gut, at the spot where his anxiety always took root.

He turned to her, smiling as warmly as he could.

My God.

How incredibly intense it felt, her anxiety.

Her grief.

When she had let go, she collapsed, becoming even smaller.

What had she been through? How had she survived? And did she realise where they were headed?

Ewert Grens hadn't really considered it – if the girl was even aware of her family. She had only been four years old when she was snatched away. What images shaped a person before that? What memories had she not yet managed to rid herself of? Was he going to pull up to a house and ask her to climb out and knock on the door of perfect strangers?

Her anxiety grew as he slowed down, pulled over to a kerb and left the car. But he had to make the call. Warn her family. If they were prepared, maybe all those stormy emotions would scare her a tiny bit less.

It took a while for someone to answer. One of the children, unclear which, a high and alert and happy voice. Grens asked for Mum or Dad and waited while the light steps ebbed away and a couple of heavier, slower ones approached the phone. Saturday, and as he hoped, the whole family was together this morning. The next voice was not as happy. The girl's father who he'd quarrelled with at the funeral. Who had basically told the detective to go to hell and, with roughly the same wording, did so again now and hung up. When Grens immediately called again, it was the mother who answered. She was just as furious, but in language that was not quite as crude, and in one of the longer pauses, between her detailed descriptions of how the judiciary viewed police officers who harassed the public they were supposedly tasked with serving and protecting, he was eventually given the opportunity to very briefly and with precision state his case.

She fell silent.

She called for her husband with a voice that barely carried.

She wept.

She calmed the girl's siblings who anxiously wondered what had happened, why Mummy was sad.

She asked again and again if Ewert Grens was really telling the truth and because he assured her that he was, she cried even more.

And when she wanted to know what day they would arrive, and he answered in half an hour, she fell completely silent and after a while dropped the phone, which slid into an infinitely long, annoying tone.

Linnea was lying on her back in the back seat of the car when he returned. She'd understood. He was sure of it now. Despite the empty gaze. She wasn't blank, shut down like before. She just felt nothing. No elation, no assurance. And if you're not on your way anywhere, it was probably just easier to lie down.

It had been a balmy August evening the last time he'd visited this house, which was the last in a row of equal-sized squares. Rotating sprinklers had chattered away on all those beautiful green lawns, and this stone path had been covered with a patchwork of scattered toys. Now the fruit trees crouched down free of leaves, and footballs and trampolines were locked away in a large garden shed. It was colder, even though he was arriving with life.

Her short steps were hesitant.

Towards a house that was new, but had a room that was so familiar.

Ewert Grens followed her slight figure, close enough to catch her if she fell back.

When, after a long moment, she pressed the tip of her finger to the damp metal casing of the bell, three pairs of children's feet began to hammer from various directions across the floor inside in a race to be there first.

Soon the front door opened.

Jacob.

Linnea's twin brother.

And when he held her, hugging the seven-year-old body, soft and hard at the same time, until she finally hugged him back, he whispered loud enough for all to hear.

'I knew it the whole time. Knew you were out there.'

Fourteen days later.

ONE LAST TIME.

Ewert Grens had regularly turned all his drawers and shelves and cabinets inside out and spread his folders all over the place. He did it again now. Searching for the note where he'd written down her contact information. One final attempt. Then he'd give up.

Earlier this morning he had checked the same register as yesterday and the day before yesterday and every other day since coming home. In the digital world, she no longer existed.

Or had he misremembered her name?

Jenny Uribe. So close to Anni's maiden name, Anni Uriba, the young woman he'd fallen in love with so long ago, who after a five-minute wedding ceremony at the Swedish embassy in Paris with two porters as witnesses had taken the name Anni Grens. Had he confused Anni's maiden name with Jenny's? Was that why he hadn't found her? Jenny Uribe had been the only person with that name living in Sweden, and there should – even if she'd moved abroad or died recently – still be some record of her residency here. Maybe he remembered the last name correctly, but not the spelling? Was there a missing accent or a circumflex or whatever those little dashes and dots above letters were called?

Two places left to look.

Among the graves in the cemetery and in the archive in the basement.

The first time he'd seen her name was there – in the bowels of the police station inside an archival box that summarised the investigation into a girl who disappeared early one morning in an ugly concrete car park. That's why he was again walking between those high shelves filled with boxes and binders and bundles of paper. Aisle 17, section F, shelf 6.

That was where it had been. One of the smaller boxes that was easy to lift down if he balanced on a rolling ladder.

Now it didn't exist at all.

No matter how he turned and twisted all the other boxes nearby.

It was utterly gone – or had he perhaps misremembered this as well?

Like last time, he had to move backwards in order to keep going forwards. Back then he'd logged into the City Police's archive computer and activated keywords from a conversation in the cemetery with a strange woman: 'MISSING', 'GIRL', 'SÖDERMALM', 'PARKING GARAGE', 'DRESS', 'PLAIT'.

He entered those keywords again.

And didn't get a single hit.

Ewert Grens was overcome by dizziness. Tried to hold the breath that wouldn't come back if he let it go.

First, the note about how to get in touch with Jenny had disappeared without a trace.

Then she couldn't be found in a single register, neither public nor the less than public.

Then there was the investigation with witness statements and forensic reports.

And now – even the data in the archive computer.

Both Jenny and her daughter had been completely erased.

Someone was trying to cover up the entire investigation. Someone in this police station.

The detective tried to stand up but stumbled, close to falling.

What was going on? Why couldn't he find what had so clearly been there so recently? How could someone so suddenly be erased?

Only one place left to look.

If he hurried – maybe he'd have time to cross her path? It was Thursday, the day he knew Jenny always visited the Northern Cemetery. That had to be the way to make contact again, unexpectedly in real life, even though she had explicitly told him she never wanted to see him again – he was known to have that effect on people. There on that bench where they first met, he would ask her to study the image he'd clicked open in that flood of orders passing back and forth between the members of the paedophile ring. And maybe, if they were lucky, Jenny would recognise her little girl. It's true that she might turn away when she saw him, they hadn't met since the day Linnea's empty coffin was lowered into the ground, when she realised his real reason for attending, but if so he'd just have to run after her and convince her, for Alva's sake – Alva, which almost sounded like an elf's name. Whose grave was another thing he couldn't find, even in the light of day, despite trying to many times.

—————

The rest of the day he sat there. On the rickety park bench by the gravel path lined with lanterns and memorial stones. With a picture in an envelope in his pocket that he never had to open. Because she never arrived. Others came, mourners who visited other graves, replanting plants and changing the contents of the vase for cut flowers, raking a little, watering a little, talking a little with someone who didn't answer any more. But not Jenny. Who once again, when he tried to remember what she looked like, faded, completely losing her features. Maybe she suspected he was waiting for her, maybe that was why she didn't come.

—————

It was late by the time he opened the heavy doors to the police station and the investigative division. Deserted. With one exception. The door closest to the lift, Elisa Cuesta's office, was ajar, the light of a desk lamp and the sound of a computer's keys slipping out.

Ewert Grens hesitated, pushing the door open.

'Can I come in?'

Detective Inspector Elisa Cuesta sat in one corner of the room with a computer in her lap on a chair that looked more like a stool. Because it *was* a stool. That was probably the only thing that could be wedged in here. And easier to get to than all the way over to a desk still surrounded by unpacked boxes.

'Everything seems to be the same, I see. Last time I had to zigzag my way through. And the box I sat on is still there as well.'

Grens remembered his last visit. That feeling that the whole world was swaying. But he settled down on a cardboard box that seemed steadier this time.

After that he wasn't really sure how to start.

'Well, you know . . . I have a question for you that might seem a little strange.'

'Oh, what is it?'

'Last time I was here, when we . . .'

'Grens – I know. That was stupid of me. I saw what kind of shape you were in, and I probably never should have knocked on your door. I know you, just like the rest of us, have way more cases on your desk than hours to solve them. But there was only a month left until she was going to be pronounced dead, and I just couldn't let her go, and I thought you might take one last look.'

'I'm sorry, but I'm not following . . .'

'So, of course, I really believed you hadn't taken in one bit of what I said. But you still solved it somehow! On a mandatory holiday that you took because . . . Linnea was rescued! She's alive! I have no idea how you did it, but I am extremely grateful, more relieved than you can possibly imagine.'

'"I saw what kind of shape you were in"?'

'Yes?'

'What are you talking about?'

'I think I said it at the time. You seemed confused. I think I even described it a bit harshly as "disorientated". That was the impression you gave me, and that was probably why I suggested you go to Wilson and take some time off, rest for a while. And then, when you came back to me again a month later talking about a completely different girl, whose coffin was under a white cross and which we had supposedly investigated and . . . ah, it just didn't feel good at all. *You* didn't feel good at all. But I'm grateful I was wrong. And that Wilson finally forced you into taking some leave, which gave you the time to solve the case.'

'"One month left"?'

'Yes?'

'And "came back"?'

'Yes?'

'And "a completely different girl"?'

'Yes?'

'And . . . What . . . I mean, have you completely lost it? I'm not following you at all, in fact I think *you* are the one who seems to be disorientated.'

'I guess it was the day before Linnea's death was supposed to be declared when you knocked on my door. About that other girl. Who was also supposedly four years old when she disappeared. I never did understand what that was all about.'

Dizziness. Which had been gone for a while, until it came back this morning, now struck him again, but much more violently.

'She was taken out of a car in a parking garage, like I said back then, and she –'

'Grens – for as long as I've worked here, we've never had an investigation into the kidnapping of a child in a parking garage. And you and I have never talked about any other girl. Just about Linnea, and about her disappearance. Which I'm so grateful that you finally took on.'

It was hard then not to fall as he zigzagged out, even though he put one hand against the wall and grabbed onto the bookshelf with the other.

He wasn't sure how he got back to the cemetery. Or how many times, in the light of the spaced-out lanterns, he wandered between the grave where Anni lay and where My Little Girl used to be and could no longer be located. The dizziness and the confused dreams were back now and tangled everything up. What had left him in Copenhagen, turning into adrenaline and sharpness and action. As the evening passed into night he sat down on the park bench, got up again only as dawn joined him, and the birds awoke. Then he started walking again. Back and forth. Until he decided to go to the grave that belonged to Linnea instead, which contained a coffin that would soon be dug up because she had no need to lie in it. He found it, thank God, right where he thought it would be. It was here that he dropped a flower with Jenny, over there in the church with the arched dome where they'd sat among the mourners.

That surely had to be right.

Maybe that's why he was heading there now. In order to stop the shaking a little, regain his balance.

And perhaps that's why right there at the church entrance he was so unexpectedly pleased to run into the priest who conducted the funeral service.

'Good morning.'

'Good morning – can I help with something? Or do you want to look around? Find some silence in preparation for the day?'

'Thanks, I just want a peek.'

'Welcome to the North Chapel. If you have any questions, I'll be here a while longer.'

They started in separate directions inside the beautiful church. Until suddenly the priest turned round, his voice a little louder, amplified by the church's interior.

'By the way . . . I recognise you.'

'I was here at a funeral some time ago, but it could hardly have –'

'You were sitting at the back. So separate from all the others. It's not every day you bury someone who's not there, a coffin with no one inside, that stays with you.'

Grens nodded, he understood exactly, and continued on into the silence that the priest had referred to.

'Excuse me . . .'

Now it was Grens who turned round to call out, and it was his voice bouncing between the rows of benches.

'. . . I have a question, too.'

'Yes?'

The priest walked a little closer, to indicate he was listening.

'You said I was sitting in the back, separate from all the others. Away from everyone.'

'Yes, I remember. It was just you. Away from everyone.'

'Me and a woman. Around my age. Short dark hair.'

'No, you were alone. And, like I said, separate, that's surely why I noticed you.'

'I don't understand.'

Grens sank down on one of the hard pews.

'The rows at the front were full? And there, on the stone slab, stood the coffin? Candles, lots of them, surrounding it. Right?'

'Yes.'

'And behind a small exhibition, which isn't here any more, but which obscured my view a bit, that's where I sat?'

'Yes.'

'Alone?'

'Just you.'

When the priest understood that they'd finished talking he left, and Ewert Grens lay down on the wooden pew and stared up at the beautiful painted ceiling. The only way to be sure he didn't fall to the floor. He lay like that for an hour, possibly two. Until he finally dared to close his eyes, a little. And make one last call in order to understand.

'Ewert? Is it you?'

Zofia.

She'd answered immediately.

'Yes. And I need your help.'

'Is it urgent? Can I call back later? I'd like to talk with you, about everything, now that Piet's finally home, but my class starts soon and the students are already filing in.'

He kept his eyes closed. Without falling.

'Slightly urgent . . . I'd say. I'll be quick. Do you remember . . . that picture you showed me in the cemetery? From the funeral that wasn't a funeral? Linnea's empty coffin?'

'Yes?'

'Where did you find it?'

'I saw it on . . . Wait a minute, I think I saved it.'

Murmuring in the background. The scrape of chairs being pulled out. Students arriving in a classroom.

'Here. Now I have it. What's your question?'

'Well, according to Erik Wilson, I'm in there somewhere.'

'Are you?'

'Yes, apparently. That's why I had to . . . Can you see me?'

She hushed her students, and the murmur ceased.

'I'm looking now . . . looking from left to right, a lot of people dressed in black and . . . Yep. Indeed. Wilson's right. There you are, at a bit of a distance from the others.'

'And who's standing with me?'

'With you?'

'Yes, do you want to –'

'This is what I'm going to do, Ewert – I have to hang up now, but I'll send you the link, and you can continue looking at this on your own, OK?'

Soon his phone dinged. The picture he'd made sure was taken, which she talked about that night at the cemetery, just like Wilson, he himself had never really looked at. He did so now. Searching. Like Zofia, from the left all the way to the far-right edge.

There. That could be me.

Ewert Grens leaned closer to the phone, dragged with two fingers across the newspaper photo of mourning funeral guests, enlarging, enlarging it a little more.

There he stood.

Separate from the others.

Alone.

———

He ran. The park bench. At Anni's grave. The one he'd been sitting on all these years, during all those visits.

That existed, right?

Drops of sweat slid slowly down his forehead and quickly down his back as he arrived. The park bench remained. And when he sat down in the exact same place as always, he could even recognise where it was uneven and where the paint had rubbed off. It was on this bench that Jenny, who reminded him of Anni, had sat down that very first time – he'd just begun to close his eyes and find some peace when the whole world shook, but it turned out to be just another human being choosing to sit down on what had always felt like his place.

Dizzy.

So incredibly, incredibly dizzy.

Had he been here, at Linnea's funeral, with . . . no one at all? Had he quarrelled with Linnea's father all alone afterwards?

If so – had he also sat here on the bench alone? Next to no one at all? Conversed with no one at all?

Did she not exist?

Was there no Jenny who reminded him of Anni?

Was there no grave for My Little Girl?

Just as there was no investigation in the archive?

Just as he hadn't visited Elisa Cuesta until *long after she had come to him* to talk about Linnea and her pending death certificate? Had Cuesta's request for help into the investigation of a missing little girl awakened inside him thoughts of another little girl Grens knew nothing about?

Ewert Grens was one of those who couldn't cry. A few times since he was a child, that was all. But now he wept. Falteringly, uncertainly. Soon with so much force that it tore him up inside. He thought of what Hoffmann, who was also not the type to cry, had said about sitting on a toilet in California trying to hold back tears that had already decided to come out. That's what this felt like. As if what had been inside for so long had decided.

Had one investigation, about a girl named Alva, been going on only inside . . . his own head?

Had he . . . invented the whole thing?

At the same time, the second investigation – the one that actually existed and according to Cuesta was the actual starting point – led him to a real girl named Linnea and a real paedophile ring that was destroyed and real children who were liberated?

He stared at the white cross, which turned blurry as those damned tears refused to stop flowing.

The grave I was standing in front of? That Jenny visited even though no one lay beneath it? Just a few rows away, yet impossible to find a way back to?

My Little Girl?

Was it . . . *my girl* that this was all about?

My little girl who disappeared when she was pulled out of a car, who I never talked to Anni about afterwards, my little girl's funeral I didn't go to – just like I didn't go to Anni's?

My own little girl lying somewhere over there in the memorial grove?

One month later.

THOSE FIRST DAYS back on the job Ewert Grens had avoided his boss's office – chosen detours to the coffee machine and taken the back stairs on his way in and out. Until early one morning Grens found Erik Wilson sitting rather uncomfortably on his corduroy sofa waiting for him. An ambush. But sooner or later, they were going to have to discuss how one of the investigative division's detective superintendents had actually spent an involuntary holiday when his only assignment was to rest. Because what Grens had hoped to keep secret was becoming very hard to ignore as the news of a busted international paedophile ring made its way not only into the Swedish media, but also into major newspapers and TV news across the rest of Europe and the United States. So on that morning Grens had reluctantly agreed to reveal every non-sanctioned step he'd taken in the investigation, from the cemetery via Hoffmann's kitchen to Copenhagen and San Francisco – and Wilson, in turn, had used every bit of his bureaucratic skill to make sure the obligatory documentation existed to make it seem like the City Police's involvement in this quite successful international cooperation had originated from their chain of command from the outset.

That was almost three weeks ago now.

The heap of papers from Birte that contained transcripts of conversations between the members of the paedophile ring across various chat forums still sat on the desk, intruding – whispering irritably as he immersed himself in other ongoing cases, even hissing loudly as he tried to sleep.

Of course, he should have got rid of it.

Carried it down to the archive. Or had it shredded. Or sent it back to the Danish National Police so they could decide the future of their transcripts.

Maybe he should even do that now. Pack it up, send it away. Allow himself to let go of an investigation that was never totally completed. Because despite the fact that neither the girl buried in an empty coffin nor the girl with no name needed to be found any more, an unsolved mystery remained. The only member of the ring who had never been seized. The one who called themselves Redcat and who, like the leader Onyx, hid behind bouncing IP addresses.

If . . . Yes . . . Maybe?

Before he finally put everything in the filing box and wrapped it up in that never-ending string?

Just one last try?

To see something he had yet to see. To think something he hadn't yet thought.

Because he really was the only one left who could do it.

Birte was long since involved in investigating new serious crimes on her endless travels around Denmark; now and then she did check in and ask how he was doing, and he always found it difficult to strike the right balance in his answers, so he usually ended up not responding at all. And he didn't want to bother Billy – just like with Hoffmann, it was important to minimise the risk of someone finding out that a detective superintendent named Ewert Grens sometimes preferred to solve crimes with the help of those who weren't police officers. That left only himself. And his methods were hardly those of the digital world. Analogue. That was his world. On a hot summer day, he'd started this international police investigation into some very modern criminals with a simple, old-fashioned magnifying glass in one hand and a small bottle of Tipp-Ex in the other – and he would finish it the week before Christmas by reading, under the light of his desk lamp, every hard copy of the paedophile network's extensive chat history.

Two thousand four hundred and fourteen pages.

A year of chat conversations between various members of the ring that Birte had managed to track down, all revolving around just one thing. Molesting children.

03-08-2019 04:09:36 Message from 873118765: *My daughter turns 11 tomorrow.*

03-08-2019 04:10:10 Message from 434876234: *I know. A shame. Already. But congrats to her! She will look really sexy in a very special present I sent.*

03-08-2019 04:11:04 Message from 873118765: *Ah. Can't wait!*

But what was supposed to be the last time, somehow also felt like the first. Grens, like Birte, had gone through the majority of this several times – but never the surplus material, which had become superfluous as soon as they had enough for prosecution. And the little he'd already read of that, he'd perceived without truly comprehending. He'd mechanically deciphered letters forming words and sentences, but hadn't been able to understand their meaning. Now he made sure he did. Twisting and turning the numbers of their addresses, searching for alternative interpretations to texts he'd previously been sure of, trying to discover some pattern in their repetitions. He spent most of his time on the pages Birte had marked 'probably Redcat' in the top right corner. Like the paper he held now – the person calling themselves Redcat was congratulating someone on their daughter's eleventh birthday and had sent a very special gift.

03-08-2019 04:11:43 Message from 434876234: *And make sure to take pics and send them back. Your daughter. Maybe for the last time as a child.*

Ewert Grens shook just as much every time.

Reflected on how this still affected him so deeply.

How it was impossible to get used to, the way Birte accustomed herself to it.

He grabbed his evening meal from the vending machine in the hallway – plastic-wrapped sandwiches and plastic-wrapped chocolate ball – and it was a relief not to have to hide from Wilson. He slipped one of his mixed cassettes into his old stereo and let the voices of the sixties sing to him, calm him. He turned off the phone, closed the door.

And started to flip the pages.

———————

What struck him first was the language. Despite the fact that the detective's English continued to be somewhat underdeveloped, still after a dozen conversations between Redcat and other members it was clear to him that the final anonymous ring member was struggling with certain expressions and formulations, clearly indicating that English was not his mother tongue. It didn't seem native to England, America, Australia or anywhere else in the British Commonwealth.

The next observation was about timestamps.

Every time Redcat communicated with one of the Europeans, it was during the day or in the evening. Never late at night, like the conversations with the Americans. Redcat must live in the European time zone, although in theory it could also be Africa, but in terms of the structure of the paedophile ring, it was more likely somewhere in Europe.

But it was only after Grens, seeking fresh air and renewed energy, had moved to a late-night cafe on Sankt Eriks Street, and continued his search with a beautiful cup in his hand and two cinnamon buns on the plate, that he made serious progress geographically, getting closer to that last one, that still unknown member. More specifically: in a chat between the ring members Redcat and Lassie. Because at the bottom of that stack of unread surplus material Lassie aka Carl Hansen from Lærdal suddenly switched from English to his mother tongue – Danish. And Redcat answered him – in Swedish.

The member with the bouncing IP address, which Birte never had time to investigate and was eventually forced to deprioritise, *lived here*.

———————

An ordinary sheet of copy paper weighs about five grams. Two thousand four hundred and fourteen pages adds up to twelve kilos. That was the bundle Ewert Grens was lifting up and down, flipping back and forth through, spreading out across his dessert plate, his table, and over every other available surface in an otherwise empty cafe.

So you too are – Swedish?

Where are you?

Who are you?

Are you in front of your computer screen right now, closer than I ever imagined, living the life of a faceless paedophile?

The answer he was searching for, the one that took him further, wasn't on any of the pages marked 'probably Redcat'. Instead it was as he arrived at those logged chats Birte had secured on the very first day from a computer they'd managed to save in an apartment above a bakery – 'Lassie' written on the page corners – that the dizziness he'd been wrestling with recently overcame him again at full force. But no longer was it coming from the confusion between what was real or not. This dizziness sprang from a sense of surprise, maybe even dismay, while simultaneously containing that wonderful tense, eager, breathlessness of something completely unexpected revealing itself. Because after closely reading about fifty documents of the members' bizarre chats to and from the Danish paedophile, the solution stood right there in front of him. In a short exchange between Lassie and Redcat about a proposed journey, a proposed meeting, their chats switched into Danish and Swedish for a second time.

First Redcat in Swedish:

08-11-2019 12:14:22 Message from 434876234: *My friend, it's gonna be so nice to finally meet you. And beautiful Katrine, of course! I'm landing at Kastrup early Sunday morning, at the agreed time.*

Then Lassie in Danish:

08-11-2019 12:16:21 Message from 238437691: *Sorry, but there's a problem. I'm not gonna be home on that day. Travelling abroad.*

Then Swedish, Danish, Swedish, Danish:

08-11-2019 12:17:30 Message from 434876234: *I'm not sure I understand.*

08-11-2019 12:18:35 Message from 238437691: *My fault. We've been planning this trip to Brussels for a long time.*

08-11-2019 12:18:57 Message from 434876234: *We had an agreement. I already bought my tickets, flights and trains. Even checked in online at SAS. Too late to get my money back.*

08-11-2019 12:19:41 Message from 238437691: *We'll need to find another day. I'm sending some extra pictures of Katrine to make up for it. They will surprise you.*

'*Early Sunday.*'

That's what he wrote. The still anonymous Redcat.

'*To Brussels.*'

That's what so-called Lassie, Carl Hansen, wrote.

And Ewert Grens knew exactly which Sunday they meant.

The morning after the police raid. The day after Grens and his Danish colleagues stormed in on already packed suitcases intended for the journey that would mean full intercourse with a stranger.

The detective dug his hidden coffee cup out from under the piles of paper.

So close.

He knew now tickets had been bought and paid for, a meeting between handle *Redcat* and handle *Lassie* had been cancelled at the last minute.

He had a date.

He even had an airline and a destination.

The only thing he needed to identify the very last member of the paedophile ring was a bit of luck, and the Sunday-morning passenger manifests for every flight that had taken off from Sweden and landed at Kastrup Airport in Copenhagen.

Dizziness, that new variety that arrived with eagerness or surprise, also seemed connected to geography. Nationalities. It had been easier to keep the images of abuse at bay when the only Swedes he'd been searching for were the victims of this crime. When they were the ones being abused and not the abusers. When *we* became the rapists his balance became so much harder to maintain.

———

The number of customers increased dramatically just before dawn when a large group of young people wearing black and a lot of eyeshadow, their voices far from sober, turned the cafe into a dance floor. Grens managed to save his sheets of paper from the hard soles of their wide heels at the very last moment. He was done anyway, about to take off. The taxi to Frösundavik was already waiting for him on Sankt Eriks Street.

———

Arriving at the airline's headquarters north of Haga Park was like a journey back in time – the long pedestrianized streets and the glass-encased buildings sent Ewert Grens straight back to the Swedish eighties, both their attitude and design. When he'd been an energetic young man open to opportunities, these buildings represented eternal growth, monopoly, self-importance, and no one – not the young police officer nor the people in these expensive salons – could have guessed that they'd one day be brought together by an invention called the Internet that facilitated crime, or that this criminality would be of the most appalling type and overseen by a criminal network called a paedophile ring. After spending the early hours of the morning outside a closed entrance, and then just as long being batted back and forth between various middle managers, unsure if passenger manifests were appropriate reading for an investigating superintendent and who then batted him onwards to another section of this glass building, at last he landed at the right mid-level boss. Who became more and more upset as he described this case to her, until she handed over the complete passenger lists from that autumn Sunday. She fetched him a strong cup of coffee just the way he liked it, guided him to an empty desk, and told him all he had to do was ask if he needed any more assistance.

That Sunday – 10 November, Father's Day – four SAS flights had departed early from Sweden with Copenhagen as their destination. From the Stockholm Arlanda and Gothenburg Landvetter airports. Really only two, both shortly after six in the morning, direct flights with estimated travel times of about an hour – but in order to get the fullest picture possible of the morning, Grens also included two more leaving a few hours later – the term 'early' could vary from person to person.

He placed the four documents in front of him on the table.

The dawn flights on the left, he'd start there based on the most likely departure time. He read each line slowly, letting one passenger name at a time sink in. Trying to spark some memory that contained connections or associations.

No.

No name on board those half-full flights stood out to him any more than any other.

It was the same on the later flight from Gothenburg, which landed in Denmark at half past ten. Here, even more seats were empty, and none of the booked ones felt the least bit familiar.

Only the later morning flight from Arlanda remained, departure a few minutes before ten and arrival at Kastrup Airport just after eleven, nearly full. A list of two hundred and twenty-three passengers.

Grens twisted a bit, softening up his neck, clapped his hands over his head using a movement a physiotherapist once taught him. It didn't help. The chair was as inhospitable as the one he'd sat in behind Birte in Lærdal's small police station. No matter how he adjusted its various handles, making the seat go up and down, tilting it this way and that, despite how he leaned forwards or backwards or to the side, still it irritated his back, made his hip throb, and his thigh ache. He felt nothing but pity for the person who spent their days at this desk.

He started from the front, row 1, seats A, B, C, D, E, F, all that extra legroom, and then read his way back seat by seat in the cabin. That's probably why it took so long.

To get to row 22, seat F, on the right side, by the window.

Arriving at last at a name he was familiar with.

———————

'I wonder: if someone books a flight, but doesn't end up taking it, would that be possible to see?'

Ewert Grens had done exactly as the friendly, helpful middle manager had urged him to do. Let her know as soon as he needed assistance.

'A vacant seat? Somebody paid, but didn't fly?'

'Yes.'

'We have those on almost every flight. Just a moment.'

Those keystrokes again. Which the whole world seemed to depend on these days.

'Three travellers. Who never boarded and therefore forfeited their money. They all booked at the lowest price, so non-refundable.'

'What about 22F?'

She turned to the computer screen again.

'Yep. That's one of them. The seat was selected at check-in almost twenty-four hours earlier.'

'And never used?'

'Never used.'

Grens returned to the desk in order to collect the papers. They now constituted evidence in a future trial.

The departing flight that internationally wanted paedophile Redcat had planned to be on.

The passenger list where the detective superintendent met a name that made him shake like he'd never shaken before.

'Was that all? Is it enough?'

Her voice was clear and distinct, not shrill at all even though he was already on his way and she was shouting after him.

'I mean, do you need the address, too? Or anything else?'

'I already know where your missing traveller lives.'

Back at the Kronoberg police station Ewert Grens dared this time to knock on Erik Wilson's door, on Elisa Cuesta's door, on Sven Sundkvist's door, and invite them all to come down the investigative division's long corridor and sit on his corduroy sofa. Finally, he could walk without feeling dizzy, disorientated, or even detached from his own workplace. And as he handed them each copies of the documents that were an extension of a coffin with no contents, he had no need to explain for very long why he was requesting backup from at least two patrol cars before making the planned arrest. His colleagues all had experience of those who lived multiple lives inside one body – the dual personalities who were experts at showing just one face to the world – and they too knew how unpredictable those inner selves could be when their performances were penetrated, and everything was over.

The toys had changed, now oblong little sledges and skis of various sizes and a bright red snowracer lying upside down just as the skateboard once did, but the stone slabs peeking through still led him to the front door of the house. The apple trees looked beautiful clad in white, and the blinking Christmas tree lit up half a snowman where the hammock once swayed.

Soon he'd have experienced their garden in every season.

Then he did just as he had on two previous visits, knocked on the round window in the front door while simultaneously pressing the doorbell, waiting for those running feet racing to be the one who opens the door.

No one came at first. Just as he expected. Neither Linnea nor Jacob, who as the oldest probably would have arrived first, were home yet. The twins attended the same class – despite Linnea having missed so much school it had been determined central to her healing and with the extra resources the municipality had allocated she was slowly catching up with her peers – and just this afternoon Grens had made sure their teacher hastily scheduled an extended field trip. The younger siblings too, Mathilda and William, after the detective consulted with their preschool staff, had packed their backpacks for an afternoon outing that was expected to go a little later than usual.

So it took longer than on his previous visit here. For the door to open.

The mother looked out, surprised.

'You?'

'Yes.'

'Again?'

'Can I come in?'

'Weren't we pretty clear with each other? I very much regret, Detective Grens, how I asked you to leave our home that first time, and how I snubbed you in the cemetery, and I was just far too shocked to thank you properly when you brought us our beloved little girl – but you stared me in the eyes and promised our family could live our life in peace. We need that. The last thing we need is more meetings with more police representatives.'

'I was wrong. Or at least not quite right. There will probably be at least one more. So let me in, or do you want me to ask my friends for help – the ones you see over there? Another just like it is watching the back of the house.'

Grens stepped aside a little so that Linnea's mother could have a view of the other end of the quiet residential street. The police car that was parked there.

'I really don't understand.'

'For the last time, I'm asking politely: please step aside so we can talk inside. At your kitchen table. I agree with you. Your children have had more than enough meetings with police representatives. And I'd like to get this settled before they get home.'

Linnea's, Jacob's, Mathilda's, and William's father also thanked the detective for his fantastic work in connection with his last visit, while expressing surprise at further meetings. He dipped slightly dry bread in warm coffee, let it melt in his mouth, before looking first at his wife and then across the kitchen table at Grens, who was similarly engaged in dipping his bread, while doing his best not to make a mess on the tablecloth.

'We exchanged some harsh words. Both you and I, Detective, said things that had no place at a funeral. But I was feeling harassed. Like you weren't listening to us. And now you're sitting here again, refusing to allow us to get accustomed to . . . well, a new stage for our family, and it sadly reminds me of that time. Like you're harassing us again.'

Ewert Grens couldn't seem to manage the dry bread. No matter how he sank it into his coffee cup brownish drops somehow ended up on the kitchen table when he fished it up again, and he used up three damp, crumpled napkins before finally giving up. He'd just have to drink his coffee the usual way.

'Well, then I'll get straight to the point. Waste as little time as possible. My errand today concerns these.'

While the cat meowed at its water bowl like last time, when the detective had realised its stripes were not grey but reddish, he moved aside the breadbasket and his own cup to make room for the first document.

He watched both parents for a long time.

'There are so many different ways to celebrate Father's Day.'

He turned now to the father alone.

'This year you'd planned to spend that particular Sunday in Denmark. Early November. You even booked and paid for a ticket. Departure from Arlanda a couple of minutes before ten in the morning and arrival in Kastrup just after eleven. Row 22, seat F, right side, by the window.'

Ewert Grens had never liked carrying a firearm. During his forty years as a police officer, he'd only fired on a few occasions. And to be honest – he wasn't that great a shot. But this afternoon he'd carefully pulled on his worn leather holster, it hung there like a cross, hidden by his jacket. For reasons he hadn't yet fully comprehended, he had wanted to meet suspected paedophile Redcat alone. Maybe it was very simple, maybe he was very simple, if his colleagues weren't with him when this all began, then they could very well keep their distance as it came to an end. And it was at that moment, as the first piece of evidence was placed in paper form between them – when Linnea's father might start to realise the real reason the detective had come – that his dual nature, which was expert at showing only one face to the world, might choose now to show its other face. The real one. The sick one. The violent one. One that had long ago passed beyond any definition of what's called humanity.

———————

'I wasn't in Denmark on Father's Day. I was here and, as usual, my beloved wife and my wonderful children served me breakfast in bed. Right, Maria?'

Linnea's father had not yet looked at the document, nor did he show any signs of understanding. Accordingly, showing no signs of attack.

'Your wife doesn't have to answer. If you will look at this instead.'

Grens placed another piece of paper between them. Also related to a flight booking.

'You paid. You checked in. But you never travelled anywhere. That's what this copy says. So you may well have got your breakfast in bed since you didn't use your ticket.'

Now the father looked.

Now he read the columns Grens had circled with a felt-tip pen.

But still he revealed nothing. If he was acting, he acted well.

'I don't understand, Detective.'

Maria, Linnea's mother, had pulled the documents towards her and picked up her reading glasses to make out the small text.

'Why would Jonas have travelled to Denmark? Why would he secretly book a ticket and then not use it? What are you trying to –'

'Here. My very last document. You can both read it. Together.'

My friend, it's gonna be so nice to finally meet you. I'm landing at Kastrup early Sunday morning, at the agreed time.

Ewert Grens held out the first lines of a chat between someone calling himself Redcat and someone calling himself Lassie.

And beautiful Katrine, of course!

At the same time, he moved his hand towards his holster and made sure they both saw it.

Prepared.

For just about anything.

'I don't understand. Jonas. What's the detective trying to say? Why would you want to go to Copenhagen? Who is "my friend"? What does "beautiful Katrine" mean? Did you write this? Jonas? *Jonas! Answer me!* I don't understand what . . . *Look at me!* There's a police car at the other end of the street. Another police car . . . There, look through the window, do you see out back? Katrine – who is she? Another woman? And why are they here if that's the case? What are you not telling me? What does the detective think he knows that I don't? *Talk to me, Jonas!*'

Nothing can truly be predicted.

Not even in a paedophile ring where only two suspects remain at large.

Over his long career as a police officer, Ewert Grens had learned that no criminal ever completely resembled another. No matter how much experts and journalists and the general public tried to sort them all into the same group. Criminal patterns can be identified and repeated, but the behaviour and reaction of an individual criminal can never be perfectly foreseen.

So Piet Hoffmann's description of the second to last free member's reaction – how the leader Onyx went on the offensive, was prepared to kill in his own home, fought for his life with everything he had – wasn't at all how this last member met his final moments of freedom.

Because Linnea's father Jonas just sat at his kitchen table. At the place that had been his at every family meal for the past ten years.

Never moving.

Not when his wife screamed and hit him and demanded answers, or when a detective superintendent held a pair of handcuffs in front of him.

Maybe he had nowhere to run.

Maybe he didn't want to.

As if he had arrived. Discovered, unmasked. No longer needed to hide.

The two patrol cars that Grens had requested as backup never needed to intervene. Putting handcuffs around two unstable arms and taking the man who called himself Redcat out of the house without his children having to watch, ended up just as undramatic as the detective had hoped.

However.

Why Linnea's father had arranged to have his daughter abducted as part of the closed paedophile ring's bartering system, Ewert Grens was no closer to discovering as they walked towards the car. How do you even make sense of what goes on inside such a deeply disturbed person's mind? The interrogations that would take place over the next weeks were all about piecing together fragments of this broken man's incoherent story. The interpretation both Grens and the interrogator would finally settle on was that the paedophile ring member Redcat had been promised access to an American child in exchange. And in the twisted world the group invented together and whose moral and human rules they alone determined, this had first been what the father called 'a temporary loan' that would be explained away by a credibly staged kidnapping. An anonymous hand caught by a surveillance camera in a supermarket – while shocked parents held each other tightly. Even the girl's mother, who knew her husband better than anyone, was as convinced by it as the investigating police. And if that were so, what the deeply disturbed man *meant to be a temporary loan to a society of the like-minded*, it seemed, based on the father's fragmentary story, became much more difficult to have repaid as time went on. The macabre fantasy had turned to a tangible reality when Linnea was taken across the Atlantic. What started as a sick thought experiment turned into a real child who could see and remember and think, an exchange student that the ring members belatedly realised could expose all of her abusers if she were ever returned.

———————

When Ewert Grens left the house that looked so much like every other on this suburban block for the very last time, where he intended to experience no more seasons, it was with a kind of loneliness that both held him up and pushed him to the ground.

Despair that he couldn't help a little girl who had once been pronounced dead figure out how to live the life she'd been given back.

And with a feeling of shame at the relief he felt at not having to, not having to turn back and look into the eyes of Linnea and her twin brother Jacob.

Five months later.

HE HAD ALWAYS felt such intense fear when a plane was landing. No ability to control the conditions for continued life, having to depend on a person you had never met before, who you never decided to trust. Now he felt nothing. When the plane bounced a little too hard against the runway and the noise of brakes sounded louder and more persistent than usual, Ewert Grens sat there with complete calm. It was as if what he'd left behind him this morning diminished all other fears – as if fantasies about what *might happen* seemed ridiculous in comparison to what he'd witnessed over the last couple of days in an American court, what *had really happened*.

He dawdled while all the other passengers struggled to grab their hand luggage first and squeeze their way out of the fuselage. He was in no rush. Where he was headed, nobody hurried.

———

The trial in the US had been different from those he'd participated in over the years in various parts of Sweden. Thirty-seven courtrooms in the same building, each with its own judge, and when the bus of ten built-in cells arrived, they'd made sure the public stayed on one side of the fluorescent markings while the prisoners and their guards passed by on the other. As Onyx approached – the only name the detective would give that face – it was an older man who now looked his age, and with handcuffs and leg cuffs his steps only shuffled slowly forward. Orange suit and a yellow bracelet that indicated he was a dangerous prisoner. As his waist chain was locked to an iron loop on the floor, he was placed on the chair for the accused and waited as his hands were uncuffed so he could receive and follow along with the investigation's papers.

The last time Ewert Grens had been at the exit of this large airport it was to welcome home Hoffmann and Linnea – now he was the one passing through the hordes of relatives, heading on to the next queue, which was just as hectic as inside the plane. The same people now crowded together in a new place. Grens lowered his suitcase and took a deep breath as he sat down on it – today would just take the time it took to get a taxi.

In the courtroom, they'd sat opposite each other. The leader of the paedophile ring, in flesh and blood, so close Grens could have touched him if he reached out a little. Onyx welcomed the Swedish detective superintendent who'd come to testify against him with a smile. Not insecurely. Not apologetically. He smiled as if he were . . . well, superior, as if *only I know how all of this is truly connected*. Grens had seen those smiles before. Learned to put up with them, ignore them. It didn't work this time. Instead, his own irritation had grown to unbelievable proportions by the time it was his turn to testify, because he knew what it meant to have the paedophile leader sitting right there and following along with the visual material. Every abuse was being relived. A healthy person would signal some shame, some remorse – not smile while raping again.

So finally he made his way all the way to the front of the taxi queue and was soon able to slide down into a leather seat that smelled faintly of cigarette smoke. The traffic was heavy on the E4 highway that led to Stockholm, despite being at least an hour past the morning rush, and it felt good to lean back and close his eyes while the sun shined so bright.

———————

The prosecutor's case had been built around images that were grue-somely painful, gruesomely cruel. By the end of the first day several jury members begged the court to dismiss them. And now – on his way home with the Danish and Swedish trials against ring members Lassie and Redcat also concluded, with sentences of five and eight years' imprison-ment respectively and damages to Katrine and Linnea that weren't even enough to cover the lifetime of therapy that one day might make them whole again – Ewert Grens caught himself, for the first time in his mem-ory, sympathising with the American system of adding each charge to a total sentence, in Onyx's case a sentence of three hundred and eighty-four years in prison.

———————

He asked the taxi driver to stop outside Gate 1. That was where he wanted to get off. He'd always found walking from this direction to be the most beautiful path through the Northern Cemetery.

And beautiful it was.

An early-spring day taking the sun for a spin around the dance floor. Lawns shining after shaking off the last snows. Trees and shrubs stand-ing as motionless as headstones in the still air.

Things that were real.

He could tell the difference now. After doing what he failed to do as a young cop thirty-five years ago – asking for the professional help needed after a person loses everything. Even finding a safe place to return to in his mind when emotions became too heavy.

He had figured it out, finally. How this time it hadn't been just his ordinary fucked-up flurry – he'd stirred up everything until it was no longer possible to find a way out. He missed her so much and got close to the moment that those who knew about such things classified as acute psychosis. The type that arrived stealthily with delusions and hallucina-tions. And it was still hard to grasp, his consciousness still cloudy. What he had actually been through. They'd been right – all the others. Late one evening he'd even opened Erik Wilson's closed office door and just like last time headed straight over and sat down on the edge of the desk, which swayed and creaked as he leaned over and said: 'You pushed me out of the force.' And then waited while the man behind the desk sputtered: 'Ewert, if you're here to bark at me or complain or . . . I just don't feel like it right now, go somewhere else, and take your anger or irritation or whatever you think you need to be rid of with you.' But Ewert Grens hadn't gone anywhere else. Instead he held out his hand, and when his boss also reached out, to his own surprise Grens gathered the courage to finally whisper: 'Wilson, thank you – you saved me.'

Because he no longer needed to escape to another world when the one he was in became too incomprehensible. He would never be reconciled to people using force to control other people, never stop hunting down those who valued their own bodies more than others, but he also knew it was possible to become reconciled with yourself. With the events that add up to a life.

The suitcase he was holding was the same one Anni bought on the day they flew to Paris to get married – even the stamp of the Eiffel Tower that still sat on its upper corner had been pasted onto it by her in their hotel room – and therefore it was also the bag he always packed whenever he ventured away from the police station. Maybe he should have stopped by home first and left it there, made it easier on his halting steps. But after having to testify repeatedly on an American witness stand how the evidence had been handled during the police's initial raid, which ended up as the basis for a total of twenty arrests and the liberation of thirty-nine children and hundreds of unidentified victims worldwide, and after then describing before the court again and again how the paedophile ring had widened as Birte dug up more hellish pictures, he knew this was where he needed to go without losing any more time.

A suitcase that during his walk became increasingly awkward and clumsy so that halfway there he dropped it on the path that separated graves of different centuries.

Resting his hand and arm.

It wasn't Anni he was heading to today – instead his destination lay a couple of hundred metres to the east. At the memorial grove section of the cemetery. Which he had been on his way to for over half his life, and that only as recently as a few months ago he'd almost reached. He was going to visit her now. Their daughter – his daughter. Who'd had heart and lungs and eyes, which had opened and closed. She had been real. She shouldn't be lying there alone. He was going to talk to her, tell her what he'd meant to say to her last time, how people exist as long as other people think they do. He hoped she was wiser than him, that she understood why it had taken him so long.

And that her dreams were sweet ones.

A Note From the Author

The most important organisation I collaborated with on *Sweet Dreams* was Rädda Barnen – Save the Children – which I walked hand in hand with, they gave me so much help. I'm so grateful for their outstanding work against child pornography.

Rädda Barnen – Save the Children
https://www.raddabarnen.se

I'd also like to acknowledge three other charities doing incredible and necessary work to help so many, most of whom are children. The last charity might be the odd one – it's a church and I am not a church-man – but S:ta Clara kyrka (St. Clara's Church) in the middle of Stockholm truly makes a difference to so many.

Stockholms Stadsmission
https://www.stadsmissionen.se

Realstars
https://realstars.eu

S:ta Clara kyrka
https://www.svenskakyrkan.se/stockholmsdomkyrkoforsamling/sta-clara-kyrka

Read Boldly. Think Differently.

Continue the conversation:

Twitter: @vintagebooks
Instagram: @vintagebooks
TikTok: @vintageukbooks
Facebook: @vintagebooks

Sign up for the Vintage Newsletter to hear more about Vintage books.

www.vintage-books.co.uk

World-class writing. Beautiful design. Ideas that matter.

penguin.co.uk/vintage